C000176819

Also available from Unsung Stories
Déjà Vu by Ian Hocking
The Beauty by Aliya Whiteley
Dark Star by Oliver Langmead
The Arrival of Missives by Aliya Whiteley
Winter by Dan Grace
The Bearer of Grievances by Joseph McKinley
Metronome by Oliver Langmead
You Will Grow Into Them by Malcolm Devlin
The Speckled God by Marc Joan
The Dancer by Rab Ferguson

PSEUDOTOOTH

VERITY HOLLOWAY

**UNSUNG
STORIES**

Published by Unsung Stories, an imprint of Red Squirrel Publishing
"Red Squirrel" is a registered trademark of Shoreditch Media Limited

Red Squirrel Publishing
Suite 235, 15 Ingestre Place, London W1F 0DU,
United Kingdom

www.unsungstories.co.uk

First edition published in 2017

Paperback ISBN: 978-1-907389-41-2
ePub ISBN: 978-1-907389-42-9

Editors: George Sandison & Gary Budden
Copy Editor: Momus Editorial
Design: www.coxdesign.co.uk
Publisher: Henry Dillon

Printed in the UK by TJ International

For Jenny, my mum.

A stranger has come
To share my room in the house not right in the head,
A girl mad as birds

Love in the Asylum
Dylan Thomas

1

And of course, the weather turned Dickensian. The East Anglian horizon was crowded with low, goitrous clouds, ballooning out like new bruises. Aisling rested her head against the window of her mother's Ford Fiesta, studying their swells through half-closed eyes as the windscreen wipers gave out their rhythmic shrieks. The late sun cast an unnatural orange glow over the thatched rooftops of another unfamiliar village. Such forceful colour seemed impossible in the drizzly Suffolk countryside, and as the car turned off on to another empty stretch of hedge-lined road, Aisling wondered drowsily if the houses were on fire.

Two weeks since the hospital. The time had passed in a succession of telephone calls, rucksack-packing, and microwaved leftovers. In her journal, Aisling reminded herself in red biro that two weeks ago the world was in the warm embrace of late summer and her mother had worn a terracotta sundress that burned brightly down fluorescent-lit corridors. Now Beverley sat scrunched in the driving seat, her shoulders thrust forward under her black mackintosh as she negotiated a cluster of puddles.

Along the muddy-guttered lanes, Aisling kept herself calm by gathering the features of each passing village. As if she were a child still, and not drifting towards eighteen, she tried to turn it into a game, imagining she were a traveller moving into unknown territory: that rural Suffolk was a foreign country, with customs and sigils that she, with her suburban upbringing, must quickly decipher if she were to survive.

In Woolpit, the tall village sign showed a lone wolf guarding a pair of green children. A knight's shield heralded the flat farmland of Thorpe Morieux. Twin carved friars ignored them as they entered the pretty, gentrified village of Monks Eleigh where the Tudor cottages were daubed in that strange, traditional mixture of buttermilk and pig's blood. In the flooded lanes of Semer, where their Ford was overtaken by gleaming 4x4s, the village shop offered knitted witches alongside the *Daily Mail* and sticks of gum.

Endless stretching fields. Black earth. Road marked SLOW.

They weren't far from their two-bedroom semi in Bury St Edmunds. They hadn't even left the county. But to Aisling, the journey felt like the closing of a door.

As the car lurched over a pothole, the small boxes in the bag on her lap gave an insistent plastic rattle. She pulled her sleeves down over her cold hands and closed her eyes.

It was too serious a thing to turn into a game.

>•<

Neurology – Clinic 2 – Third floor. A youngish consultant for a change: Doctor Ross, a Scotsman with the kind of reassuring smile that made Aisling uncomfortable. It had a soothing effect on her mother, though, and for that, at least, Aisling was grateful. 'It's Beverley Selkirk. Miss, not Missus,' she said, as if she hadn't just spent twenty minutes in the waiting room compulsively folding and unfolding Elle Macpherson's face on the cover of *Tatler*.

The screen displaying Aisling's latest scans hung against the white wall. While this new doctor fetched her mother a chair, Aisling sat herself down and felt distant, perfunctory relief. *Hello, brain.* No massive growths. Nothing brutal.

More interesting was the row of ornaments lined up on a shelf above the screen: a ceramic Greek comedy mask, a lucky coin-eating Chinese frog, and two carved Hawaiian surfers with straw hair about to ride the crest of her parietal lobe. Trinkets that were meant to say: *I am a well-rounded human being – you may relax with me.*

It would take more than a few nick-nacks to accomplish that. Folded in Aisling's lap were her pale hands, blotted and sore. Around one wrist, the plastic shackle bearing her name and number remained.

'So!' Doctor Ross took his place behind the desk. 'You're seventeen now, Aisling. How'd you celebrate the big day?'

'Quietly,' said Beverley. 'Just the two of us in front of the telly. I thought it was best to avoid too much hoo-ha.'

'Oh, certainly. She'll have plenty of time for teenage kicks when we've got all this under control. You're probably looking forward to that, aren't you?'

He was trying to catch her eye. Aisling resumed her examination of his carved Polynesian tiki grinning down with eyes of shell. In nineteenth-century Tahiti, healers used sharks' teeth to drain the bad blood from their patients' foreheads. Aisling's satchel was pendulous with *National Geographic* magazines. She might have mentioned it to the doctor, but her own head was muggy after a bad night, and Beverley wouldn't like her bringing up sharks and blood in a hospital like some ghoulish little boy.

Doctor Ross wouldn't be interested, anyway. He thumbed Aisling's notes, a tome that grew fatter each time she saw it, and hummed tunelessly as he skimmed through it. There was a slight quirk of the left eyebrow, then nothing.

'Hmm.' He shut the file. 'Your middle name ought to be "Hmm", shouldn't it?' A second's silence. He turned and jerked a thumb at the screen. 'Delightful scans, though. No lesions, no abnormalities. Nice brain. Good girl. Hang on to it. However, this does rather put us back at square one.'

Beside Aisling, Beverley began to pluck at the shoulder strap of her dress. The doctor's sincere array of teeth widened and Aisling noticed for the first time the glossy blue letters of a leaflet lying on the desk:

ESCAPE YOUR MENTAL PRISON!

A pretty girl in a yellow dress stood open-armed, *Sound of Music*-style, on a grassy hill. She was shouting something triumphant at a cloudless sky stamped with the Mental Health Trust logo.

Somehow, despite everything, she hadn't expected it. Slowly, so as not to seem agitated, she slid her arms around herself and squeezed.

'I know you've hoped against hope that Aisling's

difficulties had an underlying organic cause,' Doctor Ross said. 'Something we could tinker with in a mechanical fashion. However, as delighted as I am to confirm that she's structurally sound, this result forces us to return to the examinations of my colleagues in the other departments.'

'She's not schizophrenic,' said Beverley quickly. 'They said so.'

'We know what Aisling isn't, Miss Selkirk. Her last spell as an inpatient showed my colleagues very little other than her understandable unhappiness. We can now say that the seizures are not neurological in origin. This is not epilepsy. Defining what it is, however, has proven more troublesome than we anticipated.'

Aisling stared hard at the tiki, trying to banish that last test, the one with the sticky pads all over her head. *'Go to sleep,'* they told her, as if a night on a mixed ward wasn't a nightmare in itself. *'And get the sheet off your face. You'll dislodge the wires.'* All night: snoring, machinery, beds rolling down corridors. Between the nurses' rounds, something blunt like flesh jabbed Aisling in the head and she stopped breathing.

It isn't real, she told herself. *I'm not here.*

It was meant to be the last time.

Aisling picked silently at the remains of the indigo polish on her well-bitten nails. She knew what would happen next: Doctor Ross would laugh apologetically and refer her to another specialist as if her presence in his office was a clerical error. They always laughed. Then, another office, another new prescription, and another month would pass by unchanged. A sliver of nail polish fluttered to the floor.

Had Doctor Ross been to any of the countries his

ornaments suggested? A thorn of jealousy lodged in her throat. If she were a grown man with a big, reassuring smile, she wouldn't sit in an office all day. She would buy a bundle of airline tickets and fly to every unpronounceable city on the map. When one region was explored to exhaustion there would always be another, until she was too old and feeble to mount the steps to the aircraft. Go to sleep? She wanted to wake up.

'At Aisling's age the world is a confusing place,' the doctor was telling Beverley. 'Humans establish security by pinpointing the threats of our environment and protecting ourselves against them. The symptoms of Aisling's condition make this very hard for her. Her anxiety runs amok, and, to counteract this, her imagination embellishes information in an attempt to create a more manageable environment. I understand my colleague explained to you how strong the power of suggestion is in a creative person like your daughter. Sometimes this impulse becomes too intense. The mind is forced to take evasive action – brings down a big, black curtain, if you like. Have you heard of a condition known as PNES?'

Beverley frowned. 'Isn't that what soldiers have?'

'Ah, no, that's post-traumatic stress, Miss Selkirk, but you are in the right area. Seventy-five per cent of PNES patients – that's psychogenic non-epileptic seizures, bit of a mouthful, I know – are girls of Aisling's age. We used to call them "pseudoseizures", as they come from a psychological source rather than electrical. PNES is frequently linked back to traumatic experiences in the formative years. Bereavements, nasty divorces, that sort of thing. Did you know that, Miss Selkirk?'

'I didn't. God, it sounds… horrid.' Her hand crept over the frayed denim of Aisling's knee, and Aisling robotically covered it with her own. There would be tears later. 'What can be done? I mean, if they're not real seizures, how do you stop them?'

'Oh, make no mistake, the seizures are real. And, for Aisling, I'm sure they must be very upsetting. Am I right, Aisling?' He bent his head in an attempt to enter her line of sight.

Aisling darted him a noncommittal nod and went back to picking her nail polish. On her thumb was a silver band of Celtic knotwork, a cheap souvenir from a school trip to Colchester Castle, and she twisted it sharply. The metal pinched her skin. There was a horrid smell in the office; a growing tang of disinfectant or fuel. On the canvas of her mind's eye she tried to summon something beautiful to block it out: lights twinkling on Venetian canals, the bursting colours of a West Indian marketplace, anything at all. The best she could manage was the illustration of the human heart from *Gray's Anatomy* that looked like a bedpan, and she tapped Beverley on the arm.

'Can I go out and get a drink?' she whispered. 'Please.'

The panic left her body with the words. They were all in the room again, congenial and talking, and the doctor was fixing her with an amused look, as if to say, *Nervous little sparrow, aren't you?*

Aisling inhaled through her nose. Beverley's Givenchy perfume.

'Don't be rude,' said Beverley. 'Mister Ross. These seizures. Do we know these are what she's having? Are we finally getting somewhere?'

'What I know is that all this has dragged on for far too long. I've been in touch with my colleagues in the other department.' He sat back and laced his fingers behind his head. 'We're thinking of a more holistic approach. Stress can open the gates for all kinds of nasty things, from colds to hearing voices. It's a mysterious thing but, as we've learnt, she's quite the mysterious young woman.'

Beverley fidgeted. 'I did some reading on Ritalin—'

'We must resist the temptation to go trawling the Internet, Miss Selkirk. Ritalin would do nothing for these… what have we been calling them?' he gave the notes a quick flick. 'Daylight hallucinations. Blackouts. Insomnia and whatnot.'

'You can't leave her like this. I don't know what the other doctors have told you, but one night in July—'

'It would be better for Aisling if we didn't dwell on the past,' he said, gently.

'We live in a Neighbourhood Watch area. When one's daughter—' Abruptly, she exhaled. 'People look at her.'

'Once you look the part,' Beverley once told Aisling, *'everyone else fills in the gaps.'* She was referring to the monstrously expensive Manolo Blahniks she bought for her secretarial job at a law firm, but Beverley's eyes had hovered over Aisling's shapeless jumper and unbrushed hair. They both knew what people said about her.

'The past year must have been exceedingly trying for you both,' said Doctor Ross. 'But behavioural difficulties are a product of Aisling's distress. Kleptomaniacs are not ill because they compulsively steal, they compulsively steal because they are ill.'

'Did they say that? Did they say she's a kleptomaniac?'

'They didn't. I apologise for the clumsy example. Aisling's

little spates of theft would wither in comparison to some of the wonders my colleagues have seen, believe me.' He raised an eyebrow in Aisling's direction. 'She's a bit of a puzzle, but she's no maniac.'

'She used to be so easy to manage,' Beverley said. 'All she ever wanted was her *Lonely Planet* magazines. The Head of Year was so impressed with her predicted grades, but when exams came around, that was it. Curtains. I've tried to make sense of it. It's not even like she was mixing with a bad crowd.'

Doctor Ross made a sympathetic face, and Aisling had to give him credit – it wasn't the worst she'd seen. He began scribbling on a printed form that had been in front of him since they came in. When he was finished, he dropped the pen. 'So! D'you fancy a getaway, Aisling? Somewhere a bit less dismal and institutional?'

No small effort to meet his eyes. Just a man. Was that so horrible?

Beverley spoke for her. 'She's worried you're going to put her away again.'

'Ah!' he barked. 'Goodness, no. Nobody gets put away on the NHS. Far too expensive. No, we've observed her quite enough for now. I think what Aisling needs is fresh scenery. Stimulation – gentle, of course. Often, when clever young people find life continually unrewarding, they fall into patterns of destructive behaviour. Why do you think so many kids are smashing up bus shelters? Perhaps Aisling is trying to tell us that she needs to get away.'

'Yes!'

Doctor Ross was startled.

Beverley managed to turn her own jolt into an exasperated

laugh. 'That's yes, *thank you*. Really.'

Aisling was embarrassed. She hadn't meant to speak.

Doctor Ross regarded her. 'Is there something you'd like us to know, Aisling?'

'No. Sorry, no,' Aisling mumbled. Her mother was looking at her with a mixture of amazement and annoyance. 'I'm going to do my best.'

'A rest, then. If it's as effective as we hope, she can retake her exams and show the Head her mettle. I'll recommend her GP prescribes a light antidepressant too,' he said with a quick glance in Beverley's direction. 'Just a little something to ease her down, soothe those nerves.'

'And if it doesn't work?' Beverley asked.

His pen paused mid-scribble. 'Think of this as your chance, Aisling,' he said. 'Make us all believe you've been having us on.'

2

'Tie your hair up.'

Aisling opened her eyes. The motion of the car had lulled her to sleep. In the rush to leave the house, she had forgotten to brush her hair, and, she belatedly discovered, drawing her tongue across scummy film, her teeth.

Beverley flicked the steering wheel with an irritable fingernail. 'Run your fingers through it,' she said. 'You'll upset her before you get through the door.'

Aisling found an elastic band in her rucksack and started raking through the tangled auburn mass. They passed a squat Norman church where ivy and tree roots were slowly conquering the graveyard. The noise of the battered Ford careening down the narrow lane startled a magpie, and Aisling caught the flash of its wings as it took off from the hedgerows, flying out ahead of them over the flat, featureless fields.

Her mother's eyes met hers in the mirror. 'Hey. Smile. They didn't have you sectioned.'

Aisling picked at a tangle as they overtook a tractor. 'I don't understand why it has to be her.'

'You can help her around that great big house, do the shopping for her when you're allowed out. No one's better for this job than Edy. You'll be fixed in a week, I swear.' Her eyebrow arched in the rear-view mirror. 'On your father's grave.'

The imaginary man. As the car thumped over another rain-filled pothole, Aisling saw him on the rusty prow of a container ship mastering a blue ocean somewhere. Somalia? Antigua? A sunburned, capable nomad she had never met and didn't particularly wish to, if Beverley's stories were to be believed, which, she was coming to realise, they probably weren't. The seat belt was chafing her clavicle. She gave a small growl of discomfort.

'Language.' Flick-flick-flick. 'Edythe's firm, and that's a good thing. If my mum and dad had been stricter with me when I was your age, it would've saved us all a lot of bother.'

They passed another lone bungalow amongst a scrubby cluster of birches. Aisling viewed her father on that fast-moving ship jealously, like a fragment of herself that had managed to escape. 'In writing it out, you get to be in charge,' they said in therapy. At the bottom of her bag, the journal dug into her thigh. In the two weeks since the hospital, she had written copiously in the hope that it was true, barely thinking about the words, let alone reading them later.

'You're upset. I do know. But listen: it's better than another spell on a ward. Do you like them sticking you in those noisy MRI things? I can't keep telling people it's an ear infection. What if someone thinks you're in rehab?'

Beverley had waited until that morning to tell Aisling

where they were going. After ten minutes of waiting in the car she'd traipsed up the stairs to find Aisling kneeling over the toilet, hair hanging in damp strings around her face. Beverley had slapped her pockets for cigarettes and turned back downstairs. 'See?' she said. 'Stress. They're right this time. Bring your bag.'

The sickness remained, churned up by the meandering country roads. Aisling tried distracting herself with the names of medication she'd learnt over the past two years, quick-fire, until the words ran together in a jumble of insensible sounds – Lithium, Valium, Lorazepam, Prozac, Soma, Seroquel – an incantation against the blue devils of anxiety and the pain in her temples that kept her awake at night. Light-headed, she felt herself laugh.

Beverley watched the road. After a long moment she muttered at the steering wheel, 'It's better than another hospital.'

Not better, Aisling thought. Just new. But there was no alternative. Their family was small and scattered. The relatives who hadn't died had fallen out or lost contact and, for the prescribed fresh air and greenery, there was only one place Beverley could send her for free.

Great-aunt Edythe occupied the vicarage on the outskirts of a piddling little Suffolk village where no one went to church. She was, in Aisling's opinion, the kind of woman the Witchfinder General would have employed to operate the ducking stool. To Beverley, she was everything.

'Auntie Edy, this is Bev,' the boy had said. 'Mum says she can come and live here. She's going to be my wife.' Nervously in love with this orange-haired youth who called himself Eliot, the teenage Beverley had never known anyone like Edy. So reassuringly strict, so funny with Eliot and the New Age pretentions his mother, Connie, only encouraged. Backpacking? To Patagonia? When he wasn't even willing to get a paper round?

'You're not like him,' Edy would tell Beverley when they were alone. 'You're a better breed.'

Seven months into Beverley's subsequent pregnancy, Connie died. Eliot left, presumably for Patagonia. All too quickly, the baby was born. Beverley sat by the incubator watching the daughter Eliot had months ago named Aisling. Her own parents wanted nothing to do with her. Edythe was the only one left.

Aisling had one clear memory of Edythe Enright. Car, mother, melting Malteasers. That much was good. Then the tonsil-stinging, necromantic smell of bleach. There was a lofty, chilly room and a small, quick woman who looked at four-year-old Aisling as if she were something unpleasant trodden into the carpet.

'Her nails are too long, Beverley. Children with long nails ask for trouble.'

While her aunt rattled off a list of popular paediatric parasites, Aisling turned away to the window. It was sunny outside, warmer than the house. There were silver birches for climbing at the far end of the garden, and a pond shining like a ten-pence piece. Aisling's toes twitched uncomfortably inside her best shoes. As she gazed out, dreaming of paddling, a diamond of light betrayed something on the polished windowsill below her nose.

A clump of hair. Short and colourless, complete with roots. Aisling touched it. Soapy. It stuck to her fingers, to her blouse, as she tried to wipe it off.

Beverley was told never to bring her plain, solemn-eyed daughter to the house again.

Aisling pulled down the mirrored sun visor and scraped the long strands of hair back into a ponytail. Barefaced, her eyes had the deep-lidded, sleepy quality her mother said made her look drugged. 'I am drugged,' she said once, a mistake she didn't make twice. She pushed back the visor and plaited blind.

Trees went by, forlorn and mauve in the drizzle. Ahead, a house was emerging.

'That's it, isn't it?' Aisling said.

'It's a house, not the gallows, Sweets.'

The car turned down into a gravel track. The house – this place amongst the scrawny trees her mother had spoken of so warmly – had not featured in Aisling's childhood memory. But as the car trundled down the drive, she registered a glint of recognition at the black beams striping the whitewashed walls. It was a gigantic house, to Aisling's suburban eyes; a muddle of red Tudor chimneystacks, jutting Edwardian bay windows, and, off to one side, a delicate glass conservatory like somewhere a vicar might take tea.

Beverley drove them up to the door, whereupon the engine stalled.

'Just do me a favour and put some effort into this, okay? The man said there was nothing wrong with you. Let's be thankful.'

'I don't think that's what he said.'

'You're not the one with all the qualifications. He said they were pseudoseizures – not proper ones. So stick on a smile. You can start by taking one of your pills, please.'

'What, now?'

'Mm-hm. While I can see you.'

'I had one with breakfast.'

'Which you threw up. Anyway, you've had at least two more of those episodes since we saw the doctor. How do you explain that if you haven't missed a dose?'

Aisling produced one of the packets of pills. Four 'episodes', actually. Only two had been bad enough to mention. And then there were the dreams. But her mother wasn't interested in dreams. Aisling dutifully showed her the pill, and forced it down dry.

'Good,' Beverley said, and patted her pockets for cigarettes. She popped a Misty Menthol Light between her lips. 'Stick to them. And give Edy my love, won't you?'

'You're not coming in?'

'Astonishingly enough, I do have my own life to lead. I can't hold your hand forever, Sweets.'

Aisling opened the door. The cold air swept up the trail of Beverley's smoke. 'I meant just for a few minutes.'

'So did I. Look, I didn't want to add to your stresses right now, but I actually have somewhere to be.' Aisling thought she detected a small smile on her mother's lips, the one that usually meant she'd given Aisling's old clothes to a charity shop or enrolled them both in Slimming World. 'You remember Malcolm, don't you?'

Aisling remembered. She remembered the night, two summers ago, when he waited until Beverley was asleep. She remembered the weight of him.

The rain came in and began to seep through her jumper.

'Well, Malcolm's back,' Beverley said. 'And he wants to try again. So he's invited me to stay with him for a while, just testing the waters. He's got the most glorious loft conversion in Hackney. I think I might be on to something this time, Sweets. He's just… well, you remember. And she needs a rest, your old mum. There's only so much she can juggle. You know?'

Aisling feigned Doctor Ross's smile, and the tension in her mother's shoulders visibly lessened. Aisling was worn out and could feel a headache coming. There was no sense protesting. Not in the rain, on a stranger's driveway.

'That's brilliant, Mum. When are you coming back?'

'Malcolm said I could stay as long as I like. Obviously, we'll need to take it slow, but if it all goes well…'

'For me, I mean. When do I get to go home?'

Beverley reached over and squeezed her daughter's thigh. 'That all depends on you, doesn't it?'

The rain fell with more determination. Aisling's jeans were damp. She took her rucksack and climbed out of the car.

'Hello?'

Her voice was small in the cold, high-ceilinged hall. The door was open, but no one greeted her. A large arched window framing the Tudor staircase poured watery light on to the chequered floor. Facing her were three burnished oak doors separating the entrance hall from the rest of the ground floor. She half expected a portcullis to come down behind her, locking her in.

A television blared away upstairs. *Crimewatch*. 'Boyarov was last seen on the night of 10th February, 1995. The vulnerable teenager's disappearance is thought to be connected to a playground assault, which left a fellow fifteen-year-old with life-changing injuries. However, CCTV footage from the night yielded next to nothing of Boyarov's flight. Where he went after leaving his father's East London flat remains a mystery. Can you help, after all these years? Call our Freephone number.'

Rainwater dribbled down her neck and on to the tiles. Conscious of her muddy boots, she pulled them off and placed them next to the front door. The effort she had put into tidying her hair had been undone by the wind, but there were no mirrors in the hall, no doormat, not even so much as a houseplant. The walls were a clean monastic white. The emptiness served to draw all attention to an old studio photograph above the front door. A man in clerical black. The soft focus gave him a saintly appearance, though his well-groomed hair and stately, tilted chin, Aisling thought, were those of a man who secretly enjoyed being admired. She rose on the balls of her feet to view him. The Reverend John Enright, read the plaque. 1932.

Below it, a smaller photograph, sharper with advances in photography. The Reverend again, older but still impeccably presented, flanked by two fellow clergymen: a pleased-looking man with a Red Cross armband and a tall, stooping youth in a black suit who had flinched at the moment of exposure. Aisling stared at the blur of his large, white face and thought that he must have been considered a very unimportant figure not to warrant a second, clearer shot.

The medication dissolved in her sore stomach. It was hard to think. What had Doctor Ross said? When we know nothing, we embellish. She was here to get past all of that.

'Your feet.'

Aisling jumped. Edythe had slipped in silently through one of the three oak doors. She was smaller than Aisling remembered. The top of her head barely came to Aisling's breastbone, but there were sturdy limbs beneath the cable knit jumper and houndstooth skirt. Unconsciously, Aisling had taken two steps backwards. She held the rucksack to her chest.

'I can't abide naked feet,' Edythe said.

Black Suffolk earth on the soles of Aisling's boots. It had crumbled, stuck to her damp toes. Sooty footprints trailed over clean tiles.

'Oh, God. I'm sorry.' Aisling cursed herself. Traipsing in mud and blaspheming underneath a portrait of a vicar wasn't the first impression she had hoped to present. She repositioned her feet. Only when both were safely within the confines of a black square where the dirt was less visible did Edythe appear to uncoil.

Keeping her blue gaze trained on Aisling, Edythe followed the white tiles diagonally across the floor, like a chess piece. She squared herself up six inches from her niece and looked to the front door.

'Where is Beverley?'

'She was in a hurry.'

'She drove all the way here and just turned around?'

Aisling tightened her arms around the rucksack. 'She told me to send you her love.'

'I don't want messages from you. Why would she refuse to see me? She's never done this before.'

Aisling shook her head. The room tilted a little. She winced.

When Edythe saw this, her expression hardened. 'Poor

Beverley. I can't say I'm surprised.' She held out her hand. 'Give me your bag.'

When she registered the seriousness on her aunt's face, Aisling drew back. 'You're not going to search me. I'm not dangerous.'

With one surprisingly strong pull, Edythe tugged the bag from Aisling's arms and began systematically emptying it on to the tiles. 'Six thousand British eleven-to-sixteen-year-olds carry knives,' she said, examining Aisling's toothbrush. '*Crimewatch*, just now.'

'The sharpest thing I have is a pen.' Aisling shifted anxiously, mindful of treading more dirt on the white tiles. 'I don't want you going through—'

Edythe dismissed her outstretched hand. Rummaging through the folded underwear, she came across a glossy issue of *Wanderlust* magazine. The cover showed a naked black boy leaping joyously into a dazzling turquoise sea.

'Planning a holiday?'

The magazine hit the tiles with a slap. Next was a small book bound in mossy-green leather. '*Selected Poetry and Prose of William Blake*. What's this?'

'Just poems.'

'I know, thank you. I am educated.'

Edythe opened the little volume on a well-thumbed page. Upside down, Aisling recognised the spindly illustrations, the faint lines where she had taken a pencil and circled the verses she found beautiful or hard to understand. A bring-and-buy sale, a crate of water-damaged fishing annuals, and Blake at the bottom, waiting for her. The cover was plain, but it was the quote opening the foreword that caught her, from some nineteenth-century critic shown up by time: William Blake, an unfortunate lunatic, and the wild effusions of his distempered brain.

'I thought you failed your English exam,' Edythe said.

'When I have my episodes, I try to recite. It's a therapy thing. It works.' Give it back, give it back, give it—

Edythe scanned the open page. Aisling knew the poem at once:

Dear child, I also by pleasant streams
Have wander'd all night in the Land of Dreams;
But tho' calm and warm the waters wide
I could not get to the other side.

Edythe paused. 'No. I don't think so.' She slipped the little book into her skirt pocket.

Aisling's stomach clenched. 'I need it.'

'Nobody needs books. People need shelter and sustenance. Unless you intend to eat it or set fire to it, you can do without it.'

Next, she discovered Aisling's journal. The bundle of thin sweatshirts wrapped around it was discarded, tossed to the floor.

'Don't touch that,' Aisling said quickly.

Edythe looked up. There was a trace of amusement on her face. 'This?'

'It's mine.'

Edythe picked at the binding. It was a small thing, worn at the edges. She dropped it back into the rucksack. 'You didn't pack much, did you? You'll be here as long as you need to be, and for that you'll need more underwear. I'll go to the village on Monday and see what I can find. Do you have money?'

'I can buy my own clothes.'

'Anything you need, I'll fetch for you. Money, please.'

Aisling handed over two pounds and a few copper pennies. They disappeared into the same pocket as the Blake volume, leaving Aisling feeling frail and exposed. Her jeans were threadbare at the knees. 'Like a pikey,' Beverley always said.

Edythe turned about-face. 'Bring your things.'

Aisling recovered her rucksack, scooped up the scattered contents and hurried after her. Edythe led her briskly through one of the oak doors and into a large kitchen overlooking the garden and the fields beyond. An incongruous metal dining table, like something from an operating theatre, took centre place. It had recently been wiped with disinfectant, and the odour of it clung to Aisling's tongue.

'I'd prefer you didn't use the grand staircase,' Edythe said. 'The carpet shows every speck of dirt, being plain, so I shall know if you've trodden on it.' They came to a white door in the corner of the kitchen. Edythe unlatched it to reveal a dark flight of narrow stairs, presumably once reserved for servants.

Aisling felt her way up in the dark. She imagined what it was like to be a maid carrying trays of dishes up and down these stairs, how easy it would be to tumble down. You're embellishing again, she told herself, and nearly lost her footing as, behind her, Edythe shouted out:

'Robert! I smell tobacco.'

All Aisling could smell was bleach. 'Who's Robert?'

'A man about to have his lighter confiscated. Chop-chop.' She shooed Aisling up the last remaining steps and reached around her waist to grab the doorknob. Light flooded in and Edythe pushed past.

'Bert, please. All it would take is for you to nod off. This is a timber house.'

Aisling hovered outside the bedroom door. Over Edythe's shoulder she saw a silver-haired man reclining in an armchair, his feet propped up on a footstool. His hands, brown and big-knuckled, trembled in his lap, and he grinned around a drooping cigarette.

'I plead innocence.'

'What if social services were to hear of this, Bert? You'd be taken away. You'd spend the rest of your life eating porridge, surrounded by dribbling grandmothers.'

'And pert little nurses to take your place. Worry you, does it?'

Edythe brushed the biscuit crumbs from his silver moustache. 'Mrs Bloom would only have to make one phone call.'

The unexpected tenderness disarmed the old man. 'All right. Sister Edy knows best.' He produced a cigarette lighter from the cushions. Edythe snatched it from his trembling fingers. For the first time Aisling noticed Robert's left leg, how thin it was compared to the right. A noticeable curve from the knee to the ankle.

Edythe was busily searching the rest of the cushions and the sides of the armchair. She pulled out a crumpled brown carton.

'Egyptian cigarettes?' she said, incredulous. 'Where are you getting Egyptian cigarettes from?'

'I cannot disclose my source.'

'I shall have words with Mrs Bloom when she comes on Thursday.' The carton was confiscated. Her skirt pockets bulged with contraband, Robert's and Aisling's. They smiled at each other.

'Hallo, out there. I'm afraid I've been told to ignore you.' He noticed Aisling's wet clothes. 'Gosh. Poor drowned Ophelia. I'd get warm quickly if I were you. There's only room for one invalid in this house.'

Edythe had taken a blanket from the ottoman and was smoothing it over his legs. 'Aisling, get out. You're dripping everywhere.'

Aisling dipped her head and hurried out. Robert caught her eye and wagged a shaky finger. Edythe was infuriated. 'I'm not your chambermaid,' she hissed, and left him.

Aisling shouldered her bag and followed Edythe down the dishearteningly long corridor. As they turned a corner, Edythe glanced back at her. 'Shivering?'

Aisling ducked awkwardly under a low ceiling beam. 'I'm fine.'

'We haven't had a heater on this floor for sixty years. You'll adjust.'

At the back of the house, Edythe led her up another set of enclosed stairs that groaned when trodden on, and unlocked the door at the top. The revealed bedroom smelt faintly of wet paint. Aisling felt a useless sentimental tug towards her own bedroom at home: the torn paper map Blu-Tacked to her wall, and the pile of half-finished books with the dirty mug on top. Even the fold-out picnic chair draped with the school shirt and tie she no longer needed.

Nevertheless, she offered stiff thanks. She hesitated, looked at her toes curling on the bare floorboards. 'When can I have my book back?'

'Pardon?'

'My Blake book. I want it back.'

Edythe looked like a small, indignant bull. 'You want it, do you? When you pull yourself together, perhaps then you can make requests. But all the while you keep this up...' Her eyes flicked over Aisling's thin, bedraggled body. 'You've already proven that you're unwilling to govern yourself. If therapy and medicine won't do anything for you, perhaps parameters and responsibility will.' She turned to leave and paused. 'You'll find I'm hard to deceive, Aisling. Don't try.'

Aisling watched the door close before allowing herself to sink down on to the bed. She pressed her forehead to her knees and exhaled. The lump in her throat throbbed annoyingly.

It was five o'clock. Outside, thick oaks clustered together on the horizon where the road lingered around the paddocks and up the lane to Edythe's house. A single pair of car headlights sliced through the distant woods and vanished. The familiar tingling unfurled at the base of her spine – Go! Explore!

A few weeks in the middle of a field. Then what?

She peeled off her wet jumper and shook her hair out of its plait. Edythe hadn't changed. 'Old cow,' Beverley would have said, had Edythe been anyone else. 'Gob in her tea.' Beverley was probably on a motorway now, practising charming things to say to Malcolm. Aisling was thankful she wouldn't have to watch. There were few things worse than seeing her mother live on cottage cheese and grapefruit for these men who invariably lost interest after three dates. 'When you get better,' Beverley told her, 'it'll be easier. When you get better, everything will fall into place.'

Aisling draped the towel around her shoulders. The

room, she told herself, was not so bad. There were shelves crammed so tightly with books they gave a crack of protest as Aisling prised one out to look at the title. *Within Reason: Treatment and Protection of the Defective Classes.* Some kind of pre-war scientific manual. She had hoped for a novel, but as she tried to wedge the book back into place, a few loose sheets of notepaper slipped free, and she caught one before it fluttered to the floor. In the centre of the page, in pristine fountain pen cursive: *Whitewash is extremely moral.*

The phrase struck her as strangely confessional. It reminded her of her own journal, with its creased pages and wrapping of string. 'Write anything,' they'd said in therapy, 'just get it all out.'

And she'd tried. Her Blake book said the poet recorded his visions at night when he was alone. Reading Blake was like peeping in at a dark window. Dusky words, sometimes nonsensical. Visions of The Daughters of Albion. The Book of Thel. Blake hardly gave his hasty prophecies a second look before etching them on plates of copper, surrounded by twirling celestial beings and crawling creatures from the Inferno. In bed with her books spread around her, Aisling could pretend to hear the scratching of the stylus, to taste the vapours of the acid sealing the design. Hellish alchemy to conjure angels. And though she tried for something profound in her own journal, the cognitive exercises set down by well-meaning counsellors diluted everything to a swill of bored, impersonal nothings. Today I felt as follows. I felt this because. Now I explore why.

Back in Edythe's spare room, Aisling gathered the loose pages and took the old book downstairs to the door marked Guest Lavatory. Inside was an old-fashioned enamel bath with long silver taps that squeaked when she turned them. A great grunt came from the attic as the aged pipes shunted into action and a sharp smell, like acetate, made her nose wrinkle. Stale air in old pipes. Edythe apparently didn't often have guests.

No radiator and no lock. There was already something distressing about taking off her clothes in an unfamiliar room. Worse, a mirror confronted her above the sink. There it all was. Her collarbones jutting above the washboard sternum, the reedy neck like a boy's waiting for his first beard. All wrapped up in the papery, yellow skin they said would improve once she started eating properly.

'Wreck,' she muttered.

As the bathroom filled with steam, Aisling eased her body down into the water. The book's spine was crumbling, and the loose sheets of paper were in similarly poor shape, crackling like dying leaves. Someone had smothered a section of pages in white paint and written their own notes on top. *The malaise continues*, admitted the cramped penmanship. *Today, I begin a rigorous programme of exercise to cleanse body and soul.*

Quote. Visionary architect Le Corbusier on his ideal modernity: 'Every citizen is required to replace his hangings, his wallpapers, with a plain coat of white Ripolin. Then comes inner cleanness. Without the law of whitewash we are lying to ourselves every day, we lie to others. The law of whitewash would bring the joy of life, the joy of action. Give us the law of whitewash.'

Cannot request Ripolin – costly – but may request standard white paint to cancel out wallpaper in room. White foods – beneficial? And quiet. Quiet.

'Ripolin' meant nothing to Aisling. It sounded like a brand of medicine. As she turned a page, the satin bookmark ribbon unravelled and something plopped into the bath.

She fished it out and held it to the light. A single silver cufflink, set with a small emerald; the kind of trinket a fancy gentleman might have worn at the turn of the last century. A small thrill cut through the fog. For the first time in many months, Aisling felt the urge to steal.

'Not worth it. Not one bit.'

She put the cufflink aside and turned back to the book. It was a manual of some kind, for care home staff, and heavy on the medical jargon. The chapter headings read like a list of the wounded: Blindness, Hysteria, Epilepsy, The Lame. There were words she'd never heard of. Cretins. Sapphics. Cataplexy. Sharp words, like the names of vicious sea creatures, she thought, shifting uncomfortably in the tub. And then, towards the back, where the inky annotations were their thickest:

The Blighted Youth.

Too often, we see well-meaning physicians attempt to place the disruptive young amongst the passive: the sick amongst the well; the stupid amongst the intelligent. By osmosis is the defective expected to recover himself. Indeed, such scenes bring to mind the medieval prevention of plagues – of poppets and prayer and superstitious impotence. The feeble-minded lack the innate power of development. They have little or no individuality, and would merely grow up extremely ignorant and more susceptible to physical abnormalities than their stronger brothers and sisters. By embracing those unfortunate members of society who fall so far short of the line of normal mentality, the healthy population lowers itself as a whole.

This sentence was underlined in ink so strongly the paper was almost torn.

Indeed, we endanger ourselves. By permanent segregation only is the imbecile to be safeguarded from deterioration, and society from depredation, contamination, and increase of a pernicious element. The only humane and civilised way of halting the taint is the simple procedure of sterilisation.

The tap dripped. Aisling's stomach tightened, threatening to eject the pill she had so obediently taken an hour ago. Over the page, through a haze of steam, she registered the author discussing the merits of rubber flooring and shatterproof windows.

In the margin, neatly penned: *The degeneracy must cease.*

Somewhere above her, the boiler groaned and a jet of cold water spouted from the tap, chilling her feet. Aisling's nostrils stung. Through the pipes and the pitted ceiling, the fuel-stink of acetate had seeped into the bathroom. Even as she coughed and covered her mouth, it clung to her face like a damp veil, and she hauled herself out of the bath and into a towel. She couldn't be in that room or near that book any longer.

>•<

On the tartan coverlet of her new bed, Aisling crouched over her journal. She wrote fast, messily, pausing only as a noise in the corridor below – a footstep or the natural creaking of the old house, it was difficult to tell – made her shiver in anticipation of another wave of that terrible smell. None came. What would she give for a dressing gown, let alone a room with a high-stoked fire? But as her handwriting deteriorated and the words flowed, she sensed herself entering that meditative state her doctors said was good for her, and the cold ceased to matter.

No counsellors' guidelines or cognitive exercises. She wrote it like she always did: *My name is Feodor.*

3
FEODOR

It was burning when I reached the wasteland. All of it.

Four miles out, at the edge of the trees, I watched the shock of the flames, from the ruins and the slums in the west to the brothels and the docklands in the east. One of the old distilleries erupted in a plume of white fire. There was enough gin in its cellars to burn the entire town. I thought of the dreadlocked fishermen piling survivors into their boats, turning to the bitter October sea. They have no word for October here.

My name is Feodor. I come from a place called London on a cold island you'll never see. Some of what you've heard is true. Quick little me shinned up a drainpipe and went across the rooftops just before the stampede. Quick, clever, gutless little me.

I killed Eva that day. I killed Arthur and Germaine. When the survivors come for me, I'll probably kill again.

They won't give me time to explain. So I write.

Do you like fire? I'm twenty-two years old, and I've torched more car tyres than I've blown out birthday candles. I wouldn't kick footballs or roll joints like the other boys on the grey estate where I grew up, and I wouldn't do sex, not for fun. My thing was fire. There was a relentless supply of abandoned scooters and rubbish scattered around the tower blocks. I brought it to life, all warm and purring and bright.

I blew my dad's car into small bits once. That's another story.

Did you ever play with matches? Dad smacked my legs scarlet when he caught me, a clumsy five-year-old trying to light the candle in front of Mama's icon of The Virgin. I'd singed the Holy Mother's sad paper lips. That night, I lay under my duvet and cried until my face was sore, not for Dad's shouting or the lovely painted face I'd defiled, but because I wanted to do it again.

A whole city in flames, though – miles upon miles of brick houses full of men and women I might've nodded at when I put out the bins – that's something new.

I stood at the boundary of the woods, wheezing with the smoke and the fumes from that bloody whitewash. A section of the town wall had collapsed after the fireworks emporium went up, and I had to clamber over the rubble and slide down the other side on my bony arse while newsboys and costermongers went dashing this way and that with armfuls of possessions and useless pails of water. No one followed me, not even the looters. Little laughing Feodor was the only shadow racing across the wasteland.

I get a bit funny when I'm frightened. I'm not mad. Ignore what they say.

I thought of the council. I thought of its glass spires shattering and I laughed. I thought of the people who'd trusted me. I thought of their homes in the slums collapsing into the canals and I laughed at that too. And then I thought of that long-gone place I'd nearly forgotten; of Crossways estate, those three grey towers with their sickly yellow corridors, and the rings under Dad's eyes. I'd never see London again.

I laugh when I'm frightened. Sorry.

My clothes were clammy-black with sweat and splinters of charred timber. The hairs on my arms, I noticed as I hugged myself, were singed clean away. I felt my pockets. My money, my compass and the bundle of dried fruit I'd packed that morning were gone. I'd got my knife. That was it.

I had nothing left to do but run.

Stay with me. You might be surprised.

4

'You aren't a vegetarian, are you?'

Edythe presented Aisling with a plate of what might have been pork.

'I'm not,' Aisling said. She forced a little smile. 'Thank you.'

Edythe sat down opposite her. She had regained her composure since the outburst over Robert's cigarettes and was pleased to find Aisling had bathed and changed her clothes. 'You look like a vegetarian.'

'I'm anaemic.'

'Did they not feed you properly?' Edythe didn't touch her knife and fork. Just looked across the table.

'Who?'

'At the psychiatric unit.'

'It was all right.' There was a short silence while Edythe looked expectant. 'I wasn't there long,' Aisling added. She wished she hadn't re-plaited her hair after the burst of writing that left her headachy and tired again. Edythe's eyes were moving slowly over her forehead, down the contours of her face to her chin.

'Three-and-a-half weeks, wasn't it? And outpatient sessions on top.'

Beverley must have told her. Aisling nodded and said nothing.

'That's a long time to be locked up anywhere,' Edythe said.

'They don't lock you up. I mean, you can't leave, but... there are activities and things. It depends.'

Edythe picked up her cutlery and eyed her food. 'You must have mixed with some real cases. Do they still advocate electrical treatments? I understand—'

'Not to me,' Aisling said. She pushed the gluey lump of mash around her plate, trying to avoid contact with the grey slab of meat cooling in the centre. *It could have been worse,* she thought, with the old book in mind. *It used to be worse.*

'Mrs Bloom comes up from the village every Thursday with the shopping. I've told her you'll be staying with me for a while, that you've been ill and need to recuperate.' Edythe began the methodical process of organising the two piles of meat on her plate according to colour. 'It's a small village,' she said, deliberating over a piece of whitish rind. 'The Blooms have been friends of the Enrights since my father was the vicar here. Do you follow me?'

'First impressions, Sweets. Costs nothing to smile, mind your Ps and Qs, they make creams for dark circles these days, well, you might not care, but I do...'

Whenever Aisling found herself wanting to kick and shout and swear, the image of her mother's pained face would well up, and the urge would shrivel down into somewhere she couldn't reach. Now, however, Aisling imagined Mrs Bloom picking up her telephone and informing the local Mothers' Union that there was a defective degenerate residing at the vicarage. She smirked before she could stop herself.

Edythe looked up. A long, blue-eyed stare. 'Are you going to make things difficult?'

Aisling looked at her food. It looked back, congealed and cold. 'No,' she said. 'No.'

Satisfied that the white rind was separated from the pink centre, Edythe set about flattening the mound of potato with her spoon. 'Beverley warned me you throw up more often than you eat.'

'I can't help it.'

'And I suppose that's the medication's fault?'

'It usually goes away after the first couple of weeks.'

'I saw a television programme about bulimia once.'

'Well, I'm not bulimic.'

'No, you're anaemic.' Edythe smiled around the prongs of her fork. 'I imagine you met a few of them, though. In that place.'

Aisling's fork drooped. She wished she were on the motorway with her mother, saying nothing and being ignored.

'Don't be so sensitive. Eat your dinner.'

Aisling focused on the sound of the rain clattering against the kitchen windows. Robert was in his room upstairs, watching a film consisting mainly of machine gunning. After Edythe had cleared the dishes, she stood behind Aisling's chair.

'These are for you.'

For a second, Aisling expected another pile of pork slabs.

Instead, a piece of paper was slipped under her nose, and Aisling had time to register the word RULES in crisp pencil before Edythe proceeded to read aloud.

'Item one: Bathe daily. Item two: No boys.' She paused. 'Or the alternative. Three: Do not attempt to carry out housework until told to, and only under supervision. You would only do it wrong. Four: The land beyond the house is out of bounds. You may go out into the garden once you prove your willingness to behave around the house.'

Up until then, part of Aisling still believed the list was a joke. She twisted in her seat to gauge the look on Edythe's face, but the old woman read on without acknowledging her.

'I base all things on merit. For now, it's unsafe to allow you out alone, lest you have one of your fits. Item five: No alcohol or other stimulants.'

'I don't do any of those things.'

Edythe huffed. 'You're seventeen years old, Aisling. I know what people your age get up to. Item six – and this is crucial – any change in your symptoms, any change at all, is to be reported to me immediately. I have your doctor's telephone number. If anything changes, I'm to send you back into his care.'

'Can I not go out at all?'

Edythe folded the list up and slipped it into her skirt pocket. 'You've been sitting here all evening thinking about how stupid I am, haven't you?'

Aisling looked to the window, to the dark sky and the gangly birches at the foot of the garden. There was anger inside her, straining, spitting. 'I just want to know how I'm supposed to get fresh air if I can't leave the house. Should I hang out of the window?'

'That's enough,' snapped Edythe. 'I know about the stealing. I know about the "walks". The night on the motorway. The police bringing you home. What were you doing? Hitchhiking?'

'I don't have to talk about all that.'

'But what were you doing?'

'I wasn't doing anything.'

'You could have been killed.'

'It doesn't happen any more.'

'You mean *you* don't *do* it any more.' Edythe was almost shouting. 'Don't refer to your actions as though they weren't your own. Tell me, is it true that they don't have a name for this condition?'

'They said it could be a mixture of things. Non-epileptic… psycho-something.' The side of her head was hurting, little toothy bites. 'They used to call them pseudoseizures.'

'Pseudo.' Edythe took the phrase, tested its weight. 'Meaning fake.'

'They said they're real,' insisted Aisling. Feeling she ought to say it, just so the old woman knew it: 'I just want to get better.'

Edythe placed the dishes in the sink and turned on the taps. 'Frankly speaking, Aisling, I'm not sure there's anything to make better.'

Verity Holloway

5

Ascending the servants' stairs, Aisling was too despondent to think about the ghosts of tripping servants. She was following the corridor around to her bedroom when she heard the old man, Robert, calling out.

'Edy? That you?' He was in his room. The *ak-ak-ak* of the machine guns was incessant. Aisling had to go to his door and raise her voice.

'She's downstairs.'

Robert shouted back. 'Good. Fetch me a bucket. My brain is dribbling out on to the floor.'

Aisling turned the old brass handle. Spiced air: wintergreen and whiskey. Robert sat in his armchair, both legs on a footstool, the bone of the left calf curving outwards like a withered smile. Beside the chair were a couple of dog-eared books – *The Golden Age of Tall Ships* and *Sevastopol: A Victorian Bloodbath* – and blocking the fireplace was a television on a trolley, illuminating the old man's face.

Robert jabbed at the screen with his good foot. 'Edy thinks I'll develop dementia if I stay in a room without constant chatter. I get shouted at if I summon the audacity to turn the channel, let alone pull the plug. It's a disease.'

'I can turn it off, if you like.'

'You,' he said, 'are an angel.'

Aisling stabbed the power switch. The room was suddenly different – dark and very quiet. Robert looked smaller.

'Aah,' he sighed, sinking into the brocade cushions. 'Ah, that is good.'

'"Dies slowly, he who makes of television his guru",' said Aisling.

'Who said that?'

She had spoken without thinking. 'Pablo Neruda. He's a poet I like.'

'We have a lady of letters in the house!'

The laughter in Robert's eyes wasn't vindictive. A little of the mealtime tension lifted, and Aisling allowed herself a shy smile.

'All I know is classroom Turdsworth,' he said. 'D'you like Byron? You look like a Byron sort of girl.'

Aisling gave him a sideways look. 'What, the product of incest?'

'Sit.' He reached down beside his chair and held up a bottle of whiskey. 'Tipple?'

'Can't. It's against Edythe's rules.'

'Good grief, she really wrote some? I suppose it shouldn't come as a surprise. Would it be against regulations to pour me one?' He held out his big, brown hands, palms down. They shook. 'I tend to make a mess, see.'

He gestured at a willow-pattern teacup and saucer on the

floorboards. There was an amber waterline just below the teacup's rim.

A white grin slid across his wrinkled face as Aisling measured out ginger ale from a sticky plastic bottle. 'Edy says you're a tearaway. A morbid anorexic. That's about as Romantic as it gets. Be proud.'

Aisling felt herself beginning to like him. 'What else has she said?'

'Nothing worth recounting,' Robert said. He lifted his teacup and took a shaky sip. 'Sure you don't want a tipple? I'm afraid there's no more fine china, so you'll just have to...' he mimed a piratical swig.

She wasn't used to drinking, apart from the occasional Babycham at Christmas. *'I don't want you turning into one of those chavvy kids hanging around in the underpass,'* Beverley would say. Aisling took the proffered bottle, held it to her mouth. The glassy sloshing noise was better than the taste.

'I think you're supposed to be my great-niece, aren't you? Eliot's daughter.'

The whiskey burned its way down through Aisling's chest, a good burn. 'I thought Edythe lived alone.'

'Edy could start a New Age commune in the centre of Piccadilly Circus and still live alone. I only returned to this place a few years ago. Owing to decrepitude.' He took a moment to make a face at himself in the reflective television screen. 'This is the house I grew up in.'

There was a black and white photograph on the wall above the television. Two girls in floral tea dresses stood either side of a slouching boy in uniform. A long garden stretched out behind them, flanked by tidy English flower beds. All three faces glum.

She said, 'You knew my dad.'

'Do you want me to say you look like him?'

'Not really.'

'You don't. Except for the orangey hair. And the legs.'

Robert sipped his whiskey. The rain was gradually slowing.

'Not a conversationalist, are you?' he said, eventually.

'I'm not sure what I am at the moment.' That was a half-truth. She was hungry. Drowsy again.

'Edy's been putting the frighteners on you, I take it?'

'She took away my William Blake book.'

'Poor Ophelia. You get sensory deprivation, and I get immersion therapy.'

Aisling folded her hands in her lap. 'I had group therapy a few times. Five or six of us had to sit in a circle while we passed around a beanbag. There was this one girl who only ever lasted ten minutes each session before walking out and slamming the door. It was supposed to make us connect with our peers and feel the benefit of a successful group dynamic.' She realised with slight discomfort that this was the most she'd said to a stranger for weeks, therapy included. The intimacy brayed. When he didn't look away, Aisling reached for her plait and loosened the hairband, allowing the hair to curtain her face.

'Tell me what Edythe said about me,' Aisling said. 'Please.'

'Why don't you tell me about yourself?'

'I don't like talking about myself.'

'If you don't talk about yourself, less qualified people will only do it for you. Have another.' He waved the bottle at her.

She took a swig, if only to spite her aunt.

'Good girl. Let's get the hard stuff out of the way first, shall we? You have seizures.'

'Sort of.'

'Epilepsy?'

'No.'

'See things?'

'Sometimes.'

'What things?'

She said nothing. It occurred to her with a brief, vehement stab that she had the choice not to explain herself to another stranger. She was glad when Robert sensed her dislike of being looked at. He stretched in his chair. 'Let's swap. You want to know about my leg.'

'Was it polio?'

Robert nodded. 'Idle Merchant Navy doctors.'

Aisling brightened. 'You were a sailor? Is that you in the picture?'

'Father threw me a going away party before my first voyage. Nineteen forty-eight, that was. Edy never understood why I'd want to spend my life inside a floating sardine tin. That's her on the left, looking like she's chewing a wasp.'

'Who's the other girl?'

'Connie. Lovely Connie, my other sister. She was worried after she read German U-boats were still roaming the world's oceans looking for little English boys to drown. She offered to bake me Victoria sponges every week for the rest of my life if I promised not to go.' His lips creased as if to smile. He was quiet for a moment. 'She's your grandmother, do you know that?'

Aisling looked at Connie's face, the youngest of the three, her eyes staring somewhere beyond the camera's lens. 'We don't really talk about her.'

'She and Edy had their differences, even before Elliot

came along,' Robert said. 'If there's one thing this family excels at, it's letting people disappear.'

This is my family, it occurred to Aisling. *This is my family.*

Robert was looking at the photograph. 'It was good for me, the Navy. I never passed my Eleven-Plus, but I wanted to be on the move, anywhere, everywhere, all the time. Forty years I spent at sea. And now... well. I'm here again.'

She felt a pain, like a trapped nerve.

'You must have seen a lot of wonderful places.'

He nodded. 'Oh, a few. I've had a good time of it. Seen a few continents.' He watched his reflection in the blank television screen: a wiry, silver man.

'Have you seen Mexico?' Aisling asked, suddenly.

'What's special about Mexico?'

'Dia de los Muertos. The day of the dead. I've got a magazine with me, it's got a brilliant photo essay all about it.'

'Oh, you *are* a Romantic.'

'I'll go. One day,' she said, a little tipsily. 'Every year they celebrate the return of the dead to the land of the living. They spend all night sitting by their loved ones' graves, lighting candles, drinking and singing. The two worlds weave together. And everyone's happy.' She focused on the image, trying to feel the Mexican heat in the cold room and failing. Why on earth was there no radiator to keep the old man from pneumonia? 'I want to go to a place without all this stiffness.'

'Not Suffolk, then?'

They shared a smile. He offered her more whiskey, and she took it, if only to stifle the voice that said *don't*. Her limbs felt buttery, and her tongue free.

'William Blake, in a vision, he travelled to the underworld and met the people there. And they told him that the freedom of his mind, his imagination, was "the real and eternal World of which this Vegetable Universe is but a faint shadow". And "the wide world might fly from its hinges".' She snorted. 'I don't even know what that means, but I love it.'

'Sounds like old Bill could have done with a bit of therapy himself.'

Aisling realised she was viewing the room through a golden haze of Johnnie Walker and Robert's smile was no longer quite trustworthy. She carefully rose to leave.

'Off to bed?' Robert sounded disappointed.

'I've got some writing to do.'

'Which room has she given you?'

'I'm at the end of the hall, up the stairs.'

Robert lifted his teacup. His eyebrows formed a silky silver 'V' over the rim.

6

Any hope of a whiskey-warmed sleep evaporated as Aisling struggled with her bedroom door to find the sash window open. Half a dozen limp birch leaves lay scattered on the floorboards and the room was as cold as the fields outside.

'Ugh, no...' A gust of wind sprayed rain up into her face before she could force the ancient pulley mechanism to move. It came down with a fearful crash, causing the emerald cufflink to rattle on the nightstand like a bone.

Aisling slumped down on to the saturated window seat. Robert was coughing at the far end of the hall and she felt her own throat itch. Now that the window was closed, the odour of acetate from the bathroom was strong again and instinctively she put her sleeve over her mouth to prevent it from entering her lungs.

Unexplained smells had taken on great significance for Aisling since her stay in the hospital. There, every room, every corridor, had its own distinct scent. The canteen, a cavern of that pale green paint purported to calm patients, smelt more of pine air freshener than food. Her bed gave off the barest hint of swimming pool. The routines in that place, the rolling tide of blank, miserable, or overly-excited people, the grim cheerfulness of the staff and her mother's own fidgeting unhappiness sank Aisling into sensory infancy, forcing her to experience the world through the base mediums of taste, scent, texture. Anything more sophisticated was daunting. Like the big double doors separating people like Aisling from the upper floors where the truly poorly were, if that primitive voice inside you said *avoid*, it was prudent to listen.

Fuel-stink hung in the bedroom like fog. There was not enough air.

>•<

Somewhere, a church bell declared midnight. Aisling returned to full consciousness with a wheeze. Her jeans were wet. Her face. *How long have I been like this?*

There was a figure in the garden, indistinct through the window's warped pane. It moved aimlessly about the dark lawn, heading towards the pond before ambling back to the flowerless rose bushes clinging to the trellises. Aisling rested her forehead against the glass and let the chill penetrate her skin. The light from her bedroom cast illumination over a small square of the garden, and as the figure wandered closer she realised it was the long, narrow silhouette of a man.

The man – he was close enough now for Aisling to make out the square of his jaw and the stoop of his shoulders – paced the width of the garden, pausing now and then to look up into the rain or turn abruptly on his heel, making the tails of his long, heavy coat fly out behind him. Aisling followed his erratic progress, forgetful of ever struggling with the window or breathing in that sickly odour. He sauntered closer – hair a shaggy yellow-blond – and turned his face to Aisling's window.

She recoiled. If he saw her, he didn't give a sign.

That was the moment he shifted his weight on to one foot and dropped into a long-limbed handstand. His coat-tails flopped heavily down behind his head, but the man remained motionless, unselfconscious, legs sticking up and hair sticking out as the rain set sequins on the soles of his boots.

Aisling was enchanted.

A sharp flickering in the right side of her head. With a grunt, Aisling clenched her eyes shut. She opened them, and the bedroom walls glared back, the shadows of the birch trees all over them like a dizzying web of scribbled letters. A drum roll of bone and she was on the floor, clenched, foetal, elbows and knees wired to her ribcage, jerking, jerking, and something was making the most awful choked whimpering sound, but she couldn't raise her head to see, for the violet sparks were taking over her vision and when her teeth clamped down around her tongue there was the iron tang of blood.

Quiet now. Rain. The night outside was very dark, the man gone. When she managed to get into bed, she took out her journal and a pen, and began, head swimming with exertion, to write.

Your rhythm, Feodor, could do with sharpening.

Verity Holloway

7
FEODOR

I love this waltz: Chopin's Grande Valse Brillante. *I learnt to play it – slowly – when I was eight. Mama would smile and kiss my curly head. Next stop, Royal Albert Hall. On the sofa, Dad – the big man who saw an old piano in a pawnshop, saw the five flights of stairs to our flat, and saw no problem – would keep his eyes on* Auto Trader.

'Your rhythm, Feodor, could do with sharpening.'

I sharpened my rhythm. I learnt Sinding and Debussy. When I was fifteen, Dad sold the piano to a pawnshop in Brixton. He told me it was to pay for Mama's funeral, but I smelt his breath and knew better.

The service was held in the Russian Orthodox Cathedral on Harvard Road, where the magnolia trees grow. Mama was Russian, like Dad. They came to London for work: her a music teacher, and him whatever. Mama would have hated her funeral: the smoke, the bells, the prickly bush the priest called his beard. 'There are worlds better than this one,' she told me once. 'You can drop this old shell in the Thames when I'm done with it.' In the car park, I stared at the church's onion dome, cerulean and gold, like a fibreglass turret on a Disneyland castle. Mama had eyes as black as her braided hair. How dare she leave this world without me?

In the weeks following her death, I sat at the kitchen table and practised my fingerwork, silently chasing the waltz over the sticky Formica while Dad slept. I felt the remains of Mama's presence in the kitchen: a warm black spark in my fingertips each time they struck an imaginary chord. It shot up my arms and tickled my heavy heart.

That was all so long ago.

When they put out the fires and rebuild the town, they'll say I was a sickly loner touting dangerous ideas, grabbing fame at the cost of gullible citizens. The newspapers will detail my perversities. They'll say I tortured rodents and slept with my sisters. I'm an only child, but who cares? It's what they do.

Had you seen me scramble over the wall that night, you might have recognised the boy from the posters. I tore one down and kept it.

BLIGHT

White male. Early twenties. Height: 5'7' approx. Build: Slight. Black hair at shoulder length, clean shaven (possibly to masquerade as the opposite sex in the style of deviants), pallid complexion as result of internal corruption.

Known to consort with Foreigners
and the degenerative classes.
Information leading to arrest is subject to
FINANCIAL REWARD.
Fugitive WILL NOT respond to rational

communication. DO NOT APPROACH.
GIVE US THE LAW OF REASON
AND OUR FRIEND.

Isn't that good? There's an artist's impression of me, too: a ragged rat-boy with frantic eyes like a skull wearing a wig. I used to be quite a cute little so-and-so before all of this. There was a poster of an old singer called Siouxsie Sioux tacked above the bookcase in my bedroom at Crossways. We looked quite alike when I ruffled my hair. The state of me now, though, you wouldn't leave me alone with your kids.

It's the wasteland for me, these days. Dutiful citizens don't venture out this way. New mothers won't even leave their babies in rooms facing this direction for fear that they'll be switched for a Foreign changeling in the night. All we'd ever need, we were told, exists inside the walls. Oh, you're welcome to leave, fine, if you're happy to live with runaways, eating stray cats. You can even try to come back. But Our Friend will notice. Our Friend notices everything.

The night it happened, I don't know how many hours I spent running. Each time I stopped for breath, I'd catch the smoke on the wind as if the town itself was reaching out to clutch my clothes. I went blindly through brambles, inhaling mosquitoes. As the temperature dropped and the night birds came out to sing, I realised I was chanting the rhythm of the waltz to myself, Grande Valse Brillante, *all wobbly with tears. More than once, I slipped on wet leaves and lay with my face to the ground, '1, 2, 3, 1, 2, 3', hoping for someone to find me and shoot me neatly in the back of the head. But I'd always find myself running again. The boys back home called me a dirty little wuss. I'll give them that.*

I kept moving. The forest smelt larger. The smog of the city and the fumes of the fire were far behind me. My boots touched stone and I stopped.

It was dark inside the church. I saw the moon hanging in the broken rafters. I thought of my father for the first time in months. I saw him alone in that flat, listening out for the midnight train on the Docklands Light Railway. I heard the splash in the dark before I knew I was vomiting.

There was a large slab of stone in the middle of the floor, and I draped my body over its cool, smooth length.

'I was trying to make it all better,' I said. 'Dad, I'm sorry.'

Panic made me crazy. I heard his deep, dark voice next to my ear.

'My son is missing.'

'I'm here,' I said. 'Here.'

The words were low and dull. 'My son is missing.'

My fingers dug into the stone – 'I hate you' – and he was gone.

I must've slept. The sweat on my body was cooling. I swallowed, breathed, and raised my head.

I thought they didn't have churches here any more. The dawn birds were singing and it was light enough for me to see the ceiling, fractured and ragged as if a bomb had fallen through it. Marble arches and broad twisting columns barely supported the walls and ceiling. Above me, segments of broken staircases and balconies seemed suspended by clouds of cobwebs and a thick, wet mould caking the stone.

It was then that I realised how far I'd run.

I'd heard of these places in hushed conversations, in books I shouldn't have read. No one would follow me here.

When my hands stopped shaking, I took a penknife from

my boot and placed the blade against the nearest wall. I began to scratch the words you're reading now.

If there's one name I should be carving, it's Rada.

Remember her name. I did it all for her.

Rada.

8

Two weeks passed in a seamless block of time. Each morning, Aisling would dress and walk down the servants' staircase to the kitchen where Edythe would be boiling eggs and examining the teacups for stains. The breakfast news would be audible from Robert's bedroom, and each kitchen utensil and each tea towel would be in the same immaculate state as it had been the previous morning. Strong tea, a pill. Eggs like boiled eyes. Eating these would usually result in a sudden trip to the bathroom, after which Edythe would crossly boil another egg, and keep Aisling at the table until she had at least digested some of it.

Time was on a loop.

At first, the solitude was good. Aisling was free to spend her days decorating her arms with biro flames and swallows, light-headedly sketching the view from her window, pausing now and then to scribble in her journal: places to visit when she was better, odd words and phrases scavenged from interrupted dreams.

The house was a quieter world than the hospital, and even home. Moorhens pecked for snails in the garden and the occasional tractor trundled up the lane, but as Aisling lay awake in the grey hours, listening to the gangs of foxes screeching in the fields, she found herself pining for the night-time sirens and barking dogs of her suburban home, for Beverley's bath-time singing and the laughing packs of men ambling home from the pub.

Noise was privacy. Beverley, boiling nests of noodles in the kitchen. *Clang, hiss*, singing along to the radio. Her first seizure had gone unnoticed. Upstairs, in the bathroom overlooking the red roofs of the neighbouring street; Aisling on the floor, gripping an open tub of bath salts, electric, absent.

By the end of the second week at Edythe's house, with no word from her mother, she was as weary and nervous as she had been when she had first arrived, sleeping sporadically throughout the day, annoying Edythe with her long silences and unbrushed hair. Whenever her ears caught the *clip-clop* of a horse and rider trotting by, Aisling longed to run outside, waving and shouting her hellos, ordering them to regurgitate the headlines, the weather forecast, the number of dead pheasants they'd seen along the road that day. As Aisling's copy of *Wanderlust* grew shabby around the edges, she composed postcards to Beverley as if she was free to roam the globe.

Namaste, Mum, from the banks of the Ganges!

I slept on the Zakynthos beach last night as the turtles crawled out of the sea to lay their eggs.

St Petersburg isn't cold at all when you've got enough vodka. I'm having a wonderful time, she lied. *And I feel fine.*

Bored though she was, she fought the urge to read more of the horrible book with the painted pages. Its presence in her room felt like a calculated insult, whispering on the nightstand as she tried to sleep. *Defective. Feeble-minded.* Despite this, she couldn't help but wonder who had added the handwritten notes. Who could agree so strongly with something so cruel? The notepaper was crisp with age, she decided, giving in to temptation one night. Perhaps they belonged to the Reverend Enright, or one of his black and white cohorts from the hall photographs.

I cannot sleep, she read, in a similar state herself, wrapped in a blanket while the rain poured from a broken gutter above her window. *I hear him downstairs. The children – the favoured daughter. It was never this bad before. They are driving me into it. The whitewash helped for a month, alongside clean living, but the sickness has taken root. My nerves are glass. My skin flakes. Weak teeth. Weak mind. Weak.*

Some venereal disease, laid dormant in the bloodline? A fault of the brain passed down by my forefathers? In 1704, Jonathan Swift wrote of the corruption of the senses blocking the avenues of the fort of reason. This civil war inside a man leaves him vulnerable to physical and intellectual weakness. It poisons his lineage. Hence, the mongoloid. Hence, the pinhead.

If John knew how bad it was, he would send me away. I barely believe in his God any more. But, then, does he?

Sent away. A quiet infirmary somewhere. Would it not be better? Than this?

Aisling recoiled from the words with a wave of nausea. The green cufflink glittered in her palm. She put it away and wiped her hands on the blankets.

Can the defective be cured? I put it to you, why is this our chief concern? A plague is conquered in much the same fashion as a rotten tooth. Tear it out. Tear it out by the roots.

>•<

Mrs Bloom came on Thursday. Aisling heard her rattling up the gravel drive with Sainsbury's carrier bags swinging from her handlebars. She put down her journal, leaving a line hanging on the empty page—

Feodor was afraid. But who wasn't?

—and rushed down the stairs, through the kitchen to the hall. She nearly collided with the front door as it swung open to reveal a heavily breathing figure in Wellington boots and a cycling helmet.

'Goodness me!' Mrs Bloom shook the rain off her anorak and on to Edythe's beautifully polished tiles. 'I'm here with your shopping, Edy. Still raining, I'm afraid. Oh. Hello there, love. Who are you, then?'

Aisling stared at her stupidly. 'I thought you were someone else.'

'I'm not someone else. I'm Doreen Bloom, from the village.' She took off her crash helmet and began hefting wet carrier bags full of tinned food in from outside. 'Is Mrs Enright at home?'

Aisling sank back towards the stairs. Above the door, the Reverend Enright and his companions gazed down at her from the 1940s, unimpressed. The flinching man in the black suit seemed to be shaking his head. *You thought it was mummy, didn't you?*

'It's a nice surprise to see a new face here, I must say. Who did you say you were, my love?'

Edythe had entered quietly through the kitchen door. 'This is Aisling, Mrs Bloom. She's staying with us while she convalesces from an illness.'

Mrs Bloom looked delighted. 'Poor poppet. There's a lot of it about. Get on the outside of this.' She produced a warm Mars bar from her pocket and pressed it into Aisling's hand. 'I've three girls of my own. Why don't I send them round? You might benefit from a bit of gossip.'

'Aisling isn't here to be entertained, Mrs Bloom. She's given us all a lot of grief.'

Mrs Bloom's gazed switched from Edythe for a furtive second, taking in Aisling's attenuated wrists and the circles beneath her eyes.

'Oh. Well.' Embarrassed, she turned to Edythe. 'I picked up some bleach, in case you've run out. And I've brought Bert the cough linctus you asked for. I've a spare little oil heater at home, if it's the draught that's—'

Edythe gave a sharp shake of the head. 'The cough is his own fault. Someone has been bringing him cigarettes again. This is a timber house, Mrs Bloom. If he fell asleep with one of those things in his mouth...'

Mrs Bloom smiled benignly. 'He'd make a nasty hole in the Axminster, yes love. It's not me who's giving them to him, I assure you. You ought to ask that new postman. Name's Ahmed. One does wonder.'

'I will. Thank you.' Edythe looked at Aisling. 'Do something practical, please, and take the tins down to the cellar for me to organise later.'

Aisling grabbed the bags and went, dropping the Mars

bar in the kitchen bin as soon as she was out of sight. She found the cellar door and made her way down the creaking stairs into the cool darkness. When she found the light switch she was presented with three sets of plywood shelves: 'Comestibles: Perishable', 'Comestibles: Non-Perishable', and one heaving with alcohol wipes and disinfectants. A tarnished altar cross was propped up next to the non-perishables, and Aisling chose that spot to sit, letting the tins spill from the shopping bags and roll around the floor.

Two weeks. No phone calls, no postcards. She wondered where her mother was right at that moment. Tweaking at her hair in Malcolm's London loft conversion, talking about the charming country vicarage she lived in as a girl? For one wild second Aisling considered running up the stairs and stealing Mrs Bloom's bicycle. She could cycle to a train station. She could dodge the fare and get to London, find Beverley, apologise for everything. An image intruded of Robert in his chair, staring at his useless leg. She wanted her Blake book, to recite, to calm herself. Stupidly, she began to cry. 'I want to go *home*,' she heard herself say. 'I want to go home.'

But that wasn't what she wanted. The realisation came abruptly, and as she leant back against the rough Tudor beams of the cellar wall, her mind slowed to a halt. She felt nothing towards the semi-detached suburban house she had left behind. The neighbours would have long ago assumed she had moved to start college or find employment like the rest of the neighbourhood teenagers. And as for them – the boys and girls Aisling never quite managed to befriend – if they remembered her at all it would be as the girl who couldn't walk to school without her mum beside her, or for the time Darren McKinnon scratched an inverted cross into her desk in the form room: *The power of Christ compels you, Schizoid.*

Aisling's fingernails traced the black beams in the walls either side of her. Beverley had her own life. At Aisling's age, she was living with her boyfriend, and then her baby. If Beverley decided to attach herself in a permanent way to Malcolm, Aisling could do nothing to stop her. And, to her surprise, she found she would have no inclination to. Aisling was seventeen now. In another year—

Her fingertips slid into a hollow in the wood. Pressing down, she felt something give.

In another year, she could just—

The whole beam moved. The beam shuddered up. It opened.

She could just go.

Summer, two years ago, twelve forty-five at night. The A14, somewhere near Newmarket. Aisling's memory was strong and sharp. Black, peaty smells of the farms either side of the concrete. There were sleeping pigs a mile or so behind her. She had climbed the embankment to stare at the lumpy shapes of them, snoozing outside their sties in the heat of the night, before moving on. Bare feet on warm asphalt.

'Where to?'

A lorry had stopped and the driver, a round man with a tired face, was calling down to her from the cab.

'Where are you going?' she asked.

'Calais,' he said. 'D'you not have a bag?'

'Calais?'

'France, via Dover. Wine wholesalers. What are you doing out here with no bag?'

'Can I come with you?'

'Now, hold on. It's the middle of the night.'

'I need to go somewhere.'

The driver peered down. 'They pyjamas?'

Aisling nodded.

'S'not right.'

Aisling shrugged.

They sat in the lay-by, waiting for the police to arrive. The driver offered her one of his Marmite sandwiches which she nibbled cautiously, as if taste might bring her pain.

The anorak he draped around her shoulders smelt of stale pork pies. 'I'm not sitting you up in the cab. Police mightn't like it. There's some who'd be less than kind to a kid out here at night, know what I mean?' He prattled on, regardless of whether Aisling was listening. She wasn't. 'D'you know how many fatalities were on the A14 last year? Two hundred and twenty-two. Some of them were little'uns like you. S'not right.' He watched her pick at the sandwich, knees drawn up to her chest. He frowned. 'You not going to talk to me?'

Aisling stared angrily at the empty road. 'I could have been miles away by now.'

'Folks at home all right?'

She paused. 'It's okay.'

'What's all this about, then?'

'I'm waiting.'

'Waiting.'

'Waiting for something.'

'And you thought you'd find it in Calais?'

'Worth a try,' she muttered. He laughed. She didn't.

Off to the left of Aisling's vision, someone was emerging from behind the stationary lorry's cab; a small person, bent down and creeping. The driver watched them quietly as they started to move diagonally at a run across the carriageway. He opened a flask of tea and poured.

The figure was awash with light – a boy with slim legs, curly hair flying – but the oncoming oil tanker was travelling too fast to stop. Aisling gave out a shriek and found herself on her feet, dashing out into the road just as the boy disappeared beneath the four pairs of wheels. The great gust of hot air whipped up by the oil tanker threw the whole weight of her loose hair over her eyes, blinding her as the arms of the driver snared her around the waist, hurting the bones there. The tanker steamed noisily ahead into the darkness, oblivious to the small person under its wheels.

The driver was dragging her away. 'Bloody things. No sense of self-preservation.'

She fought and struggled.

'Rabbits,' he said. 'Stupid bloody rabbits.'

As the roar of the engine faded and the road was again empty, there was nothing in its wake.

9

'Ophelia! You're just in time for the adverts.' Robert lifted his one good leg to indicate the stool that had become her customary place.

But Aisling stood still in the open doorway, her face unusually flushed. 'I found the priest hole,' she said. 'I found the priest hole in the cellar. That's what it is, isn't it? One of those old hiding places.'

Robert noticed her quick, shallow breathing and switched off the television. 'Sit down. I won't be able to catch you if you faint on me. What has Edy been saying?'

Aisling did not move. Robert thought he caught the crackle of static electricity on her clothes. 'She hasn't said anything. I found it. Look.' In her fists, his cigarettes, her Blake volume and papers, pale and limp with mould. 'It was full of this stuff. She's been using it to hide the things she takes from you and me. This is my book. Why would she do that?'

Robert reached out slowly, coaxing her forward until he

could touch the damp paper with the trembling tips of his fingers. Aisling's jeans were wet at the knees, but her smile was bright. His expression betrayed nothing.

'I was putting the shopping away in the cellar, and then… well, it doesn't matter. You could fit two people in there. I crawled right inside.' She felt giddy, ecstatic. The tears of the afternoon now felt childish. 'There was all this mushy old paper, like essays. Bundles of them. Look.'

She flapped a grey slice of paper at Robert, who, without his glasses, squinted at the cramped handwriting.

The First Law—

The Second Law concerns—

—give us the law—

Quiet.

Robert frowned. He took the bundle from her and placed it on the floor on the other side of his chair where she would not see it. The paper shed white flakes of paint over his hands and he wiped them on his thighs, grimacing.

'There was an old book in my room,' Aisling went on. 'About sick children, and people like me, how they should be locked away. And someone had written inside of it, a sort of a diary, and *this* – this stuff – is the same handwriting. Edythe's putting it where I'll find it. She's playing mind games with me. Why would she do that?'

'You're bleeding.'

Aisling looked at her hands. Long white things attached to longer, whiter arms. Fingernails, lined in red. 'Ow,' she said. '*Ow.*'

'Give me those filthy things and fetch the medicine chest. It's on the mantelpiece. There should be some antiseptic, thanks to Edy the Vigilant.'

Aisling drifted over to the medicine chest and took it to Robert who made her hold out her hands. He silently removed splinters and bandaged them. He insisted on checking her elbows and knees, scuffed and mauve with fresh, secret bruises, clicking his tongue and muttering something military in regards to the fraying hems of her jeans. She ordinarily hated to be touched by strangers, but the trembling of Robert's hands made them seem like small, gentle animals.

When he was quite certain there was nothing left to patch up, Robert sat back. 'Do you want to talk about it?'

'Did you know it was there? The priest hole.'

'That's not what I mean, now, is it?'

Aisling looked at her bandaged hands. 'I must have caught them on the brickwork.'

'I've punched the occasional wall in my time. I know what the results look like.' He gave her another steady, silver-browed look. 'This house has that effect on people.'

It was almost a minute until they spoke again. Robert gallantly attempted to pour her a teacup of whisky, splattering the armchair and his trousers in spicy-scented droplets.

'My head hurts,' Aisling said.

'Did you catch that on the brickwork too?'

'Mmm. No. Stabby.' She pinched the Celtic ring beneath the bandages until the pain subsided. 'I'm glad to have Blake back.'

He watched her touch the pages with ragged fingernails. 'I wouldn't want to get you in trouble, Aisling. But we have a small problem here, don't we?'

'Please don't tell Edythe. I wasn't snooping around. I won't go down there again.'

It was a lie, of course. Robert's raised eyebrow indicated that they both knew it.

'I won't go telling on you. But when potentially infectious bodily fluids are concerned, there's not a lot your Aunt doesn't notice.' They smiled at each other, but their faces swiftly dimmed. 'You understand, don't you, that you are my responsibility? As a grown-up, I must, if it comes to it, pick up that phone and speak to your doctor.'

A look of fear flashed across Aisling's face. With only a hint of difficulty, she met his eyes. 'I understand,' she said. 'But it was a silly accident. I've been healthier here than I ever was at home.'

He exhaled heavily. 'All right. Let me tell you about the priest hole. It was a rainy day during the war. We were playing indoors, my sisters and I. Connie was hiding behind the shelves in the cellar and got her dress caught on a nail sticking out of one of the beams. She struggled a bit, got her fingers into the wood to prise herself free, but she was stuck fast. Had to call Edy and I to help her. And, as you know,' he spread his hands, 'the beam is false. Three moderately strapping children pushing on it was all it took to activate the tilting mechanism, and up it swung. I got the bottom end straight in the jaw, *thwack*. The cavity behind that beam is where a very daring former owner of this house – Elizabethan, I should think – once hid a couple of very frightened Catholic priests to save them from the hangman. They have them in old houses all over England, courageous pieces of design. Our father, the Reverend, knew nothing about it, and there's no record of it in the Victorian plans for the extensions. Before that, it probably hadn't been disturbed since the 1500s.' He flashed her a begrudging smile. 'And Aisling Selkirk is here for two weeks and finds it straight away.'

Aisling lifted the teacup and studied the ripples within. Her mind drifted. After a long silence, she spoke. 'Who gives you all these cigarettes?'

Robert drummed the arm of the chair. 'You are not to tell a soul. There's a chap who comes to the house. He's researching the Russian émigrés who came over here in the twenties, for a book. There was a famine and one of my father's church colleagues helped with the relief effort. But look, don't tell Edy. She's afraid I'll be taken away to a nursing home if some do-gooder notices I'm here. He's been coming to visit for a couple of months now, nice and discreet, while Edy drifts off in front of *Countdown* in the afternoons.'

'He's blond, isn't he? I've seen him in the garden.'

Robert seemed surprised. 'Blond? No. Bald as a cricket ball.'

She hadn't thought of the strange, yellow-haired man at all since that first rainy night spent sitting on the window seat. The sight of him standing on his hands, long legs sending a carefree victory salute to the sky – *Up yours!* – flashed in her mind as clearly as if she had been handed a photograph.

Robert's silver eyebrows scrunched. 'You've seen someone in the garden?'

'I thought I did. I have vivid dreams. It's the seizures. Sometimes I find it hard to, you know. Tell the difference.' Aisling paused, testing the silence. 'Can I ask you a strange question?'

'I would love you to.'

'Do you ever feel as if you're only ever half here?'

Robert tapped his bent leg and grinned. 'Long John Silver feels as if he's three quarters here.' He instantly looked guilty for deflecting her seriousness and shifted so they were eye to eye. 'Go on, Ophelia.'

'I can't remember finding the priest hole. I can remember which beam it was and I know what it felt like to move it. But I can't remember going inside. I don't remember hurting my hands. I should know, but I don't. It's like sleepwalking.'

'Is this something frequent?' he asked.

'They're called "petit mals". You just drift off for a while. Wide awake, but not present. Some doctors call them "absences". But they don't last long, and you tend to stay still, just staring. You don't just get up and...' She looked at her knuckles. 'What else have I forgotten?'

'Perhaps these absences are why these happened.' He laid a tremulous brown paw on her bandaged knuckles, light as a moth. 'To bring yourself back.'

'I want it to be that simple, but,' she met his eyes, 'Robert, if I'm absent, where am I going?'

At that moment, Edythe's voice came from the servants' stairs.

'Aisling? The bath is dry. You haven't bathed today.'

The teacup jerked in Aisling's bandaged hands.

Robert took the cup and settled it on the floor. 'Panic not. I'll tell her you tripped. She'll scold you, but that'll be that.' Robert grasped her sleeve as she scooped up her Blake book and stuffed it into the waistband of her jeans. 'Listen. Don't go looking at nasty things in your bedroom, eh? You've enough on your plate. Don't go worrying about anyone's horrid old diary.'

'I won't,' she lied. And she was gone.

10
FEODOR

I've done some foul things in the course of my little life. But I'm at my worst when I mean no harm.

It's been years since I made this chapel my home. But still, every night, I lie here on the mattress I dragged from a tramp's abandoned hideout and think about everything I've managed to ruin. It's grown around me with time, thick, a scar.

The family that took me in owned a pawnshop in the town. First, they gave me a room and a job because they felt sorry for me. Later, they hid me.

There was Germaine, the nasty little squirt. I can still see him standing over my bed. 'There's people who'd give good money to know you're here.'

Then Arthur, his father. What a man. The best.

And Eva. She was expecting Arthur's second child when they came to take her away.

I think about making a proper tribute to them on these walls, but what would I say?

I killed them. There you go.

There were more, but I don't know their names. When the fires went out, they buried them in a long pit, sprinkling the bodies with buckets of white lime before tossing in the next layer of dead. Empty houses, unclaimed wages and a bit more food to go around. The pit's outside the town walls, so no one ever visits. In the winter the land floods. When I can't sleep I think about them, lying there under the ice.

My Mama's body is buried in London's Plaistow East Cemetery, under a plain, tooth-shaped stone. Not a word about her music, her laugh, or the magic she worked on Dad's black moods. I visited it once, saw for myself how they'd erased all trace of her. I never went back.

People were kind, to begin with. The boys in my class hassled me a little less, and the teachers spoke to me a little more. A few of the neighbours we'd never bothered to meet knocked at the door offering shortbread and tins of beans. Londoners are cold people, on the whole, but they love a sudden death.

At Mama's funeral, I was fluttered over by a flock of saggy-breasted women I'd never seen before. They hugged me without invitation, told me how they'd worked with her in the factories when she'd first arrived in England, that she was a tough old bird and it was all such a shock. Their husbands and kids loitered around the graveside, suspiciously eyeing the Cyrillic prayer books and the odd way we had of crossing ourselves: right to left, not left to right like the Catholics. A few of the women sniffled through the service, and I wanted to slap them. If I managed not to cry, what right did they have? Their watery humanistic crap made my chest burn. 'You'll always have your memories.' 'She'll live on in your heart.' As if grief were an embarrassing smell that would go away if you sprayed enough air freshener on it.

Dad went under quickly.

The grieving widower is given three months to get it all out of his system. After those first long weeks of visitors and Interflora deliveries, he is expected to politely keep his grief to himself. The phone calls trickle away to nothing and the foil-wrapped lasagnes cease. Life, they kept telling us, would go on.

Time goes on. Life doesn't.

From now on it was just Dad and Feodor in a pokey fifth-storey flat. It didn't take long for us to slip off the community radar. The other boys on the estate had always thought I was queer, so they gave me a wide berth. Most of the time it was just me, walking up and down the concrete walkways linking the towers, flicking my lighter in time with the metronome in my head while Dad went off on one of his drives. I'd never hated Crossways before. The tower I grew up in was a gothic place sprung up from the earth, my very own fortress against the London skyline. I liked the flickering artificial light and the dripping in the stairwells when it rained. Even the rattling lifts and the slamming doors were okay with me. But now Mama was dead, the estate was one enormous concrete tombstone – here lies Feo and his dirty, noisy, insignificant little life.

Plans came to me. Politicians said it all the time – 'Clean up the streets'. I could get up at three in the morning and throw petrol down the stairs. I wanted to see my fellow lowlifes – all twenty-seven storeys of them and their beetroot-faced babies – get up and do something.

I was too small for big shit like that. I bought food and did laundry. I lit candles beside Mama's icon of the Virgin. Told clever stories to the neighbours when they caught me in the corridor.

'Your dad in?' No, he's asleep. No, he's working. No, he has the flu.

'How's school?' All right. I like PE. Watch this handstand.

I suppose it was inevitable that I got ill, but I was still furious about it. Lights in my left eye. They'd come on before a killer headache, and I dreaded the sight of them, like bad water trickling down a gutter. Once that started flowing, it wasn't long before the room was spinning and I'd be heaving like I was trying to bring up a kidney. The GP said I might never be safe to drive a car. Not even a scooter. I didn't have a respectable tumour in there. Just a crappy old head.

I dropped school in September '94. I was fifteen. Dad didn't notice. Dad didn't notice much at all.

Mr Benedict, the bachelor along the hall with the paunch like a sack of sand, started helping me out, which was great, especially when he introduced me to his friends. They all wanted to give me money. Dad had lost his job at the docks and my paper round wasn't enough. My cute Siouxsie Sioux face was morphing into hollow-cheeked adolescence and I needed new shoes, but Mister B and his friends didn't mind. I told one of these men I'd always wanted a pair of Dr Martens, and he drove me to the Army surplus shop and bought me a pair of paratrooper jump boots with someone's name in felt-tip pen on the tongues. He was funny, that one – L, he called himself. All elbows, and hair like a rusty scouring pad. He had a girlfriend and a couple of kids in various locations and looked alarmed when I said more than six words in a row. But he'd pay me to sit in the back of his Metro while he

slithered all over me and went on about how he was waiting
for some relative to pop their clogs, and then it'd be Brazil,
the West Indies, all that. Bye-bye, crappy Crossways.

I said to him once, 'I reckon everywhere's crappy if you
give it a chance to be.' Running away wouldn't sort it. Maybe
if people didn't run away so often, they'd fix places up.
Someone should put up a fight, at least. L looked at me like
I was retarded – 'What, you?' – and my eye started with the
lights. It wasn't worth saying another word.

Dad would drink himself to sleep while the sun was still
above the tower blocks. He'd always enjoyed a few with
Mama. It was their Friday night thing, cuddling in front of
the TV watching Humphrey Bogart (*As fast on the draw as
he is in the drawing room!*) and Margaret Astor (*She's been
bad – worse than you could know!*) on Mama's flickery video
of The Maltese Falcon. Dad liked to think he was Bogart.
Looking back, on a good day, he did have a certain charisma.
No one would put up with him otherwise. When he slapped
my face he would straight away hug me tight and call me his
little crumb. I still can't stand arms around me.

Now Mama was gone, he rarely moved from the sofa,
preferring to piss into an empty milk bottle than walk six feet
to the bathroom. It was my job to stand tall, deepen my voice
and convince the corner shop staff that, yes, I was eighteen,
yes, all that Smirnoff was for tiny wee me, and no, I didn't
plan to drink it all in one go, ha ha.

That's when I met Rada.

Dad would talk at me when I was in the room, and at no
one when I was away. I'd hear him sometimes, ranting on in
his baritone English (never Russian – 'To hell with that filthy
place,' he used to say) as I came up the stairs from the corner

shop or Mr Benedict's flat. 'Rada', he'd be moaning. 'Rada.'
Rada, rada, rada.

Sometimes I'd surprise him, slam the door behind me and shout, 'Rada, what? Rada, who?' He'd look up from the sofa, the capillaries livid in the whites of his eyes, then demand to know where I'd been, and why I smelt of petrol and aftershave, you secretive little invert, you disgrace to your mother's memory.

I threw down my coat, knocking over the takeaway cartons piled next to the bin. The noise made him wince. 'I've got money. Money, remember what that is? What's Rada? Do you even know what you're gabbing on about? Never mind me, what would Mama think of you now? I wish you'd just die. I wish I'd just die. Don't yell at me when I pay for this shit, when I mop up your mess.'

We'd go on like that, flinging accusations across the living room until, surprise, he'd burst into embarrassing tears I could hear from my bedroom as I lay on top of the duvet, boots on, watching the stray headlights skim across my curtains from the road.

How long would this last?

'I need a priest.'

He said it one afternoon as I sat playing Sinding's Rustle of Spring silently on the kitchen table. He'd been quiet for hours. I'd thought he was asleep.

'Dress me.' I saw him trying to heft himself up off the sofa. 'Get my coat. Where are the keys?'

'You can't go out. You look like hell,' I said.

'I need a priest.'

'You need a shower.'

'Feodor. You'll get me to the church.'

'Oh, sure. I do everything else, don't I? Why do you need a priest? Do you want an exorcism?'

He became aware of the large stain on his trouser leg that had been there for a fortnight and rubbed it uselessly with his sleeve. 'Get me down to the car. Where are my keys?'

'You don't seriously believe you can drive.'

'Then you drive!' he spluttered. 'Get the bloody keys!'

I was due a migraine. Never mind driving underage, if I got dizzy at the wheel I might plough us both into a lamp post. That sounded all right, actually. One way to test Mama's theories about other, better worlds.

'Dad, sit down. You're going to fall.'

He slumped back down into the cushions. 'I'm having one of my headaches. Do the thing you do. Put your hands, yes. Do the thing to me.'

A hangover's not a headache, I nearly told him. But I did it like I always did. My palms flat on the wrinkled plane of his brow. I wasn't a faith healer or anything. I just had an unusual way of dealing with the morning after.

'I'm cursed,' he whined, and I felt his fingernails through my sleeve. 'I've done this to you both. God, I need a priest. God, I'm so...'

This was my father. My big, booming father: a sweaty lump of flesh with funny-coloured eye sockets, cringing under my touch. I sat on the arm of the sofa, easing him down.

'Shut it,' I said, testing his brow for the source of pain, lightly exploring blood vessels. It tastes like smoke, a headache. Like burnt rubber and liquorice. My father was sick, I could taste it. Sick in his depths.

He was whimpering nonsense now, like a man fighting a fever. 'My boy, my little crumb. You shouldn't be here. The *things I've done. Rada. And your mother. My wife. My son.'*

I couldn't concentrate. 'Shut. Up.'

I applied gentle pressure to his skin. There, above his left eye. 'This is your own fault,' I told him, tracing the marble swirl of pain. 'You won't eat. You won't drink the water I bring you. If you die on me, what then? A foster home? You can't do that to me.'

He was nodding pathetically, tears leaking from the crusty corners of his eyes. Had he not smelt so foul I might have kissed his cheek to reassure him, but the pain was rising from him now, leaving chalky condensation in the back of my mouth. He allowed his corned-beef hairy head to flop back into the cushions with a grunt.

It was done. Sod's law being what it is, I couldn't fix myself this way. Maybe I'm just unfixable.

I'd felt wisps of my father's emotions once or twice as I tended to his headaches. On one occasion I thought I heard him swearing at me when his mouth was closed. It wasn't something that kept either of us awake at night. I didn't think I was Mystic Meg, but then—

Along came Rada.

I knew little about Dad's life in Russia. He hated to be pestered. Yet here, inside my head, was a girl called Rada in a town called Rostov. Here was a lake called Nero, wide as a sea, and a youth called Yuri. This was my dad, this Yuri. Rada was his sweetheart, one of a handful.

Lake Nero was three metres deep and froze so thickly in winter you could drive a car on it. I knew this because Dad knew this, just as he knew it was the night of 8th March 1959, and that he had agreed to meet Rada in secret by the lake's edge. Nine o'clock. The date was indelible.

I saw domed churches and ramparts. I saw cornfields and factories. But most of all, I saw Rada.

Yuri liked to meet his girlfriends in secret. He and Rada had been meeting by the lake for two months, ever since she'd first visited the railway cafe where he sold tea to grey-faced travellers on their way to Leningrad. He didn't love Rada, but she was older than him, just enough to make his friends congratulate him on his catch. Rada was a cheerful blonde, not grouchy like Irina or bottom-heavy like Veronika. Yuri would take biscuits from the cafe and they'd share them, cuddled up at the lake's deserted edge with the distant city lights lying still against the surface.

I spread my fingers out against Dad's forehead. I saw the deep ripple of the water as Rada tossed a cold pebble with her slim white hand.

'I'm going away to England soon.'

'What's there?' he said.

'Everything.'

There was paperwork in her bag. Red crosses on official-looking letterheads.

'It's taken my mother and I years. But we've found something grandmother lost.'

Grandma could take a running jump. Rada's eyes were full of emotion, and that made her kissable.

I knew what was coming. I didn't want to watch.

For thirty-five years, my dad had replayed this moment. I saw it as he did: coated with guilt so thick it clogged my throat and forced me to gag.

Rada in his arms; the warmth beneath her blouse. It happened quickly. Juvenile anticipation interrupted by a gentle push from her, a word he didn't quite hear or understand, *a touch of skin, a shove, angry words. He was embarrassed – he hated to be embarrassed – and when she tried to stand he wouldn't let her. He hadn't meant any harm, he hadn't, but she was stronger than he thought and when she struggled out of his grasp, cursing him, he lost all control.*

If I had just pulled away and walked four feet to the door, maybe none of this – none of this terrible, unnatural mess – would have happened to me.

Meanwhile, in 1959, Dad hadn't anticipated the slipperiness of the frost. As he lurched after Rada, shouting about dim-witted reactionary women, he stumbled, grabbing her coat-tails as he went down hard on his kneecaps. Rada spun and yanked at the hem with both her hands, and the force of it coupled with him releasing his grip surprised them both as it sent the girl backwards across the frosty grass, and down the short, steep bank to the water.

A glutinous numbness covered him.

She was in the lake. I heard the splash as her heavy overcoat forced her under, and then the second splash as she came up floundering. Somewhere in the harsh space between a choke and a shriek, she called to him: 'Yuri!'

Dad watched.

I felt his dull, mechanical surprise. A girl has fallen into a lake, *he thought.* What will happen next?

A moment later – how long, I couldn't tell – he got up and took two small steps to the lake's edge. Rada's pale face was like a coin in the water. A mermaid. I heard the pretty similes forming in his mind as the girl thrashed, open-mouthed, in the dark lake. He was almost excited by the sight, because she'd said no, hadn't she, and now look at her.

No one was hollering for blankets. Dad wasn't whipping

*off his coat and diving in to save her. One short scream and
it was over.*

*A crescent moon emerged from the clouds. Yuri watched
it for a moment, his breath coming in smooth streams before
him. At his feet, Rada fought against the dragging weight
of her coat. Her fingers stretched desperately for the frozen
bank. Dad was thinking about a tattoo he'd seen on the arms
of the hoarier menfolk of Rostov:* What a woman wants, God
wants. *Yuri considered this as he observed Rada's slowing
struggle and wondered if God wanted her to climb that
bank just as much as she did. It was odd, he thought, how
he couldn't muster the energy to care. He ought to be on his
knees, grunting like a fisherman and hauling this endangered
female up into his sturdy, gentle arms, should he not?*

*He looked to the onion domes in the distance and wiped
his nose.*

*I watched him stuff the scattered English letters into Rada's
handbag and nudge it with his toe until it toppled, tumble-
tumble-splash, into the lake beside its flagging owner.*

*When Yuri turned his back and walked away across the
dark field – the careless shuffle of a drunk – Rada and I were
left with each other, joined at the eyes, drifting down into the
dark water, drifting into the quiet.*

*When I came to, it was to the sight of my father's watery
blue eyes locked on to my face with horrible sobriety.*

'Vyed'ma,' he whispered.

Witch.

I grabbed my coat and legged it.

*Mr Benedict was unlocking his door as I hurried around
the corner. Either side of his trainers were carrier bags full of
lager, and he smiled when he saw me.*

'Afternoon, Feo. Me and the lads are getting together tonight. You'd like to see the lads, wouldn't you?'

'Great,' I managed to croak. I was shaking at the knees like a cartoon character. 'Tonight?'

'Nine. Your old man'll be all right?'

My boots thumped away down the corridor.

I bought a sausage roll from the Spa shop. I gathered together some loose sheets of newspaper blowing around and took them under one of the concrete walkways where I set them alight. I smothered a small panic when I thought my lighter was out of fluid, but the paper soon caught the flame and I sat there, under the walkway, warming my sausage roll until the fire fizzled out and the wind chased the blackened remnants of the horoscope pages away across the grass.

I wouldn't go home that night.

First thing tomorrow, I'd go to the Army recruitment place on North Road. They'd cut my hair and give me a uniform and I'd never have to think of myself as anything but part of a unit again. They'd send me away. Screw what I'd said to L about Crossways and sticking around to fix it up. I didn't even want to destroy the place any more. I wanted out.

A puddle shimmered chrome in the wind, reminding me of the lights in my eyes. Fine, then. If the Army wouldn't take a boy with a bad head, I'd heard you could do fairly well living rough if you were smart and stayed away from the heroin. The Salvation Army would feed you and, if you were really lucky, some places offered proper beds at night, and showers. I had skills, didn't I? At least two skills. It hadn't occurred to me until then, but when my father died I'd be free to go wherever I liked.

I laughed because I was scared.

What the hell had I just seen?

The back of my mouth tasted of railway cafe biscuits, and I spat into the ashes to get rid of it. My hands reeked of Dad's sweat. I washed them in the puddle and wiped them on my thighs. New calluses on my fingertips. I crammed them in my mouth and sucked.

What could I do now? Believe what I'd seen? Climb those stairs and ask my father if he let a girl drown thirty-five years ago? Question time, Daddy: are you a girlfriend-murdering bastard? And what do you fancy for tea?

Maybe he killed Mama, too.

Now my mind was going to hysterical places. Of course he didn't kill Mama. Mama died of a stroke. One day she was fine, the next she was not. It happens all the time, all over the planet, and yes, it hurt more than I thought anything could hurt, but that won't change things, will it, Feodor?

My father hadn't cried at the funeral. Neither had I, but I'd been holding it in. That was pride, not, I don't know, evil? Perhaps the ability to crush emotions is in the blood. A survival reflex. How else could I stand Mr Benedict and his parties and his—

There was gristle in the sausage meat. I was going to leave it on the tarmac when I noticed an old tramp settling down for the night on one of the benches by the playground no one ever played in. My legs were heavy as I walked to him.

'Cheers, sweetheart,' the tramp said, squinting up into my face as I handed him the food. He wasn't old, as I'd first assumed. He laughed huskily as he registered my gender before cramming the remains of the sausage roll into a hole in his beard. 'Sorry, mate. Can't tell these days.'

It was getting dark. I could smell other people's dinner

floating out across the estate: tinned spaghetti hoops, curry, chips. To me, it was the scent of someone else's world. I felt uprooted.

I could see our window from the park. The lights were on. Had Dad fallen in the shower again, I wondered? Was this the same Yuri who had fled to England and found himself a job with all the other immigrants, loading container ships at the docks with his big biceps? Had a killer really courted my mother?

Somehow, I knew Mama had died without ever knowing about Rada. For thirty-five years he'd barely admitted it to himself, until grief unwound his coils of defence. There was a curious feeling, though, crawling over me. Now that I'd seen Rada, what was I supposed to do with her?

'Oi! Count Dracula. Whatchoo staring at?'

Three guys were loping towards me across the playground. One in front, a thin boy with a Nike tracksuit and spray-tan, fixed me with a grin that meant bruises. Strangers, all three of them, but that didn't matter. Nothing brings you back to reality quite like a punch-up.

'He's gonna howl at the moon,' joked the smallest, who couldn't have been more than fourteen. He'd shaved his head so closely he weirdly resembled an ageing skinhead shrunk to half his natural size. He strutted up to me, looking for approval from the third boy, a big lad with bottle of something blue in his fist, two-thirds empty and sloshing against the glass like antifreeze.

'He's looking for business,' said this big one. 'Aren't you, little fag? We know what you get up to.' He unscrewed the bottle; the dubious blue liquid disappeared between his teeth.

I stood still as the tanned one began to circle me, scanning from the roots of my unwashed hair to the toes of my boots. 'My mate says you're a he-she. His mum's a nurse up at the hospital, and she says when you were born the doctors didn't know if you were a boy or a girl 'cause you'd got this weird, shrivelled thing between your legs like one of them monsters from Alien.'

The little skinhead giggled. 'That's nasty, that is.'

'It's Chernobyl, yeah? After the fallout, all the Communists were having freak-babies with no eyes and stuff.'

It was always the same with this sort. They were waiting for me to say something that meant they could teach me my place. I still wonder if this was to avoid admitting what they really wanted: an excuse to get close, to lay on hands.

'Chernobyl was in '86,' I said.

That did it. The tanned one stopped circling and leaned in. We looked into each other's eyes. 'You what?'

'Six years after I was born.'

'So?'

'So were your mum and dad siblings or are you just crap at maths?'

The kid's whole head turned Spam pink. 'Piss off, he-she! Your dad's a lush. Everyone knows. Your dad's a drunk and your mum's dead, and you're a fag. So piss off.'

On the bench, the tramp pulled his coat over his head and turned his back to us.

The biggest boy pointed his bottle of blue at me. 'You don't belong here. My family's lived here since this place was built. I was born here. My little girl's gonna be born here, come April. You're a freak. You're the one who goes round setting fire to stuff. You're not even English. What are you doing here?'

I laughed at this. 'I don't know. Are you in charge?' My

neck felt floppy, and I tipped back my head to look over the boys, up at the scudding night-clouds. Whose idea was all this? Where did he live?

'He's full of it, this one. Hey! Count Dracula. Wakey-wakey.'

I drifted back down to find the tanned boy grinning inches from my nose.

What else was there to do? I slugged him in the face.

In a blur of nylon, the boy toppled backwards into the little skinhead, who made a noise like a cat being hit with a hammer. The biggest boy reacted, bottle in hand. I smelt the tobacco on his knuckles as his fist connected with the base of my throat, and even with the choking and the savage impact of the concrete against my spine, I felt better than I had all evening. This I could deal with.

Three pairs of boots in my guts. Three pairs of fists in my ribs. The tanned one, a furious splodge on his cheekbone where I'd hit him, was screeching as he battered me, telling me how he was gonna kill me, gonna kill me, gonna tear my stinking ears off, and he continued his murderous tirade as I grabbed his ankle and wrestled his skinny orange body to the ground. The other two descended on me with glee, and I was euphoric with adrenaline by then, smothered by the writhing, crushing weight of them, thrashing out my frustration with my little fists and straining lungs – 'I hate this place, I hate my life, I hate myself and I hate you, I hate I hate I—' until there was a weight on my hips, a fist in my hair, and someone produced a can of deodorant and blasted me full in the face.

I lay there, blind and wheezing. As sometimes happens during a fight, serene thoughts floated across the surface of my mind. Must be good to be blind, I found myself thinking. People being kind, helping you cross the road, and you'd never know *how ugly you are, or how ugly everyone else is, and people will always be gentle, always do the looking-after—*

And then a boot connected with my skull.

When I came to, I was lying with my cheek against the tarmac. A yellow stripe ran under one limp hand, and I stared at it from a hundred miles away, allowing the aches and the strange burns to rouse my body. Knees, hips, ribs. Defiant heart, still beating. They'd dragged me to one of the quiet by-roads beside the park and left me in the shadow of yesterday's rain. My money was missing, and my coat and jumper were bunched around my armpits as though they'd planned to leave me naked but changed their minds.

They'd beaten me up, and it meant I was normal.

A white van came shooting around the corner, and with a grunt of pain I rolled myself on to the grass verge and out of its path. The three boys were still in the park, a safe distance away from me. I could hear them laughing at some new distraction, and I was about to limp back to the flat with the proof of my normality when I saw them behind the flaking red bars of the climbing frame. Four figures instead of three, one doubled over, staggering at the centre of a frenzied dance.

The tramp.

I stood there motionless, as my father had, thirty-five years ago. Watching.

The tramp had somehow latched on to the tanned boy's hair. The other two were all over him, fists and boots and teeth, and when the tramp's legs buckled under the weight of them the biggest boy upended his bottle of blue stuff over the man's head, drenching him for the cold night ahead. Whoops of laughter.

I broke into a run.

The boys were too preoccupied to notice the small figure clattering towards them. The tanned one was still laughing at the tramp when I whipped out my lighter. By the time I snatched up the can of deodorant from the tarmac it was too late for him or any of the others to stop me, and even I was surprised at how easy it was to compress the aerosol, flick the ignition and—

His tracksuit went up like tissue paper.

I'm horrified now. I feel guilty now. But shock insulates the brain.

So I watched.

The boy was screaming. Bubbling and blackening, the melting nylon stuck to his palms, eating the tender skin as he tried to bat out the flames.

He wouldn't be punching anyone for a while.

The other two had frozen. I could see the big one's tonsils. The little skinhead looked as if he were about to cry. Only the tramp moved, scrabbling away to the bench where he snatched up his few belongings and ran. Probably sensible, what with his being drenched in alcohol.

I don't remember deciding to run. Only the tang of smoke clinging to my clothes as I went, head down, pounding over the road to the flats. My heartbeat battered my bruised throat as the boy's howls faded behind me. Turning a corner, I pulled my hood over my ears. In the orange street light, I imagined that the whole estate was burning; that I'd vanquished the concrete ogre, burned its castle and its minions, and that soon nothing would remain but ashes. Ashes, Feodor and freedom.

I felt so good I scared myself.

When I reached the fifth floor, Mr Benedict was waiting

for me. I halted, unsure whether to deny everything or turn tail and run.

But the unshaven face was smiling. 'Oi,' he called to me. 'Weren't going to stand us up, were you?'

I let him lead me down the corridor to his flat, even as Mrs Sekibo from number five-oh-nine pushed past us with Sainsbury's bags and averted eyes. If the neighbours were aware of the nature of Mister B's parties, they kept quiet. At that moment, anything was better than going home.

'You smell like a tart's bath,' Mr Benedict chuckled as he opened the door to his wallpapered kingdom. 'What've you been rolling in?'

'Bit too much Lynx,' I mumbled, and he laughed again, his paw hot and large against the small of my back. I had the chance to glance back at the empty corridor. The echoes of lifts and grizzling babies: so ordinary.

Despite all the weeks I'd been visiting Mr Benedict's flat, I was never prepared for the smell. Stale washing-up water in the kitchenette sink and the leftover whiff of fried breakfast eggs. He hadn't cleaned his fish tank since my last visit. Ronnie and Reggie, the two goldfish, hung sluggishly behind the green glass. Next to the tank, one of Mr Benedict's awful girl band mix-tapes was playing on an old eighties ghetto blaster: 'baby' this and 'maybe' that. My head pounded.

Mr Benedict plucked at my damp jumper. 'Look at you. Don't you own no clean clothes?'

'No.' I shrugged him off. I was shivering and sore.

There were packets of peanuts and ready salted crisps scattered over the coffee table. In spite of the stench, my mouth watered.

Mr Benedict flopped heavily into his customary armchair.

'Gary's coming over to see you tonight. Sort yourself out. You reek.'

I remembered Gary, the one with the Jesus forgives tattoo and the tense, toothy face like a nutcracker. I couldn't deal with Gary that night. I already felt as if a car had reversed over me. I went to the bathroom and locked the door.

Mr Benedict's medicine cabinet was a depressing jumble of indigestion tablets, poppers and wrinkled tubes of eczema cream. I found some aspirin under a tub of Vaseline and swallowed them down with a palmful of tap water, splashing my face with the rest.

I closed the mirrored door and got a shock.

I looked dead. Properly, clinically dead. I'd never seen my face so white; it was almost mauve. I pulled down my eyelids to find the capillaries there purple and furious. Zombie movie eyes. My tongue was ruddy and throbbing, and a smear of blood – mine or someone else's – was dried across my chin like war paint.

My face was nothing compared to my head. My brain was boiling. I'd read in the papers about boxers leaving the ring and then being found on the toilet the next morning, blue as that kid's drink. The thought of falling asleep in a stranger's flat frightened me, never mind dying. I wanted to collapse into my own bed, but Dad would be draining a bottle by now and I couldn't face him. More than anything, I wanted my piano. I needed to sink into some Chopin, something plodding and soothing. If Mama was right about better worlds, maybe music was a doorway.

Mama. It took the ambulance twenty minutes to get to the flat. Dad was no use at all, made me do the phone call, and afterwards, when the paramedics slowly put their equipment *away, no… I couldn't let it engulf me. Not here.*

I leant my forehead against the mirror and closed my throbbing eyes. 'Get money,' I told myself. 'Get it and go. It's doable.'

In the living room, the ghetto blaster was louder than before, and Mr Benedict was thumping his fist on the arm of the chair.

'Will you turn that shit off?' I growled.

'My house, my tape.'

'They're abusing that piano. Do you know what I'd do to have my piano back?'

'Oh yeah?' He raised his voice and jerked his chin in the direction of the kitchenette. 'Why don't you ask L to buy you one?'

L was here. He was watching me from the doorway, orange fringe flopping into his eyes. He was thirty-ish, but always managed to look like a teenager shocked to find himself in an ageing body with ingrowing hairs and a mortgage to pay. He was giving me one of his meaningful stares, as if we had some cosmic, Biblical connection and Saint Sebastien was about to wander into the flat with a torso full of arrows and a tray of Hobnobs.

I'd never been so relieved to see him.

'I just popped round,' L said. 'I, ah, thought I left my keys here.'

Mr Benedict waved a dismissive paw. 'He came to keep an eye on you. And he's leaving now, aren't you, L?'

L was bashful. He'd gone soft for me; everybody knew.

'Have you had your tea?' L asked me.

'I haven't had anything. Can I?' I asked, turning to Mr Benedict. 'Whatever you've got.'

Mr Benedict let me have some crisps and a can of Stella. I took off my coat and dropped it on the floor before taking a long, lukewarm swig of the beer. It tasted like carbonated fish tank water. Still, I devoured the crisps and made appealing eyes at L. He always had a full wallet for me.

Under the racket the girl band was making, I registered sirens in the distance. An ambulance, a police car, the whole circus. Had they ever come for Rada like that, I wondered? Had they found her at all?

L picked up my coat from the floor and smoothed it over a chair. I'd forgotten he'd bought it for me. He led me to the corner by the window. I licked my fingers where the salt stung my grazes.

'Your hair's getting long.'

I could see the park over his shoulder. 'D'you like it?'

He offered me more crisps, which I descended upon. His mouth twisted with concern. 'Are you sure you're eating right? You're looking gaunt.'

'I'm all right,' I said, mouth full. He was treating me like one of his kids. 'D'you have any cash?'

L blanched. 'I thought we were a bit beyond that.'

I must have glared at him, because he fell silent, shyly running his eyes over my hair and my clothes, until his expression stiffened and I stopped chewing, convinced he magically knew what I'd done.

'You're bleeding,' he said. 'Your ear's bleeding. There's dirt in your hair. What have you been doing?'

'Assault course,' I said. My head felt like a dropped egg. 'I'm going to join the Army.'

An ambulance was almost in the park now. There were blue lights against the skateboard ramp, twirling, twirling.

No army would take me now.

I took L's arm and tried to lead him away from the window, but he planted his hands on my waist and wouldn't let me move. 'Let's go somewhere,' I said. 'Take me for a drive. I've missed you.' I should have said something enticing about Venezuela, or Argentina, or wherever it was he was always banging on about, but my brain had slowed to syrup.

'Tell me what's wrong.'

The room tilted as I extracted myself from L. Lights in my left eye, bad water meaning more pain was on the way. Not now, not now. People were emerging from their flats to gawk. Shortly, a police car sped down the by-road below the window and parked diagonally, blocking the view of a group of women congregating at the park gates. Two officers emerged. They'd take a statement from the tramp when they found him. He wouldn't know my name. The little skinhead and the big one, though…

I felt L's hands on my shoulders. 'Hey,' he murmured against my ear. 'Talk to me. Have you been in a fight? Did someone beat you up?'

'Yes,' I said, airily, watching as the ambulance reversed out of the park. A tiny hiccup of a laugh escaped me. 'And no.'

Five storeys below, the police were cordoning off the park with blue tape. I'd never burned a person before. I was so used to bringing things to life with fire that the possibility of killing had never occurred to me. Had I maimed? Or killed? A queer, alcoholic feeling came over me, as if I were about to fall.

What would Mama say if she knew?

L's body pressed against my sore back, insinuating. 'Feo,' he whispered. 'What have you done?'

My body gave up. A loud ringing noise pierced my head like a siren as my stomach lurched. 'Gonnapuke!' I managed to grunt, scrambling for the bathroom. The door flew open as I fell into it. I'd left the taps on. Water cascaded over the sink's edge, and my knees buckled before I could reach the toilet. I found myself face-down on sodden green carpet. No, pink. A pink carpet that smelt familiar.

I was in my parents' bedroom.

L was gone, Mr Benedict, and his music too. The urge to vomit had dried up completely. The watery lights had stopped.

I was sprawled at the foot of my parents' bed. The air was rancid with old chip papers and my dad's bottles of wee. Mama's empty space. The table topped with her glasses, her silver wristwatch, her small Bible. We hadn't dared put them away.

Dad was in bed and not drunk on the sofa. The next shock was that he was awake and looking at me.

'You're back,' he said. He wasn't blinking.

I'd make it right if I could. *Was that my voice?*

A cold rivulet of spittle dribbled down my chin.

'Don't go,' he said.

Drops of rain batted against my eyelids. I looked up: no ceiling, only sky. I was lying on the cold tarmac outside, curled, foetal, beside the ashes of my newspaper fire under the concrete walkway.

I laughed. And then I was gone.

11

In her room at the back of the house, Aisling held the Blake book to her chest, allowing the cold leather to dampen her jumper. A day had passed since she discovered the priest hole. At dinner Edythe had immediately latched on to Aisling's damaged hands, but, after a vigorous encounter with iodine, Robert's story about an accident on the stairs prevented any further questions.

'We ought to get a light bulb fitted,' Robert told her. 'It won't do, having people hurting themselves.'

'Clumsiness shouldn't be catered for,' Edythe had argued. 'Father managed without the electric light. You'll be wanting a paraffin heater next.'

As the autumn wind buffeted the trees outside her window, Aisling mentally retraced her steps down into the cellar. She recalled the battered iron cross, a relic of the Reverend Enright. She had been writing in her journal that morning, something about a church, perhaps the one they'd driven by on the way to the house. And there her memory failed. It was as if a huge paintbrush had smothered the afternoon in pitch.

Beside her on the coverlet lay her open journal, littered with scribbled notes from her therapy sessions with Dr Weber all those months ago.

'Do you know what dissociation is, Aisling? Dissociation is that funny feeling of unreality. Of looking down at your hand and thinking, "Is that really mine?" I think we've all done that once or twice, haven't we? In small ways, dissociation can be useful to us. It can make you feel as if you are in control. Have you ever found yourself very upset and thinking, "This can't be happening"? I know I have.'

There was a woman on Aisling's ward with a high, boyish voice and old-fashioned manners. She was convinced the hospital authorities were piping The Beach Boys into the wards through the air conditioning vents. Every night she lay awake listening to the faint whine of 'Good Vibrations', and during the day she would ask passing patients to put their ears to the vents and tell her what they could hear. Soon she was taken off her regular medication and given a dose of something that made her ears roar. She lived in the same world as everyone else, then. But was she any happier?

Beside Aisling's journal lay the other book, *Within Reason: Treatment and Protection of the Defective Classes.*

I cannot think, said the notes. *I need quiet.*

'Who were you?' Aisling asked the empty room. 'Did you ever get better?'

The priest hole was quiet, it occurred to her. If someone wanted time alone in this house, what better place was there?

When Aisling took a peep through the crack in Edythe's

bedroom door, her aunt was dozing in front of *Countdown*. Aisling turned and crept back along the corridor to the main staircase. The air was sharp with the smell of acetate. Aisling had been sick twice that morning, unable to bear the heaviness of even a glass of water inside her with that oily smell hanging around. It was as if the house were decaying around her, succumbing to something old and foul.

'Ophelia. Come in to see me, girl.'

Reluctant to give up her mission, she nonetheless turned back to Robert's doorway. He beckoned her inside. The floor was spattered with droplets where he had done his best to pour her a drink.

'How are you today?'

'Why?'

'I have something to share with you. Close the door. Sit.'

She did so, watching his face all the while. When she was settled beside him, he huffed at the suspicion on her face.

'Kept your secret, didn't I?'

'Yes,' she said.

'And you kept mine. So how about another?'

Her stomach twisted. Still she nodded.

'His name,' Robert said quietly, 'was Mister Morgun.'

'Whose name?'

'Your diarist. I thought my father cleared out all his things many, many years ago, but it's a big house. We evidently don't know every nook and cranny. Edy isn't toying with you. I couldn't let you go on thinking that. She's spiky, my sister, but she isn't knowingly cruel.'

'But my things. And yours. If it isn't her?'

'It's a coincidence. I'd come to the same conclusion in your position, but you mustn't take it as anything other than a hurtful fluke. My fags and your book, yes, no doubt Edy stashed them there. It wasn't me. But they aren't important. It's *these* I worry about.'

His gaze travelled to the mushy old papers on his table. Black mould crawled along the edges where the ink chanted its litany: *The First Law, The Second, The Third.* Aisling's ring bit into her thumb. She hadn't realised she was twisting it.

'Ophelia, generations of families have lived in this house. In that time, plenty of people have been happy, but plenty will have been unhappy, too, and Mister Morgun was one of the unfortunate ones. He lived here in the forties when Edy and Connie and I were small. He assisted our father around the parish. Somewhat reluctantly, I believe, not that one notices such things until it's too late. He was very ill, Aisling. And very angry that he was so ill.'

'He said, *"The degeneracy must cease".*'

'I was a little boy at the time.' Robert sighed. 'I hope, whatever happened to him, that things turned out better. But more importantly, I want *you* to be well. Whatever you read in these and in that book, it was written in another time. There are things people said casually ten years ago that are utterly repugnant now, let alone…'

It struck a chord, though, didn't it? Or you wouldn't have said anything. Her silent look said as much, and there it was. She saw his guilt. She got up and went to the window so as not to face him.

'*When* you get better—' he began.

'I could be stuck with this forever.'

'When you get better, you need a plan. Morgun didn't have one, or if he did it was hopelessly self-loathing. But you are made of sterner stuff. You're Edy's niece, after all.'

Aisling's forehead clonked softly against the windowpane. A plan? The idea of having a job, of functioning or even looking like an adult, was completely beyond her imagination.

'I missed a lot of school. But I want to travel. I can work in a shop for a while, save my wages.'

'Five pounds an hour isn't going to get you to Mexico. Great Yarmouth, maybe. How's that?'

Aisling's chest tightened. For a single second, she hated Robert with hot venom. 'I don't care what I have to do,' she said, as it passed. 'Anyway, someone like me is hardly going to be overrun with job offers.'

Robert sighed crossly. 'Oh, come on. You're not foaming at the mouth.'

'No,' she retorted. 'I heard it again and again in the hospital. Even Mum admits it. Employers only pretend they don't discriminate. There are laws, but they don't stop them gossiping about you, or keeping you in the stock room where no one has to talk to you. Everyone from school will be in college now, or getting ready to go. They'll have jobs and salaries and houses. I feel like I've missed the boat.'

'Life isn't as linear as all that.' He watched her brush a lank tendril of hair away from her eyes, big, fixed on the floorboards. The flat plane of her chest rose and fell. 'There's nothing wrong with you. If you can stop letting people like my sister tell you you're, well, "defective", to borrow a term, life will be easier. This is just something you have to deal with. Like my peg leg. Sod everyone else. You're the one who has to live with you.'

Aisling screwed up her eyes and shook her head. 'I'm

sorry. Can I bring you some tea? Do you want me to switch off the TV?'

Robert stretched in his chair. It was a relief to see she hadn't hurt him. 'You could open the window,' he said. 'I feel like having a puff.'

Robert lit his illicit treat while she leant against the window frame, cautiously savouring the novelty of fresh air against her skin.

Nothing wrong with her? Edythe thought otherwise. That woman, Mrs Bloom, the look on her face.

'Whoopsie-daisy.'

The cigarette slipped from Robert's fingers and smouldered on the rug. Aisling snatched it up. 'It'll be more than "whoopsie-daisy" if you torch the house.' She replaced it gently between Robert's lips, and his eyes twinkled his gratitude.

'Dear girl, you don't know the half of it.'

When Aisling turned out into the corridor, the fuel-stink hit her full in the face. She managed to walk to the top of the main staircase before having to steady herself against the newel post, concentrating on controlling her gag reflex.

She raised her eyes to see a battered black overcoat gliding up the main staircase towards her. For one thrilling moment, Aisling thought of the blond man turning cartwheels. But it wasn't the blond from the garden. It was an older man, an unfamiliar man. One who smelt appalling.

A jolt of instinct shot up her spine. *Run*, it said.

The man paused on the top step. His head bobbed awkwardly near the ceiling like a white balloon. At the sight of Aisling he hunched his shoulders and appeared to shrink into his coat, stiff with dark stains as if it had been left to hang in a garage.

'You're new,' he said.

His face loitered on the border between foul and fascinating. His bulging cheekbones appeared to be trying to pierce the papery skin, and his lips, which he nibbled and licked constantly, fluttered with flakes of dry skin. Aisling noticed his odd lack of eyebrows and eyelashes. Bald as a cricket ball.

'You're here to see Robert,' she remembered, covering her nose as politely as she could manage.

The man quirked the milky lumps of muscle where his eyebrows should have been. 'You're new and informed. Tell me, when did the family decide on this wallpaper? I don't think much of it, do you?'

Despite the stench he had a shy, schoolmasterly air that Aisling found reassuring. He looked as though he might offer her his hand, but after a moment of thought he clasped both neatly in front of him, tensing slightly as though they gave him pain.

'But you wouldn't know,' he said. 'Of course you wouldn't. Tell me your name.'

'Aisling. I'm Robert's great-niece.'

He touched his collar thoughtfully with broad, bony fingers. 'An aisling is a ballad in old Irish. When a poet wrote an aisling, his motherland would appear to him in the form of an ethereal woman. She is known as the Spéirbhean, the sky woman.'

'Speer-van?'

'She's a messenger. She brings word to the poet of the revival of his fortunes. What a lovely omen for a Thursday afternoon.' He smiled, baring bloodless gums. 'Though I must say, it isn't healthy to believe in omens.'

Aisling looked into the man's face. *What else did he know?* 'I like poetry. I like William Blake.'

But the man's eyes drifted over her head, regarding the wallpaper. Busy floral stripes, regimental and cluttered at once. He followed them up from Robert's room at the end of the corridor, through Aisling, standing with her arms tight around herself, and up to the staircase and the room she slept in. 'Mmm. No. Blake was mad.' The man looked at her. Abruptly, he asked: 'Do you believe in omens, Aisling?'

The comment about Blake stung her back into shyness. She shrugged.

'No,' he said, seemingly to himself. 'No. Well, good. My name is David.'

He prounced it 'Dah-veet', like someone from a European city with cobbled bridges over slow-winding canals. 'Are you from France?' she asked.

'France? No.' The big head wobbled uncertainly. He rubbed at one eye with the back of his hand. 'Somewhere altogether colder. Well, a long time ago. But no, I'm...' He couldn't seem to decide.

'Are you a traveller, then?'

David wriggled his bony shoulders. 'This came for you,' he told her, and pressed an envelope into her hand. 'Oh, and Aisling? You dropped this.'

The cufflink glittered invitingly against the fish skin flakes of his chewed nails. She didn't remember having it with her, but pocketed it nonetheless. David and his smell wafted towards Robert's room without another word.

The Blake book dug into her thigh and she hurried down the main staircase, inwardly laughing at herself for being frightened of someone so unthreatening.

Down in the entrance hall, the kitchen door was open. There was a pale wash of daylight over the chequered floor, and she made a game of hopping barefoot across it, one white tile at a time, *slap slap slap*.

She hadn't realised how desperate she'd been to see a new face.

The kitchen was predictably immaculate. *'Tidy house, tidy mind,'* Beverley would have said. *Tidy mind, empty head*, Aisling corrected her. She caught herself smiling and felt guilty. As mean as Edythe was, Aisling felt for her. Every day the same house, the same rooms. Enough to make anyone mad.

Resting on the marble sideboard was a pewter dish bearing a shopping list and a folded ten-pound note. It was the first money Aisling had seen since Edythe made her empty her pockets on arrival.

Ten pounds. She glanced over her shoulder. How much was a train fare?

Her hand wavered.

'No stealing,' she whispered. She was here to get better.

She paused and listened for the television in Edythe's room. If Robert's guest was here, Edythe was asleep. The cellar door opened soundlessly. She made her way down the dark stairs, gripping the wooden banister with one bandaged hand.

When she turned on the light, the priest hole was open. The beam had been left at half-mast, exposing the hiding place.

Aisling inhaled. Edythe knew.

It was damp and very small. Aisling thought of the priests who had once knelt where she was now. In the 1400s, they'd hanged Catholic dissenters from the church ramparts in Bishops Stortford, not far away.

There, on the floor, stacks of mouldering papers. Faded magazine clippings offered miracle shampoos for ageing men and fortifying tonics to invigorate the blood. Most of the notepaper was beyond legibility. Scraps of compiled statistics were framed by brambles of scrawled commentary.

Eleven stone ten. Eleven stone two. Ten stone nine. Words bled where ink met moisture. *Healthy body, healthy mind? Healthy mind, healthy body? Does it not stand to reason—*

Aisling dropped the papers. It was too quiet to think.

She shuffled backwards to the light of the entrance and opened the letter David gave her. Inside the envelope was a postcard of Queen Elizabeth's tiara-topped head. It smiled up at her, inviting her to read.

Hi Sweets!

London is fast and gets under your fingernails, but terrific fun. Saw Les Miserables *at the theatre last Friday – very long, very miserable! Hope you aren't miserable. Are you eating and taking your pills? Malcolm bought you a teddy bear from Harrods. Expect a package soon.*

Kisses,

Mum

PS: You'd love the Tower of London. Ravens!

Aisling read the message twice, then the envelope. Edythe's address in Beverley's round, irregular handwriting. The cream edge of a sheet of hotel writing paper peeked out.

Hello Edy! London calling!

Her mother wrote like an excited teenager. Malcolm was wonderful, his loft conversion heavenly. There were restaurants, art galleries, afternoon espressos and more shopping than she could handle, even with Malcolm flourishing his credit card like a magic wand. Aisling's mouth twisted as she envisioned Beverley assuring herself that *this* time was the *right* time, fretfully smoothing her skirt until Malcolm praised her outfit, squeezing into support tights and worrying what her choice of wine would say about her personality.

She turned over the page.

We're not being too hasty, Beverley had written. *We'd like more time. Malcolm says there are boarding schools for college-aged kids. That could work out well for all of us. Don't know about fees yet, but Mal's job is flexible and he's so keen to help.*

She's a clever girl. But you know what worries me. If she's poorly all the time she'll always be dependant.

I'm glad she's with you.

Up came the memory from the black well. One o'clock in the morning. The weight of him. Beverley, snoring gently down the hall. *'How tall you've got. Like a model. You've never had a boyfriend, have you? But that's nice, that's nice. You don't belong to anyone.'*

She crawled on her numb knees out of the priest hole. She went quietly up the cellar stairs to the kitchen, and up the bleach-scrubbed servants' stairs to the first floor where Edythe's afternoon game show was coming to an end. She still slept. Aisling went quickly along the chilly hall to her bedroom. Two plastic popper-packs of tablets waited for her on the nightstand. *To be taken with water once daily. Do not exceed the stated dose.*

She took both packs down to the guest bathroom. There was no lock, so she sat on the floorboards, one foot braced against the door to prevent it opening from the outside. Taking a spare roll of toilet paper from the cistern, she tore off several metre-long strips and laid them out beside her. She opened each pack and popped the little white pills out on to the paper in three long lines.

'You've made your decision,' she whispered. 'This is mine.'

For the first time in weeks, the East Anglian sky was clear. A pale glow of late-autumn sunshine lit up the fields surrounding the house, stretching into the hazy brown boundary of the horizon. At first it had been unsettling for Aisling, the suburb-dweller, to see the sky meet the ground in every direction. No hills or settlements to break up the endless line, only low, linear hedgerows and the occasional distant church spire.

It took three flushes to get rid of the pills.

When she was satisfied her medication was on its way to the sewers, Aisling walked barefoot down the main stairs, under the benign gaze of the Reverend Enright and his companions, and silently out of the front door into the shock of the September air. She crunched her way over the gravel driveway, around to the back garden. When she reached the birches she held one knobbly trunk and looked out across the fields to where the rooks rested in the naked treetops. Somewhere unseen a moorhen trilled and scuttled.

Her mind turned to the ten pounds waiting on the kitchen sideboard. She had never run away with a purpose before. Robert's well-meaning questions only highlighted all the skills she didn't have. One seizure in front of strangers on a railway platform and she'd be back on a ward.

She held out her bandaged palms, grubby and pink where the bark had pushed aside the gauze. An unfamiliar calmness had settled in her core. She was going to be ill now. It was her decision.

She took the Blake book from her pocket and thumbed the smooth edges. That man, David, was right. Everyone had thought Blake was mad, greeting chimneysweeps in the street as though they were Saint Paul, seeing God peeping in at his bedroom window. Blake was ridiculed all his life. He died a penniless outsider, buried in a cheap grave. *That must be what happens when everyone thinks you're crazy,* she thought. *They push you away until you disappear.*

'Father, O father, what do we here?
In this land of unbelief and fear
The Land of Dreams is better far
Above the light of the morning star.'

Her voice wavered as a rogue tear spilled down her cheek. She flicked to the frontispiece, where a curmudgeonly portrait of the poet scowled up at her. 'You always know just what to say, you miserable git.'

'That doesn't rhyme,' someone said.

Aisling dropped the book and spun around. Standing in a patch of goose grass on the other side of the fence, a slender, scruffily dressed young man was holding up his palms in apology.

'I wasn't spying!'

Aisling held the birch trunk like a shield. 'How long have you been there?'

The man shook his head vigorously. Shaggy tendrils of dirty blond hair fell over his eyes. He wore a sleeveless coat of brown leather and tough, muddy boots laced up to the shins. 'I don't mean no harm,' he was saying. 'I didn't know anyone was here. I was just walking. And you said something. So I answered.' He backed off as if to leave.

'Wait. No. You've been here before. Haven't you?'

The man picked bashfully at the tarnished chain around his neck. 'Hard to tell. It's all a bit the same out here.' He darted a glance past Aisling's shoulder and over the autumnal farmland surrounding them. 'Are you quite all right?'

There was a gentle Northernness to his voice that she hadn't expected. He looked more like a punk or a ballet dancer than anything from Sheffield.

'I've seen you,' she said, with relief. 'You turned a cartwheel in the dark.'

'So *you're* the spy,' he grinned. Confident now, he smoothed his long hair down over his ears. 'Can we swap names? I'm Chase.'

'I'm Aisling.'

'Ashley?'

'Aisling.' *Means something to do with magic messengers and poets.*

'Oh. Not too good at this, am I?' He produced a brown paper bag from an inner pocket and held it out to her. 'Would you like a bit of fudge? It's very expensive.'

'Where did you get very expensive fudge?'

'Nicked it.' A grin.

Aisling declined politely. Chase took a large hunk and bit it in half. She eyed him from behind the tree. His eyes were a smokier green than Aisling's, prettily foxy. They rolled back with pleasure at the taste. Around his gymnast hips, a leather belt was heavy with pouches and compartments. The bone handle of a utility knife was stained with what she hoped was blackberry juice. He reminded her of the Afghani tribeswomen she'd admired in *National Geographic* magazine: gorgeous, green-eyed, not to be messed with.

'Do you live around here?' she asked him doubtfully.

'Not really,' he said, licking sugar from his fingers. 'Sometimes. I was wondering about you. Why are you all the way out here in the sticks?'

'I'm staying with my aunt.'

Chase stopped chewing. 'What, here?'

'She's the daughter of the old vicar. But the church is closed now, I think. There's no vicar any more. Just the house.' She glanced back. Edythe would wake up soon.

Chase remained quiet, his tongue skating nervously across his lower lip. Aisling didn't know what to say. Her mother's magazines piled up next to the bath said that males were a separate species with separate rules. Faced with an attractive man like Chase, she felt large and ugly and ashamed.

'I like your hair,' said Aisling, to break the silence.

'Thanks. I like your bandages.'

He offered the bag of fudge again and Aisling popped a piece into her mouth. Melting violets and cream – heavenly after weeks of boiled eggs and overdone pork.

'Good, innit?' Chase smiled.

'You stole this?' she asked, mouth full.

'Yeah. But the merchant's a rich one. I don't take from the proletariat.'

Aisling briefly considered relating her own stories of thievery, but it was keenly apparent that nothing she could say would impress a man like this. She remembered her face was probably puffy with tears, and she rubbed it with her sleeve.

'Were you having a cry?' he asked.

'I thought I was alone.'

'Is it your aunt? Did she do something to you? You should come with me.' He was bouncing on the balls of his feet. 'I've got a friend. She's good to people. Anyone who spends too much time out here's gotta be a bit,' he stuck a finger in his ear and pulled a face. 'Oh. You cringed.' His hands automatically went to his hair, which he smoothed anxiously down over his ears like a helmet. 'I'm classically bad at this meety-greety business.'

Aisling twisted the ring on her thumb painfully. 'You might not want to talk to me if you don't like people,' she mimicked his gesture, 'like that.'

Chase cocked his head like a dog. 'Is that why you're out here?'

She shrugged. She had expected him to be disgusted, not inquisitive. 'I was supposed to be getting well.'

Chase's cheeks were raspberry with delight. 'Oh, wow. Gosh. I mean I ought to have guessed. Not in a bad way, I just, only...' He leaned towards her as if imparting a secret. 'You're the first one I've met, that I know of.' He jerked his blond head in the direction of the fields behind them. 'You should come. We're sympathetic. You needn't worry.'

Aisling was unsure. She held her rising excitement in check. 'You don't know me. I could have some horrible, mind-bending disease.'

'So could I. Isn't life exciting?'

He offered his long, tanned hand, which she took without thinking. She swung a leg over the small wooden fence and perched on the top while Chase made a gentlemanly display of kicking aside the nettles to make a path for her. 'She loves

114

to meet new people,' he was saying. 'Do you like chickens? She's got three in a pen: Rum, Sodomy, and The Lash.'

Straddling the fence, Aisling looked back at the house. Robert's window was open; he was probably getting cold. Her jeans were wet around her bare ankles.

Chase placed a hand on her back. 'You coming?'

'I can't.'

The corners of his lips drooped. 'Was it the sodomy thing? Because that was a joke. I mean, that's what we call the chicken, but not for, y'know, any reason.'

'I can't keep running off. That's all anyone ever does in my family. It isn't fair.'

'Oh. Not even for a little while? Just with me?'

The hand on her back was warm and solid. Her shoulder blades stiffened. She didn't know this man.

She slid off the fence just as Chase lunged out and caught the hem of her jumper in his fist. 'Don't go that way!' He laughed with disbelief, but his grip was tight. 'You never want to go back that way.'

She knocked his hand away, scoring his skin with her ragged fingernails. Before he could stop her, she bolted back across the wet grass to the safety of the house.

Underneath the birches, blushing and sore, Chase was left rubbing his hand. When the girl disappeared from view, he noticed her little book lying forgotten in the brown leaves. He scooped it up, picking the mulch off the worn cover before slipping it into his coat.

As he turned back to the woods, a magpie took flight across the open land.

12

Eggs were boiled, tiles were mopped. The rain returned, flooding the lanes.

Funny, thought Aisling, how nothing had changed in twenty-four hours. She didn't know what she had expected. Like stepping up to a pneumatic drill in the street and taking her fingers out of her ears, perhaps. It was guilt, she supposed, that had made her brace herself. She saw the whole production chain behind each dose she missed. The scientists tinkering with chemicals she had never bothered to look up. The tests, perhaps cruel, on rats and volunteers. And then the completed pills, those little miracles of science, packaged up by factory workers wishing recovery and health into each box. Could they sense her ingratitude? As she passed through the hall on the way to her bedroom, the Reverend Enright's blurred companion seemed to shake his head. *Defective.*

The bedroom was sharp with furniture polish. On the edge of Aisling's bed, Edythe perched, small fists clenched against the houndstooth of her skirt. When Aisling came up, the first thing she noticed was the rucksack beside her, fastened and bulging with clothes.

Aisling closed the door behind her. The shaving mirror on the chest of drawers reflected a fairground version of her face, all eyes. Her folded towels were gone, as was her hairbrush and bar of soap. A pair of yellow rubber gloves lay limply in their place.

'I was asleep,' the old woman said quietly. 'When you did it.'

The toilet hadn't backed up. How could Edythe know about the pills? 'I went outside,' Aisling admitted uneasily. 'But I'm inside now. I didn't run off. That's a good sign, isn't it?'

'I see. But tell me this. I lock my door when I'm not in my room. I always have. So I must have been sleeping. When you did it.'

She didn't understand. 'Why is my bag packed?'

Edythe was up off the bed and across the room, her face inches from Aisling's sternum. 'This is my *house*,' she hissed. 'My *father's* house. Not yours. Not Eliot's. Mine.' Her body trembled, blue eyes lividly wet. She went to the bed and produced, from behind Aisling's rucksack, a wooden jewellery box.

Aisling was backed against the door. 'What is it?'

'*It* has sat on my dressing table for more than fifty years. My father carved these roses himself, hunched over his desk after services. I treat the wood with polish. I repair the lining when it frays. I keep inside it my correspondence, my keepsakes, my most cherished possessions. You wanted your poems back. So you crept into my bedroom and had a good look around. But once you'd found the book, you didn't stop, did you? You couldn't help yourself.' Edythe drew a deep breath. 'My father's emerald cufflinks. One is missing.'

No.

'Turn out your pockets.'

Aisling shrank back. 'No.'

'Turn them out.'

'I haven't stolen anything.'

'I've been in touch with your doctor. Tomorrow, I'll arrange a taxi to take you back to Bury where your mother will be waiting.' Edythe's lips stretched with satisfaction. 'She left London as soon as she heard.'

Aisling's mouth opened, and no sound came out. The chemists, the rats and the factory workers collectively exhaled: *Well, we tried. To Hell with you.*

Robert's voice travelled up from the bottom of the stairs. 'Edythe,' he called to her, thin with exertion. 'Remember she's poorly.'

'Oh, "poorly",' Edythe sneered. 'And that gives her the right to steal from me?'

Aisling's head was moving from side to side, a puppety swing. 'No.'

'No?'

'I've never been in your room.'

'Then you'll gladly empty your pockets.'

There was a series of thuds and creaks as Robert attempted to haul himself up the stairs. 'Edythe, come downstairs. We can—' A bang. 'Bloody! Edythe, come down and we'll discuss this together.'

'Stop it, Bert, before you hurt yourself.' The old woman

stared at Aisling. 'I've gathered together your possessions. All of them.'

Aisling watched with distant dismay as her aunt produced a small book bound with string from her skirt pocket. 'That's my journal,' she heard herself say. 'What are you doing with my journal?'

'Beverley warned me you like to squirrel things away. Eliot was the same. But even he didn't write incoherent filth like this.'

'That's private.'

'I can see why.' She opened the book and read: *'I'm going to tear your stinking ears off, he screamed. I hate this place and I hate you too.'*

Panic was rising. She felt she was moving through tar, wading against Edy's quick, sharp rage. 'They're just stories, bits from dreams. I was told to write. I'm doing as I'm told.'

Robert shouted again. He was close to the door, but tiring fast. 'Edythe, that's enough, she's had enough.'

'You were told? Then I'm sure your specialist will want to see the results,' she said. 'Do you know how many television reports there are of withdrawn youths committing violent crimes against those who care for them? Do you know how many of them leave a trail of warning signs? Plainly speaking, Aisling, I feel threatened by you. The gentleman on the telephone was very concerned. Being a danger to others is, I understand, a very serious matter. Not to mention what you do to yourself.' She looked pointedly at the bandages on Aisling's hands. 'Now. Empty your pockets.'

Aisling's throat was tight, as if Edythe was squeezing it. *Thud, drag,* and the hard *clack* of a walking stick on each warped step. Backed against the bedroom door, the squeezing sensation in Aisling's throat spread to her lungs. She was dizzy, cramped. The thought of Robert with his withered leg, coming to defend her. If they sent her back to hospital, she would likely never see him again.

'There's no use making faces,' Edythe said.

She wanted to crush herself, crumple, disappear.

I could, she thought, *I could—*

What?

Aisling put her shaking hands in her pockets. Another, stronger Aisling in another dimension would have hurled the cufflink across the room, made a wild, incandescent last stand. Feodor would have. *I've lost,* said a calm voice inside, and she believed it.

With a cry, Edythe snatched up the cufflink from her outstretched hand. She held it in her open palm for a long moment, allowing it to cool in the draught from the window.

'You absolute beast,' she said. The shock of confirmed suspicions overcame her rage, and the hard edge faded from her voice as she traced the delicate settings with a fingertip. 'Connie thought them too ostentatious to wear to church, but he looked so fine in them. A gentleman, my father. With his spectacles and the slick of pomade in his hair. It was thin, of course, but I was proud to walk out in the village with him. At the summer fetes, the emeralds would glimmer like eyes while the curate slouched beside him. Ugly, jealous man. The contrast—' She swallowed heavily. 'When father died, Connie couldn't appreciate their worth. All this tosh about material possessions. She gave them to *your* father, a runny-nosed seven-year-old. He played with them like toys. I couldn't allow that.'

The thought of Edythe out in the village, a proud girl in a

Sunday dress with a father she idolised, was somehow eerie, as though the pictures in the hall had shifted to display lingering signs of life.

Aisling heard the weightless monotone of her own voice: 'My book was in the priest hole. Not your room.'

'Priest hole?' The old woman's face grew taut with contempt. 'Who have you been talking to? That priest hole. What have you been reading?'

There was pressure on the door behind Aisling, and she stepped away as Robert emerged from the stairwell. His face was mottled and purple with exertion.

'Edy.' He leaned heavily on his stick. 'I promised I'd keep it quiet. It was such a minor thing.' He inclined his head in apology to Aisling. 'I don't lightly break confidences, Ophelia. Forgive me.'

Aisling took him by the elbow and led him to the bed. As Robert eased himself down, Edythe paced the parallel lines of the floorboards with her quick, light step.

'My brother has been keeping things from me.'

Robert growled. 'Let it go, Edy. She's in a big old house all day. She's bound to explore.'

'The hole is *sealed*. You were at sea, you won't remember that whole dreadful business that followed. But I shall never forget it, Robert, and you encourage her.'

Aisling's jaw clenched. 'It was wide open.'

'And how would I go about opening it at nearly eighty years of age? You've been reading the old newspapers. I'll bet you found something frightfully interesting, didn't you? And that cufflink—'

'She told me about the priest hole and the book long before you discovered the cufflink missing.' Robert lowered his voice. 'And Edy, there are things left down there. His papers. Things she really oughtn't have to see.'

'Father destroyed them all. And you side with her?' Edythe was on the verge of tears, and it only enraged her further. 'I do everything for you, you deceitful— Everything.'

'And I'm grateful for it,' he replied. 'But these seizures make her forget things. Perhaps the priest hole was showing a little. She may have forced it open and then lost the memory of it. Perhaps she did go poking about in your room, but that doesn't mean there was any malice involved. Don't punish her like this, Edy. What good will it do?'

A light went on inside Aisling's panic-stupid brain. 'David.'

Edythe all but yelled. 'There! She admits it.'

'He was here yesterday,' she said. 'He told me you were asleep and then he gave me the cufflink. Robert, he'd come to see you. Robert, say something.'

Edythe and Robert looked at each other. Horror, unmistakable.

'What in God's name have you been telling her?'

Robert was baffled. 'Only that he— She may well have—' He sighed, wiping his hand over his eyes. 'Oh, Mister Morgun. Enough. I suppose I told her quite enough.'

High on the roof, the weathervane shrieked and spun west. 'Enough,' Edythe said. 'Yes. I think we've all had quite enough.'

Verity Holloway

13

That night, Robert stayed with her. They sat on the edge of her bed, watching the shadows creep down the walls as the evening waned. Robert smoked his Egyptian cigarette.

'If I was going to throw a fit, I'd have done it by now.'

Robert nodded. 'That's jolly good news.'

'Very jolly.'

'Jolly in the extreme.'

He had tired himself out climbing the stairs and couldn't muster the energy to tackle them again.

'Do you think I did it?' Aisling asked him.

'Edy said your pill containers were all empty.'

'I flushed them. It makes no difference. Do you think I did it?'

'I think,' he said kindly, 'whatever happened, you are not the guilty one.'

She picked at the fraying wool of the tartan bedspread. 'I'm sorry I gave it away. About your friend.'

He cocked his head kindly.

'David. The man.'

'Where did you get that name? Did you read up on this place?'

'He was here. We spoke.'

Pity wrinkled his brow. 'This bloody house.' He gathered himself. 'You probably saw him in the photograph downstairs. Big chap. Rather unfortunate-looking. David Morgun. I had a feeling, when I knew which room Edy had given you. I'm not a believer in ghosts. But time has a way of folding back on itself, I think. Especially where tragedy is concerned.'

But he wasn't a ghost, she wanted to say. *I spoke to him.*

She could say anything she liked, now. No one would believe her.

Aisling studied her knuckles. Her journal was gone, her private world cracked open. Her Blake book was missing, no doubt snatched up by Edythe too. Night was bearing down.

Where was Beverley now? Not with Malcolm, that was certain. *'They don't like drama,'* she told Aisling, over and over. Men were a mooing herd easily spooked. Did Beverley hate her? Wouldn't it be natural to? She gave the ring on her thumb a slow twist. One, two, eleven.

Robert was leaning on his stick, watching her closely. 'Hello. We lost you for a moment.'

'I'm very tired.'

'I should let you sleep. If you need me, at any time of the night, no matter how unholy, I want you to knock on my door. We will then proceed to get fantastically drunk together. Go out in style. You understand?'

'Yes, sir.'

'Clever girl.'

Robert paused, knowing not to touch her, and settled for an affectionate scrunch of the face. He took his stick and began the slow descent to the main body of the house.

Sleep came without warning and was easily shattered. She had dropped off fully dressed, like Beverley after a bad night out. It was only when she rolled over to write that she remembered her journal was gone.

She turned her face to the window where the open curtains framed the night. Somewhere, a television played what sounded like late-night news. She eased herself up to rub the life back into her cold toes. How many hours until the taxi came for her? What would she say to comfort Beverley?

She rested against the headboard as her eyes adjusted to the darkness. There were too many niches in the small room. Too many nooks for shadows. Someone was using the guest bathroom; she could hear rushing water, and the sound muddled her brain. Liquid darkness. At the base of the bedroom door, a huddled shape blackened the woodwork like a stain of deep oil. Aisling's toes prickled as the blood began to circulate.

She traced the outline of shoulders, then haunches, down by the door.

Habit nudged. Had she taken her medication? By now, the little white pills were on their way to the sewage works. She imagined them bobbing around in the collective slurry of East Anglia, and smiled weakly.

There, amid the black stain: the slow movement of a small white hand.

'Hello,' she whispered.

The oil stain turned in her direction. Big black eyes like an Orthodox Jesus.

'Who's that?' The boy's lips moved, but there was no sound.

Aisling waved a greeting, but the boy seemed not to see. His small body was tense; teeth white and bare like a cornered terrier. 'Come out,' he said, aloud this time. 'Come out, or I'll cut you.' A brittle East London accent.

The figure became clearer, as though a dim haze of daylight had entered the room, illuminating a black cloud of curls and a jailhouse pallor. Aisling felt no fear.

'Who are you?' the boy mouthed. His voice faded in and out like a broken radio. 'How did you get in?'

'Are you one of the priests?' she asked him. 'The ones who hid here?'

Bafflement on the boy's face. 'Our Friend got rid of all the priests.'

'Who's your friend? Hello. I'm here, look at me.'

Aisling watched his eyes flick blindly around the room. He rose on his haunches, as if to run. 'This is my place. Find your own.'

With that defensive phrase, something clicked. Aisling shifted closer on the bed. The haze of interrupted sleep gave her courage.

'I know who you are,' she said.

'You don't.' A rattling intake of breath. 'Stop fucking around and come out where I can see you.'

The face wasn't what she expected. It was harder, more sharply defined. A shadow of stubble. He had grown older, but the eyes were unmistakable.

'You're Feodor.'

His face. Utter dismay. 'Go away.'

'I've been dreaming about you.' She edged slowly to the end of the bed. Perhaps she was dreaming now, but who cared? The air around this boy smelt of dust. Still he could not see her.

'You didn't like that, did you? When I said your name.'

'Don't think I'm stupid,' snapped the boy. 'You'll regret it.'

She rose into a kneeling position, watching him intently for any sign that he could see her. Her fingers uncurled and she extended her hand, reaching for the white oval of his fearful face. She was close enough to hear the phlegmy flutter of his breathing. He stared out blindly, bottom lip twitching, as she stretched, straining, until her finger met the quivering tip of his cold nose.

She shot back as if she'd been burned.

The boy sprang up and bolted down the stairs, seeming to pass through the closed bedroom door like a shadow. The clatter of his boots echoed in the enclosed stairwell, leaving nothing but the dusty, sweaty smell of him in the bedroom.

Aisling sprawled, panting.

'Jesus. *Jesus.*'

Flesh.

She was up and following him without a thought.

The first-floor corridor was oppressively dark. For a second, she couldn't remember which way to turn and had to drag her hands along the walls for balance, following the smell of tobacco coming from Robert's room near the servants' stairs. Her insides churned with every childhood fear imaginable, the hungry promises of darkness, of silence. Moving faster, she clung to the possibility that nothing had happened, but logic was no comfort. She had just reached out and touched a nose. The possibility it could be the nose of someone *who was not there* represented a nightmarish loss of control.

She had to find that boy.

Robert's room was ahead; a sliver of light showed under his door. She imagined the boy – Feodor, *her* boy – creeping into the old man's room while he slept. The thought appalled her. She rushed to the light, head bent to avoid the low beams of the ceiling, and opened the door. Robert slept deeply in his chair, cheek resting on one large hand. A paperback lay at his feet: *The Battle of Jutland: Naval Tactics in 1916*. The familiar smell of Egyptian cigarettes hung heavily in the air, clashing with the alcoholic tang of Edythe's cleaning fluids on the skirting boards.

Feodor was nowhere to be seen.

The sight of Robert grounded Aisling in reality. What was she doing, rushing around a dark house with her brain full of boys and dust? Touch meant nothing. The mind could fabricate it as easily as a dream. She'd met fellow patients who had only to hear the word 'pin' to felt the real, sharp prick of a needle piercing their flesh. *Two options*, she told herself. *Either a character from my dreams is alive and running around this house, or I'm an idiot who flushed her pills.*

Tea, toast and sleep. Aisling took the servants' stairs down to the kitchen and shakily boiled the kettle. She drank with her back to the window. Dawn couldn't be far off. The door to the cellar was slightly ajar, and the sight of it brought back a fragment of the evening's adrenaline. She put down her mug and flexed her bony ankles. She had to move, get the blood pumping.

The cellar was cold as pond water. She turned on the light and rested on the top stairs. No boy down here. The sounds of Edythe's television were far away, and the cellar, with its whitewashed walls, felt secluded and lonely. *Only fitting*, she told herself. For comfort or punishment, she couldn't tell.

The priest hole, naturally, was open wide.

She crouched and squinted into the depths. Her mind turned to the frightened Tudor priests, sending up pleas to heaven from their hiding place. Beverley hadn't raised Aisling in any faith and disliked the subject because churches reminded her of dead people, but thinking of the priests, an impulse took her. There was a well-chewed carpenter's pencil on one of the shelves. From her pocket she took a torn remainder of the creamy hotel envelope with her mother's handwriting around the edges. Self-consciously, she began to write.

God(dess?)

I want to be her daughter. I want to WANT to be her daughter. A deal – I'll take care of her. I'll swallow the wanderlust and be good.

But you, you have to clean me up. All the black stuff in my head. Do the magic.

Aisling.

She crawled into the entrance and reached up to place the scrap of paper on a ledge at the far end, above the stack of mouldering old notes. The ink murmured to her. *The First Law, The Second Law, The Third.*

'David Morgun,' she whispered.

No sooner had she said it than a prickling began in the soles of her feet. She shuffled backwards on her hands and knees, needing to get out of that cramped space, and fast.

Standing in the sickly light of the single bulb was a long black pillar of a man topped with a bald white head.

I've gone mad.

David was smiling. 'You couldn't resist,' he said. He used the gentle voice he'd addressed her with before on the stairs where he'd looked so humble, but in the harsh light his face was a sweaty greyish white, his eyes too bulbous in their rheumy sockets. He looked…

'Dead.' The word slipped out before she could stop it.

David quirked the hairless lumps of his eyebrows. 'Oh, Aisling, no. I'm alive. Very much alive. Very.'

The muscles in her legs had turned to concrete. *I should be running. Why am I not running?* She wedged herself into a corner. The door seemed suddenly so far away. He was dabbing at his mouth with the sleeve of his coat. Its stink reached out to her. Fuel and smoke eager to invade her healthy lungs. 'How did you get in here?' she wheezed.

Calmly and without ceremony, David spat out a tooth.

Aisling snatched up the heavy old crucifix leaning against the wall and brandished it.

'Oh,' said David, smiling weakly. 'Oh, you see, I thought you told me you weren't superstitious.'

The tip of the crucifix wavered. 'I know what you are.' She swung it experimentally, a holy baseball bat. 'You're in my brain. The photo in the hall, it's you.'

The tooth lay between them on the stone floor, yellow and real, glistening with spittle.

'You told Robert you felt as though you were only half here,' he said. 'What an insightful way of putting it.'

'If I wait long enough, you'll go away.'

'Your mention of Blake jogged a memory. When he wasn't

preoccupied with tigers and chimneysweeps, he once said something very astute. *"If the doors of perception were cleansed, every thing would appear to man as it is."* Cleansed, Aisling. Made pure. Wouldn't you like that?'

He extended one white, big-boned hand to her, slowly, as if reassuring a frightened dog, and she watched with horror as the sinews slid beneath his shrunken skin when he took the end of the crucifix and relieved her of its weight.

'You mustn't be frightened of me.' He placed the crucifix gently on the floor behind him. 'There. Quite real, and quite alive. But perhaps only half here.'

Still her legs refused to move.

'You're in an awful lot of bother now, aren't you?' he said. 'But it is for the best. I myself was in a similar situation, only I found the strength to transcend it. I didn't know you were here until quite recently. I don't like to linger in that bedroom, you see. The priest hole, well, it was a hiding place of mine, once. To tell you the truth, by leaving it open I had rather hoped to give your aunt a little fright.'

'Is the boy here too?' Her voice was a thin croak.

David's eyes sharpened. He came towards her, priestly hands hovering over his chest. 'A boy? What kind of boy?'

The smell of him was atrocious. 'Just, I don't know.'

'Now look here.' His voice was clipped now. 'Is there someone else in this house tonight? Aisling?'

She shook her head helplessly, and David's patience snapped. His hands clapped down on to her shoulders, heavy as dead meat and just as cold. A scream burst from her: 'Robert!'

David released her instantly, struck by the sudden noise. 'Please,' he cried. 'You'll hurt yourself.'

But once the first scream was out, others followed, big, raw screams she didn't know she had inside her. She had never made a noise so loud. She chanted Robert's name again and again, a deluge, as David waved his palms, afraid to touch her: 'Quiet, quiet, you're hurting me now, you're hurting— Ah!' He shielded his head with both arms, giving her the opportunity to duck past his body and bolt for the stairs.

David was after her, snatching at her hair, ungainly with humiliation. Aisling was faster and managed to reach the wooden stairs, hands first, clambering desperately. Halfway up, a hot wave of pain blossomed in the centre of her forehead – *snap!* like a bite – and her muscles slackened in surrender, her body sliding back to the floor. David was upon her, black-bodied and white-faced. He held her down, his flaring white nostrils blasting solvent breath into her face.

'You want a way out. Don't you?'

She kicked at him, hammered at his chest with her fists. 'Yes!'

'It's taken root in your cells, in the electrical signals skittering around your head. You're muddled. It's hurting at this stage, isn't it? Your head, your chest? Bowels, maybe? Visceral pain.'

Aisling's arm broke free, and she caught his cold face with the back of her hand. He fell back on to his knees. She hauled herself up the cellar stairs and tripped though the door into the kitchen. Slamming it shut, gulping clean air, she snatched a gleaming frying pan from one of the hooks above the stove and held it aloft, ready to bring it down on David's head when he burst through the door. It wavered pathetically; it was one thing to hit a man when he was charging at you, but another entirely to brain him as he stumbled into your kitchen. She shot across to the dining table and dragged it to the cellar door as a barricade.

Just as she was wedging it into place under the doorknob, David wheezed out at her from the keyhole.

'When you vanish off into one of your petit mals,' he said, 'where do you think you go?'

She whacked the pan against the keyhole and he said no more.

Dawn was coming. The door remained closed and the cellar beyond was quiet.

When Aisling's breathing slowed sufficiently, she put down the pan and dashed out to the front hall. The chequered tiles were clean as ever in the dull wash of morning light. One of the photographs lay on the tiles. A neat crack split the glass across the three clergymen's chests. The 1930s portrait of the Reverend Enright hung at an angle, his tranquil gaze now aimed at something low and unseen.

She looked to the staircase. The first birds were awakening in the trees surrounding the house. Back in the kitchen, her tea mug sat on the table, undisturbed.

With effort, she walked past the cellar door. Then, she climbed the servants' stairs and opened the top door.

'I've gone mad.'

The dirt and chaos Edythe spent her life fighting had swept down the hall like a tidal wave. Light bulbs hung shattered in their fittings. Missing floorboards bared the guts of the house. There was the sturdy Victorian plumbing. There was the mangled electrical wiring, torn from the walls like roots from soft clay. The remains of the guest bathroom door lay several metres from its customary place, its bronze plaque twisted into a horseshoe, as though the room had been blown apart from the inside. Black blast marks tiger-striped the walls. The paint crumbled beneath her questioning fingers.

Dull fascination drew her deeper. She stepped slowly down the hall, crunching over broken glass and hard, unidentifiable chunks of matter.

Edythe's bedroom door was locked. Further down the hall, Robert's refused to open. Some mechanism in Aisling's brain kicked into motion; a black curtain dropped, allowing to her pick her way calmly across the wreckage. Robert's china teacup, the one she had filled with whiskey two nights ago, was smashed into two neat pieces at the top of the stairs. She touched the broken cup with her toe. It made a real sound: fragile, clear.

'Where are you?' she whispered.

A rustling sound. Aisling stopped breathing.

It came from the guest bathroom. Stepping over ruined floorboards, she braced herself and looked inside. This was the epicentre of the fire. The walls were black, the paint peeling like birch bark in high summer. The enamel bath had all but melted, and there, balancing in the remains of the window, was a nest. Three magpie hatchlings glared at her: spiky, big-mouthed things, huddled together with extended necks. They shrieked in unison at Aisling's intrusion. Above them, a gash in the wall revealed the grey sky of morning, absurdly naked and pale.

Her brain was picking up speed. *No bang, no sound, nothing at all.*

A pain in her big toe made her glance down. A fat bead of red blood, brimming. She reached down and extracted a shard of glass from the neck of a bottle.

Edythe's detergents. Aerosols, polish.

'Little rockets.'

Aisling wiped the blood on her jeans and gave the Celtic ring on her thumb a sharp twist. All real, so far. All coldly genuine. But what about the woman at the hospital, she reminded herself: the sweet, polite woman who heard The Beach Boys wherever she went? *'You tell whoever has that radio in their room, dear, you tell them I haven't had a full night's sleep in weeks. We have to* live *here with that noise.'*

Down in the kitchen, where the sink glistened and the cooking utensils hung untouched, Aisling sat on the table.

'Something's happened to me,' she told herself. 'And it's okay. It's okay because I know something has happened, and I know I flushed my pills and that I'm scared of going back on a ward and of Mum being upset— But I *know*. If I didn't know something was wrong, then I'd be in trouble.' She squeezed her eyes shut tight. There was pain in her chest, just as David had said. Her stomach griped. 'Robert said… Robert said it doesn't make me a bad person. Robert said… I'm not…'

But where was Robert now?

She turned to Blake to calm herself.

'Dear child, I also by pleasant streams
Have wandered all night in the Land of Dreams,
But though calm and warm the waters wide,
I could not get to the other side.'

Her mug was still on the table, the rim sepia where she had sipped weak tea before dawn. Beside the mug was a note written in schoolgirlish cursive she didn't recognise.

My dear Reverend,

My family were shaken to hear of the events last week and would like to offer our condolences and prayers. Fanny and May are so terribly upset and anxious to do anything they can to help. If you ever need someone to take your little girls in while repairs are made, do call on us. As for our friend Mister Morgun, we are all praying.

Florence Bloom.

The hand holding the paper shook. 'What happened here?' she breathed. '*When?*'

The cellar door loomed large in the expanse of the kitchen. Aisling was down the stairs and into the dark space before she knew it. Cold air around her neck. The faint residual smell of the past. No bald man down here. No Feodor. No one to touch her, or hem her into a corner.

David's yellow tooth, dry now, lay conspicuously on the ground. She picked it up and, after a moment's inspection of the brown creases, slipped it into her pocket. *It should be with me,* she told herself. The thought was rootless, almost not her own.

And then she did the only thing that seemed logical. There was the slit black mouth of the priest hole. She got down on all fours and crawled inside, scraping her knees on the damp stone. Her letter to God was no longer on the ledge, but the loss didn't matter. A foetal curl felt most inviting, her wounded hands tucked under her chin. Submerged in the wet dark.

In the half-sleep that followed, she came across the memory she had never meant to keep. Malcolm. He tore her map of the world in his haste to shut the bedroom door. A great crack severing New Zealand.

14

Chase was going to need new boots. They didn't smell too attractive on the rare occasions he took them off.

But what a day, he thought, as he tramped through the undergrowth, a lanky figure in a mud-spattered coat. The kind of day Tor would call 'fruitful'. He'd made a new friend, a sickly-looking ginger girl with interesting bandages, and though he'd managed to scare her off in his usual style, he now knew what not to do in the future. *Plus*, he thought, feeling the small green book in his coat pocket, *I've got a reason to see her again*. Providing he could find her. But he knew this land like an extension of his own body: every thicket, every hillock and every hiding place a familiar sight. The presence of someone new in his territory sent subtle ripples of awareness back to him.

I'm like a spider in his web, he thought cheerfully. *A friendly spider.*

A brief squint of worry crossed his face as it struck him that the girl might have expected him to gallantly hand the book to her straight away. Would the delay make him look like a thief? Tor told him plenty of stories like that, where a lady dropped her handkerchief as she fled a masked ball at midnight. What the hero did with the handkerchief was crucial for the 'happily ever after' part Chase so enjoyed, though he wasn't sure how the hero was meant to tell the difference between an ordinary lost hankie and a covert signal of undying love. Tor never explained those details, even when he begged her. 'Do you want to take the bloom off?' she'd say, and no, he didn't.

He dropped down on to a fallen tree and flipped through the worn pages. The pictures were good and gory. He liked the one of the muscular old man on all fours, staring out with white eyes full of horror. He wanted to hear the ballad that accompanied it. He knew it was a ballad; written down they were tall and blocky, like this one. It was bound to be a chiller, something to make his heart race as he tried to sleep alone in the woods.

But the girl had said she was *like that*, hadn't she? Chase wondered what someone *like that* was doing, reading a scary ballad to herself. Perhaps the ballads had *made* her *like that*. And if that were the case, would too many scary stories eventually make him like that, too? That was a chilling thought. He shivered to himself, half-smiling.

Nature was calling. He shuffled to the nearest bush and didn't bother to glance over his shoulder before unbuttoning his trousers.

'Down by the holly bush, down in the muck, wizzing in widdershins, wizzing for luck.'

The recent rain had collapsed the side of a small hill, creating a precipice over a six-foot gulley. Chase poked the crumbly soil with his boot. There were white slivers of shell where the forest had been a riverbed thousands of years ago. A young tree jutted temptingly over the drop. He sprang up the hill, catching the branch easily with both gloved hands. It bounced as he pulled himself up to dangle above the gulley. Two swings with the spring of the young wood and – 'Wheee!' – his boots were hurtling up past his head. The shriek of pleasure startled a dozing wood pigeon in the canopy above. 'Sorry!' he laughed as it took off with a racket through the trees. His coat-tails flew out behind him as he dropped down into the gulley and landed lightly on the balls of his feet.

'Hollow-bones', Jobi called him. *'Chase the cat'*. It made him blush, even though it was true. Jobi was like that to everyone, flashing his smile around the place like a prince bestowing honours on his courtiers. Chase had been in winter clothes last time they'd met. But that was Jobi's style; he made his grand exits, disappeared just long enough for his friends to become nervous, then strolled back into their lives with souvenirs and stories. Dangerous places, beautiful girls, swashbuckling rubbish he'd probably fabricated on the spot. No, that was unfair. Jobi was brave in a way Chase only dreamed of being, and Chase couldn't wander the wasteland the way he did without wondering if Jobi had passed this way recently, if Jobi had washed his face in this stream or tasted the blackberries from that bush.

No one cared when Chase wandered off. Jobi had adventures. Chase slunk away.

He picked himself up and began to move east, deeper into the safety of the wasteland. The cool of twilight was creeping in, and Tor would want to see that book.

15

Aisling's braid was a wet rope against her shoulder. She was awake.

Eyes open. Brain ticking into life. Exhaustion mingled muddily with dread. It was still night. There would be enough time before morning to clean up and change into fresh clothes. She couldn't go back to her mother smelling like – what was that? She inhaled and was mortified. She put her hand between her legs but found no wetness there. At least she hadn't lost all control. Edythe would have loved recounting that to Beverley, loudly and in front of Robert for good measure.

She raised a hand and planted it against the wall to orient herself. To her confusion there was a shelf above her head, and her blind fumbling dislodged a troop of nick-nacks that bounced and shattered around her.

'Shit!' Aisling scrambled to her knees. *What have I done, what have I done, what have I—*

She shrank back down against the wall, widening her eyes

to catch the slightest detail of her surroundings. At her feet, her shaking hands made out a wooden doll with straw hair and what might have been a china mask, cracked in two. Little noises: toppling stones, flying insects. A spatter of drizzle against the dry skin of her lips. She shivered hard.

She had wandered again.

The wind buffeted the clouds aside, and a dim sheen of moonlight allowed her to count the walls encasing her. Three and a half, a square stone room. The door had been smashed in as if a car had hit it, taking most of the surrounding brickwork out. No roof, save a few bare beams and a chunk of plaster.

It was pointless trying to recall what road she had taken. The back of her head jangled with the unmistakable aftershocks of a seizure. At least the texture of her clothes was familiar, and she snatched up those details, rubbing her palms over the too-short jeans and the thin cotton jumper reaching down past her hips. She had gone to bed in those clothes. It occurred to her that it might not be the same night.

She hauled herself up, colliding immediately with something dangling above her head. She yelped; candles, hanging by their wicks, clattered like a gibbet full of bones. There were racks of the things all around the room, and she felt a dumb pang of relief. Traditional candle-making, quaint and East Anglian. She can't have wandered far.

Now to walk through the night and turn herself in at the nearest roadside pub, to whine to a barmaid, 'I don't know what's happened, I want my mum, I'm scared.' She felt a dig of self-disgust. No. She had to do this bravely.

She picked her way over the debris to the hole where the

door once was, and belatedly remembered to be cautious for discarded needles. *HIV on top of everything else,* she thought. *Fantastic.* Her bare feet were wretchedly sore, but as she stepped outside they found smooth cobblestones in the dark. Straining, she made out the silhouettes of gaunt houses lining a road peppered with puddles and potholes. Each building was a scarred face, windows without glass, doorways without doors. A sycamore sapling had erupted in the middle of the road. She touched a leaf, felt the ridges of living veins.

Aisling turned her back to the tree and struck out in the direction of the moon. *Walk far enough and I'll be somewhere else,* she told herself. Anywhere but that strange, empty street.

Slap-slap went her feet, echoing clammily in the dark. Her brain rattled with mental jumble. Squashed terraces gave way to knots of warehouses. Steel girders and oil drums flaked and pitted like rotting fruit.

The sky was gradually mellowing to a dim grey. In the half-light she caught a cat crossing the street ahead. It paused, seeing her. Aisling puckered her lips and made a friendly noise. The cat shot away somewhere unseen. How she wished she could have her Blake book, even only for a minute. Just long enough to calm her down and tame her thoughts.

She stopped to rest in a grassy gap between the skeletons of two uninhabited houses. A stream ran in a gulley and she knelt beside it, noticing her bandaged hands as if for the first time. A black residue darkened the fingers like the frostbitten explorers in *National Geographic* and she immersed them to the wrists in the cold stream until the bandages unravelled and slithered away. As she stood, a lump in her pocket scraped her hipbone. A tooth. Two long brown roots, sharp to the touch. She stared at it, trying to recall why she'd pocket such a dirty relic. A needly sensation danced around her shoulders.

Has there been an accident?

A bare arm caught her around her ribs, squeezing the air out, and a hand clapped to her mouth before she could yell. The sky tilted over her face as she was hauled off her feet and into one of the houses through a broken wall.

A hard male body pressed against her, squashing her into a corner. A stark black thought: *I'm going to be raped.* Then: *violet fudge.* Her knee jerked in an instinctive jab to the groin, but the man countered the movement, scooping his arm under her leg. He held her there against the wall, like a dance partner, whispering a jumble of apologies, 'I'm sorry, be quiet, be very quiet, please, shhhh!'

It was then that she saw his face.

'Chase!' she cried into his hand.

'*No,*' he whispered. 'If we're heard—' He glanced over his shoulder, wedging their bodies further into the corner of the room. He looked back, his green eyes pleading. 'Trust me. You don't want that.'

Outside, feet tramped slowly over gravel. Chase appeared to be praying. He squeezed her tightly, pressing her cheek against the cold of his gold earring. 'I'm not gonna hurt you,' he whispered. 'But you've got to do what I tell you. Yes? Say yes.'

She nodded against his ear. Then, as though it mattered: 'I dropped my tooth.'

'Your tooth? Where?'

She pointed at the stream's edge.

'Stay.' He was back in less than five seconds. 'This?'

It plopped, cold, into her palm. 'Thank you.' From a gap in the unfinished wall she could see a thirty-foot perimeter wall of stone. It curved around the street, corralling the buildings. There was no indication of where she had walked from, or where to go. Her heart tripped back into a gallop. 'We're bricked in.'

'Uh-huh.'

'We can't get out.'

He was looking at her as if she was a child.

'This isn't Suffolk, is it?' she said.

The footsteps were closer now. They looked at each other.

'You know how you told me you were,' he stuck out his tongue and crossed his eyes. 'Right? Well, I'm okay with that. But right now, I need to know if you can run.'

A ridiculous memory of PE uniforms and plimsolls. 'Sort of.'

'I need you to run in that direction, straight down between those buildings. There's a mound of rubble, a big mound, where the wall's been smashed. You need to get up it, over it, then wait on the other side for me, out of sight. And be church mouse quiet. *Dead* church mouse. You get it?'

She nodded. 'Dead mouse.'

She was shaking. Chase gave her arms a vigorous rub. 'You,' he grinned, 'really smell. I'm not gonna abandon you. All right?' He picked up a sack from the floor and slung it over his shoulder. With his earring and his smirk, he looked like a sailor on leave.

Again, the crunch of footsteps over debris.

'See you on the other side.' He was off across the street

and scooting up a drainpipe. From her hiding place, Aisling watched as he pulled himself up on to the roof and skittered easily across a bare girder, hair bright in the rising dawn. A small thing was moving in Chase's wake: the cat. It sprang up on to a wall and settled down to watch as the young man skipped across the rooftops with his leather coat flapping like a tail.

Somewhere off to the right, heavy feet on gravel. The cat rose into an arch and fled.

Time to leave. Heart thumping in her throat, Aisling slipped out into the street. The hole in the perimeter wall was plain to see now, a hundred metres away at the end of the main avenue, a pile of stone and twisted wire. She would have to run in plain sight.

In plain sight of what? She found she couldn't consider it.

Sparks of pain as crystals of grit worked inside her blisters. As she hurried to the gap in the vast grey wall, she found herself marvelling. Castle walls, Blitzkrieg, 'Keep out'. Or 'Keep in'. She planted her sore hands on the cold stone and began the ascent, praying that Chase didn't expect her to be half as agile as him. Her biceps struggled where the morning purges had made them pathetic, but after a couple of painful slips she found she was getting into the climb. Near the top she stopped for breath, standing upright to give her knees a chance to recover. Then she did what all humans unthinkingly do when they reach a high point in the landscape. She turned to assess the view.

What she had thought was a deserted village was in fact a deserted town. Between buildings of black brick and slate were passageways, broad thoroughfares and jail-like structures with concrete yards she recognised as schools.

Clock towers slumped shoulder to shoulder with chimneys and the hollow husks of dead oaks. Pub gardens broke their enclosures to sprawl out into the streets. Far off, there may have been lights, but she couldn't trust her eyes. Encircling the town as far as she could see, the high wall.

Below her, a figure stood in the doorway of one ruined house. At first she thought it was Chase and she paused, allowing him to see her balancing with difficulty on the rubble. The figure shifted in her direction, tucking his white chin into the lapels of his coat like a pigeon in a rainstorm. He raised an arm in greeting, hesitantly, above the bald white ovoid of his head.

Why did she wave back? An expression of intense gladness spread across the man's bulbous cheekbones; she could see it even in the dark. His arm hung in mid-air, fingers spread wide, as if to grab.

Aisling scrambled up the last remaining stones and then down the other side, jumping the last six feet to fall awkwardly into the wet grass below. Chase was there, lounging on a rock with a sack full of loot.

'Flex a bit as you land,' he said. 'Your knees'll thank you.'

On her backside in the grass, Aisling felt like the hinges of her bones had fused shut. She wanted to tear off her dirty clothes, bin them, bathe.

'I think… I think I know that man,' she panted. 'You know him, too – don't you?'

Chase said nothing, picking the dirt off his bootlaces. She looked back at the wall with its bomb-blast hole, unable to process what she had just seen. 'Please. I need to go home.'

Chase swung the heavy sack over his shoulder. 'What you need is a bath and some proper food,' he said, lifting her to her feet without permission. All traces of his earlier fear had evaporated. He was once again the big, happy blond she had seen turning cartwheels in Edythe's garden. 'You're lucky I was having a snoop back there. Do I get a "Thank you"? Gallant rescue, and all that.'

She couldn't speak. She nodded stiffly. That seemed to satisfy him.

'Something you do often?' he asked, shepherding her into the field where the dewy ground was stony and slippery at the same time. 'Standing out in the open like that, shoeless?' He nudged her with his shoulder, failing to coax a smile. 'Hey. I'm reuniting you with your Mister Blake. Are you mates, by the way? He doesn't sound like someone you could sit down and have a sandwich with.'

'You've got my book?'

'Yep. When you did a runner, it was on the ground. I wasn't sure about following you, y'know? Fellow in leather chasing a young girl. But I reckoned it meant a fair bit to you. So I looked after it.' His expression reminded her of a child hoping to impress a favourite teacher. 'Is that a smile?'

The relief was so enormous, the trembling almost ceased. 'Thank you. Did you— Did you like it?'

'Tor read me some. I can't make sense of words once they're written down.' He glanced at her. 'I s'pose that makes me stupid.'

'No, I... Of course not.'

The ground was uneven with roots, and there were thistles to avoid. Ahead was a crowd of silver birches at the opening of a large wood. Chase seemed to be intent upon entering it. Thanks to the exhaustion or the prospect of being sent back to hospital, she found she was strangely unfazed.

'You said I wasn't in Suffolk any more,' she ventured, with every hope he had been wrong. Rural Suffolk and its neighbouring counties were all largely the same, with their flat expanses of tilled black earth. This place was more like, well, she didn't know.

Chase switched the sack to his other shoulder. It clanked. 'Thing is, I'm not one for maps, so I can only *vaguely*— Oh, hey, come on, don't cry. I'm on your side. Do you need a cuddle?' He held out his arms to her awkwardly, and she moved away.

'I'm not crying,' she snapped. 'I'm cold. And I'm in so much trouble. You have no idea. When I get back, my aunt and my mum—' She had to break off the sentence, because Chase had thrown a small package at her. She caught it just before it hit her in the face.

'Those,' he said, 'are almonds roasted with honey. They're sticky and yummy and you'd better be flattered 'cause I'm giving you my last ones.' Aisling hesitated and Chase became mock-stern. '*Shouldn't* do this, *need* to do that. Stick 'em in your gob. I'm not carrying you if you pass out.'

She took one glistening nut and chewed on it. 'Thanks.'

The mouth of the woods: an engulfing tunnel of trees. Aisling thought she saw the white flash of a magpie gliding silently through the depths. Perhaps she was embellishing again.

Chase nodded smartly and smoothed his hair down over his ears, an unconscious gesture she was getting used to. 'My pleasure,' he said. 'And we'll tell your aunt I kidnapped you.'

>•<

The past came to her in vivid slices.

Locks were forbidden, on doors and on diaries. No trip to the toilet without teacher, no walk to school without mummy, no private place to rest. Nevertheless, swimming out of the hot darkness of Aisling's dreams was a padlock. She was at school again: the science department on a noisy lunchtime. Shoulders hunched to quieten her long, conspicuous body, she stood at her locker, staring inside at the notepads and scattered biros as if they might stand up and speak.

'Looking a bit peaky today, Aisling. Looking a bit pale.'

A boy from her year was walking by with one of the older girls.

'I'm on suicide watch,' he said. 'I'm keeping an eye on you.'

The girl swung her bag against the wall, *scrape, scrape*. 'We won't get a table. Hurry up.'

Time tilted. The boy was beside Aisling now, raking his gaze over the postcards tacked to the inside. The Welsh river view with trees and boulders, the museum postcard of Blake's ladder to the moon, a tiny figure clambering out into space: *I want! I want!*

Don't look, she longed to hiss. *Mine.*

'My brother's training to be a doctor.'

Scrape, scrape, went the girl's bag. Aisling pulled the door of the locker open just enough to create a barrier between herself and the boy, but when she dared a look there was nothing in his face to suggest malice. She softened slightly. 'Yeah?'

He laughed, she sounded so suspicious. 'For real. He's starting his second year. He told me something that might help you, actually.'

The girl laughed and sauntered away. He leaned in closer to Aisling, so close that she could see the styling gel drying in scales along his hairline. 'Yeah, my brother knows a lot about people like you. You're pretty interesting, actually.'

Something tightened.

I'm not interesting.

He removed her hand from her locker door, closed it and faced her. 'See, they didn't used to do all this special treatment with counsellors and all that. They just used to take one of them ice picks, and they'd put the pointy bit just under the eyelid here...'

I'm not here.

The row of locker doors shuddered like thunder as the edges of the padlock, she discovered later, cut into her eyebrow. The hand he had used to slam her head into the locker disappeared into his pocket, and he was off and away as if he had done nothing more than pat her on the back.

She was far away when someone tittered. And from the padlock at school she was sucked downwards to the lock on the bathroom door at home, up to her ribs in bathwater, dabbing at her swollen eye. The scent of Beverley's jasmine moisturiser as she cried outside the door. That particular night existed under the thickest, blackest tar imaginable, and it was into that Aisling found herself sinking, thrashing in the pounding heat and down into guilt and forgetfulness.

16

A stare was another kind of touch. She felt it and cracked open one eye to find Chase's nose inches from her face. He bit his bottom lip to suppress a smile.

'Good morning, good morning, the raven said as he pecked at the eyes of sleeping Fred.'

Aisling recoiled. Everything ached, like the time she'd had flu when she was eleven. She remembered the fever-dreams, snakes wheedling into her clothes.

Chase shuffled closer, smiling still. 'No one's eaten your eyeballs. It's just a rhyme.'

She was lying on a small sofa with her legs dangling over the end. On top of her was a thick eiderdown with spots of discolouration. She was hot, sweating.

'What's happened?' she asked.

'You've had a good rest.'

'After what?'

'The walk. You walked. With me.'

'I didn't.'

Chase giggled.

'Where is this?' Her voice was croaky. She sounded like someone else.

'Good grief,' he laughed. 'You never shut up with the whys and the hows. Sit up, come on.'

He put a pillow behind her back, and with effort she pulled herself up. She wasn't wearing her own clothes, but a thin nightdress that may have been a bed sheet in a previous life. The room was like something from a war film. Walls of clay were lined by big, rough beams, criss-crossing to take the weight of the ceiling with the help of corrugated iron sheets affixed to the walls like rusty plasters. A high platform housed a mattress and blankets, and in the cave below it was a paper-strewn desk and shelves lined with tiny bottles, catching the light with different coloured and textured contents. The floors were made of wooden packing crates, dirty with raw earth, and a rifle hung from an exposed root above the fire, gathering dust.

The furniture told a different story. In every available nook, there were chairs draped with lace antimacassars. Worn pink brocade, chintz and jolly stripes competed for attention like a Women's Institute bric-a-brac sale. On a moth-eaten rug was a coffee table laden with junk: cigar boxes, dirty spoons, a china cake stand loaded with rusty bicycle bells and other salvageable scrap. *Guerrilla grandmothers*, Aisling thought, and could have laughed if it weren't for the ache in her head.

Chase prodded her shoulder. 'Hey,' he said. 'Cause they're the best thing after a long snooze, I picked you some lovely mushrooms for a fry-up.'

She followed his gaze over the sofa to where a brown-skinned boy in grass-stained clothes was chopping the stalks from a basket of mushrooms and spring onions. 'Hello,' he smiled at her. His voice was pleasingly soft, like his face.

Chase smacked his lips. 'With butter and garlic, please. Tor says they're good for making me heal when I catch myself on brambles.'

'What's Tor?' Aisling asked.

Before Chase could explain, there came a voice like the crackle of burned sugar.

'Introductions, Chase, remember. They always come first in polite conversations.'

Behind Aisling's sofa, where the boy chopped mushrooms, a woman was emerging from another, lower room. She was short and wide as a door, with a black Louise Brookes bob and heavy-rimmed glasses. She walked with lumbering difficulty, but smiled with the warmth of a practised hostess. 'Hello there, Aisling. Are you comfortable? My name is Victoria Craig.'

'Call her Tor,' Chase said. 'She likes her friends to call her that.'

Tor scooped up one of the mushrooms from the boy's basket to taste. 'Chase has already decided it's imperative we become chums.'

'I'm famished.' Chase bounced on his heels. 'Do we have any onions?'

Tor waddled to one of the striped armchairs adjacent to Aisling and lowered herself down. There was swelling in her ankles, a purplish bloating. 'Go down and raid the pickle jars if you're desperate.'

'What about meat? I fancy a bit of fish.'

'There's nothing fresh. You've eaten it all. I don't know why I don't nail the door shut when I hear you coming.'

'But the pickled ones are all vinegary.'

'That's rather the point,' Tor smiled. 'I'm sorry, Aisling. Please, are you up to taking a little breakfast with us?'

Aisling gathered the duvet around herself. 'I get sick in the mornings. But thanks.'

'That's quite all right. Relax, and know that this is the safest place you can be.'

Chase hadn't been listening. 'I miss fish,' he said. 'The ones from the river in town come out all wonky. Apparently some guy hooked a trout last month and it came up with little stumpy leggy bits. He ate it, obviously, so nobody ever got to see it, but he said the legs were boneless, like noodles. I remember when you could get proper fish, big, normal—'

Just as Aisling was about to ask a question, Tor interrupted. 'You know what I miss?' she said. 'Bread.'

Chase groaned in agreement.

'Hot buttered rolls, fluffy and white and *ooozing* with butter. Oh! And pasta. Have you ever had pasta made for you from scratch? All slippery with oil and sea salt. Carbohydrates are the devil's work, and I adore him for it.'

'I can get you some bread. Next time I—'

'No, they mix it up with sawdust and the yeast is a thousand years old. I'll keep my memories of real food intact. Oh! Look who we've woken up.'

Rats. Three of them, brown, white, and black, scurrying out from behind a sheet of corrugated iron. Aisling instinctively tucked her duvet under her feet.

'Hello, friends! Well rested?' They assembled at her feet like children. Tor noticed Aisling recoiling. 'They're perfectly clean and tame. Aisling, meet Mister Black, Mrs Brown and Señor Blanca.'

Señor Blanca, with paws as pink as porcelain, pottered over to Aisling and sniffed her hand with a querulous nose.

'Good morning,' Aisling said. The rat blinked his button-black eyes.

Tor was reaching under her chair. 'I have something for you, young lady.'

It was her Blake book, slightly warm, as if Tor had dried it by the fire.

Aisling resisted the urge to bury her nose in the familiar crinkles of the pages. 'Oh, thank you. Thank you.'

'I'm impressed by this. You're what? Nineteen?'

Seventeen, she was about to say, though at that moment she couldn't be sure.

'It's good to see a young person taking an interest in controversial literature. I myself was once slippered for reading a novel about a lady offering sanctuary to a disgraced knight. Racy stuff. Mother was appalled.'

Aisling barely took it in. The firelight was a painful yellow and her stomach was beginning to gripe. Chase was so close, nearly resting his head on her knee. Her eyes watered.

Tor cocked her head. 'Where are your parents, Aisling?'

'Patagonia? On a ship.' She looked at Tor and blinked, mouth slack. 'I don't know.'

Chase's handsome face was crinkled with concern. 'She's still a bit weird,' he commented. 'D'you reckon she's properly poorly?'

Just then, the boy peeling mushrooms gave a squeak. 'The signal's back!'

He had a little wind-up radio set. Over the crackles and

whizzes of static there was a tinkling, like bells, and the boy's face softened into a sad smile as a piano waltz revealed itself, *1, 2, 3, 1, 2, 3.* Everyone stopped to listen.

'He used to love playing us this one,' he said.

Clarity did not come the next morning, or the one after that. Aisling drifted in a honeyed state between sleep and wakefulness, too drained to raise her head for more than a minute. She was vaguely aware of taking single bites of food when it was offered by hands that may have belonged to Chase, dreamily registering the transitions from morning to afternoon and evening to night by the gentle undulations of temperature and sunlight.

On the third day, she opened her eyes.

She was down in a lower, darker part of the house, snuggled in a nest of duvets. The air was pleasantly cool on her puffy eyelids, sore with grit. Perhaps she had been crying.

Her bed was beside a long wall of jars stacked up to the earthy ceiling. She recognised preserved onions, gherkins and sliced carrots. There were cabbage leaves curled up like scrolls. An enormous apothecary jar she couldn't imagine Tor or Chase lifting, even together, contained a knot of pinkish snakey creatures. There were peaches suspended in golden jelly, apple segments and monstrous strawberries from what must have been an incredible summer. If a new Ice Age were to descend, Tor and her friends were prepared.

Upstairs, the little radio warbled to itself, incomprehensible interference and code. Finding her jeans and jumper crisply laundered on a stool near her bed, Aisling shimmied into them before making the difficult transition from lying to standing. The pickle jars showed her reflection, limbs bent at strange angles as she steadied herself against the beams in the walls. *I look like Bambi*, she thought. *Done by Dalí.* With one more glance to check her appearance wasn't too horrid, she took the short flight of dusty stairs up into the main body of the house.

Light and air. The door and windows were all open, and the breeze coming in to meet her was fresh. It ruffled some papers tacked to the wall, delicate pencil portraits she hadn't noticed before. Scores of them. Long-haired boys were preserved in slack-jawed slumber alongside profiles of drowsy girls, heads drooping into open books. The occasional solemn-faced child was cocooned in blankets, arms clamped jealously around dolls and toy boats. Aisling recognised a likeness of Chase snoozing by the fire, hair in disarray, earring glinting.

There were voices in the garden, and the cheerful clinks of spoons on china. She shielded her eyes and stepped out into the light.

There wasn't a garden, as she had first thought. Gardens as Aisling knew them had fences, and washing lines, and sheds. The house was in the middle of a shallow bowl in the landscape, ringed by a corona of tall trees. By the door was a patch of blousy cabbages with purple-tipped leaves, and a row of fragrant tomato plants. Around the corner, a lean-to in need of repair housed a pile of firewood under a tarpaulin and a few farming tools lumpy with rust. There were other vegetables growing in patches around the house, rambling happily up cane frames or spilling out on to the grass. Almost everything growing in the clearing was functional, bar a climbing clematis smothering a window frame in white stars.

The house itself was a marvel. She could now see that half the building was underground, with the rest emerging from a grassy lump much like the community air raid shelter the council had bulldozed to build her primary school. There was a photograph of it in reception, black and white, flanked by nameless local men holding spades and bottles of beer.

From the trees encircling the bowl, the house would be invisible.

She found Tor and the pretty young boy sitting at a small table together, drinking tea from floral cups. Chase was lounging barefoot on the grass beside them, his blond hair bright in the sunshine. They had been eating a breakfast of eggs and fruit. Tor's lips were smeared with purple juice.

'Look at you!' she cried, seeing Aisling. She was at the head of the table with a sprig of white clematis flowers tucked behind her ear. 'Walking on your hind legs.'

Chase jumped up, offering her a chair that looked as if it once belonged in a Parisian cafe. 'I've been waiting for you to wake up,' he told her, so thrilled that his voice threatened an adolescent tremor. 'I stayed beside you the whole time. I really did. This is the first time I've left you.'

Tor chuckled at Aisling's expression. 'Creepy thought?'

Chase flushed across the cheekbones. 'To make sure she was all right. It's confusing sometimes, waking up in a new place. I know.'

Aisling sat. She looked up at the sky. Clear blue, with a hint of mauve in the atmosphere, a flawless summer morning. 'I hope I haven't been a pain,' she said. 'I've taken up quite a lot of your floor.'

'You needed the rest,' Tor assured her. 'It wouldn't do to ignore the body when it says "stop". Now, I really do insist you take some breakfast with us.'

'I could,' Aisling said. 'I'd actually love to. That's so strange. I'm usually sick in the mornings, but now I'm not sick at all.'

'The air's good here,' said the boy. He was younger than her, fifteen, maybe, self-contained, with dark eyes wide as a deer's.

The air *was* good: alpine and crystalline. No city grit to filter through her lungs. She suddenly wanted her *Wanderlusts*, to compare the experience with that of other travellers. Fear followed. How would Beverley punish her for running off? Would she go through her bedroom with a bin bag, scooping up handfuls of novels and notebooks for the recycling collection on Friday? '*You couldn't want them that badly,*' she would say, '*if you didn't take them with you.*' Aisling was momentarily disorientated enough to lose her grip on her teacup, causing it to slosh warm tea over her fingers.

Tor was polite enough not to visibly notice. She served Aisling a hard-boiled egg sliced in two with a dollop of spicy chutney from one of several open jars. 'To health,' she said, and they all murmured their agreement as they reached for second helpings. A bumblebee bobbed past the table, heading for the blooms on the runner beans.

I've been very ill, Aisling reminded herself, for it seemed like a statement in someone else's diary. *My name is Aisling Selkirk and I've not been very well. But today, I'm all right.* She picked up the boiled egg with her fingers and felt the white flesh yield, bouncy and smooth. She took a bite with some chutney. It was wonderful. Everything was wonderful.

Chase, who hadn't stopped grinning since Aisling had emerged, poked her elbow. 'That's a nice ring you're wearing. Who made that?'

Aisling swallowed, shrugged, took another bite. The ability to eat without nausea was irresistible. 'I don't know,' she said, mouth full. 'It's just a cheap thing I bought years ago. At a castle.'

'A castle!'

'Colchester Castle, I think? There was a lot of Roman stuff.'

'Colchester. Not heard of that one. Tor, did you ever hear of a Colchester Castle?'

'Chase likes to think he's seen the universe entire,' Tor said to Aisling. 'He hates to be reminded that it's bigger than he'll ever know.'

Chase snatched a peach segment from Tor's plate. 'I haven't been to Colchester,' he said. 'But I will, 'cause Aisling will take me. Won't you? And I'll get a nice ring for myself there.' He munched open-mouthed, swinging his shoulders like a pleased little boy.

Tor dished out some more chutney on to Aisling's plate. 'Aisling probably shouldn't be taking anyone anywhere for a little while.'

A looked passed between Tor and Chase. Aisling missed it, distracted by the pretty boy quietly offering her a cup of tea. 'I washed your feet while you were sleeping,' he told her, topping up her cup, first with milk from a blue china jug, and then with tea. Puckered pink licks of scar tissue lightened the dark skin of his forearms. 'You had cuts, but they were shallow. If they itch at all, do let me know. I have a little cider vinegar. It will help.'

'That's really kind,' Aisling said, careful not to stare at the scars. 'I'm sorry, I've forgotten your name. I'm all fogged up from sleeping so long.'

'Georgie,' the boy said. His voice was light, but steady. He may have been older than Aisling first estimated. 'I'm Georgie.'

A mischievous smile crept across Chase's face. 'Georgie was a little frog, a'hopping through the meadow. But when he caught a handsome fly, he couldn't bear to swallow.' He circled the table to tickle Georgie, and the boy snorted, curling into a ball on his chair. It was an old routine.

'Flies have a right to their lives.' Georgie got up, batting away Chase's wiggling fingers. 'But, well, so do frogs.'

Chase watched him gather the dirty plates and walk back to the house. He stretched, indolent in the sunshine. 'Everyone's got a right. I like that.'

'Everybody,' Tor echoed. She was looking down into her lap. Something was moving there, fidgeting against the faded black corduroy of her skirt. One pink, whiskered nose quivered into view, then another: rats.

Aisling laughed. 'I thought I dreamt them.'

Tor lifted one big-bottomed rodent up on to the table. It sat there, happy to preen its velvet ears beside Tor's teacup. 'Did you dream a lot, Aisling?'

Chase interrupted. 'You would've. Our Georgie made sure you were topped up with lettuce tea. Knocked me clean out when I had a sinus infection last spring and couldn't sleep for pain. It's a funny story, actually. I was climbing a tree to get to the mistletoe growing at the top—'

'Above dirty water,' Tor added. 'And thin ice.'

Chase grinned. 'Big splash.'

'He hauled himself out – miraculously, considering the weight of that coat – and managed to walk here before collapsing on the doorstep like a bad actress. He was feverish for two days, thrashing and bleating the entire time.' She affected a sullen Northern accent: *"I'm 'ungry, gerroff me, I'm gonna die."* Not like you, Aisling. You were like one of those dreamy antique post-mortem photographs. Artfully arranged. Very quiet.'

Chase agreed. With a queasy sensation, Aisling imagined them crowding around her as she lay unaware: the broad woman with the intelligent blue eyes, handsome Chase keen to miss nothing, and Georgie, feeding her something potent and secret as she stirred. 'What was it?' she asked, so consciously casual it sounded ridiculous. 'The name of that tea?'

Tor petted Mrs Brown, the rat, with her fat fingers. 'Georgie is our little doctor. We don't like to rely on anyone but ourselves.'

Aisling wanted to repeat her question, but was startled by the rush of Chase's breath in her ear. He'd slunk up close without a sound. 'I got a present for you.' From somewhere he had fetched a long hessian sack. He knelt down and put his whole arm inside, making a show of rummaging before pulling out a grimy bottle of wine by the neck. 'Proper medicine.'

Tor snatched away the bottle. 'And where did you get this?'

Chase sat back, pleased to have his secrets.

Tor gave him a gentle kick with her bare foot. 'Well?'

'It looked lonely all by itself.'

Tor turned the bottle over in her hands, reading the label.

'And did anyone see you take it?'

'Hey, I could be offended! I'm discreet.'

'You could be in gaol.'

He was delighted. 'What does it say? Is it posh?'

'I'll put it in terms you'll understand: we couldn't afford this. Not if we all clubbed together, sold everything in the house, and handed you over to medical science. This is nice wine. Too nice.'

'Well, good. It's a special occasion. Aisling's awake. And she's happy to be here.' He leaned across the table, whispering loudly. 'Guess where I found it. Have a go. I'll give you one clue.' He put his index finger to his lips. 'Ssshhh!'

'Oh, Chase.'

'Yeah. Down *there*. In a guard post, no less. It wasn't even manned any more. None of them are. What a fine time they must've been having on duty. While inside—'

'That's enough, dear.' With the edge of sternness in her voice, Tor sounded as if she were dealing with the gamekeeper of her grand estate. 'And how is poor Aisling supposed to feel? With you here, leading her to believe she's among thieves?'

'It's *looting*, not nicking. Looting's like recycling. And I never take from the proletariat. Come on, Tor, I'm not a bodysnatcher.'

'Good people can still set bad examples.'

Chase was in a full-blown sulk now, scuffing at the dirt. The childishness, coupled with his height and physique, was hopelessly endearing. Aisling raised her teacup over her smile.

'I can drink it myself,' he grumbled.

'Not a chance,' Tor said. 'Fetch four glasses, and bring

Georgie outside to join us. Tell him we're toasting your criminal downfall.'

When Chase had bounded off, Tor placed the sleeping rat on the table and dragged her chair up to Aisling's until they were knee-to-knee. 'You must think we're horrid.'

'Oh, no. I was thinking how lovely it is here.'

Tor gave a husky chuckle. 'You're the most well-mannered teenager I've ever come across. And for that you can stay here as long as you like.'

'It's tempting. I mean, it's so warm. The *air...*'

'You certainly notice it the first time. And we've a small bay behind the house – you've never seen water so clear.'

Aisling touched her knuckles. The skin was pink and sore.

'Could I use your telephone?'

'Rest first. You're weaker than you think.'

'I know, and you've been really kind. But I should tell someone I'm here.'

'Chase told me about all the *shoulds*. The thing is, you've caught us in the middle of a power cut. Happens all the time out here. One never knows when it will ping back on.'

'Do you get a postal collection?' She could send a letter. A postcard.

Tor reached across the table and gently placed her hand on top of Aisling's. It was heavy and soft. 'No, dear. Not now.'

There was laughter in the house. Aisling saw the small shape of Georgie flit by a window, pursued by Chase, galumphing at him like a lanky-legged monster. Tor looked on like an indulgent mother. She patted Aisling's hand, inspected the healing grazes on each knuckle. 'Do you see that tree up at the top of the hill? The youngest tree, with the roots like little feet? Yes. You can go up to that tree. You may sit under it and read when you want to, even swing on the branches if you're able. But you can't go beyond that tree. That is our perimeter. This is our place.'

'Once you prove your willingness to behave,' Edythe had said. But Tor's instructions were gentle, and they made sense, she supposed. The countryside worked differently to the suburbs she was used to. Stray from your regular path and you might cross a dangerous bull or a shooting party. So Aisling accepted Tor's instructions, just as she accepted the older woman's gentle scrutiny of her fingers, splaying them apart to check the elasticity of the grazed flesh.

'You'll have the hands of a debutante again in no time. I'll get Georgie to feed you plenty of mushrooms, or— Oh. Did I hurt you?'

Something sharp had scraped Aisling's hip. She worked a finger into the pocket of her jeans and came to something cold and smooth.

'Now there's a brute,' Tor murmured, looking at the gnarly old tooth between Aisling's forefinger and thumb. She held the thing at arm's length. A yellow chunk of bone, with dried brown blood on the twin-pronged roots. Even the rats stared.

Chase and Georgie had come outside with four mismatched glasses. Chase immediately latched on to the tooth. 'Grim! It looked smaller in the dark. And *blood*, there's blood. Oh God, and I *touched* it. And then I had breakfast. With my *hands*.' He rubbed his palms on his filthy trousers gleefully.

Aisling was unable to think of anything sensible to say. She found herself dwelling on frightening things: on blackened wallpaper and baby magpies. It was better to focus on Chase pressing a glass into her hand, his healthy skin and clear green eyes. The clamouring inside her quietened down.

Georgie poured the wine. They put the tooth on the table, a macabre centrepiece among the floral china and jars of jam. The four of them silently toasted, to what they weren't certain; the tooth had their attention, dominating the table with its size and ugliness. Even Chase's fascination turned cold. Eventually, Tor, with her sense of propriety, silently covered it with a white napkin.

Chase broke the silence. 'This is all right. Better than that paint-stripper home brew we cooked up.'

Georgie brightened at the memory. 'What was that name you gave it?'

'Uncle Chase's Tasty Bothways Water, tastes just as good coming up as going down. Georgie'll tell you, Aisling, even Tor was plastered. She tried to show us how to fold a crane out of a napkin, and when she couldn't do it, she just got madder and madder, and she'll never admit it now, but she swore like—'

Tor coughed. 'Yes, we don't mention that episode any more, do we? Why don't you take Aisling out to the bay to get that filthy tooth clean?'

'Like a good boy?'

She glared at him over her glasses. 'Like a slightly-less-horrid boy.'

Chase took Aisling along a dirt track leading up and over a hill behind the house. Yellow-flowering gorse bushes snagged at their clothes. The breeze picked up as they neared the mouth of the bay, the trees sighing as if, seeing two small people tramping through their ranks, they were murmuring their approval.

They came to a stretch of shingle enclosed by rocks and rooty trees. The flat water was the clear yellow-green of a cat's eye. Of Chase's eyes, too, she realised.

'I've never seen the other side. Not even with a telescope.' He hung back by the track, holding their glasses. 'Are you gonna wash that thing?'

She took it down to the water lapping against the shingle. She wished she had a scrubbing brush, or the thing Beverley used to take the hard skin off her feet. *Drop it, then,* she thought suddenly. *Drop it if it's so disgusting.* She opened her palm under the water. The tooth rocked back and forth, but there was no tide to take it away. That seemed to decide it.

Chase had drained his wine and started on hers. They sat down together on the shingle and she showed him the tooth.

'It's still pretty hideous,' he said.

'I found it in my aunt's house. Everything was so clean there, she was obsessed, but this thing…' she trailed off, unable to anchor her words to a memory. The fog following a seizure could last for hours, but *days*, she wondered? What if there was permanent damage this time? She took her wine glass from Chase and held it up to the light, watching the streams of bubbles rise and burst and fade.

'Tor's house hasn't been clean since it was built,' he said. 'She's talking about setting you up a proper bed downstairs, you know, and she was saving that spot for a permanent bath. She usually does it by the fire and makes me and Georgie look the other way. She must really like you.'

Hesitantly, she turned her face to him. The fabric of his

trousers had been patched and patched again, and she followed the tracks of stitches over wiry muscle and bony kneecap. The words came out in a tumble. 'Look, I know I've only just met you and you've all been really kind to me, but people must be worrying about me. I need to get back.'

'To your aunt? She made you cry. You're smiling here. Look. You're doing it now.'

She was, and she was ashamed of it. 'They'll think I've run off again. I mean, I have, I've done it, but it's never a conscious thing. I've never,' she squeezed her eyes shut, 'I've never been anywhere like this. I've never seen anything so lovely. There's too much to ask.'

'You said "again". You'd run off again.'

'Yeah.'

Chase made a dismissive noise, as if to him everything was clear. 'Folks don't run away for fun. I know people who, well, they're different. They're showing off. But you? With your *shoulds*? Maybe those people you talk about are the selfish ones, trying to keep you somewhere you can't stand to be in.'

For a second, she was shocked. She looked out at the water. There was nothing in the distance, no outline of coastal hills, no seabirds hovering in the ozone. The intense *take-me-with-you* feeling that usually accompanied a clear horizon was strangely absent. The wine left a trail of sparkles down her throat.

Chase regarded her, tanned arms encircling his knees. 'Why not just enjoy it?'

17
FEODOR

I used to like imagining what happened after my disappearance.

It's forty-eight hours, I think, before someone's officially listed as Missing. In films, there's always a picture of the lost kid smiling with his arms around a Labrador. There weren't many photos of me at fifteen. Mama took plenty on disposable Kodak cameras when I was a baby in the eighties. Me, curly-haired and scowling, on Dad's knees at the piano. She'd posed him there, of course. It was her who taught me to play. He preferred to sit off to one side with his face behind a newspaper, shielding himself from disappointment when I touched the wrong key.

I bother myself wondering how long it took him to notice my absence. I see him as I last saw him, rigid in bed with the covers heaped on top of him, leaving my mother's side bare and cold. Had he sat there in bed all night, thinking? Had I crossed his mind at all?

So how would it go? Mister Benedict, though slow to catch a joke, wasn't stupid. He wouldn't draw attention to himself. Of all of them, L would be the one with sufficient imagination to see me huddling under a railway bridge somewhere. He'd make the call from one of the payphones outside my block. I can see him having to enter each booth before finding the one on the end that hadn't been vandalised. The anonymous tip-off would be his style, thinking of that girlfriend of his, though if there was a chance of reward money being involved later on, I reckon he'd wait. Patagonia. Jamaica. I bet that man never once left the UK.

In my head, the policemen who come to my door wear those tight blue uniforms you see in the American crime shows on late night TV. My father would squint at them. He'd look terrible under the fluorescent hall light, and growl something in his suspicious immigrant accent about the time of the night. Cue the sad music. The cops would see the kitchen crammed with empty bottles, the takeaway containers piled up and reeking, and the biohazard disaster we called the bathroom. Poor kid, *they'd be thinking,* poor little bugger. *In my bedroom, they would take photographs. Bed, unmade. Mama's candle with the Virgin Mary.*

That's where it all comes unstuck. The matches under the bed. The pile of lighters, some spent. The library books with their missing pages, plastic jackets crisp and black.

'Mister Boyarov,' they'd said, 'when did you last see your son?' And he wouldn't remember. Tuesday was identical to Monday, and Monday was identical to any other day. But the police would have realised by now, I'd gone on Wednesday, right after that kid copped it in the playground with the burning tracksuit. It didn't matter how hard I tried to

imagine it any other way. There wouldn't be a smiling picture of me in a file anywhere.

At first, I liked being The Missing Boy. I'd never have to spend five days a week stacking shelves or scanning barcodes. No weekly shop for me, no bank account, no number seven bus to Croydon. I'd escaped. I was cleverer than everyone I'd grown up with. I was the one bold enough to reject it all. In those first few weeks of freedom, because I was vain, I even brought Rada into my story. I'd disappeared, just like her, and my disappearance created a kind of symmetry that made me feel important. Rada had been denied her life, and now her killer had been denied his only child. Gorgeous.

That was all years ago.

I woke up this morning feeling like I'd spent the previous night swallowing rocks. The rabbit had looked okay when I found it, but it must have passed that twenty-four-hours-in-the-open rule. It's high summer; I should have known better. It's the lack of sleep. It's like it was when I first came here, crouched in the corner with my knife in my hand, checking the entrances for intruders in a regular sequence, three seconds on each, keeping time, keeping watch.

I talk to them, the people waiting just out of sight. I don't recognise my own accent. Did I always talk like that? And who am I going to ask? This is the wasteland. Nothing but squirrels and birds and the people who watch me. And they're not chatty.

Like an old man, I leave my bed at the first sign of dawn, go out and forget why. Sometimes, horribly, I almost forget the way back, wandering uselessly in the boots I've repaired too many times. I try to keep the daily routines I've been living by these past few years – water, Feodor, set the oilcans up for the condensation, or what are you going to eat tonight, idiot, it's not like you can pop down to the Co-Op – *but rational thoughts slide past me like the shadows across the floor, and I lie there, getting hungrier, weaker. My kidneys ache all the time now. I forget to be worried. I'd like to forget everything, but I'm not that far gone. Not yet.*

I was fifteen when I went missing. I'm twenty-five now.

When I first ran towards this building with its churchy arches and open door, I was ready to be discovered at any moment. Even after making myself a den here, I'd spend the nights rehearsing what I was going to say when they found me. As if sorry ever did anyone any good.

I don't mean the police. They might as well not exist, now.

Months passed. Just as I dared to wonder if they'd forgotten me, things started happening. Noises in the shadows, flutters of air against my eyelids, teasing me just as I was sinking into sleep. I couldn't venture out for food. I couldn't sleep. My hipbones were so pointy, I couldn't lie on my side without bruising myself. It was part of the punishment. They would stretch it out for as long as they pleased, letting me get thinner and lonelier, and then, only at the very end, they would sweep me up and take full satisfaction for the things I'd done.

Once, I felt one of them touch me. Right here. On the nose. I'm on the brink of being found.

>•<

As strange as the situation was, Tor's house had a set of routines, and in the days that followed Aisling's arrival it didn't take long for their regular rhythm to make her feel at ease.

Mornings began with strong tea brewed by Georgie on the stove while Chase doodled arrow-shot hearts on the steamy windowpanes. There were the chickens to attend to: Rum, Sodomy and The Lash. One, they were yet to discover which, laid tastier eggs than the others, a fact that stirred up squabbling at teatime. Then came a leisurely breakfast out in the garden, with the boy Georgie frying mushrooms, boiling eggs and selecting jars of fruit from the cellar, depending on whether Tor was in a 'purple mood' or having an 'orangey day'. To Aisling's fascination they seemed to source all their food independently, and when it surfaced that Tor, arthritic hips creaking, would spend an hour every morning rummaging in the woods for mushrooms, Aisling decided to eat a little less than she might have otherwise.

After breakfast, they all helped carry buckets of water up from the bay and poured them into the home-made sanitation unit bolted to the side of the house, the reliability of which Aisling preferred not to ponder. Tor would wash in an old-fashioned tin bath in front of the fire without a care for her modesty. She was never at rest, always knitting, or sketching or surveying Georgie's graphs detailing which seeds to plant in the coming weeks.

Georgie turned out to be a fountain of skill. There was nothing he didn't know about plants and nutrition, and through their brief conversations carrying trays back and forth from the garden, Aisling gleaned small facts of his life: that Tor had found him on the streets, a little boy wandering without so much as a pair of shoes. It had shocked Aisling, not least because he recounted the events so dispassionately. That had been years ago, he told her. He now saw Tor and the house as his responsibility. It gave him satisfaction to take care of the creaky old place, especially as Tor supported his ambition of expanding the garden to include a smokehouse for meat. He had even constructed the small crystal radio that caught sporadic blasts of distant piano that Georgie claimed was played by an old friend.

'It's always best,' he told her, 'to focus on the good times.'

Chase, it transpired, didn't live with Tor and Georgie officially, and it was normal for him to disappear for days at a time, sometimes weeks. When he chose to sleep at the house, he curled up on the hearthrug like a mongrel and, despite using his rolled-up coat for a pillow, he awoke as cheerful as ever, smelling of soot and morning dew. Aisling had shied away from his attention at first, wary of being made fun of, but within a few days it became apparent that cruelty wasn't in his character. He beamed, he sulked, and quickly beamed again, and for all his bravado, he really cared what other people thought of him – especially Aisling.

Coming noisily into the house with the sack over his shoulder, never saying where he'd been, he'd upend it at her feet. Bundles of scrappy books. Because he couldn't read, he relied on Aisling to reveal the titles of his finds. Mouldy old volumes, covers missing, fragments of diaries fading like whispered conversations. The ones he prized the most were the horticultural textbooks, hand-illustrated with coloured inks. Georgie used them to plan a herb garden.

Once, he brought her a pair of ankle boots, precisely her size.

'Where do you *find* these things?' she would ask him.

He would shrug, as though it were obvious. 'Town.'

One morning, Aisling sat on the grass outside the house, scanning one of Chase's books for amusingly archaic sentences while the hens scratched the dirt in their enclosure. Tor was sitting behind her on a stool, working at the knots in Aisling's hair with her big, gentle fingers. 'One more bird nest to untangle and we're nearly there,' she said.

'Oh, here's a lovely one: *"As autumn draws a russet curtain across the gaiety of summer, the gardener's first responsibility is to the health of that most bulbous of guests, the onion."*' She giggled. 'That's gorgeous. It must be so good to grow all your food yourself. It's something everybody talks about and never ends up doing.'

'It can have its drawbacks, like when you're sitting by the fire on a winter's evening, dying for a mug of cocoa, but I wouldn't go back. I couldn't.' Her voice was familiar now. Aisling loved the syrupy depth of it.

'Mum gets our food from Sainsbury's.'

'And what does your mum do? You've been awfully cagey, madam. I want to know everything.'

'She's a secretary. Nothing exciting. Actually, I think she'll be packing it in soon. She's got this boyfriend.'

'Ah. The wifey type?'

'Girlfriendy. Wife sounds middle-aged. She doesn't look old, but she thinks she does. She was about my age when she had me, and it's like she's still waiting for life to go back to normal.'

'That's sad.' Tor made a parting with her fingers, separating two fine auburn curtains. 'You like it here?'

Aisling took a deep, long breath and let it out slowly. She couldn't remember feeling so serene.

Tor was pleased. 'You feel right here. Don't you?'

'I feel *better.*'

'That's perfect. Now look, I hope you don't mind me

bringing it up, and please say something if you'd rather we didn't talk about it, but Chase mentioned that prior to coming here you had been having a wee bit of difficulty.' She was speaking like a nurse in an old film, talking about *some poor girl in a spot of bother.* It was a nice way of approaching the subject, Aisling thought. With her strong hands confidently working at the knots in the nape of Aisling's neck, Tor went on: 'I just wanted to say that we're *simpatico.* We're fine with it. I'm sure you're aware that many people aren't.'

One of the chickens had found something tasty in the dirt. The other two hurried over to bully a share for themselves. Aisling half-heartedly scanned the open book for another funny passage, but found she couldn't focus. Tor's hands had stopped moving.

'What do you call an epileptic in the garden? A seizure salad.'

'Oh, my word,' Tor said mildly.

'My PE teacher said that to some boys while we were doing netball practice,' Aisling said. 'I'd gone up to him to ask if I could go to the loo, and he hadn't seen me coming. When he realised I'd heard, he sort of froze, staring at me like he was deciding how to cover it up, but then this weird grunting laugh burst out of his nose. And the boys took the cue and just squealed like little pigs. I think they were embarrassed, but there was real laughter in there, too. Like they were releasing tension.'

She picked at the grass. It felt good to tell someone.

'And did you report him?'

'There were so many things. If I'd reported them all, I don't know.'

'And here, if the worst happens, and we discover you've,' Tor searched for one of her elegant euphemisms again, '*taken a turn*, what should we do?'

Aisling felt her pockets for the folded list of instructions Doctor Ross had given her prior to leaving for Edythe's house. Aside from the tooth and a scrap of an old receipt, illegible now, there was nothing on her. 'It's not epilepsy. They call it "pseudo". All this black stuff descends on me and I forget where I am. Don't call anyone. I don't want any more of that.'

'I was hoping you'd say that. You see, this is the best possible time to tell you what you may have suspected. We don't have a telephone.'

Incredulous, Aisling turned to face Tor. 'How do you live without a telephone?'

'Blissfully.'

'God. And you've got oil lamps, haven't you?' It was absurd, but she hadn't noticed the lack of light bulbs. Everything worked so fluidly at the house that it hadn't occurred to her. 'And the stove, I saw Georgie putting logs into it. Do you not...?'

Tor nodded. 'No electrickery. Not here. You see why I wanted you to take it slowly? This is all going to be a surprise for you. I'm doing my best to avoid it being a shock.'

All at once, the little details of the place struck her. The merry chittering of birdsong instead of distant engines. Good air, as Chase had said. Even the summer sun soothing her muscles made no sense when she thought hard about it, because her mother had worn a dress at the hospital before the autumn had arrived and the days turned drizzly. That had been weeks ago. And what kind of people didn't own a telephone? But the questions were impossible to grasp for more than a moment. They were forced aside by stronger images that demanded attention – the tooth, the melted bath, disfigured, cadaverish – but their absurdity made the task of sorting them into coherence seem insane. The alternative, to disregard them, was smiling down at her, just as Tor was: safe and right and good.

She looked up at Tor, shaking her head slowly. 'This should all feel frightening. Why doesn't it feel frightening?'

Tor laid her heavy hand on the crown of the girl's head. 'You said it yourself. You feel *better*. Now look at all this pretty hair.' She gathered it up in both hands, draping it over Aisling's shoulder. 'We've beaten the knottymonsters. Why don't you wear it down today? You don't get to see those fiery tones when it's tied up, and I think that's an awful waste.'

'Fire,' Aisling said. It always came back to that. 'I can't get rid of these burned things. It wouldn't be so horrible if I knew what they meant.'

Tor considered this. Her plump hands skirted the nape of Aisling's neck to caress the shells of her ears. 'When I was a little girl,' she said, 'a neighbour of mine had a lovely pony called Moppet. When the weather was fair they kept him tethered to one of the trees in their garden, with a trough of water and nice things to eat. During the summer balls one year, my neighbours held a party for children there. All the sprogs from the fine families were invited, along with their parents. It was magical. There were candles glittering in glass jars, and a cake twice the size of me. Old Moppet was thoroughly spoiled, so many girls and boys patting his head and giving him sugar cubes. Well, after a time, all the little bodies crowding around him must have got too much, he was startled. He bolted. Tied to a tree, he couldn't go anywhere but around and around. And, of course, the children were all running off in different directions, there was paper strewn around from the party games, and before any of the grown-ups had time to deal with Moppet, someone had knocked over one of the jars with the candles in them. It wasn't a big fire, just a few bundles of tissue paper carried around the garden in the wind. A couple of the dads managed to chase down the papers and stamp them out before the grass was too badly singed. But, you know, I never got over the *shockwave* of the adults' fright. For the longest time, if I were anxious about something my first instinct would be to double-check if there was water around, just in case. I refused to wear big skirts in rooms with candles in them, and I certainly never left wrapping paper lying around at birthdays. Even now, when I have a nightmare, it's that Chase has got himself trapped in a barn somewhere and dropped a match. All traumatic events have to be dealt with eventually. Fear, like fire, leaves a mark.'

Fragrant smoke was rising from the house's chimney. Georgie must have started on that batch of chutney he had been talking about. Aisling focused on the static image of the charred bathtub for a moment longer and, for the first time in days, she felt unwell. Instead, she tried to mentally link the two halves of Tor's life: a privileged childhood, with friends who owned ponies and parents who held garden parties, followed by a house in the woods with no electricity.

'Where is Chase today?' Aisling asked.

'If you have any ideas, feel free to share them,' she said, but there was no humour in it. Aisling watched her scan the trees surrounding the clearing.

'He goes to that town, doesn't he? I remember it. There was a high wall.'

'That's good. You can remember when you relax.'

A pigeon came clattering out of the woods, interrupting Aisling with her lips parted. Then followed a pair of black rooks leaving the higher canopy. They were startled by something moving towards the house with a rhythmic, throaty noise like a huge cat hacking up fur lodged in its craw. *Krrmph! Krrmph!*

Tor stood, tilting her head in the direction of the wind. The source of the noise was getting closer, amplified by the bowl in the landscape. Georgie came outside, rubbing his hands on a tea towel. His dark eyes were wide.

Aisling rose up on to her knees. She was poised to speak before, but now there was a cry inside of her, mounting pressure in her throat. The coughing was at the lip of the woods now, a raw, sick sound. Georgie looked to Tor, who shook her head, tersely. *Krrmph! Krrmph!* went the sound, and then, carried downwind from the trees, a sharp, petroly smell triggered a memory that hit Aisling like a blow.

Chase came stumbling out of the woods. He was bent at the waist, clutching his ribs and the tree marking the boundary of Tor's land, spitting out a stream of sputum. His usually tanned face was a ghastly yellow, and no sooner had he spat out one mouthful of fluid, more coughs dislodged another stream. 'Ugh,' he spluttered. 'Shit.'

Tor was across the yard. She seized Chase by the shoulders. 'My God,' she cried. 'You silly, stupid boy. Get inside. Cough it all up. Cough up a lung.'

They made Aisling stay outside. She shivered in the yard,

looking back at the woods. Only the sighing of the leaves, the far-off lapping of the bay.

She slipped a finger into her pocket and touched the tooth.

Verity Holloway

18

In her sleep, Aisling visited the wreckage of Edythe's house.

The fire had done as it pleased. Upstairs in the hall, rain had weakened the ceiling's remaining plaster, leaving the Tudor roof bare to the beams, like the ribcage of a whale. She moved through the corridors as if inside such a creature, gliding deep in the silent darkness of the sea. There were no stars or lights from the A-roads to prove the existence of a wider world. The house was alone.

She found Doctor Ross in the melted remains of the bathtub. He was wearing the same colourful monstrosity of a tie he had worn when she last saw him and, as then, he smiled hugely for no decent reason. Resting on his lap were her medical notes, spewing out papers and letters like an overfilled sandwich. At first she was frightened that he had come to take her away but, apart from a single glance at her entrance, he ignored her.

There were three children sitting cross-legged on the blackened floorboards: a boy and two girls, prim in their

Sunday best. The little boy wore a sailor suit and cap. A stubby cigarette hung limply from his lips. The room was veiled in soft tendrils of smoke.

'John 14:2.'

They all looked to the blackened sink where a broad man stood in the shattered remains of the bathroom mirror, reading from a Bible. Mister Morgun. David. Like the photograph in the hallway, his face was a white blur of movement, a featureless smear atop a long, broad body in clerical black. 'John fourteen,' he repeated, his voice rising emotionally from that bony chest. *'In my Father's house are many mansions. I go to prepare a place for you.'*

Doctor Ross was writing in her notes, chuckling softly. Aisling strained to read, but he shifted away from her view.

'In my Father's house are many mansions,' David said again.

The little boy took a long suck of the cigarette. The familiar flavour plumed towards Aisling, and she knew the child was Robert, legs as yet untouched by polio.

'Let not your heart be troubled. Every citizen is required to replace his hangings, his wallpapers with a plain coat of white. Then comes inner cleanness,' said David.

One of the little girls smiled nastily at her shoes, leather buffed to a fine sheen. The other was anxious, looking from David to the doctor, and then to the door. That was Connie, Aisling realised, the grandmother she never met. A deep blue streak of sadness passed between them. Connie tried to mouth something at Aisling, but froze. The blurred face of David turned to Aisling, staring without eyes. Connie shut her mouth and looked guiltily at the floor.

'In my Father's house are many mansions, whitewashed

and clean,' he said. 'With doors to close and doors to lock and doors to hide behind. Lead us not into degeneracy, and forgive us our defects.' He opened his mouth, a dark slit wider than a letter box, and with the smooth motion of dreams, Aisling slid back against the wall where the charcoal was thick. David had Robert's cigarette in his big, white hand, and his voice cracked with emotion as he let it drop.

And then, with the sound of shattering glass, teeth. Hundreds of teeth rocketed from his open mouth, clattering across the room like coins from a slot machine. Connie and Robert were hit, chests and hands taking the brunt of the tiny missiles, and when Aisling saw her face in the broken mirror, scores of yellow molars had embedded themselves painlessly in the thin flesh of her temples.

In panic, she turned and ran – and rolled off her bed, face first on to Tor's gritty wooden floor.

When her heart had slowed to a normal pace, Aisling crept up the stairs to the main room. In her bed on the mezzanine, Tor was a motionless lump. Georgie slept without a sound, curled on his side with the sketches of his smokehouse beside him. Chase was sleeping on the floor by the low fire, arms and legs splayed like a child. He was awake before she spoke, conscious of movement in the room.

'You'll bother the rats,' he growled, but there was a smile in his eyes.

'Are you feeling better?'

'Lousy. But I've 'ad worse.'

'I think I'm remembering things.'

'Put the flags out,' he smiled.

She got down and whispered to him. 'The town. I want to go back.'

He gave a small whimper as he tried to roll over. He was still in pain. 'Oh, bloody hell.' He flopped back on to the carpet and looked at her. 'Why? You've got everything you need here.'

He was limp as a cat, flat stomach bare where his grubby shirt rode up. In her half-sleep, Aisling wanted to lay a hand on him, but he had been so sick after coming in from the woods, heaving and hacking until Georgie's medicine had calmed him down. Aisling couldn't bear to be touched when she was ill.

There was a crack across New Zealand.

What?

She didn't know.

'I could teach you to read.'

It was something her mother would say. But his eyes were alight before she could take it back.

He breathed for a moment. She heard the leftover rattle of his lungs. 'Gimme time.'

FEODOR

When Dad hit the talkative stage after the first three beers, he'd tell a story from when Hitler's army surrounded Leningrad, trying to starve the Russians into surrender.

It went like this: An old woman woke in her bed to find the Devil, in the shape of a wolf, savagely biting her feet. She screamed and howled, but the Devil wouldn't let go. She prayed to God, but the Devil wouldn't let go. Finally, she stopped screaming and she stopped praying. She looked the

Devil in the eye and said, 'Fuck off!'
  The Devil fled the house.

> >•<

Over breakfast the next day, Aisling counted three weeks since flushing her pills.

When the time came, her GP told her, they would ease the dose down by ten milligrams every couple of weeks. She'd experience a little nausea and some tiredness in the afternoons. But when she'd gone home and looked it up, she'd found the forums and the blogs and the Yahoo Answers.

RX: POISON. FREE YOURSELF TODAY with my pamphlet 'Big Pharma, Big Brother', downloadable for only $5.99. 100% gluten free, cruelty free, vegan alternatives to the addictive, dangerous 'medication' the industry forces you to swallow.

Beverley, reading the computer screen over her shoulder: 'Nobody's actually vegan, Sweets. It's something people say to make themselves look middle-class.'

I've come off morphine cold turkey and I've come off Citalopram slow and I'd take the morphine any time srlsy. The moodswings were worse than when I was sick. Dizziness like a rollercoaster. Actual headshocks. *rage face*

'Don't read those things,' said Beverley. 'People on the Internet don't know anything.'

Flush.

Three weeks without a single pill and Aisling felt wonderful.

She breakfasted with Tor in the garden as usual. Chase

had brought them a sack of coffee from an undisclosed source. While the rest of them set up the breakfast table, Georgie took his own plate of fruit out to the back of the house where the foundations of his smokehouse were. 'I'd like a conical roof, I think,' he had said, shyly presenting Tor with his drawings of supporting walls and doorways. 'We'll be far better prepared this winter, just you wait.'

At the table, Aisling curled her hands around her cup, watching Chase's face through the rising steam. He had been quiet all morning. Tor had uttered a total of three words to him, two of which had been 'Stop it', when his hiccuping coughs had interrupted the flow of conversation.

Aisling's ankles flexed beneath the breakfast table. She prodded at Chase's boots, tugged at his trouser legs with her toes.

He munched his fruit slowly. 'I'd like to read your poems,' he said at last. His voice was husky from coughing.

She'd forgotten the promise, but the thought of sneaking out had her nodding enthusiastically. 'I can help you.'

Tor was clearing the plates. At the mention of Chase reading, a muscle in her forehead twitched.

'We don't get to learn,' he said, cryptically. 'Where I'm from.'

As soon as Tor lumbered off to the smokehouse to assist Georgie, Aisling pounced on him.

'Have you thought about it? Will you take me?'

He had turned pink around the cheekbones. 'You're asking a lot,' he said.

'We can go at night. What's stopping us? Tor doesn't have to know.' It was exciting, like sneaking out with friends to drink cider in the park. At home, kids her age flew up and down the road under her window, laughing shapes dipping in and out of the street lights. She thought her turn would never come.

'You said you were always running away.'

This stopped her. 'I want to come back afterwards,' she said. And she did. She didn't want her mother, or her bedroom at Edythe's house or even the park with the kids her age. She wanted this place.

Chase wouldn't look at her. 'I go back to collect useful things.' He was struggling with words. 'Not 'cause it's fun.'

'But I shan't hold you up now. I'm stronger. I'll be able to climb that rubble, no problem.' It was true. It had only been three weeks, but already she had put on weight and looked better for it. She studied her wrists. Not yet strong, they were no longer ropey with tendons and vessels. Surely Chase could see it.

'It's not that,' he said. 'It's Tor. She told me to be careful. 'Cause of your illness and that.'

Oh. She lowered her eyes and found she had been picking at a painted carnation on her cup, scratching at the enamelled petals with her ragged thumbnail. 'I can go on my own.'

She looked up and saw him frozen with his coffee cup resting on his lips. 'It's dangerous,' he said.

'I'm quite capable.'

He blinked once, slowly, so she could see the capillaries in the moist creases of flesh. She thought back to his retching coughs, leaning on the boundary tree like a man three times his age. Perhaps he was asthmatic, she told herself. They hadn't talked about it since. None of them had.

Tor was coming back, hobbling sorely on her bad joints.

Chase sucked the gritty dregs of the coffee from his cup. 'I'll take you,' he whispered. 'Tonight.'

❯•❮

In the honey-glow of jam jar candles, they formed a drowsy circle under the apple trees. Tor luxuriated in her evening bath indoors. Chase took up the most space, sprawling on the grass, looking better, while Georgie nursed a cup of tea. Draped in a blanket, Aisling diffidently laid the Blake book out on the grass and showed them the pictures. Chase wanted explanations.

'What about him?' Chase asked. 'He's about to get his hands burned.'

He pointed at a picture of a small boy walking through dark woods. A bright flame had burst into his path and he was heading towards it fearfully.

'That's "The Little Boy Lost",' Aisling said.

'Read it to me?'

Fairly certain there was no trace of mockery in Chase's request, she summoned a clear voice:

'Father father, where are you going?
Oh do not walk so fast!
Speak father, speak to your little boy
Or else I shall be lost.
The night was dark, no father was there,
The child was wet with dew;
The mire was deep, and the child did weep,
And away the vapour flew.'

Chase crawled closer, blew his hair out of his eyes. 'Vapour, huh?'

'Blake was strange,' she said carefully. 'He saw things. Spirits appeared to him in his cottage and made him write things down. He'd sketch portraits of angels. Well, they said they were angels. They taught him new printing technology, way beyond his time. And they gave him prophecies. He'd sit alone at night, just frantically taking down everything the spirits were telling him, pages and pages about disasters and revolutions and...'

Chase's face made it clear he was envisioning puffs of smoke and ghostly groans in the night. 'Like a fortune teller?'

'A seer,' Georgie said, not entirely with approval.

Chase grinned at him. 'Say a spirit wakes you up at witching hour, Georgie, and tells you to take down a letter for him. What d'you say to that?'

'I have enough of my own chores.' The boy was distracted. He picked at the grass. 'Chase, I'm not sure.'

'Give over.' He turned back to Aisling. 'So these spirits, they'd have him draw fire and forests. What good's that?'

Again, she scanned for ridicule, but he waited so patiently for an answer she found she couldn't think. Something in his phrasing felt designed to tease her. '*Say a spirit wakes you at witching hour...*'

'Were they even right?' he coaxed.

'The visions didn't always make sense,' she said. 'A lot of the time, they look like moral stories you'd tell to kids. But if you look long enough they hint at other things. Like when you can only half-remember a nightmare the next day. Some of Blake's visitors claimed to know the Devil.'

As she said it, she tried to think of a joke to hide behind, something about Blake needing to get more fresh air. But Georgie's face was thoughtful as ever, and Chase was studying the illustration with interest. Fire and a lost boy. His brow crinkled in concentration, and she wanted to take the book back before he could do anything to it, snatch it or tear it or hurl it into the undergrowth where it would take hours to find, by which time the foxes might have taken it, if foxes were interested in paper, which they probably weren't, but still…

Seeing none of this, Chase chewed his lip. 'I'm no seer. I'm a dunce,' he said. 'If you ask me, the bright light's scary, but so's the wood behind him. The boy's got no choice. He's in the mire and you can drown in those, I've heard of it happening. Gotta take the plunge, I reckon. Take his chance with the unknown.' He raised his blond head, shrugged. 'Or get fried, whatever.'

Georgie lifted his tea to his lips. In the candlelight, his forearms seemed wrapped in marbled endpapers. *What does someone have to do to receive burns like that?* Aisling wondered, feeling a fool for bringing up the subject of fire. Chase handed the book back smartly, and with it safely in her lap she saw his bravado at last. He was afraid of being wrong.

'I like his poems,' Chase said. 'They're like messed-up nursery rhymes.'

That, it occurred to her, would explain her rock-a-bye instinct to recite them when agitated. *Child,* she spat at herself.

Chase rolled on to his back and rested his boots on the apple tree's trunk. In the encircling woods, fireflies made their bumbling progress, something she could never hope to see in the paved suburbs of home. Unsettling but somehow acceptable. As long as she didn't question too hard.

Upside down, Chase tugged at Georgie's trouser leg.

'How badly d'you want to sleep tonight?'

'No,' he said. 'No, no. I'm not listening to one of your stories.'

'It's not a story. This one's true.'

'Oh, they're all true. Until you laugh at me because I believe them. I spend whole nights awake because of your imagination. If I'm sleepy tomorrow, my calculations for the smokehouse will be wrong, and then it will fall down and there'll be no kippers for you.'

'But all this talk of mires,' Chase wheedled.

'I know that one.'

'She doesn't.' One long finger jabbed at Aisling, who was still preoccupied by fireflies. 'And she's survived a close encounter.'

In the dark, Georgie's wondrous expression reminded her of a baby seal's. 'You've seen him?'

'I don't know what either of you are talking about,' she said.

Chase was grinning fit to burst. 'We're talking about how I rescued you from torments unimaginable at the hands of Our Friend.'

Georgie turned his eyes on Chase. 'Have you told Tor?'

'No! Can you imagine? She'd never let her out of the house again. She'd knit her a straitjacket.'

They were making fun of her. Aisling straightened her back, hoping that by appearing taller they would think her less of a target. Not that that strategy had ever worked. They couldn't touch her, she told herself; she hadn't told them about her own solitary writing. But the wariness scratched at her. Perhaps she'd told them too much. 'I don't know your friend,' she said.

Chase sparkled with mischief. He flipped over into a cross-legged position and pulled two of the candles close to him so that he was the focus of attention. 'Gather round, kiddies,' he said. 'Who wants to take their medicine?'

Georgie cast Aisling a long-suffering look. 'It's going to be horrible.'

'Well, it was horrible,' Chase said.

'But you'll make it more horrible.'

'Grown-ups are talking, Georgie, shut y'gob. Aisling? You'd like a story, wouldn't you?'

Before she had time to decide, let alone respond, Chase was off, palms in the air like a priest about to launch into a sermon. 'So! This story begins before I was born. Before Georgie was born. Like, eons before, 'cause he's a baby. Tor was there. She won't talk about it. It's all too raw for her, too terrible to—'

'Is it all going to be like this?' Aisling asked.

Georgie sighed. 'All of it.'

Chase pretended to slap him, but dropped the silly voice. 'Old folks say it's hard to tell young people how different it all was, before. The earls and the duchesses and the little children heirs to fortunes they couldn't imagine. When the Archduke Ratcliff's son was born, he had glassblowers craft him a rattle filled with diamonds. When his wife called it a tawdry bauble the Archduke tossed it on the fire. There were wild parties, coming out balls and solstices. Dynasties so old you could believe they were created out of stardust, along with the earth. And there were priests. Blind scribes, holed up in chapels out in the wasteland, groaning with gold. It was the greatest honour for a family if their child was selected to drink from the blinding chalice and spend the rest of his life out there, writing and writing as long as they lived.'

A snort of derision forced its way up Aisling's throat. 'No, no way,' she stopped him. 'What's a blinding chalice?'

To her surprise, Georgie answered. 'Ethanol,' he said. 'Taken from the gin factories. It attacks the optic nerve.'

'And people drank it? Deliberately?'

Georgie cleaved to his teacup. 'I said it was going to be horrible.'

'Who's telling the story?' Chase crawled closer to Aisling. His voice dropped, soft, like the halo of candlelight encircling his blond hair, and despite herself she fell into the role of listener, letting him take her where he wished. 'Imagine it. You've been sent to the chapel by your weeping parents. Your last sight in this world is the pen and the sheets of vellum before you on the desk where you'll spend the rest of your life. The sting of the alcohol on your tongue.' His eyes flicked to the sky with a hint of a smile. 'Channelling, they said. Guidance whispered through the doors between the heavens. Build schools for orphans, they'd say, or feed the cripples who live in the causeway. A little bit of good amongst all that decadence. The council would be given copies of anything readable, and they would act on it. Always, even if the message said, I don't know, "Present all terriers with cummerbunds". It was taken very seriously. Those ruined houses I found you in, Aisling, they were all homes for the poor built on the orders of the blind scribes.

There were hundreds of them, once. And then...'

Georgie put his hands over his ears.

'One night,' Chase said, 'out in one of the wasteland chapels, the old abbot was reviewing the week's scribblings. Piles of meaningless scrawls, wasted ink. He was wanting his bed. But then, something caught his eye. There it was, in the neatest handwriting you ever did see. Now, that wasn't unheard of – some of the scribes were educated and could still grip a pen with some skill – but the boy who came up with this was the dim son of a dim family eager to get rid of him. Barely knew which end of the pen was the sharp one. And yet here was this message, right in the centre of the page like a wedding invitation.

'So what was the abbot to do? What they always did when something came through. He sent it out to the council. The message was strange, he thought, but perhaps it would make sense to the worldly types back in the town. At least that's what he said afterwards, maybe to save his skin.'

'So what did it say?' Aisling asked, waiting for the daft punchline.

'I happen to have a copy.'

Georgie scrambled to his knees. 'Fibber, you don't!'

'Behold.' Chase had a leather dispatch folder, and inside it was a sheet of paper, folded many times.

'You mustn't let Tor see that,' said the boy. 'It'll go straight on the fire. And how do you know what it says? You can't read.'

Chase faltered, losing the glamour of the storyteller for a moment. 'Jobi won it at cards,' he said. 'And he read it to me. And he let me keep it, 'cause I'm man enough to shoulder one of Tor's tellings-off.' He held the hallowed piece of paper out between his fingers. 'Aisling can read it. She'll do it in her poem voice.'

Aisling's stomach tightened. 'If this turns out to be a dirty limerick, or—'

'Just read it,' he said, with a quick glance back at the house where Tor could be heard humming to herself in the bath. 'Quietly,' he added.

It was the kind of handwriting people had before computers, artistic and hard to decipher. But then it would be, she reminded herself wryly, if the writer had his optic nerve burned away by moonshine.

With the eyes of the boys on her, she began:

'There is not a single hair left on my body. They say it may never grow back. I am a just man, a man of intelligence. But this place and these people corrode me. Muscles wasted, animal spirits all gone. I am a pseudo-man.

'The remedy is in my reach. It is within reason. It is.'

By the time she had finished the short passage, the hairs on her arms had all pricked up. She glanced up at the woods around them, distracted for a moment by the eerie dance of the fireflies winking in and out through the trees and over the warm grasses. The words were as good as meaningless and yet somehow, as Georgie had predicted, horrible.

The boys looked at her. Her solemn reaction seemed to satisfy them both.

Chase went on: 'Strange, said the councillors. Amusing. Something to talk about at the summer balls. The town was preparing for them at the time. Gardeners laying out boxes of rambling roses to dangle from the windowsills, washerwomen boiling yellow dye for the debutantes' gowns. The bakeries made cakes as tall as grown men, and the bands practised new waltzes paid for by the richest households. Firework factories, portrait painters, toy-makers, cooks, cleaners, courtesans. Every year the same rituals for the pleasure of so few, taking up the labour of so many.'

A moth came fluttering down over their heads towards the lure of Chase's candles, a tremor in the light.

'And then they found him.'

Georgie looked to his tea. Aisling couldn't catch his eye.

'Fishermen were gathering cockles down in the mire below the Queen's Teeth. Those are the cliffs not far from one of the chapels in the wasteland. They thought he was a corpse at first, and he would have been had they found him an hour later. They pulled him out, got him to the nearest chapel, but the state of shock was so deep, it was as though he had no thoughts at all. When they pressed him as to how he'd ended up in the mire, he didn't seem to know. And here's the creepy part: not a hair on him. Not one. They held out doubt. Perhaps the mire had some caustic quality. His clothes were burned, and his skin was blistered, but after three weeks in the chapel, bathed and nursed, there wasn't so much as a whisker.'

The moth set off on a different course, leaving a shadow, then a ghost of a shadow.

'They thought he was the man who wrote the message,' Aisling said.

Chase nodded. 'They panicked. In two thousand years of recorded history, no human being had ever manifested after communicating through the Doors. No one had prepared for this. The abbot kept the man in rooms deep under the chapel. As people started to read the new message circulating the town, ripples went out. A madman's been found, they said at first, and that was no crime back then. Another thing to chortle over at the next ball.

'But the man was the queerest thing. He said nothing, but he listened. There wasn't much to do in those chapels, 'cept gossip, so he heard a great deal. How the carts went out in the morning to the town and brought back barrels of forbidden wine and tobacco. How the children of the rich sent for schooling in the chapels avoided the blinding chalice, getting the cushy overseeing positions with the nice robes and the steady salaries. He started to talk. Not to tell anyone anything, no. He wanted to know the most successful merchants by name, their personal fortunes, how much they paid their workers. The young novices brought their friends to look at him, holed up in his cell. As more and more people came to see him, he sat straighter, his spine like a ramrod, even though he was this bald, funny-looking brute. He looked like a displaced king. As stories reached town, more people wanted to see this man. Important people. They wanted to boast that they'd seen the freak. But when they met him, they were unsettled. He wasn't a man like any from the town. It was as the message had said, a pseudo-man.

'Finally, the council summoned him. He was brought out, handcuffed, and sat in the centre of the chamber with the councillors all around him, staring at his big, bald head. Without waiting for the judge to begin questioning, he spoke.'

Here Chase adopted a deep, regal accent that would have been comical were it not for the needling sensation at the base of Aisling's spine.

'"*This place,*" he said, "*is flawed. But somewhere so small* can be worked with, the roots of degeneracy can be plucked out. A rotten tooth must be extracted for the sake of the others." The councillors were furious. Now, in those days, there was a public gallery in the council chambers. That day, it was packed. The judge ordered the man to be silent, but it was the people in the gallery that wouldn't shut up. They wanted to hear him. Someone threw an apple core at the judge and got dragged away. The trial went on for days, and the man's supporters grew. Soon people set up camp outside the court just to hear what he'd said. And to talk about his hair. Just as the message stated, it never grew back.'

'So, the message,' Aisling said. 'Did he say how he got it to the boy in the chapel?'

'Now that's tricky. The message disturbed him greatly. First, he claimed he didn't know how his private writing had ended up there. He was from another place entirely, he said, a terrible place of injustice and cruelty. But as they pressed him, and more people came to the trials to watch, he seemed to swell up. He put on a show. *"I chose the boy,"* he said. *"I opened the doors of his perception. I chose you all, this place,"* he said. And then the accusations...

"'I notice the abbot isn't here to watch me today. Pity. But then he has so many whores to attend to in his room, one can't blame him. Well, it's a building full of the blind! How difficult is it to smuggle in a few trollops?"

"'Even the lowliest labourers' children are more intelligent than those of the ruling classes. This balance should be overturned. It is madness that the rulers of tomorrow should be feeble-minded children selected by virtue of blood."

"And these parties I see you preparing for. Dipsomaniacs and libertines running riot. History is unkind to those who

dance while the walls crack around them.'"

'How much of this are you making up?' Aisling said.

'Well, they're not his actual words. I wasn't there. But it's what he said. And people listened. The judge tried to have him sent back to his cell, but the audience had heard too much. *"Let him speak,"* they said. *"He came through the Doors. He chose us."* Plenty of prostitutes were happy to admit they'd been paid to visit the chapels, and everyone knew the noble families spent their days dribbling in their massive houses, waited on by jaundiced girls from the slums. Half the people witnessing the trial had their knuckles rubbed raw preparing the town for the summer balls. All those parties, all that pleasure, and yet normal families were having to choose between feeding their children and heating their homes.

'Within weeks of the man being found in the mire, a mob battered down the council doors. They tore up the chamber, beheaded the statues of Justice, and cracked all the convicts out of their cells underground. Out came the man, hairless as ever, blinking back tears of thanks. And then The Remedy began.

'People called him Our Friend. And he was. The council recovered from the riot, but he continued to speak out against corruption. He organised night patrols to stop the sons of rich families coming out and molesting the girls working the streets. Popular stuff. *"A new age of reason, cleanliness and quiet,"* he called it. The authorities couldn't catch him. Too many people were willing to hide him. People from all over town travelled to hear him speak. Beautiful speeches, they were. People left weeping. The summer balls were in full swing, but at his orders, the richest families with the least security were robbed in the night, and the money was given to the paupers in the slums. Men tattooed his name across their chests. Women left their husbands to follow him. "Our Friend" was a slogan daubed on the walls of every street, in white, his signature colour. That kind of love, it's a weapon.'

Georgie spoke: 'My grandmother was given a crib by one of his followers. It came from a mansion, she said. There were rubies in the headboard. She picked them out and pawned them for winter clothes. To her, Our Friend was a kind of god. He had come from another world, she said. What other explanation was there?'

One of the candles was guttering, and Chase cupped the rim of the jar in his hand, coaxing the flame to grow. 'But then he got a bit carried away.'

Georgie glanced back at the house, and Chase seemed to understand. He lowered his voice.

'Different these days, isn't it? No priests, you'll have noticed. No lords and ladies and summer balls.'

Those dizzy, disjointed memories of waking in a wet, dark room. Fragments of sky in a broken roof. Aisling shook her head. 'So the man led some kind of revolution?'

'Aye. A bloody one.'

'The Remedy,' Georgie said.

'It started with the sweating sickness. That winter, old people were dying off in scores. The weakest children went next. Within a fortnight, the infirmaries were overrun with people wet and shivering from top to toe. The council were as much use as a paper umbrella, so Our Friend promised everyone showing symptoms somewhere safe to recover.'

Reasonable enough. Nonetheless, Aisling's fingertips

crept over the Blake book, seeking the reassurance of the worn leather in the dark.

'There was a place people spoke of,' Georgie said. 'The Quiet.'

'Somewhere secret, under the earth,' Chase supplied. 'Somewhere Our Friend built for the sake of all. But when the quarantine didn't stop the spread of the sickness, he sent the families of the infected down there too. Just in case, like. Whole streets. It was their weakness that let the plague in, he told them. It pained him to say it, because he loved them, but it was their tolerance of foreigners coming in from the wasteland, spreading their germs and their immorality. They'd been too soft. And once you're soft in the head, you're soft in the body. 'Course, people were terrified. Started killing strangers on sight. Our Friend closed the dance halls and the unions. Shut the churches. When people are scared, you can do things to them they'd never allow otherwise. And he did.'

Chase stopped speaking, apparently unwilling to go further until Georgie, smiling weakly, bid him take a sip from his teacup.

'When Our Friend became,' Georgie shrugged, 'well, king, I suppose, The Quiet was his greatest tool. Nobody knew where it was, but everyone knew of someone who'd been taken there. The councillors, of course, and the ruling families. All gone. And after the sickness, anyone considered, well, wrong.'

They didn't look at her. Neither of them.

'And the man,' said Aisling. 'Our Friend. Where did he come from? Did anyone ever find out?'

Chase shrugged. 'Spoil my story, if they had.'

'So what happened to Our Friend in the end?' asked Aisling. A small sound from Georgie. Not the protests of before, something fragile. Chase heard him and swallowed, the spell of his storytelling snapped. 'Kings fall,' he shrugged. 'That's just how it goes.'

'Some kind of counter-revolution?'

Georgie gazed up at her through the wavering firelight. Somehow, she had managed to amaze him. 'Do you not recall?' he asked. 'I would have thought your poet-seer was one of the first—'

At the nudge of Chase's boot, Georgie looked away and started collecting the teacups. 'Our Friend still walks,' Chase said. 'Some say he lost faith in us. That we never earned his love. But the man from the mire is no longer the feared leader or even the friend of the people. Just a living ghost.' Chase widened his eyes, a flourish of green to end his story. 'And Aisling's seen him.'

'What was he like?' Georgie asked her.

Aisling flared with annoyance. She had been drawn into the story and now Chase had spoiled it. She pulled at her ponytail, letting her hair fall and hide her face. 'I can't remember.'

'She shouldn't be here, by rights. She should be wherever he takes 'em. Down in the deep, in The Quiet. I've heard them, Georgie, in the tunnels at night. The crazies, the defectives. Howling, like mad dogs.'

Georgie wouldn't listen. 'It's not right to joke about it.'

'I'm not joking. Jobi's seen him, too. And I tell you, if we lived in the town and not here, we wouldn't be having this conversation, 'cause we'd be too damn scared. He's still at work. He's got his people.'

Aisling stood, let the blanket drop. 'I have to go to the loo.'

'Uh-oh, scared shitless.'

'Shall I stand by the door?' Georgie offered, but she was already across the yard, hot in the face and clutching the Blake book, furious fingernail-moons in the leather. In the outhouse, safely out of sight, Aisling twisted the ring on her thumb, hard. *Crazies. Defectives.* After using her illness as an obstacle he could place where he fancied, Chase was going to try and weaken her will to visit the town with silly stories, as if she were a child. Her fault as much as his. She'd talked too much. Given him something to use. She squatted over the bucket and listened with resentment to the boys chattering away thoughtlessly like all those people who could go wherever they pleased.

When Aisling came back out into the garden, Tor had finished her bath and was standing in the doorway wearing a dressing gown of ragged yellow satin. Georgie had already trotted quietly back into the house. Chase, like a dog caught stealing from the dinner table, hung back, head down, kicking at the grass.

Tor held out her hand to Aisling.

'Come to bed, dear. Before the fireflies whisk you away from us.'

Verity Holloway

19

She dreamed of Doctor Ross's office, of the international ornaments above his desk. *I'm going*, she wanted to tell him. *I've gone.* And in the dream, the boy Feodor slouched beside her. He had traipsed some kind of pink, noxious gunk all over the sterile hospital floor and was playing with a plastic cigarette lighter. *Flick. Flick.*

'You shouldn't be here,' he told her.

When Aisling opened her eyes, Chase was sitting on the steps leading down to her bed.

'You were talking in your sleep,' he said.

'About what?'

He wouldn't say. 'You'll need this.'

It was still night. She got out of bed, already dressed, and he presented her with a bundled-up coat of green wool with military piping on the cuffs. It was too broad across the chest and made her hands look minute, which would have pleased Beverley. *'You're not that mannish,'* she'd tell her, *'not really.'*

'I love the pockets.'

'You can fit books in them,' said Chase. 'I thought of that.'

A fanfare of snoring from the living room made them both freeze guiltily. They grinned at each other.

'Don't get too excited, all right?' he whispered.

'I'm ready.'

He jerked a thumb at the living room. 'If Tor wakes up, we're scuppered. Georgie not so much, but I'll have to sweet-talk him into keeping schtum later. If we leave now, we'll be in town by dawn. We'll have a quick look around before it gets too crowded and be back here by breakfast. I'll say I took you foraging. Is this what you want? Is this okay?'

She nodded tersely. He was moving too slowly for her liking.

The tree at the boundary lurked like guilt. She was struck by the brightness of the stars here. Without the malignant glare of light pollution she could make out constellations she had never seen before, and even a reddish speck that may have been a planet. In the enormity of the universe, one night of sneaking out wouldn't make a difference. The brightest star blinked at her, as if in agreement.

Once they were up the hill where their voices wouldn't travel, Chase began to natter. He was nervous, pointing out the leaves most likely to give you a high if you smoked them, and the yellow eyes of the toads squatting in the grass. She wanted to savour every detail of the forest at night, but Chase kept a marching pace.

Dawn crept in and lightened the forest enough for them to travel side by side on a well-beaten path. Chase began to relax. 'Give us a poem,' he said. 'Do the one about the madman. About the night. I want to learn that one.'

'Mad Song?'
'Mad Song!'
Aisling willingly recited:

'Like a fiend in a cloud,
With howling woe
After night I do crowd
And with night will go.'

Chase tramped beside her, grinning widely at the treetops. Smiling herself, she continued:

'I turn my back to the east
From whence comforts have increased;
For light doth seize my brain
With frantic pain.'

Chase gave a shriek of laughter. 'I can't *wait* to read. I'm going to read to you, when I know how. Stuff you've never read. And I'll read to Tor while she's knitting. And I'll read instructions to Georgie while he's building the smokehouse. I'll read history, and stories. There's so much to catch up on.'

His enthusiasm was energising. She couldn't imagine getting to Chase's age – twenty-five? twenty-six? – without reading a single word. 'Did you really never get a chance to learn?'

His nose crinkled. 'It was sort of a religious thing.'

'What religion forbids you from reading?'

'It's not so much reading as writing words down. It's like putting the spoken word in a cage. They don't believe it's right. We don't. Look, all of that stuff, it can wait, can't it?'

Of course it could. He gave her a thankful look before turning his face up at the soft umbrellas of chestnut leaves. 'I'm gonna be just like you. With a little practice.'

And here's me, she thought, *wanting to be you.*

The woods were thinning out. As Aisling's pleasure at exploring somewhere new increased, so did the guilt. She kept imagining Tor up on her mezzanine, trusting that her young friends were safely in the beds she had made for them.

'She won't be angry, will she? She's never minded you going.'

As hard as he tried, Chase was incapable of covering a lie. 'You saw the wall of drawings, right? The faces? Those are all people she's looked after at the house. You wouldn't think it to look her at, but she worries something terrible. Every time Georgie gets a scratch, she's thinking it's gangrene. Every time I go to town to root around for junk, she's certain I've been arrested, or beaten up, or drowned. She had a bad time during The Remedy. Looking after people's her way of, y'know. Coping.'

All those people, sleeping in the bed she had just left. 'Did you know them all?'

'No. Before my time. Well, there was one. But now there's just Georgie.' He patted her shoulder. 'And you.'

Up ahead was a rusty railway carriage ensnared by brambles. Chase hopped inside without hesitation. In the grass around the carriage were signs of residency. Aisling kicked at a rusty frying pan. Anything of use had been taken or had decomposed, along with the lonely soul who had lived there. Around the door, Chase's arm appeared, wearing a boot with a floppy sole like a mouth. 'Light!'

shrilled the boot. 'Has seized my brains!' His blond head followed. 'All clear. Now, memorise this bit like you've got to come back alone.' He saw her expression and shrugged. 'Tor'd be more upset if I came back alone than if you did. You eat less. Ready?'

She stepped inside the humid carriage. 'What am I looking for?'

Chase gave the floor a kick. 'There was a tramp who lived here years ago. We called him Big Bear. He had hands the size of cabbages, and there was hair all over the backs of them, black as pig bristles. And here's where we buried him.'

When Chase whipped a sheet of corrugated iron up off the floor, she thought she was about to see a skeleton in a rotted tramp's parka. Her eyes adjusted. Another joke. It was a short flight of steps chopped into the black earth and fortified by wooden slats. The steps led down into a tunnel so dark that only the mouth was visible, moist and veiny with roots and tubers. Perhaps there was a body down there, melting quietly into the sod.

Chase had a cigarette lighter.

'It's easiest on your bum. Scoot!' He plopped down on to the ground and slid into the blackness.

In a moment of hesitation, Aisling called down, 'Can't we go above ground?'

'Where's the fun in that? We could die down here. Come on. This was your idea.'

With a small prayer, she got down and slid into the tunnel. As her boots touched solid clay, Chase flicked the lighter and recovered the entrance behind her. His face was already smeared with earth where he had thoughtlessly scratched an itch. When Chase lifted the lighter over their heads, Aisling could make out bright veins of ultramarine pigment in the outcroppings of rock.

The tunnel was more elaborate than she had first thought, with thinner corridors leading away from the main walkway. As Chase guided her along the tunnel, Aisling was surprised to find signs of human habitation. Sconces for candles had been scraped out of the earth, accompanied by floorboards, cricket bats, and fence posts tacked to the walls, marking sub-tunnels, alleys and bunkers: Hammer's End, Lover's Lane, The Long Walk, and, disconcertingly scratched into what could have been a wooden spatula, The Bitch (QUICKSAND).

Chase led her onwards. 'We're nearly into the town, now. Sometimes, you're so close to the surface, you can hear people in their living rooms over your head.'

Beside a dark archway, the word CULAPSD blared in drippy paint. Aisling peered inside. Clods of clay and rock blocked the way like congestion in failing lungs. He hadn't been joking, she realised with a touch of claustrophobia; they could die down here.

'Some of them used to be sewers,' Chase said. 'They flood in the autumn, freeze over in winter, then crack. Whole families came to live down here during The Remedy. Not families of engineers, though, crucially.'

She stayed close to his back. It was impossible to tell how far they had walked, with nothing but blackness beyond and behind them. As they turned another corner, his lighter flickered over a tunnel opening marked Sorry Street, and she stopped, squinting into the depths. There was water in the bottom of it, stagnant.

Aisling lingered at the opening. She tested the puddle

with the toe of her boot. It could easily have been the gentle sway of the water, or the gathering darkness as Chase went on without her, but there, at the end of Sorry Street, she could have sworn…

But no. No, she wasn't the sort of person who should allow her mind to wander without restraint. And what would Chase think of her, jumping at shadows?

Up ahead, he had stopped. 'You coming?'

When she didn't answer, he hurried to her. Light flooded Sorry Street, and Aisling saw man-sized grooves in the walls like sentry boxes, too dark to see into. Chase's whole body stiffened. The lighter winked out. With Chase's arm around her waist she was pulled backwards into the darkness, propelled left down a narrow tunnel, then left and left again, until she was nauseous, tripping on her own feet as Chase insisted on more speed. 'What? *What?*'

'Shurrup,' he hissed in her ear, and dragged her left again. *Four lefts*, she told herself to remember. *Four sudden, frightened lefts.*

At last they stopped. When Chase flicked the lighter back into life, they were inside a bricked chamber, and the bones of his sternum rippled as he panted. A set of rotten wooden stairs led to a trapdoor in the ceiling. Dizzy from the sudden propulsion, there was a horrible moment when Aisling thought she was back in Edythe's cellar, and the thought made her heart judder in her throat. *Get a grip*, she told herself.

They stood together for a moment, Chase with his head cocked to one side, looking back the way they had come.

'Wait here,' he whispered. She could only nod.

He sprang up the stairs, skipping over the rotten steps,

and gave the trapdoor a hard shove. A quick listen, and he was up and out of sight.

With the lighter gone, Aisling was left in thick darkness listening to the swish of her eyeballs moving in their sockets. What if he never came back? Archaeologists would find her skeleton in three hundred years and create a plastic model of her face, like the forensic scientists on television. *This was a girl stupid enough to go exploring down unstable tunnels alone, how sad, but ultimately a cautionary tale.*

Worse was the knowledge that whatever she thought she had seen inside Sorry Street, Chase had seen it too.

At that moment, the trapdoor opened and Chase appeared in a strip of daylight, a grin plastered across his face. 'Come into my parlour, said the something to the other thing.'

He hauled her up into an empty room with a wooden counter and layers of empty shelves and cabinets. The floorboards were wet where a lead pipe had crashed down through the roof, creating a slide for rain and leaves.

'We're not going to fall through the floor, are we?' she asked.

'One of these days. 'Til then, this is my own private entrance to the town. These openings are dotted all over the place, but this one? No one's cottoned on to it yet. I should stick a lock on it and live here.'

Chase kicked a panel of wall so hard a chunk of plaster fell to the floor with a *splat*. He gave one of his naughty laughs. *We shouldn't be here*, Aisling thought excitedly. The fear that had grown in the tunnels fizzled to nothing.

The newspaper pasted over the windows was turning green. The front door was boarded up from the inside, and the nails had long ago thickened with rust. Above the door frame, Aisling could just make out a dark carving in the wood: three names.

'I knew someone who lived here,' Chase said, when he saw her looking.

She stood on tiptoes to read it. 'Arthur. Germaine. Eva.' She turned to find Chase looking at his feet, smoothing the hair down over his ears.

'Yeah,' he said. 'Them too.'

She moved to the counter. Worms had started on the wood. A dark ring remained where someone had once put down a hot mug, an unnervingly human detail in the otherwise dilapidated scene. 'What was this place?'

He brightened. 'Pawn shop. Pawn with an A. They had some great stuff. This coat, actually. I thought it'd be gone by the time I scratched together the money for it, but no, they held it for me on faith. Good people.'

'It's a shame to let it just…' Aisling trailed off, looking over at the names above the door again. 'Why did Arthur and the others leave?'

She must have looked nervous. Chase came and stood before her, and he surprised her by taking one of her hands in his. He shook it gently to punctuate each word: 'We don't have to do this. We can go home.'

It was too uncomfortable. She twisted from his grip and ducked under the counter to investigate the kitchen. The back door was hanging by a hinge, leading into a greenhouse shattered by falling roof tiles. A bush engulfed the exit, festooned with a white web of caterpillar eggs. Chase stood where she left him, chewing his lip.

She was crunching over glass when she caught her reflection in one of greenhouse's grubby panes. She paused.

That ordinary face she had never liked – changed somehow – his hair, ginger-brown, alight at the temples with frizz and the kinks of a restless night. Lips thin, chapped. Eyes darkly ringed for the want of sleep. Like someone having an adventure.

If you saw me now, you wouldn't believe it, she thought. To whom, she was unsure.

She forced her gaze away and pressed through the bush blocking the door. The web of caterpillar eggs clung to her eyelashes. She faltered, trying to catch the sticky threads between forefinger and thumb. She felt Chase push past her, a crunch of leather against brick, and her eyes were open.

They had emerged into a walled trash-heap. What once was a small urban garden was now the receptacle of overturned wheelie-dumpsters, a festering collection of takeaway food containers – candy-coloured cartons declaring Sweetness For Bitter Times! – and a mouldy sofa missing its cushions. Chase brushed the brick dust from his coat. 'Now,' he said, 'you follow me. You don't dawdle or wander off. You don't talk to anyone. You don't *tell* anyone *anything*. Just do as I say. All right?'

'All right, boss.' She tried to catch a smile from him, but he was already off across the garden and under the loose fence panels.

Behind the garden was a weed-choked railway bridge crossing a canal. They edged their way along the narrow strip of earth between the bank and the backs of crowded terraces. Spouts emerged from the canal wall, one for each building, dripping sullenly with household refuse or worse. *No falling in*, Aisling thought, and, as if summoned, the corpse of a small cat came floating towards them from under the bridge, aglitter with bluebottles where the jaws parted in a silent yowl.

'If there was a better way in,' Chase grunted, 'a way that bypassed The River of Certain Dysentery, trust me, we'd use it.'

Aisling concentrated on her footing. 'Does it really give people dysentery?'

'When it's feeling friendly, yeah.'

'What's this place called?'

'River's the river, town's the town,' Chase said, with that big-eyed incredulous look he sometimes turned on her. He laughed. 'You. It's like talking to an alien.'

They came to a low wall. He was up and over it in one smooth motion, leaving Aisling to scramble and flop her way over.

'I wouldn't make a very good burglar,' she apologised.

'Just as long as you make a good spy, we're laughing. You're well behind enemy lines, now. The dragon's lair. Boggart-country. Scared?'

'A bit.'

'Fear not. I'm a professional.'

They were behind a warehouse. Like the pawnshop, it was derelict. The back door, nailed shut, bore the warning: TRESPASSERS WILL BE—

CONGRATULATED, some wag had supplied.

Out in the street, few people were about. Dawn turned the puddles a mournful grey. Chase kept Aisling close, moving discreetly along the gutters. An old man putting his bins out grunted a polite 'Good morning' to Chase, and he nodded curtly in return, pushing Aisling on. His shoulders were tense beneath his coat. But there was nothing to be afraid of. The early morning traffic hadn't yet emerged on to the narrow roads, and the cramped terraces and grocery shops were as still and quiet as dolls' houses.

They passed a shop window displaying hookahs and tins of tobacco. The shop was closed, but she could see a man standing at the counter, writing on a newspaper and taking a spoonful of porridge. Breakfast at home had always been a hurried affair. Beverley hated being seen with food in her mouth, preferring tiny pastries that deflated into nothing after one bite. What was she eating this morning, with Malcolm? Aisling couldn't quite think of it. Not yet.

The streets were narrowing in a Mediterranean fashion, bleeding off into red-bricked courtyards and alleyways overlooked by balconies heavy with laundry. Shopkeepers arranged piles of cheap tat: pocket watches hanging in rows and moth-eaten fur stoles once the height of fashion. There was a gradual increase of people around them, and Aisling hugged herself as she walked. *No one's looking at me*, she told herself. As Chase turned a corner, a woman leaving her house gave him a brief look of what might have been alarm before hunching her bony shoulders and striding away. Perhaps he had startled her.

At a corner cafe, two old men were setting up a chessboard. On the windowsill, a radio broadcasted a man's voice over swirls of interference:

'The fifth law concerns environment. An individual may be rescued from corrosive influences by a plain room, white and clean. Such rooms are provided by Our Friend. Any citizen concerned for the health of a friend or neighbour may apply for such a room at any post office, and a representative will arrange an appraisal post-haste. Give us health, give us reason, give us the rule of Our Friend! The sixth law concerns diet, and the importance of physical vi—'

The voice was overwhelmed by a wave of static carrying the faint trill of piano.

'Chase, listen!' Aisling whispered as one of the old men fiddled with the aerial. The other stared at the chessboard as if he had heard none of it. Chase took her by the arm and led her away.

Ahead of them was an expansive market square where traders were setting up for the day. This she could relate to: noisy Sunday markets in Bury St Edmunds. Tracksuits for a tenner alongside French cheeses and crystal healing. Striped tarpaulins brushed neighbouring shopfronts where deep grooves in the brickwork showed they had done so for decades, even centuries. At the square's centre, a paperboy coughed and spat on the stone steps of a waterless fountain.

'Keep close,' Chase muttered. 'We'll have a nose around.'

They dawdled amongst the stalls where vendors unloaded crates of dull saucepans or sorted the limpest of vegetables from limp bunches. The sickly scent of rotting vegetation mingled with the nutty richness of cooking oil firing up on the food stands. A hollow-cheeked woman was preparing a wok of noodles, sleeves rolled up revealing a pair of goldfish tattoos, green with age.

Chase led the way through the gathering throng of morning shoppers, looking shockingly tall and healthy amongst so many sallow, underfed people. The furtive glances he received were not so much admiring as astonished. When a pockmarked girl on a jewellery stand called to Aisling, 'Real pearl, real pearl, you wanna try?' she felt strangely ashamed, and was glad of the distraction of fine rain on her face. A knife-sharpener, something she had never seen in her life, fired up a coal brazier and watched the smoke drift across his neighbours' stalls. 'How's that stiletto holding up for you?' he called to Chase.

The two of them fell into conversation. Aisling stood off to the side, holding herself by the arms.

'Do you know what dissociation is, Aisling?'

I'm hungry, she reasoned with herself. *I've been up all night.*

She gave the ring on her thumb a sharp twist.

Chase was recounting some heroic, probably-fictitious feat to the knife-sharpener when a whistle startled Aisling out of her thoughts. It piped at her from the edge of the marketplace where the stalls ended and the alleys began. She looked away, but again:

Wee-woo!

A minuscule old woman. She was smiling at Aisling from a crack between buildings, where her wizened body would be invisible in the gloom were it not for the bright white of what looked like – no, extraordinarily, it was – a judge's powdered wig topping her head. With Aisling's acknowledgment, the woman grew bold, taking one heavy white wing of the wig, beckoning with it.

Chase had extracted himself from the knife-sharpener, and took Aisling's elbow to lead her on. 'Come on, I made you promise. No talking to strangers.'

Aisling resisted. 'She wants me to go over there.'

'Ignore her. She's a prayer seller.'

'Prayer *seller*?'

He tugged at her coat. 'Oh, don't be a pain. You called

me "boss", and everything.' But the old woman had opened her arms in a welcoming motion Aisling found difficult to resist.

'Good day, young people,' she said, drawing the wig across her face flirtatiously. 'It's time to raise the veil.'

The woman was all collarbones and broken capillaries in a shapeless patchwork dress. But her eyes were keen as a jackdaw's under the bizarre wig, and she held Aisling with them lovingly as she stepped cautiously into the alleyway. The woman laid hands on her, pressing gently on the epaulets of her coat.

'*Heavy* guilt on these shoulders, the *weight* pressing down on these bones, oh! I can help you. I will lighten that load.'

'Uh-huh. And our pockets,' said Chase.

The woman shot him a glare. 'You'd let her crack? Like a faulty teaspoon?'

Chase urged Aisling deeper into the alley and out of sight of the market traders. The old woman was indeed selling something from a crumpled briefcase open on the ground: small cards bearing handwritten slogans.

'I've got no problem with you or how you live,' Chase warned her. 'But if you try anything funny with her, there'll be trouble.'

'Trouble? You want to talk about trouble, with my husband twelve years dead?' She turned to Aisling: 'A growth in his bladder, my poor angel-man, it swept him away fast. Been together since babies, he and I.'

'I'm very sorry,' Aisling said quietly.

'And you, blondie, you want to talk to me about trouble? I had two brothers before all of this madness, and you know where they are now?'

Chase didn't feign interest. 'I don't know. Where are they?'

'I. Don't. Know.' She thumped with her foot. 'It's so often the way, isn't it, with those who speak up? People drop off the map. Get taken. Quiet! But the veils, the veils between the worlds, they're kind. The child is reunited with the mother, the lovers meet at last, the wanderer finds home. A flutter, a tear in the gauze, and one sees through.'

Veils. Aisling remembered staring at Dr Weber's silk scarf as she talked about dissociative dreaming, winding and winding a smidgeon too tight around her neck. But the old woman was settling into her patter now, crooning at Aisling with grandmotherly charm.

'As per the old way, I write the name of your choosing on the card, burn it in my hearth. Proper copper cauldron, with rosemary for remembrance. The ashes, I cast from a wasteland-facing window on a night with a kind wind. Your message will reach your intended as they sleep, no matter the distance.' She splayed the creamy cards, cut from cereal boxes. Aisling read them. *I'm so awfully sorry, I loved you most, despite everything*, and, heartbreakingly, *Please don't die.*

'The whole service for a penny,' the woman said, and when Chase took Aisling by the elbow to lead her away, she turned her bright eyes on him with surprising scorn. 'I'm proper cunning folk, and subtle. Unlike some, Foreigner. Let her make her choice. I know men like you. No man at all. Eh? *Gotcha.*'

His hands went straight to his hair in that guilty way, and the woman tilted her chin with triumph. With a blush spreading over his cheekbones, Chase produced a coin and pushed at the old woman. 'Get a move on,' he muttered, and busied himself looking out at the market.

Only one card held her attention.

A pencil came out of the old woman's wig. 'The name of your intended one here, dear. No need to divulge your own.'

Robert.
I am well.

Aisling handed the card back, and it disappeared under the wig.

'The next kind wind, your message will be delivered. A good day and a good life to you.' She nodded at Chase. 'And to you, blondie. Good luck.'

They hurried away into the gathering activity of the market. When Chase was satisfied they were not being followed, he chuckled to himself.

Aisling was on the verge of laughter herself as they hurried along, looking behind to check the alleyway existed at all. 'That was the bizarrest thing,' she said.

'You're the bizarrest thing. We've been here ten bleeding minutes, and you're already breaking the law.'

'That was illegal?'

He snorted. 'You're precious, you are.'

Precious. And he was off, bouncing on the balls of his feet towards a stall laden with bicycle wheels. *'I know his type,'* Aisling heard her mother say, in a voice that cut through the commotion as a tired-eyed woman with a brood of excitable children ploughed past her. *'They feel sorry for the ugly ones.'* Aisling tucked her hands into her sleeves and walked faster. The little light went out.

'Why did she call you a foreigner?' Aisling asked, when

Chase had got his hands sufficiently greasy fondling bicycle chains he had no intention of purchasing.

'Who?'

'Her. Just now. The prayer seller, she distinctly called you a foreigner.'

'Dementia. Dunno. Hey, dirty rags!'

She looked around for a literal washing line of stained linen as Chase scampered away to inspect a stall peddling ink drawings of nude fat women atop enraptured bishops.

Reluctantly, she joined him. 'Oh, that's lovely,' she grimaced as he waved a sheet in front of her face, depicting what may have been a sex act or a violent sport.

'Controversial, but all above board,' said the vendor, an incongruously prim little man and also the artist judging by his inky fingers. 'If poetry's more to your taste, I've a lib'ry of epics here for your enjoyment.'

'Read me a scary one?' Chase asked Aisling, and she picked the nearest pamphlet from the rack, an intimidatingly long poem entitled *The Fall of The Pale Prince*, written by hand. With Chase leaning in close, as if to witness the alchemy of written letters becoming living sound, she read the first stanza:

'Now, wise children, listen well,
To the tale your mother tells,
Of seasons past, before your time,
When she herself was young and fine,
A girl of vigour, loyal and true
To fatherland and mother too.'

Aisling sucked in her cheeks to keep from giggling.

'Flip to the back,' Chase said. 'There might be a massacre.'

Sure enough, the final page of doggerel was wreathed in funeral lilies where the final lines stood out in bold black:

'She warns you well and warns you stern
Of strangers, dear, who'd see you burn,
Of dark-tongued ones who lie and scheme,
Seduce the young, infect the clean,
Who come in secret, leave like snakes,
With graves of babies in his wake.'

The poem concluded with a drawing of an open coffin containing the body of a boy with a dark halo of matted hair. A noose was drawn tight around his neck, the coffin wreathed in flames.

'I do big prints of that, if you like it,' said the vendor. 'Dead popular.'

Chase seemed upset. He nudged her onwards, leaving the little man to place his unappreciated work back on its rack.

They trudged back into the centre of the market. 'So, you know she'll just light her fags with that prayer card. If you wanted to send a message home, you might as well have tied it to one of these ladies.' He jabbed a boot at the pigeons pecking under the stalls.

He was upset that he couldn't read the card. 'It said *Robert*,' she freely admitted. 'He's my great-uncle.'

Chase huffed, a little noise of relief. 'Hey, he's not one of the ones who made you cry, was he? 'Cause if it was, you should let him hang. No use sending good wishes to them who'll wipe their arse with the paper.'

'That's disgusting.'

Chase wasn't laughing. 'Hey, if Robert and your other people wanted you safe so bad, they'd have found you by now. People put up posters for their missing dogs, y'know? I'd've known if they'd sent someone out for you, and they haven't. That's disgusting.'

A deep flush forced itself up into Aisling's face. Her knees lost the knowledge of how to bend. She tried to call Chase back – he stomped moodily ahead – but glitter obscured her vision and she knew she was seizing. The world tottered sideways, and she backwards into a pair of beefy arms. Chase had come back. He must have. But when consciousness returned all she could see were open pores dotting a snouty nose. The stranger's breath was ripe with port and raisins.

'Your boyfriend has a sweet tooth.'

His finger looped through the buttonhole on her lapel. There was a ring on the finger, gold with a glistening tiger's eye. Aisling struggled feebly as the man wedged her up against a stall, but her arms were numb and her tongue a slab of plasticine. Chase was somehow by her side again, shouting something she couldn't decipher. The stranger let her go. And then she was on the cobblestones.

'Got your oily hide!'

The operatic boom turned heads all across the square as the stranger seized Chase by the scruff of the neck. Kicking and swearing, Chase's long body dangled as if he weighed nothing more than a furious cat. The stranger, however, was huge in all dimensions. His bristling fur coat only served to increase his bulk, and his face, alight with triumph, was topped by a crown of glossy black hair, standing up as if a charge ran through it. 'Where you been, boy, hmm? Got yourself a girl?'

Chase squirmed, but wasn't afraid. Aisling shuffled backwards against the leg of the stall. Her hands had clenched into claws as a result of the drop in blood pressure and she pressed them to her sweat-sheened face. 'No,' she panted. 'He hasn't.'

'Oh?' The man used the bulk of his chest to push Chase back into the table. 'I'm glad to hear it, what with his disgusting, entirely justified reputation. Did you steal her from someone, too? Spirit her away? Or do you only steal things coated in chocolate?'

Chase winced. 'Never from—'

'*I never take from the proletariat*,' the man whinged. 'What does that make me, your doting dowager aunt? I earn my wealth. You're a tick on my arse.' He turned his face to Aisling and switched to a conversational tone. 'It's the sugar. These boys, they love it, like little hummingbirds. You sure he's not your boyfriend?'

Aisling flexed her tingling fingers. 'I'm sure.'

'She's sure,' Chase gritted.

The neighbouring traders lost interest. Aisling took in the crates of sweets surrounding her. Baskets of toffees in gold foil and trays of out-of-date chocolates were piled beneath the stall, ready to be displayed. Wrapped in paper were marbled slabs of fudge, and she remembered Chase plying her with them in Edythe's garden. It seemed a hundred years ago. The crates were stamped with a pretty oval design she had noticed in the pawnshop garden, Sweetness For Bitter Times, underlined by a bold, flourishing signature: *Borghese*. This, she assumed, was the name of big man, and when she looked up she met his brown-toothed smile.

'See something you fancy? I'd treat you, gladly, but I'm

running a little low on stock. Idle hands taking as they please.'

Borghese looped his little finger through Chase's earring and tugged just enough to cause pain.

An assistant came to the stall with another crate of sweets. He looked like a man who had spent a long life careening from one fistfight to the next. 'That'll be the last of the liquorice, sir,' he said.

'Thank you, Wilson. Don't forget to purchase flypaper, will you?'

'No, sir.' The old man paused to jerk his jaw at the boy in his employer's grip. 'You got him, then, sir?'

'Debating which hand to chop off first, Wilson.'

The assistant barked a laugh and loped off into the market. To Aisling's surprise, Borghese took his hands off Chase and relaxed entirely. From his pocket, he took a tin of snuff and inserted a delicate pinch into each nostril. 'Your problem, of course, is that you're dim,' he sniffed. 'If I were anyone else, just *think* what I'd have done to you by now. Gruesome.'

'It won't happen again.'

'Oh, grovel. Grovel harder.' He turned his big, brown smile on Aisling. 'I manhandled you. No apology will do. Snuff? It's cherry.'

Chase dropped his voice to little above a whisper. 'Jobi,' he said. 'Where is he?'

Borghese rolled his eyes. 'Not here, thank my vengeful God.'

'It's been weeks.'

'He'll be holed up in a nice love nest in the wasteland somewhere. Have patience.'

'I've had patience. This isn't normal.'

'It's precisely normal. You're whining.'

'I'm not whining.'

'Where is he, I miss him, I love him loads, waaah.'

Chase wrinkled his nose. 'He could be my brother, y'know, we're not that different.'

'Oh, as if that stops your type from dabbling. Now look, you've upset your girlfriend.'

'I'm not anybody's bloody girlfriend!' Aisling snapped, hauling herself upright.

The two men stared.

Borghese was the first to recover. 'Darling girl, you are quite right. Have a lemon drop. You know, I have my fingers in a number of pies, and one of them is professional mourning. You have a face for it. Need a job? I can drape you in black crêpe, but you provide your own tears.' He waved a yellow candy in front of her nose. She wouldn't take it.

'I'd like a lemon drop,' Chase said.

'Tick on my arse! Open up.' He popped the yellow sweet between Chase's parted lips and offered his ringed hand regally. 'Kiss it better,' he said, and Chase coyly did. All the while, Borghese was regarding Aisling with interest bordering on rudeness. 'I like her. She doesn't talk as much as you. And she's new.'

Mouth full, Chase shrugged. 'Shesh knock inkorkank.'

'She's new, and that makes her *extremely* important.' Borghese licked sugar from each of his snuff-brown fingertips in turn, eyes firmly on her. 'Give me your name.'

'It's Aisling,' she said, ignoring Chase's warning look over Borghese's shoulder, cheek bulging with the lemon drop like an anxious hamster.

Borghese gave a slow, approving nod. 'Memorable.'

Chase removed the lemon drop from his mouth and prodded Borghese with his sticky finger, eager to turn the conversation away from Aisling. 'You're not bloody listening. If Jobi comes by, or anyone who might know where he is…'

'I'll send a telegram to your oh-so-permanent address. He's fine, Chase. He's more streetwise than you are. And if your positions were switched, he wouldn't be here bothering me about you.'

A sherbet-pink blush blossomed across Chase's cheeks. All his emotions were so close to the surface that Aisling suddenly pitied him. How awful to be so easily penetrated.

'There's always a chance,' he said quietly, scuffing the cobblestones with one muddy boot. 'When he's tipsy he'd only have to tell the wrong person.'

'Tell them what?' Aisling asked.

Awkward silence. Borghese looked to Chase with an expression she sensed he didn't often reveal – true astonishment.

'What?' she said. 'Do I not get to know?'

The blush on Chase's cheekbones spread to his neck.

'Oh, my giddy aunt.' Borghese took a monogrammed handkerchief from his sleeve and sneezed away the brown remnants of snuff. 'Chase, take your young lady somewhere else, somewhere fine and clean, and stop stewing over things you cannot change. All things, know what I mean? Take a gumdrop. Stick it in your face and don't argue.'

There was a commotion from a stall behind them as a stray dog attempted to liberate a stick of salami, and Borghese took the opportunity to evict them both, miming a closed beak at Chase as three young men in overalls sauntered by, openly eyeing his height and clear complexion. They were halfway down the row before Aisling glanced back and found Borghese watching her. He called to her, 'Where'd he find you, new girl?'

Pigeons fluttered.

'Don't,' Chase said, and led her quickly by the arm. They left Borghese leaning against his stall, staring after them with an expression Aisling couldn't read. 'I gotta get you home,' Chase said, under his breath.

They left the market. In a nearby street, a house was in the process of falling down, and people had gathered to watch. Aisling saw a bedroom in cross section: wardrobe doors hanging open, shirts rippling gently. A man in overalls shouted at Chase as he tried to push past.

'Oi! Do you want to get squashed? The supporting wall went this morning. I don't want a repetition of Coldwater.'

'Coldwater?' Aisling asked Chase.

'Coldwater College, derelict for years. All the little kiddies knew not to play in it in case it collapsed, so they played in the garden instead.' Chase shrugged. 'No one told them buildings can fall down sideways.'

They changed direction down a broad thoroughfare of factories studded with sash windows. The clatter of rowdy families drifted from some of the rooms; others were empty, the windowpanes so filthy they might have been bricked up. From the ground floors came a rhythmic mechanical noise like a chorus of old washing machines. She considered mentioning Blake's dark, satanic mills to Chase, rattling off a few lines to make him smile. But a boy with atrocious sores around his mouth sat on the pavement, strumming a guitar with an upturned gas mask at his feet. Poems didn't seem appropriate.

The half-hearted drizzle started again. In a daze, Aisling followed Chase. In her head, the strangeness of it all – *this isn't right this isn't right* – bobbed like a cork in deep water. People were queuing up a grand set of steps, sitting under shawls and oilskins. Some of the women had babies, jostling them gently. The few men assembled kept quiet, frowning at newspapers to discourage strangers from approaching. Aisling was about to ask Chase what they were waiting for when she saw the banner clinging to the bricks above the great double doors.

DAILY BREAD.

The door was flanked by statues of women holding books of the law to their breasts. Pigeons loitered on the stumps where the heads had long ago been hacked off, and Aisling remembered with unease the council from Chase's story. As he guided her closer, she could see inside. Officials inspected white tokens, lifting them to the light to check the watermark. At long tables, uninviting bricks of black bread were doled out, one for each token. A handful of men old enough to have grandchildren stood watch by the door, batons in hand. 'Winnow's norphans,' the leader said, as he paced the line. 'Winnow's norphans.'

It was like the historical newsreels of Russian peasants waiting for rations when there were none to be had, nothing Aisling's upbringing had prepared her to witness. Chase was by her side, and she didn't resist when he gently moved her on. She spoke slowly, weighed down by a sense of shocked shame she'd never felt before.

'Tor said she missed bread.'

As she said it, a small girl came down the steps and passed them, loaf in hand. She was no more than ten, but her jaw was set like a boxer returning to the ring.

Chase called after her. 'Mind you don't drop it. You'll make a hole in the pavement.'

'Eat shit,' the child said over her shoulder, and scuttled off down one of the cobbled alleyways.

Chase led them in the same direction, between a clump of two-up two-downs engulfed by a profusion of Virginia creeper. He chattered on, though Aisling barely listened. 'That black stuff's half potato peel, half sawdust. They'd be better off eating shit. Mind out.' He steered her away from a puddle where a hunk of chicken skin lay rotting. 'We can get breakfast, if you like? I've got a bit of money.'

Food was the last thing she wanted. Along one of the buildings, the enormous phrase WITHIN REASON had been stencilled, now faded to a whitewashed ghost. She thought of the lunches Beverley packed for her just before she was taken out of school: cheese wrapped in plastic, single chocolates in foil. Little mouthfuls, quick to eat so she could sit in the toilet with the door locked, where no one could see her. And the notes: *Have a sunshiney day, Nil desperandum*, and towards the end, *Do your best.*

'"Winnow's norphans." Widows and orphans of what? The Remedy, was it called?'

'Stuff's happened,' he said, reluctantly. 'Since then.'

Someone was behind her. Aisling stopped and looked back.

'All right?' Chase said.

Nothing but the boy with the guitar. A woman leaned out of a top-floor window, shaking a dusty rug.

'Nobody's following us.' He held out his hand. She didn't want to take it, but found him lacing his fingers with hers and tugging her onwards. *I'm not your girlfriend*, she wanted to say. *I'm not anyone's.*

The lake. The pavement dropped to a shore of brackish mud. She placed her boots at the edge, aligning her toes to hang over the brickwork. Tiny crabs skittered in the sludge below.

She knew the smell of stale smoke, of old fuel and Edythe's bathroom chemicals. Her skin prickled, wet under the armpits and the hollow between her breasts.

Chase looked out over the distant water. 'Some say it's like the paraffin they put in the streetlamps when they were working. I reckon it's more like the smell of old dogs, you know, when they've given up.'

'It's not natural.'

'The mud? Oh, it's not the mud. Vapours come in from the water. Up through the tunnels. If it gets bad and you breathe too much, you get sick. That's what happened to me the other night.' He shrugged. 'The papers try to tell us it's smog left over from the decadent times before The Remedy. But I tell you, I'm not the only one who reckons it's him. You know who I mean. You think it, too.'

That jangling in the back of her head. But once she had stood at the top of Edythe's staircase. Once there was a black overcoat gliding. 'I thought you were making it up.'

She looked to the horizon. The wreck of a great ship was marooned in the black mud. It leaned heavily to one side, portholes streaked with the droppings of pigeons colonising the rusting cabins. The funnels pointed skywards, all but one stencilled with an enormous red cross which had slammed into the bridge with the force of a felled tree, crushing the place where men had once consulted charts and turned the wheel. The words WITHIN REASON were daubed across the hull in white paint.

Mudlarks in thigh-high boots waded through the slurry, arms black to the elbows where they dove down for trinkets. There was a small commotion when one unearthed a violin. They horsed around with it for a short while before throwing it back to the sucking mud. The ship lurked beyond them, a skeleton in the mire.

Chase was watching her. His voice dropped, became soft. 'It was good here, once. Just so you know. Not perfect, but, well, not this.'

Her coat had slipped from her shoulder and the cold crept down to her skin. A gaggle of girls came charging past them, and she was swept back from the edge. Teenagers, like her. 'Come on, it's gonna go!' one shouted as they dashed down a covered alley. Did Aisling see them dodge someone at the mouth of the alley, someone just out of sight?

'I want to go back the way we came,' she managed. 'I want to see the building fall.'

He took her down the covered alley – no lurking figures there, or none that cared to show themselves – to a red-bricked, needly building with a clock face frozen at ten past three. No one stared as they took the flight of stairs zigzagging up to a balcony that bounced gently as they set foot on it. From there, they could see over the striped tarpaulins of the marketplace, far away to an expanse of unoccupied tenements in the shadow of a high wall, the blackened wrecks she inexplicably found herself in, weeks ago.

A breeze whipped their hair, and for a moment Chase was unable to see her watching him. *You could easily be a dream*, she thought. The product of magazine covers, tribal photographs, old footage of punk boys in Camden who dressed like they didn't care and no one could make them. Something animal, too. Something she half-glimpsed.

She looked across the streets to the collapsing house. The building was sinking to its knees. Someone had created a cordon around the area from torn bedsheets and a scattering of cafe chairs with paper signs attached: DANGER! No one ran for cover when the chimney swayed, though many watched from the sidelines and from tenement windows, blank expressions on tired faces.

A memory jumped to the fore: *'Close your eyes,'* came a voice as her body slid inside the CT scanner's red rim of light. Aisling felt a terrible fraud. Out in the waiting room, some of the people flipping through *Good Housekeeping* may have had tumours in their heads and there she was, frightened of something she could barely remember happening.

'It was horrible,' Beverley said. *'I heard you call out, and I found you lolling about on the toilet and you couldn't speak. You just pulled on me, pulled me right down until your face was in my chest, and you started to jerk. Jerking like someone was shaking you by the shoulders. Twenty seconds of that.'*

Smoking more and eating less, Beverley was the witness the doctors called *'Vital in piecing this together'*, as if Aisling were a plate that had slipped off the drying rack. *'I won't be long,'* Aisling promised as the nurse came to take her through to the machine.

Back in the town, a shout went up. The building fell in on itself.

On the other side of the thoroughfare, walls that barely saw light before were revealed, thick with old soot. A shriek emitted from an open window where the dust whooshed harmlessly into someone's downstairs toilet.

The rubble ceased to tumble. Someone cheered.

'Winnow's norphans,' came the distant call. 'Winnow's norphans.'

The wind whipped Aisling's hair across her face, and she caught a fistful of it, stuffed it down the back of her collar. The scales of rust on the railing had sliced the pad of her thumb from tip to joint. She raised the thumb to her lips for the tinny taste of blood.

'Chase?'

He looked at her.

'I think I've gone mad.'

'Is it nice?'

'Yes.' Her breath hitched. It sounded like laughter. 'Yes, it is.'

Verity Holloway

20

Seamless, how they ended up back home, back in their beds, without detection. Chase left her on her mattress beside the pickle jars, and he paused at the door before coming back to arrange the duvet over her, as if it might not occur to her to seek warmth.

Aisling stared up at the jars. Her head was blank as she dozed. Once, she thought she heard the front door swing back and hit the wall, an angry sound that may have been a dream. No further noises followed. She allowed the silence to swallow her, and drifted.

Soon enough, a shy knock on the door made her jolt under the duvet. It was Tor, bringing her a cup of late morning tea.

She shuffled in, smiling, in one of her fisherman's jumpers. A twig was caught in the wool under her elbow. 'No mushrooms today,' she said breezily. 'But I've a clutch of eggs ready for frying. Georgie might chop up a cabbage for bubble and squeak if we're lucky.'

'Thank you.' Aisling took the hot mug. Tor's fingers

were sooty with graphite, and Aisling remembered Chase's words about the wall of faces. When would Tor add her face to the collection? Was she waiting for a 'mission accomplished' moment, when the household would wave Aisling off, confident and healthy, back into her normal life? That, she knew now, would never happen.

I should say something, she told herself.

'I've been lying around like a rock.'

God, she sounded like Beverley. The tiptoeing before the screeching row. Aisling took a gulp of hot tea. It tasted peculiar.

'I need to start repaying you for all this,' she told Tor steadily. 'I need to give you something in return.'

Tor was quiet. She eased her sore joints down on to the stool by the bed, ignoring Aisling's boots, caked in dirt from the tunnels. On noticing them, Aisling's heart tripped into a guilty gallop, but Tor's eyes were gentle. 'You've gained a little confidence,' she said.

'I've been thinking.'

'Always dangerous.'

'I've been thinking about all of this. This place, and you, and Chase. The way I ended up here. And I don't want you to be upset, but I don't know how else to put it. It's just important, I think, to say it out loud.'

Tor nodded silently. Aisling inhaled.

'None of this is real, is it?'

The older woman gave a stunned laugh. 'If I'd known you were a philosopher, I'd have booted you out weeks ago.'

'No, it's okay. I think I've worked it all out now. And I don't mind that it's not real. I'm happy here.'

'Because you're happy, it can't be real?' Tor's expression

was pitying. It was the same look Chase sometimes turned on her, and she wondered if that, too, was a product of accumulated memories of people's stares. 'Oh, Aisling.'

'But it isn't sad,' she said. She sat up and took a gulp of tea, enjoying the burn of it. The hard part was out of the way. 'It isn't. I've gone mad. And going mad is a form of being set free, isn't it? It's like letting go.'

'Mad is not a kind word to use.'

'But it feels like it's mine, now. I can finally do what I want with it.'

'You do have that right, yes,' Tor said slowly. Worry had crept into her voice. Then, the unexpected; she leaned down close enough for Aisling to smell the malty warmth of her body, and kissed her on the head. Her teeth whistled as she did so. *Ssss. Pseudo.*

Pseudo-seizures, they called them. Mad was not a kind word, Tor was right. It conveyed a violence that frightened people. But pseudo was like a sigh. Pseudo was unreal. Pseudo could not hurt.

'I'm just so happy,' Aisling said.

Tor nodded slowly. 'Happiness counts.' It was then that Aisling noticed her looking at the dirty boots. A defeated look had settled over her soft face. 'Chase left this morning.'

'Why?'

'A friend of his hasn't been seen for a while. He's not one for sitting and waiting for news.'

The relief of Aisling's confession collided with jealousy and disappointment. 'Someone called Joanni, or Jobi?'

'He didn't want to wake you, so I told him I'd say goodbye on his behalf. We'll probably not see him for a few weeks. Maybe even months. That's just what he's like, I'm afraid.

Coming and going as whim dictates.'

He'd said he couldn't wait to learn to read. Aisling finished her tea. A grassy taste lingered on her tongue. She wanted to lie back down and doze.

'You know I'm doing everything I can for you, don't you?' Tor said. 'I only want what's best. So does Chase, in his silly way. That's what this house is all about. Striving for the best.'

Tor smiled. The wrinkles around her eyes were slack and soft, like the hide of a hairless cat. She looked exhausted.

Aisling asked, 'Did you sleep all right?'

'I was disturbed.' She sighed heavily, and Aisling was careful to show no reaction. 'I hope I didn't wake you, but we had a visitor turn up unexpectedly, and rather early.'

Relieved she wasn't referring to the difficult sneak across the living room, Aisling was curious. 'You get visitors?'

'No. Well. This was someone I used to know. Though it's clear to me I don't any more. Life, life.' She wiped her hands on her skirt, leaving graphite smears on the cotton. 'And you? Did you have a nice night?'

'Oh, yes. I needed it.'

>•<

One night, two nights, three nights.

She'd been touching everything compulsively since returning from the town: the pickle jars, the walls of her bedroom, even her own arms, tugging at the hairs to be sure they were anchored to real roots and real nerves. She dissected her food, watching the fibres of meat stretch and separate. Tor and Georgie stared, of course, but they didn't mean any harm. They wouldn't hurt her. Perhaps they couldn't.

She began to write again. Lying on the grass, she sketched out lesson plans for Chase. Short sentences in capitals and cursive, *Hello, my name is C H A S E.* The first lines of the poems he liked so he would recognise the sounds, see them crystallised. *Hello, my name is F E O—* She paused. The words looked unreal. Everything did.

On a fresh page she set herself questions. Was Tor's house part of the sealed, internal world of a dream, or reality embellished as Doctor Ross had said? Either way, if she had invented Chase, surely he wouldn't have his own independent life? Surely he wouldn't have a boyfriend in London with a glorious loft conversion, too.

The gnarly old tooth was rubbing her hip in her pocket. She sketched it in the margin, a totem pole of teeth. Before the seizures started, she had wanted to be a travelling artist, lugging sketchbooks around in a leather satchel and drinking black coffees in gallery cafes. But then Mrs Howard, the school careers officer, had said, *'It's nice to see you taking an interest, but speaking practically, Aisling, artists aren't happy people. No money in it. It's one of those things like being a pop star, you make it big or fail hard.'*

Which was this?

What if it was possible to wield this place, to make it exactly how she wanted it, as an artist might? *Wield,* she wrote, next to the teeth.

The slim figure of Georgie blocked the sun across her page. He had brought her a cup of tea. Since Chase had gone, all he seemed to do was forlornly boil the kettle, listening to the bursts of piano on his little radio.

'Hello,' he said shyly. 'Tor said you'd like to help me with the smokehouse.'

She smiled up at him, feeling a warm confidence she wasn't accustomed to. 'You have beautiful skin.'

Tor, who was sealing jars of pickled cucumbers at the breakfast table, looked up with disapproval. 'She thinks she's dreaming us.'

Georgie brightened. 'Oh. Could you dream me a bit taller?'

Aisling whispered up at him, 'I just wish I'd dreamed up a world with flushing toilets.'

Georgie spluttered with giggles.

Tor took an empty mason jar and dusted it on her sleeve. 'I'm not sure I like being imaginary,' she said. There were still moments of doubt, largely because Chase wasn't there to tell her yes, there was a tunnel below the forest, and yes, there were queues of hungry people like Soviet Russia and a ship that looked like a dead animal. Did it all matter? No, she thought as she sipped her tea. Everything was within reason. And she was *happy*.

Told held up the jar of pickled cucumbers. 'Reminds me of a museum of anatomy I once visited.'

Aisling grinned. Georgie didn't catch the joke, but laughed anyway. He settled down on the grass with her and showed her his plans for the smokehouse, indicating calculations with his babyish fingers, smooth with scar tissue.

'What happened to you, Georgie?'

He didn't mind her asking. 'An accident. I had a friend, he never meant to do any harm. They don't hurt much, any more.' His black foal eyes darted up at Tor, immersed in her work. His voice dropped as if imparting a secret. 'I miss him.'

He soon perked up as they went over the construction plans. 'Soon, we could be totally self-sufficient. If we divide labour and work carefully with the seasons, there'll be no need—'

'To go elsewhere?'

Again, he glanced at Tor. 'If at all possible, I'd like to have the walls done in a week. Give us time to set the roof up and experiment with smoking techniques before the cold weather comes.'

Aisling finished her tea, grimacing slightly at the aftertaste. 'Where's Chase?'

He pretended not to hear. 'I've considered salting meat. You pack the flesh in salt until it sucks out the moisture, preserves it for months. I just need to source the salt itself, but I'm not sure.'

She edged closer, until they were elbow to elbow. 'Do you want to go for a walk with me?'

When he saw her look to the woods, Georgie was startled. He whispered, 'Beyond the boundary?'

She nodded.

'*Why?*'

'Why not?' She rolled drowsily on to her back and stole a glance at Tor, upside down, trimming excess wax. Slung around her broad hips was a belt with a service revolver in the holster, sharply shiny. Aisling had never seen a real person wearing a gun before.

Tor noticed her staring.

'You look tired, dear,' she said. 'Why don't you have a little snooze?'

Another day without Chase. An amendment had been made to the wall of faces.

Aisling saw it while Georgie taught her to caramelise onions. His small body pressed unthreateningly behind hers, holding the handle of the pan and shaking it lightly, letting the butter melt into a yellow stream. Aisling glanced back at him to say 'It smells amazing,' and noticed something different, something looking at them. But then Señor Blanca, the little white rat, made a bid for the open door and, at Tor's shriek, Georgie unlooped his arms from Aisling's waist and went chasing after him. Aisling finished the tea Georgie had brewed for her. After that, she forgot the wall.

One lazy afternoon, Tor gently roused Aisling where she had nodded off in an armchair. She and Georgie had prepared a surprise for her.

Down in her room, Georgie beamed with pride. The pickle jars had been transferred to new shelves. In their place, one of the overstuffed chintzy chairs from the living room was arranged invitingly next to a small oil lamp for reading, and a footstool with elegant Queen Anne legs. They had unrolled an old rug over the floor beside the bed, and against the wall two beanpole tripods were lashed to a broom handle. In the centre, on pegs, hung a freshly knitted pair of socks.

'Do you like it?' Georgie asked. 'It's all for you.'

Aisling gazed around the room. It was the strangest feeling, of slotting in without a struggle. Of being liked. Tor indicated a tower of wooden floorboards elevated by bricks. 'And here, a place for our resident librarian to keep her tomes.'

She couldn't help herself. 'Oh, thank you! This will be perfect for Chase when he gets back. I'm going to teach him to read.'

'Yes,' said Tor uncertainly.

Georgie said, 'We thought it was about time you had a permanent place with us. What do you think?'

Before Aisling could respond to that heavy word – permanent – Tor clapped her chubby hands. 'I think it's high time it was tea time. Georgie?'

The sun swept slowly across the living room. Aisling dozed in the armchair by the crackling stove with the Blake book on her chest, her eyelids flickering as dreams sailed by, leaving nothing more than ripples in her memory. She rarely dreamed nowadays. Sleep was a blank, quiet chamber, and she surrendered to it easily and often.

While the silence of Edythe's house had made her nervous and exposed, Tor's house, with its routines of gentle exertion and fruitful labour, had a soporific effect. As her wasted muscles gradually regained strength and her skin returned to its natural smoothness, something inside her was growing heavy and warm. She could almost perceive its treacly weight on the cusp of sleep, smothering the thoughts of Chase and that strange town beyond the boundary tree.

'*Ease her down,*' said a voice in the faraway dark. '*Soothe those nerves.*' She swatted at it drowsily, her limp arm flopping to the floor. The rest of her slid off the armchair with a thud.

Aisling swore softly. She had only meant to rest her eyes.

The Blake book tumbled after her, straight into the empty teacup on the floor, splitting it in two. Behind her cherry blossom modesty screen, Tor snored in the tin bath. The three rats congregated around the fire, preening their ears.

Aisling ran her fingers through her rumpled hair. Something had changed in the room while she slept. Not the reappearance of the bath, or the cherry blossom screen, nothing so obvious. But she sensed it nonetheless. As she stretched her back and looked around, eyes adjusting to the patches of late-afternoon sunshine illuminating the piles of junk and bootprints on the floor, she saw it.

The wall of Tor's drawings. A new piece of paper had been added to it, taken from the back of a book. The tear was still crisp. Aisling crept towards it, careful not to wake Tor. A needly sensation shivered across her shoulders.

Her face, looking back at her. Hers.

Like the other portraits, Aisling's had been rendered while she was sleeping. Curled barefoot in the armchair, hair streaming over her shoulders where her head drooped, she looked as vacant as a corpse. The unpleasantness of it almost stopped her noticing that the portrait had been pinned over another, older picture, while the rest had respectfully been given their own space.

Gingerly, for she was almost afraid to let the thing touch her, she slipped a finger under the fresh drawing and lifted it. Pencil lines, soft with age. She revealed the tendons of a throat captured in charcoal. A tapering chin followed, and a slight smile tweaked one side of the lips. The other side drooped gently, a hint of a habitual sneer rendered lovingly.

She glanced over her shoulder. In her warm bath, Tor

slept. Georgie was out in the garden, gathering herbs. She raised the paper, watching as a narrow nose emerged, delicately shaded. Clear, confrontational eyes under thick black brows like that old singer, the punk girl. Dark curls, grudgingly brushed.

The tip of her index finger gave a cold throb.

'Feodor.'

All at once, she remembered.

Barely able to think, she snatched her coat from her bed and made out through the front door, leaving the portrait of her hiding Feodor's youthful face. Something in her pocket bumped against her thigh, a knife wrapped in the page of a book. Chase's knife, stained with blackberry juice. He must have slipped it into her coat before leaving.

'Left suddenly, did he?'

As she hurried out across the garden to the trees – with what purpose, she had no idea – she was dismayed to hear Georgie calling after her.

In his hand was a rabbit, dead and dangling. 'I was going to let you help,' Georgie said. 'With the smokehouse.'

She paused at the boundary tree. She didn't want to look at him. He sounded hurt.

'I will,' she said. 'Later.'

'People come and go all the time here. I never have the chance to settle with anyone.'

'Chase was asked to leave. Wasn't he?'

'He broke a rule,' Georgie said miserably.

'Who was Tor's visitor the night he left?'

'Visitor?' His surprise was genuine. Tor was keeping something from all of them. He made a small step towards her. 'Come back from there. I'll make us some tea.'

'Tea? What's in that tea? I've done nothing but fall asleep since Chase left.'

'Nothing. Just a little, a little something.'

To ease me down. The blood roared in her ears. 'You've been drugging me.'

Georgie turned. 'I'm getting Tor.'

'No, Georgie.'

He flushed. He tucked his hand under the rabbit's limp neck and laid it on the grass. He inched closer to the boundary tree, cautiously, as if its spindly boughs might reach down and snatch him up. 'They all want to go back. In the beginning.' He glanced over his shoulder to the house and lowered his voice. 'Please. You'll get in so much trouble.'

'Georgie, I don't know how I ended up here. Try to see it from my perspective. I think—' She took a harsh breath. Here it was, saying it out loud: 'I think something terrible happened in the house I came from. And even if this isn't real, I think what I saw there was. Georgie, if you know something, *please.*'

He held out his hands. She wanted to run straight back to him, back to the yard where she could learn to smoke meat and keep chickens and forget all about burned-out bathrooms and doctors who told her never to lock doors. But then she remembered Chase turning cartwheels in Edythe's garden. He was the element she couldn't bear to lose.

'I'm dreaming you,' she said. 'You're an invention.'

'No. None of us are.'

'I'm sick.'

'You mustn't say that. You mustn't go. Our Friend will get you.'

At that moment, Tor came toppling out of the house with a towel around her. She was dripping and pink from her bath, and when she saw Aisling standing at the tree with her coat on, her round cheeks whitened.

'Not sick, dear. But very rash, if you think you'll find what you're looking for out there.'

Tor took a step forward, and Aisling instinctively backed away. The gun glinted in her free hand, a winking silver eye. 'We have to muddle through somehow, Aisling. You may not understand yet, but it's all for the best. You're happy. Come here. Come home.'

'Feodor's been here.'

Tor's shoulders drooped so suddenly that she almost let go of the towel. Georgie spun to look at her, eyes wide, and caught the guilty rise of blood in her neck and cheeks. He picked up the dead rabbit from the floor and held it to him, like a toy. 'Feo died,' he said softly. 'He died in the big town fire. You said. We had a memorial. We planted the boundary tree. I cried. Tor?'

Tor turned her face away to the house, to the chickens, to the vegetables she planned to pick that day. A look of awful defeat passed over her. She hoisted her towel close and met the eyes of the two young people staring at her. 'There's only so much I can control.' She raised the gun. 'I'm quite good with this. I can nick you safely, shins, upper arms. If you move suddenly, I could get a blood vessel. A bone. I've no way to fix you if that happens. Please.'

Aisling's feet twitched, aching to go. 'What's so terrible about out there? I've been out there.'

'I know you have. And so does Feodor. Believe me, Aisling, you don't want him to catch you. Him, or worse people.'

Time muddled. First Aisling felt a hot pain, like a slap on sunburn. Then a crack made her jump. After both these things, she saw the bark of the boundary tree beside her explode as a bullet penetrated it, shards of wood peppering her coat and face. Last, she saw Georgie, his mouth contorted into a silent 'O' as he rushed to Tor, who had dropped her towel, sobbing. The gun lay in the grass at her feet.

Time reared up. Aisling bolted into the woods. The last thing she heard as she sped across the fallen branches and the gullies was Tor's voice: 'We love you here. We love you.'

21

She couldn't remember the bloody poem.

The railway carriage had been in this direction. She was sure of it. But there was nothing waiting for her in this part of the woods, nothing but fallen pine trees making the journey maddeningly slow. In an effort to remain calm, she chanted Blake to herself:

'You don't believe – I won't attempt to make ye.
You are asleep - I won't attempt to wake ye.
Sleep on! Sleep on! While in your pleasant dreams of
Reason you may drink of...

'Something something. That's a tricky one. Okay. Um.'
She murmured the words to herself as she picked her way across a series of rotting logs:

'Mock on, mock on, Voltaire, Rousseau,
Mock on, mock on, till all is vain,
You throw the sand against the wind...'

And then it drifted off. She stopped, clenched her jaw in search of the next line.

'*And the wind blows it back again*! Yes. Everything's fine.'

Except she wasn't sure who Voltaire was. And Voltaire, whoever he or she was, did not exist here, just as supermarkets did not exist, or the Gregorian calendar. *You were born in June?* Georgie had asked. *Where's that?* Where once she would have thought nothing of turning to the Internet or opening an old-fashioned encyclopedia, now she was struck by the awful possibility that if she didn't know it by now, she would never know it at all.

She looked around her at the featureless woodland. How could she have almost memorised *Wanderlust*'s features on the pre-Incan ruins of Columbia, but lack the most basic knowledge of navigation? And why, come to think of it, did she assume that she would find Chase? She had a small knife, a cigarette lighter and a coat. Her younger self would have had fun in these woods, imagining tiny creatures watching her from behind the curly fanfares of bracken. Little eyes and little minds wondering who she was. But sooner or later, it would get dark.

'If thought is life
And strength and breath,
And the want
Of thought is death…'

Panic threatened.
Wield. Come on.

What would the therapists say, in their cardigans and modest heels, smiling questioningly? *You believe that by flexing a mental muscle, as it were, you can affect – control, even – the fundamental rhythms of the universe?*

Her resolve wavered. 'Well,' she said to no one. 'It's worth a go.'

She straightened up, brushed the moss off the bottom of her jeans, and continued to where the landscape began to rise in a steep hill. Tor's cries still echoed in the soreness of her cheek where the splinters had caught her. But she hadn't lapsed into a dream-state to just be pinned by more rules. *Never lock the bathroom door, you can't learn to drive with your condition, let me see you swallow that pill.* She crunched through the leaves with gritted teeth. If she was mad now, she was mad on her own terms.

As Aisling climbed the hill, she realised with cautious excitement that this was the first time since living with Edythe that she had been fully, consciously alone. It was like old times, when she was still allowed out by herself, walking to school or picking up groceries when Beverley felt depressed. She could almost envision a cycle path ahead, or hear the rush of traffic on some nearby A-road, just out of sight. Then, as if her idle mind had willed it into being, her boot struck a rusty tin of beans and sent it spinning down the dirt path and into a clearing. The clatter startled a magpie grubbing in the undergrowth and it soared over her head and up to the lead tiles of the forbidding spire of a church.

I'm back, she thought, and reflexively began to retreat – what good it would do – but the wood was the same as ever, the air as clean and silent as before, with the hint of waves crashing on an unseen shore. It was a church, all right, but not Edythe's father's. The same nave, spire, big arched door. But while Edythe's church lay politely dormant, this was a wanton wreck. The magpie pecked at the vines wheedling in and out of the roof's bare rafters, throwing clods of moss down into the cavity of the building. Impatient roots had long ago disrupted the path to the entrance, splitting it up like an old spine.

There was something about the place that nudged a distant part of her mind. High on the roof, the magpie hurled down another clod of moss. Seeing there was nothing good to eat beneath it, the bird took off over the pines with a shriek. The thought was gone.

She had to squat and shuffle under the rotting porch door. A deep thrill went up through her spine: this was the kind of discovery that happened long ago, when the world was unfettered and unmapped. Eyes adjusting, she saw that there were no pews or furnishings in the cavernous space, no stained glass or discarded Bibles. Slowly, she made her way to the centre of the chamber, noting the small, regular indentations in the stone floor, suggesting long, narrow rows of desks. Between each pair of deep indents were soft, rounded ovals, shuffled slowly into existence over decades. She paused to settle her boots into one such hollow, and her mind wandered. She could almost hear the *scritch-scritch* of nibs.

But this was a bad place for her imagination to take control. One of the columns supporting the roof had collapsed, leaving blocks of masonry scattered across the flagstones. And there, in the far corner, in the ruins of a small sub-chamber, was the tumbledown shape of a tent.

She had already stood there long enough for anyone who knew the church and its quietest corners to creep between her and the exit. Aisling took out Chase's little knife. On seeing the blunt edge, her inner voice remarked unhelpfully, *What are you going to do? Methodically saw his head off?*

She was about to obey that voice and crawl under the door again when curiosity intervened. Chase had shown her an entrance to the tunnels beneath the abandoned home of a tramp. It was possible that there was another here. With blunt knife half-heartedly brandished, she walked to the tent as quietly as she could.

Tent was too grand a word. A slapdash system of ropes and sticks held up a large blue tarpaulin. A curtain embroidered with discoloured sunflowers hung halfway over the entrance, weighted into place with lumps of rubble. Inside was a mattress succumbing to wet black rot. Blankets were cast indiscriminately around the tent along with spent matches and chalk stubs littering the flagstones. Sweetness For Bitter Times on a cardboard carton mashed into the floor.

No personal effects remained, save a fragment of mirror, grubby with the prints of absent fingers. Aisling raised it to her face as though she could catch a glimpse of whoever had lived in this lonely space. In the blue glare of the tarpaulin, three dried rivulets of blood formed a fork down her cheek. *'I'm good with this,'* Tor had said. Aisling wished she could stop replaying the look of distress on the older woman's face.

It wasn't too late to turn back. She had been careful to take note of unusual trees and interesting formations of roots across her path. *Of course*, said that helpful voice, *everything was bound to look remarkable and noteworthy to her, coming from a street with three bus stops on each side of the road.* Seeing her own helplessly stupid expression in the mirror, she put it down.

She tried moving the mattress aside to look for a hidden entrance. The mould on the underside was thick. It sucked at her fingers. She sat back in disgust, and the littered matches crunched under her feet. As if in answer, a scuffling sound came from the chapel's entrance. Aisling froze.

Ducking under the door was a man. He was short in stature and gaunt, with a Rasputin-wild beard that was crusty with food and snot.

For a moment, in which Aisling's heart beat so hard she could feel it in her teeth, the evening clouds shifted and cast a wash of light down through the rafters between them. She prayed it meant he couldn't see her.

The man was muttering intently, a stream of rhythmic mm-mm-mms broken by more distinct fragments: 'How could— Couldn't do— Not a— Water for the— Knife in the— No— Should? No… Yes? No.'

Without moving, for fear of giving herself away, Aisling searched the room for some crevice she could slip into until he left. But aside from a large rock in the room's centre, there was nowhere close enough to dash to, and he was trudging slowly towards her now, a heavy bag slung across his narrow body. Before the spark of resolve left her, Aisling took a breath and stood up.

At once, the man halted. His eyes bulged, and for a moment she was sure he would turn and sprint away. But as the shock faded from his face, he regarded Aisling with his chin tilted into his chest, like a guilty dog. Slowly, very slowly, he removed the satchel hanging across his body. The hem of his shirt rode up to reveal a flash of hipbones, splashed with bruises fresh and fading. He put the heavy bag down and came to her. Aisling was fixed where she stood, unable to speak as his dark eyes met hers, with what? Dread? Disbelief? When they were less than a metre apart, and Aisling was standing in the mildew-sweat stink of him, the man raised his right hand, as if to wave hello. When she didn't react, he extended his bony index finger. The breath hitched in Aisling's throat. She knew what he would do.

He placed the cold tip of a finger firmly on the end of Aisling's nose.

'Real,' he croaked.

His hand hovered in the space between them. For some unfathomable reason, remembering so keenly the cold, electric sensation of her fingertip against his skin that night in Edythe's house, Aisling wanted more proof. *Do it again*, she thought, and as if she had said it out loud, his tremulous hand came down upon her wrist. The nails pinched where the broken tips rasped against tendons.

'Really here,' he said. 'Aren't you?'

This was not the Feodor she knew. This skinny man with terrible breath and hair matted almost into dreadlocks was stroking the softest part of her wrist, stroking, testing, his little finger a wishbone waiting to be snapped, and just as she decided she'd had enough, his voice shifted from quiet fascination to a hoarse growl of threat.

'You ain't taking me nowhere.'

She wrenched away her arm and caught him off balance. She burst into a run. He tripped after her, a skittering whippet of a man, but he moved slower than his size suggested and Aisling was at the door, about to duck under, when the chase came to an abrupt end. The hand that had touched her nose was pawing at the small of his back. The other trembled against the large chunk of stone in the centre of the chamber, the knuckles white with effort or pain. With a whine, he collapsed.

Silence draped itself over the chapel. The magpie returned to the roof, listening for further signs of the outburst that had disturbed his scavenge. Aisling saw the glint of the glossy beak through the shattered rafters. Feodor was still.

This. Is your chance. To escape.

As Aisling's thighs began to cramp, the magpie resumed pecking about on the roof. Hunks of moss began to rain down upon Feodor's prone body. One green chunk dropped into the mass of greasy hair. A second bounced off the rim of his slack mouth, sprinkling dirt over his hollow cheeks. Feodor didn't so much as twitch. With a small prayer that she wouldn't regret it, Aisling stood and walked back to him.

Despite having collapsed so many times herself, Aisling had never seen anyone else pass out. When Feodor's body hit the floor, she had been assaulted by a jumble of thoughts: *he's dead! A trick! Disease, go!* Now she found herself tilting his head to inspect the sickly tone of his face. The skin was too thin. It reminded her of papyrus behind museum glass. Was that what she looked like, she wondered, when Beverley found her on the bathroom floor? Something fragile and not to be touched?

She brushed the moss from his face. A knife lay by his side, and she had the presence of mind to tuck it into her pocket along with Chase's, though both blades would have struggled to slice blancmange. Feodor smelled like Beverley did when she was dieting too strictly, a whiff of almonds on each shallow breath.

'Alive,' she said with relief. His fall had dislodged his shirt, and again she was confronted by the jagged landscape of his pelvis, bruises pricked where fleas had flocked to the tasty pools of blood. She grimaced. 'After a fashion.'

And now what? If he sprang into life, he'd only attack her again, but the thought failed to worry her as much as it ought. She had survived being shot at and the experience had left her elated. More than anything, she knew how terrible it was to wake from a dead faint to find oneself alone. She slipped her hands under his armpits – *I'm mad, that's my excuse* – and began, with difficulty, to drag.

The mattress *squished* as she lugged him on to it, and she noticed with embarrassment that at some point during the journey he'd wet himself. Should she strip him before the ammonia started to burn his flea bites? She sat to catch her breath before realising that fleas liked to jump. And there were drying puddles of vomit all around. How could she have missed them the first time?

'What am I doing?' she panted. 'What am I doing?'

The wings of Feodor's ribcage fluttered; the brittle palpitations of a moth.

Poor thing should be in a hospital, she thought, but did they have hospitals here? An absurd image sprang to mind of a pair of paramedics jogging into the chapel, lugging an ECG machine. *'Are you able to answer me, Aisling? You've had a little seizure. I'm just going to take off your shoes and do a test of your reflexes with this stick. It won't hurt, but it will feel a bit weird as I run it along the sole of your foot, okay?'*

She bit her lip. It brought her back. She pulled her sleeves over her hands and stood up, stomping the drying mud off her boots. Fleas or no fleas, she could do as she pleased.

Twilight was coming. Her rational side told her to take a chunk of chalk and leave a message on the floor. *Had to go. Get well soon.* The windows on the chapel's west side were lit up in slender, Gothic relief, displaying the east walls smattered with a seemingly endless mass of – Aisling blinked – writing.

She stepped out into the main chapel. Here were walls of words arranged in columns, scratched in chalk and later carved from the soft rock. Silky beneath her fingers like the soapstone moonstruck hare in that therapist's waiting room – what was her name? Aisling couldn't recall. Something in the side of her head was tingling, and she pawed at it unthinkingly. She knew this wall just as she knew the words, just as she could envision Feodor scrawling them in haste, glancing over his shoulder at every crack and rustle of the woods outside.

She walked the length of the wall, taking in its enormity. Feodor must have had years to do all this alone, but the writing had not been updated for some time. Awaiting carving, the final chalk paragraphs were beginning to fade.

I just wanted to make—better

—thought that was the point

—all—fault

s—

RADA

Aisling felt lightheaded. All those hours she'd spent scribbling in her journal; meaningless, therapeutic waffle to pass the time. *My name is Feodor. Stay with me.* The man on the mattress shifted in his stupor. A bubble of mucus throbbed in one nostril.

Veils and doors and things passing through.

...treacle in my hair. Germaine took me to the garden and cut it, thick, sticky clumps on the grass with the rest of the rubbish...

...people came from everywhere to see me. Treated me like some kind of, I don't even know, Prince? Like the one they called...

'This is insane.'

It went on for metres and metres. Fractured paragraphs of guilt and storytelling.

What I did, I did for the good of the people.

'What did you do?' she whispered. She read as fast as she could, skimming over illegible sentences carved hastily in bad light. But Aisling could find no trace of whatever crime he was supposed to have committed. It was as if the reader was expected to already know. Black mould had crept across the walls where the constant stream of stagnant rainwater slowly trickled down from the gutters. Whole passages were coated in foul wet blossoms of the stuff. Her skin itched just looking at it.

Rada rada radad dad ra—

Finally, her eyes fell upon a full passage.

The first pair of friendly eyes I saw here were Arthur's, a man in a big brown hat patiently waiting for a logical reason for a boy to be lying inside a broken barrel in the street. I would've liked to hear it, especially as the barrel had recently been full of something black and sticky, and I had no memory of thinking what a great idea it'd be to climb inside for a sleep. I remembered Mister Benedict, all right. I remembered L, and worse things. But this?

Arthur. I couldn't tell if he'd lift me up and brush me down or give the barrel a good kick and send me rolling off down the street.

'That,' he said, finally, 'looks uncomfortable.'

Home: Arthur opened the door and a waft of something delicious hit us. In a kitchen hung with herbs and knives, a woman with a shaved head was reading a book and stirring something on the stove. A stocky boy about my age straddled a chair, playing with a rubber band. From his light coffee colouring, I guessed he was Arthur and the woman's son. When I came in, he sat up straight. 'Mum,' he said, and it startled her.

'I found a little boy,' Arthur said.

The woman put down the spoon, but not the book. I heard a hiss as the food began to stick to the pan. Her voice was low and (to my teenage brain) totally irresistible: 'A little—? Why, he's at least the same age as Germaine. Look at his lip, there's a moustache there, almost. Where did you find him? Is he... Did you...?'

'Perhaps, and no,' said Arthur.

She turned her sexy voice on me. 'Are you homeless, young man?'

'Yes,' I said, quickly. A sweet glob of treacle dripped out of my hair, and I licked it off my chin.

They sat me in front of a bowl of red goulash. They watched me eat in silence, all three of them, around the modest dining room table in a storeroom crammed with boxes of all kinds of junk. The shelf above the son, Germaine, was packed with battered toys. A wind-up dog dangled over the edge as though *it would fall at the slightest vibration. I couldn't stop glancing at it, willing it to drop on to his head.*

Arthur led the interrogation. 'Where are your parents?'

'Dead,' I said, and filled my mouth with bread. Something in the back of my brain flickered, a guilty image of Rada, really dead, really really, and I bit my tongue.

'And so you live on the streets?' Eva asked.

I looked down into my food in case the joy swelling inside me slipped out. Eva had already made up her mind to keep me. I stuck the spoon in my mouth and made an effort to look tragic.

'Why haven't I seen him, then?' the son said, and my joy evaporated. He looked me hard in the eye, and I stared back. 'I'd've seen him.'

'Germaine, do you know what social privilege is?' Eva said. 'No? Then don't participate.'

'You have to keep moving,' I said quietly. 'People don't like you settling down.' I thought of the tramp on the bench in the playground, lowing like a heifer as the boys drenched his parka. 'Last place I was in— I had a friend. Proper arthritic old guy, but all right, you know? We chose the wrong place to sleep one night, and— And the things they did to him, miss. I tried to fight them, but—' And all of a sudden I was crying into my goulash. Really crying. I surprised myself.

Germaine regarded me with undisguised loathing. But Arthur, to my amazement, placed his hand on my arm.

'Lad, there's no explaining to do. If my wife agrees, I have an offer to make, and I hope you'll take it.'

'Yes,' Eva said, 'he can work in the shop, can't he? He can help Germaine stock the shelves.'

This didn't please Germaine. 'You're already having

another baby. What do you need him for? Where's my say?'

'You have a bed, a job, and food you don't have to pay for,' said Eva, mildly. *'That's quite enough.'*

Arthur agreed. *'We can offer you a place to sleep. Nothing fancy. And you earn your keep.'* But then the look he gave me made the food in my mouth turn to concrete. *'There's one condition.'*

On the mattress, Feodor gave a little snore. Flakes of dry skin fluttered in the shudders of his breath.

My first job! The first real job I ever had, and the only one. Six months of sweeping the floor, lugging crates and polishing old pewter tankards with cloths that made my hands go black. I worked from seven in the morning until seven at night, and I'd never been so happy in my whole life. We'd have breakfast together, all four of us, at the table in the storeroom before the sun came up. I want to freeze the image of them as they were. Arthur, serious and silent at the head of the table, looking over that week's sales and loans. He never relaxed, never took off his big brown hat. He probably slept in it. His straight-talk with the customers and his firm hand with Germaine. No slaps, no yelling, just the occasional 'Now then, what's this nonsense?' This was a proper man!

And Eva. I'd never seen a woman with a shaved head before. It's—

Aisling paused. The derelict shop in the town, the names above the door. Something else troubled her. Despite all his talk of a new life with a new family, no one seemed to be looking for Feodor. What's more, Feodor didn't seem to care.

It's amazing what you can just accept.

They told me I had to be mute. I could talk when it was just the three of them there, behind doors. Anywhere else, I had to pretend I couldn't so much as sneeze.

I told myself I'd wandered into one of those communes for religious weirdos, without cars and TVs. Maybe the government had let them have some land. It made enough sense, and enough was all I needed. If I had to be quiet in front of strangers in return for a warm house where no one ever threw up in the sink, that was fine by me. They even had a cranky old piano they let me play, and that was the best thing of all. I was half-watching Eva for the moment she'd whip out a Bible and do the 'Give in to Jesus, you grubby little heathen' bit, but she didn't. She reminded me of my Mama, the way she half-smiled all the time, always reading something, her own person, not just somebody's wife.

Amazing what you can just accept.

The sensation of itchiness spread down Aisling's sides, and she hugged herself.

That autumn, Eva taught me how to speak 'like a gentleman'. The silent act was bound to fall flat at some point, Arthur kept saying, and how many total mutes did one come across? That in itself would draw attention. And what about the inevitable moment when I dropped a box of cash on my foot and swore in front of the customers? 'People will talk,' Arthur said, 'even if you don't.' Eva (so pregnant that I kept thinking she'd topple over) took down the gardening books no one ever bought on account of the sun never shining, and she used them to teach me how to speak so I didn't sound funny. We sat in the garden with cups of tea, struggling with the clunky sounds of old words in my mouth. "A com-i-cal enough vegetable, the leek, with his hairy head and weedy, un-ath-let-ic legs, but how in-val-u-able an addition to one's garden." Eva, I sound like a knob.'

But Eva smiled at me. 'You sound like yourself.'

She didn't know what I was really like. I don't think she would've understood.

Those first few weeks, the nightmares still came. I was in Mister Benedict's flat, lying on the bathroom carpet while his guests filed in to tug at my clothes and blow smoke in my eyes. Always it ended with L kneeling by my head with his stupid orange hair. 'You can turn a bad place good,' I told him, and again he laughed, 'What, you?' before pouring a cold can of lager down my spine. I once woke up to find Germaine in the doorway, his wiry hair illuminated by the moon in the window behind him. 'I'll catch you talking in your sleep one day,' he said. 'Then we'll know what's what.'

Germaine hated Feodor, and they fought whenever possible. The boys competed for Arthur's favour, and Eva was grateful for Feodor's eagerness to help in the kitchen while Germaine stomped off to meet his friends. He even offered antenatal nutritional advice, something Aisling didn't think someone who'd lived their entire life on takeaway pies ought to be giving.

'You've got to be careful with tinned fish, it's the mercury, bad for babies. I saw it on the telly.'

'I think you've got a bit of Foreign in you,' Germaine said one day, while his parents dealt with customers. 'There's

*something queer. Where'd you come from? You're like a short
little Foreigner.'*

*He punctuated each word with a kick to my ankle. I
carried on cleaning the medals an old soldier brought in that
morning. Arthur and Eva let me sleep in their house and eat
their food, but I assumed bashing their son's head in would
be the limit of their hospitality.*

*'I know someone who'd like to meet you, mute boy.'
Germaine flicked one clean medal off the counter and on to
the dirty floor. I forgot all about hospitality. We were the same
height, so I only had to swing my right hand, still holding the
cleaning rag, and knock him in the sternum. He tripped back
into the wall, a big, dark patch of moisture on his shirt where
the flammable grease sank eagerly into the fabric.*

*'If you're not careful, Germaine my lovely, I'll set a fire
under your bed one night and burn a chunk out of your arse
so you'll never sit straight again'.*

A thick flap of mould covered the following passages
nearest the floor. Had Feodor done something to Germaine?
Was that the terrible event that led him to flee to the chapel?
That abandoned pawnshop, chalky with soot. Where was
that family now?

*The old soldier came to ask for an extension on the loan
Arthur granted for those medals, but Arthur was out fetching
the salted pork Eva had a craving for, and Eva herself was
in the garden, dozing with a book in her lap. Germaine was
out with his mates, as usual. I reminded myself I was mute,
keeping my tongue firmly between my front teeth as I went
out to deal with him.*

He wasn't as old as I'd originally judged him, this soldier. Maybe fifty-something. He walked as if his hip was hurting him, and with no stick to lean on he resembled a lopsided badger ambling out of his sett. When I gestured to the empty shop, indicating I was alone, the soldier huffed so hard that tufts of his beard wafted like plumes of smoke.

'Buggeration. I don't suppose you know if he's in an amenable mood today, d'you, your boss? I need the pennies. I have cats to feed. Imagine me outrunning a bailiff.'

The soldier dropped down on to the pew pushed against the wall for the unlikely event of a busy day. Lots of people blowing off loans, leaving collateral. Arthur was doing well to hide his concern at the falling profits, but I noticed the frown lines under his big brown hat.

When it became apparent the soldier was setting up for a long stay, I took off my apron and dropped it on to the floor before hopping over the counter. To my delight, he was missing two fingers on his right hand. This guy had seen some action. When he caught me staring, I mimed fetching a glass of water.

He patted his anorak pocket. 'Got a sandwich. Sardines.'

I still hadn't mastered the art of conveying the long streams of information you take for granted when you're free to make noise. You probably don't want to sit there too long, I wanted to say. If Germaine comes back with his mates, they'll make a joke of your hand.

'Oh, just bloody talk! I'm no fool. And you're no mute.'

I nearly dropped.

'Name?'

I chewed the tip of my tongue. Eva was still outside. When she was engrossed in a book, you could drop a piano out of *the window and she wouldn't flinch.*

'Come on. Name. What do they call you? Raggy-hair? Loppy-face? He Who Gawps?'

'Feodor,' I said. It came out of me like a hiccup.

'That a lisp, Theodor?'

'Feodor,' I said, louder. 'With an F.' F for, If Arthur walked in, I was fucked.

'And your boss, when's he back?'

'Just popped out to the butchers.'

'Today? Well, he'll be there for a fortnight, the summer quails are delivered today. Everyone wants one. Why didn't he send Germaine? Little shit out gallivanting, I take it?'

I smiled. 'Maybe you should come back.'

'You're no son of Arthur's. Least not via the wife. What are you?'

What could I say? Arthur and Eva hadn't decided what to tell people. Idiot apprentice, Germaine had suggested, and Eva had shouted at him. A retard was a seriously bad thing to be around here, I was learning.

'You're horrid pale, boy. Once upon a time, they recommended people get a good hour of sun per day. You never saw children with the coughs and the rickets, like you do now.' He lowered his voice and leaned towards me, anorak crunching. 'In some ways, them old days was better.'

A woman and her two galloping children came past the window, and for the brief moment when they looked as though they might come in, the soldier stiffened up.

'Where do you hail from?' he asked, when they were gone.

'Bow.'

'You'll have to be gentle with me. Got knocked on the head by a falling roof tile in the last war.'

'Bow.' *I softened my accent, thinking of Eva.* 'East London.'

'Good there? Bow, East London?'

The old fantasy of the tower blocks sheathed in flames lit up inside me, and I didn't know how to feel. Mama had a phrase she used whenever the subject of horrible estates came up. 'Just a place on the way to somewhere else,' *I said. The soldier patted the pew. I sat.*

'So white you're almost green. I could've mistaken you for a little prince, all done up in rags.'

My clothes were hardly rags. Eva had washed the hoodie and done a good job of repairing the ratty hems of my jeans. But I liked the soldier. I may have been out of practice, but there were no veiled intentions in his words that I could hear.

'I am a prince, actually,' *I said.* 'I'm taking some time off.'

'You see, I knew from the off. That, I said to myself coming through that door, is an unusual boy. That's a boy who oughtn't be polishing old men's medals. Watch that boy, I told myself. Mute act all part of it, I assume?'

'My regal accent gives me away.' *I used one of Eva's new words. Regal. I was happy.*

The soldier rubbed the stumps of his missing fingers absently. 'And is there a king in charge of this Bow of yours, pale prince Feodor? A queen?'

He didn't want to hear about my parents, I realised with relief. This was still a game. So I straightened my back and crossed one leg over the other, all queenie, and it made him chuckle into his beard.

'Well! There's a queen,' *I lisped.* 'She's got a palace. You see her on the news sometimes, giving out prizes, stuff like that. She does a speech at Christmas, but I've never seen it.'

'And does she wear a crown, this queen?'

'No! Well, she does on stamps. In real life, she wears these nasty flowery old-lady dresses.'

The soldier listened patiently. 'And is she a good queen? Do you like her?'

'Nah. She can't make decisions, or anything. The Prime Minister does that.'

The soldier groped his pocket for the sardine sandwich. The foil was flecked with cat hair, which he picked off. 'Well, golly gosh. And now you're here. Different sort of place altogether.'

'I like it,' I said.

'Easy journey? Getting here?'

'Arthur found me in a treacle barrel on the side of the road.'

'And what were you doing inside a treacle barrel on the side of the road?'

'Don't know.'

'How does one come to be inside a treacle barrel on the side of the road without knowing why? And don't say "drunk". You're a clean boy. I see it.'

I'd been on the brink of giggles until he said that. A clean boy? Me?

'Left a bad lot?' he asked gently.

What would Mama have said? 'Worse than some, better than others.'

'And what do you like about it here? Don't tell me, the big old pleasure mansions on the east side? Everyone secretly likes looking at those. The long stained glass windows all lit up at night. Or the gin factories! I bet you like the smell of the juniper when the morning deliveries come in.'

'To tell the truth, I haven't seen any of that stuff. I've hardly been outside since I arrived.'

'Arthur's not playing the slave-driver, is he?'

'No. No, he's brilliant. I love Arthur.'

'Well, we all love Arthur. Even when he won't budge on a loan. But what's all this business with you being mute? It's not like Arthur to insist on something silly like that. It was his idea, I take it?'

'It was. And I don't know.'

'And you just did as he asked?'

'Yes.'

'Didn't ask questions?'

I resented his tone. 'Well, there's a lot of things I don't understand. Like, why's there no electricity? Where does Germaine go to school? I don't think he does go. And what is half of this stuff? Like that.' I pointed at a metal frame housing what looked like two rolling pins controlled by a large cog. 'What the hell is that?'

'You don't have washing mangles in Bow?'

'There's a launderette down the high street.' I must have looked furious, because the soldier threw back his head and laughed. He slapped my knee, again, nothing sinister to it, so I forgave him for laughing at me.

It had been a wet week, and the stumps of his fingers were pink and sore. Without thinking, I reached out and closed my fist around them.

We sat like that for a while, saying nothing.

He withdrew from me almost reluctantly. The stumps, where the flesh had been sewn shut around prongs of bone, were soft and rounded, the angry colour gone. The soldier's eyes were suspicious.

'And how did you do that, pale prince?'

'Mind over matter?' I suggested cheerfully. I knew nothing back then. Nothing.

'Well, *misguided treacle boy, whatever it is you are, you're new. And I have just what a new boy needs.*' The soldier *reached inside his anorak and handed me a small packet. It was like a business card, only the centre was a foil-wrapped strawberry bonbon that popped out when I squeezed it. I glanced at the card. A cameo image of a woman with a huge hairstyle holding to her lips what looked like a dick on a stick. A signature squiggled underneath the woman, and the tagline:* Through Sweetness, Light.

'*My Mister Borghese will put you right. You need money, he'll get you money. Need to find someone, he'll know how. And his peanut brittle is unsurpassed.*'

'*So I should go and find this guy?*'

'*I reckon you'll prove sufficiently interesting to warrant a personal visit.*'

Before I had time to ask him what he meant, the shop door opened with a tinkle of a bell, and I was up on my guilty feet. It was a tall young guy with blond hair sticking out in all directions like he'd been sleeping in a bush.

'*That leather coat in the window,*' *he said.* '*It's for sale, isn't it?*'

The old soldier chuckled. '*There's no use asking this one, mate. He's mute.*'

At the mention of Borghese, Aisling's heart tripped up. As she stepped past another wide strip of mould, something in her chest turned cold.

My teeth turned bad with sugar. I lived on gifts of fudge and lemon drops and coffee beans covered in chocolate. And love, I went sickly with love. My followers wrote poems to

'The Pale Prince'. They drew pictures of him with streams of hearts beaming out from his palms, sang songs in pubs and in parlours to their children.

My what? Followers? Oh, yes. It happened fast.

Soon after my meeting with the old soldier, they came. At first, they pretended to look at the shelves of dancing shoes and the badly-stuffed stoats, but it was me they wanted: staring, smiling, coaxing eye contact. The man with the baby with the sore on its forehead; the woman lugging the dog with the bad eyesight; the couple unable to have kids. 'Is it true?' they asked. 'That you took the pain from Mister Borghese's manservant's fingers?'

Arthur knew nothing.

'Profits up twenty per cent on last month, Eva. It won't last.'

Then, the gifts. Treats blocking the shop door at opening time. Bottles of gin with labels tied to the necks – Remember little Adam's bad leg – handkerchiefs sewn with the initials of sick grandmothers, honey jars with letters taped to the lids, pocket watches, leather gloves.

Visitors filled the shop from morning to closing time: 'We want to see the boy.'

'Germaine is on an errand,' Arthur said.

'Not your son. The new boy. He looked kindly on Mrs Morten's ugly daughter, and the scars from her pox faded overnight!'

I crouched on the back stairs, listening through the bannisters to the voices of these strangers, getting louder and more urgent with each passing day.

'Did he polish those spoons? I must have them.'

'Bring him to my factory tonight. We all need to hear him speak. Our Friend is weakening, they say.'

Arthur did his best, but by the end of the week, I was a problem he could no longer ignore. He banished me to the kitchen, but the visitors broke in through the back yard and Arthur had to wield a pair of coal tongs to stop them from dragging me out into the street.

'He cannot speak. I do not know what you've been told, but while these malicious rumours continue, you are not welcome in my shop.'

It was as he struggled to force the crowd outside that a girl I'd barely noticed amongst the surge of bodies threw herself across the counter and grabbed a handful of my hair. I was terrified as she pulled my face close to hers.

'When Our Friend hears of this,' she hissed through rotten teeth, 'you're done for.'

I don't remember the first boy they threw off the clock tower. It sounds terrible now, but back in Bow you'd hear of the craziest things happening on drunken nights out, and it didn't touch you. Once, two men walked into a pub, got this guy they'd been looking for, held him down on the table he'd been drinking at and whacked off both his hands with an axe. The news-stands the next morning said HATCHET HANDS HORROR, and I cut the headline out and stuck it on my wall. It was the same here. Wild things happened, and people went 'Ooh,' and 'Dreadful,' and then forgot.

The second boy was taken up by two men in full view of the midday shoppers. Arthur came in one morning with a pint of the goat's milk Eva liked, and they went into the kitchen together. They stayed there for a long time before Arthur came out alone and told Germaine and I what had happened. The first was considered an accident on account of the old railings being so wobbly. He'd been a good boy, from a family people generally liked. But this second boy, he was almost identical to look at as the first. And both boys, both dead boys thrown off the tower, were almost identical to look at as me.

I was forbidden to leave the house.

'I told you never to speak. Not to anyone. You're new,' Arthur said. 'Don't you have any idea what that means for my family? All this talk of tower blocks and cities far away. Don't you see how people will think you're mad?'

That's when they sent me away.

The guy with the blond hair and the leather coat came one day. He and Arthur talked, and that was that. I was to go and live in what Arthur called 'the wasteland'. A place for wasted things. There was a woman there who'd look after me. It would all be all right, Eva said. But she clutched Germaine to her, and I knew she was afraid.

>•<

When Feodor awoke, he was almost tearful, looking about the chapel with incomprehension before fixing on the hem of Aisling's coat, her tangled hair, her expression of concern. He sank back, shuddering. 'Jesus,' he exhaled. 'Christ.'

Aisling forced a reassuring smile. 'It's all right. I moved you,' she said. 'Sorry. I didn't want to make it worse.'

'Someone's always dragging me somewhere,' he muttered. Full sensibility had not yet returned. 'Hey, your knuckles, I can... I can do someth— Hey.' He was reaching for her hands when his grey eyes widened almost to the limits of their sockets. Aisling shifted backwards in anticipation of another lunge, but instead of throwing himself at her he flopped on to his back, hands scrabbling at the wet patch between his legs. 'What the hell? What did you—?'

Aisling averted her eyes. 'It can happen when you move someone unconscious. It's happened to me a few times. I should have thought. Sorry.'

'What, so you let me marinade in my own piss?' He scrubbed at the fabric, as if his broken fingernails could absorb the worst of it. 'How long have I been out?'

She blushed. Of course he'd be hostile. Why wouldn't he be?

'Fifteen minutes,' she said. 'Maybe twenty.'

Damp black curls fell over his eyes, and he viewed her from under them, secretive, thinking.

'And now I get to see you.'

The shape of the chapel amplified the distant sounds of the shore. The tide must be coming in. She tried to imagine the place on a sunny day, with the light dappling through the rafters and the flagstones warm, but instead all she saw was the lake down beside Tor's house, the way the pebbles in the shallows were the same green as Chase's eyes. She wished he were here.

'Do you have some spare trousers?'

The huff could have been dismissal or pain. 'Every time you've been here, I've known,' he told her. 'You're quiet and you move well with the shadows, but I've seen you. So don't talk to me like I'm stupid.'

'No, don't get up, you'll faint again.'

He glowered, but did as he was told.

'When it happens to me, it feels like I'm walking around in my own dead body afterwards. Words float around in my head and I can't grab them.' She pulled her coat around herself tightly and shrugged. 'I've never been here before. You're confused, but it passes.'

'Am I confused about this?' His arm snaked out and he brushed her nose with all four fingers.

It was a gentle enough gesture, but his fingers were wet, and she flinched. 'That didn't happen here,' she said. 'You'd slipped into my bedroom.'

'Unlikely.'

Aisling didn't know where to put her eyes, and settled on his dangling left hand, twitching finger by filthy finger, as if striking notes.

'Do you miss your piano?' she asked, and instantly regretted it.

'Yeah, you've been here,' he growled as she glanced guiltily at the writing on the walls. 'Had a good read, did you? You know, at first I thought you were a spy for Our Friend, someone coming to smother me in my sleep. But you don't have a clue, do you? What are you? Sixteen? Seventeen? Gangs of men with dogs come year after year, and they never get close. And now there's you.' He lay there on the filthy mattress, looking her over with cool disinterest. 'So what's wrong with you?'

'They don't know.' *Because it isn't a real thing, it's a pseudo thing.*

But Feodor appeared real enough, more so than she'd like, up on his elbows, checking the tent with fresh agitation. 'What've you taken? Empty your pockets. Let me see. Come on, move.'

The wildness in his eyes worried her. She moved slowly. Her knife, followed by his, and then the cigarette lighter. She laid them all out of his reach. In the half-light, a small lumpen thing cleaved to the blade of Feodor's knife, a sticky something from her pocket. Aisling covered the tooth with her hand. If Feodor had seen it, he didn't let on.

'I'm not here to steal from you,' she said, with the rotting roots pricking her palm.

Feodor eyed the knives before they disappeared back into Aisling's pocket. Another wave of lethargy carried him off, staring up at the ceiling, staring at nothing. Worry niggling inside her empty stomach, Aisling wondered how she was meant to extract herself from the situation.

'I've got no food,' he said, 'and if I did, I wouldn't share it.'

'I just wanted to make sure—'

'I'm fantastic. I'm about to nip down to Boots for some antibiotics and one of them body-building milkshakes.' He writhed against the mattress. Something in his back was making him grit his teeth. Mentally, she listed the items she could bring him: toothbrush, bedding, shaving razor. What was she thinking? Would she let someone like this loose with a razor?

'Look, get me water,' he said. 'From the barrel out the front, get me a drink.'

He meant the rusty oil drum she had seen on the way in. No wonder he was ill.

'I was on my way to the town when I found you. I can get a doctor.'

Feodor stared. Through his open mouth, Aisling could see the dark residue of his last meal caked over his molars.

'What, then?' she said. 'You're obviously seriously ill. Do you even have a way of washing those trousers?' When the mouth didn't close, she waved at the piles of vomit: one, two, six. 'If you stay here, you'll only get worse. That black stuff, it's toxic mould. I've read about it. In the Middle Ages, people ate grain covered in it. Masses of people had fits in the streets until they just rolled over and died. They thought it was judgement from God.'

Feodor blinked at her. 'Were they right?'

'If you'd let me tell someone you're here.'

'You can't just wander into town.'

'There have to be doctors there. I could get them to come here so you wouldn't have to walk.'

'No and no and *no*.' He scratched at his scalp, eyes squeezed shut. 'I'm not welcome there. You ain't, neither.'

'That's not true. I've been there.'

The hand scratching his scalp turned into a fist, and he tugged at his hair so hard she half expected to see the dirty hank come loose. 'I know! I followed you. I saw you down in the tunnels. *This* close, we were, at the mouth of Sorry Street. You had that idiot look on your face like, *The rules don't apply to me, I'm having an adventure!* And then Chase the Wonderdog came and whisked you off before I'd decided what to do with you. How did you persuade him to show you the tunnels back? 'Cause I bet it wasn't the same way I did when it was my first time.'

She chose to ignore the challenge in his face, meant to suggest something she'd rather not think about. 'You know Chase.'

Feodor laughed. He laughed hard, until pain bit into the small of his back and he curled up, panting. 'Tor's told you nothing. And that's not your fault. It's what she does. But she told me a fair bit about you. How you think this is all a strange little dream. Yeah? Pretty blond boys and fairy-tale houses in the woods. And how you think you're special here, because everyone's going, "A new girl, a new girl," and that we should *keep* it that way. I bet no one gave a shit about you at home. And that's what scares me. 'Cause that's how it starts.'

Aisling was already on her feet.

'You're thinking you should've left me on the floor,' he said. 'Anybody else would've.'

'Oh, what?' She spun around and shouted at him. It caused a satisfying echo, even under the broken rafters. 'You know, I've read nearly everything on these walls, and I can't see a single decent reason for you living out here in this toxic archaeological *tomb*. When Chase took me through the tunnels, we came up into Arthur and Eva's pawn shop. No one had lived there for years. Why?'

His face froze in a mask of dismay. She had expected him to laugh, spit at her, anything, but the flaky line of his mouth drooped, and he looked so canine, so emaciated. *He's lived here for years*, she thought. *Alone.*

'You need a doctor,' she said quietly.

Feodor shook his head. With difficulty, he rolled on to his side, his wrists crossed like a body trussed up. His fingers twitched, striking those invisible keys. 'You tend to think of it as a dream at first. It's sort of, I dunno. Safe.'

There was wetness on Aisling's face, and she felt for the wound on her cheek. 'I used to write about you in my journal. It was like you were telling me all about yourself, and I had to write it down. And my aunt found my journal and she said, she said it was sick, all the things I'd written. That you've written, over there. I had to explain to her you were a daydream I used to have. That you're not real and you don't mean anything.' She emphasised the last words as if they could make him disappear. Reluctantly, she met the steady contact of his eyes.

'You're lucky I can't get up.'

He shifted closer to the edge of the mattress. The light fell on his face in such a way that Aisling almost saw the old Feodor, the boy who played the piano for his mother's praise and liked to burn newspapers in the park. She wanted to shave him, to wash him, to round out the hard contours of his bones. 'Have you tested yourself yet?' he asked her. 'Feel your face. If you can bleed a little, you can bleed a lot. I used to—'

'I don't want to know.'

'Ask me how long I've been here. Not here, in this room. Here.' He stretched his hands wide in an all-encompassing gesture that showed the white cracks in the dirty skin.

'No.'

'Ask me.'

'I'm leaving now.'

'Ten years.'

Her cheeks flushed as though he had slapped them.

'Those people left me offerings like I was some kind of saviour. I'd come from nowhere, just like Our Friend, they said. I liked it. I didn't have to *do* anything to be important to them. But then I started to see it. Anyone who spoke out about Our Friend, anyone who got sick, or depressed, or wanted the old religion back – they had a way of disappearing. You could be put away for drinking too much, or being born with one leg shorter than the other. Unwed mothers, asthma, interpreting dreams! Degenerates. Enemies within, dirtying the water. I hadn't seen how bad it was while I was shut up in Arthur's shop, but when they kicked me out…' He swallowed painfully with the exertion of speaking. 'I couldn't stay with Tor, not while all that was going on. So I did what you did. I went back. My people helped me hide fugitives down in the tunnels, get them out into the wasteland. We rioted. And I got them close, I got so damn close, but… Look, I know what it's like to think you're the molten centre of the universe, but there's history here, and people moulded by it. All the dukes and the duchesses before my time, and the blind priests and the summer balls. There's ancient cave paintings a few days' walk away. They didn't sprout up just for you. 'Specially not for me. I don't pretend to understand it. It's like there's a thin boundary between where we were before and wherever we are now. And you were almost through it when you touched me on the nose that night. But you're here now. And it's not just you, you know. Not just me. There's three.'

Aisling turned and crossed the floor as fast as she could without running. As she ducked under the door, Feodor's shout came echoing after her. 'Leave the knife, leave it, ah!' He had rolled off the mattress. 'You walk off with that and I'm dead.'

Aisling sent it skittering off like a pebble across water. 'Get up, come at me, make me believe you've been having me on.' But he looked at the knife and did nothing. Hauling himself back on to the mattress was exertion enough.

'Go back to Tor,' he told her. 'Have a quiet little life growing beans.'

She staggered out into the darkening woods. A pine tree offered a low branch to slump against. A slick of black mould was stuck to her sleeve; she scrubbed it against the bark.

None of this is real. You. Are. Mad.

Chase could be out sleeping under a bush by now with his

real friends, like that Jobi character he was so preoccupied with. What had led her to believe he wanted to see her at all? It was her fault he'd been sent away. She stared at his knife, trying to imagine his hand around the hilt. *Do something useful and stick in it your wrists*, said a cold-eyed, hateful Chase in her imagination.

Beside the chapel, the bracken fell away to a chalky slope, and Aisling slid down it into a gulley of tall plants topped with spikes of star-shaped blooms beginning to close for the night. With a pang, she recognised them from one of the arcane gardening books Chase dragged home from the town.

Asphodel, white sentinel of the tomb. With its blooms as sharp as tears shed alone, the asphodel is as hard to kill as grief itself. My regrets, says the asphodel, follow you to the grave.

Pushing through the throng, she came to stone steps cut into the ground, smothered in moss. The steps seemed to lead into nothing but, as she brushed aside the thick stems of the asphodels, Aisling saw an opening of blue-veined brick and her own reflection in the dark gleam of shallow water.

Sorry Street.

22

The first thing she saw as she wriggled out into the light was a shelf labelled Non-Perishables. Tins of Spam. Bird's instant custard. A jar of Heinz quince jelly glinted at eye level, bloody and dull.

Aisling was lying half-inside the priest hole in Edythe's cellar. It was unmistakable, down to the caustic tang of bleach rendering the thought of jam and custard unbearable. Her elbows cracked as she lifted herself up. It was the priest hole all right, a closed hollow in the wall, leading nowhere. She stretched, gave the interior wall a solid kick.

The journey from lying to standing took as long as a full tour of the house. She made it to the cellar stairs before needing to sit, resting her chin on the heels of her hands as the blood slowly coiled up into her tingling fingers. The light bulb hung above, the first artificial light she had seen in... she couldn't recall. Harsh and tawdry, leaving angry blotches in her sight.

She hauled herself out into the gleaming kitchen. The

daffodils outside bobbed gently as a midday breeze stirred the garden. The oven had been used recently, and the warmth was a balm to her aching joints as she leaned against it. The kitchen door was open, but there was no sign of anyone out in the oak-panelled hall or in the living room beyond. A statue of the Virgin stared placidly down at the chequered floor. Had that been there before?

The servants' stairs beckoned. As she scaled the first few uneven steps, dizziness swept over her and she dropped into a crouch. The door swung slowly shut, leaving her breathing unsteadily in the dark cavity as the house sighed around her like an old ship. How had she forgotten the foibles of brick-and-mortar buildings so quickly? There were many things she had forgotten, Aisling realised, as her fingers slipped through tiger stripes of soot on the walls, stretching down from the door above her. Scars visible in slices of daylight.

Something was coming. Someone else was in the house: Edythe, Robert, who else? The slap of a man's dress shoes followed by a clamour of women's heels tottering across the kitchen towards her. She shrank back, waiting for the door to fling open and the light to hit her, but nothing came.

Aisling returned to the kitchen to investigate. The house was silent. On the table, a beautiful bronze jelly mould waited to be filled. A Mrs Beeton recipe book lay open: General Observations on creams, jellies, soufflés, omelets & sweet dishes. *She tried to imagine Edythe focusing the taut elastic of her energy on something as frivolous as a wobbly red jelly. Scattered across the worktops were crumbs, crusts, empty tins of salmon. A discarded butter knife drooled soft yellow fat in the sunlight. There was even a tea towel on the floor, a hanging offence under Edy's regime. Aisling picked it* up and wiped the soot from her fingers.

Drifting out in the conservatory, Aisling discovered tea cooling in four Wedgwood cups. A currant bun christened with a fresh bite reminded her how long ago she had last eaten. The food looked fake, somehow. Like waxworks.

Aisling stood very still under the warmth of the summer sun. Energy like dust motes reeled around the room, unable to settle. One wicker chair was overturned.

Aisling twisted her thumb ring. A spool of time unwound. There was a girl in the garden. She sat on the grass beside the pond, where tall white flowers swayed in the breeze. One of her long socks had rolled down to her ankle, and the leather sandals were unbuckled. When she saw Aisling coming down the conservatory steps, she didn't move. Chin tilted up in an adult fashion, she called out:

'Will Mister Morgun be all right?'

As Aisling made her way across the lawn towards the pond, she could see the neat waves of the little girl's hair had come unpinned on one side, that there were cake crumbs down the front of her dress. She looked as though she had been ushered outside in a hurry, and was now alone.

The girl repeated her question. Aisling tried one of those false adult smiles she disliked and hoped the little girl would fall for it. 'I expect so, yes.'

The child took in Aisling's stained trousers and coat as if hoping this visitor might be some kind of country brigand.

'You can't see the little bathroom from here,' she said. 'That's where he was. I heard it.'

It.

Aisling sat on the grass.

'I knew he'd do something,' the girl said, a hint of emotion creeping into her voice. *'Edy knew, as well. And do you know what she said? She said, "Good".'*

Aisling followed her gaze up to the windows of the first floor, to the back bedroom where Aisling had stayed all those weeks ago. Robert's bedroom window was open. Lace curtains fluttered surrender.

'Your pockets,' said the girl. 'Show me.'

Aisling turned them out. Two winking emerald cufflinks. A gentle ripple went out across the pond.

'Daddy will want those back,' the girl said. 'Mister Morgun borrows them without permission sometimes, he dresses up, the silly sausage. Daddy was positively fierce when he found out.'

A gentle breeze skimmed the pond. With it came the first wisps of smoke over the roof. No more than a whisper at first, and then a deep, black sigh.

Aisling looked at the girl.

'You're Connie, aren't you.'

Connie smiled. 'This is yours, I think.'

Edythe's jewellery box, pulled dripping from the pond. Strange awareness came to Aisling, touching the clasps to lift the lid. The box wasn't smashed. Connie, her grandmother, was a child. The proper order of things had jostled out of place to make room for her.

Inside the box was her note to God.

'It turned up in the cellar one evening,' Connie told her. 'We'd cleared it out the day before, the whole show. Daddy thought he was seeing things.'

'I know how he feels,' she murmured, turning the scrap of paper over. Not her mother's hotel notepaper, not any more. Inks of all colours flooded the torn page, vapours of pink and *indigo. A tiny figure was twirling out of blue heaven. Like a copper thread, it fell down into a hell of bony cliffs and a wide, black marsh below. Aisling touched the grass beneath her. Not as solid as it was. She could have been at home again, gritty-eyed at 2 a.m. with her books spread around her on the duvet. She should have been. But when she thought of the blankets lying heavy over her head, her shallow breaths in time with the tick of the clock in the hall, the marsh was somehow the friendlier option. In the picture's centre, above the falling body, was familiar scuttling handwriting. She looked uncertainly at Connie, who smiled.*

'William Blake wrote this,' Aisling said.

'He did.'

'Just before he died,' she said.

'Yes,' said Connie.

Smoke trailed out across the fields. A magpie called for its mate. Connie took the paper from Aisling's limp hand and read in her clear young voice:

'Were it not better to believe Vision with all our might and strength tho' we are fallen and lost?'

Slouching on brick, chin on chest, Aisling stood in the long puddle of Sorry Street, lips plucking at words that wouldn't come. As full consciousness washed over her, the muscles in her hands gave a sharp twitch. Chase's lighter almost slipped from her grasp, and she was fumbling and swearing lest it fall into the water where something bumped, glimmering, against her boot.

A glint of emerald and spoiled silver. She cupped the

cufflink in her palm as she had that long ago evening in the bath. David Morgun, bald and white. David Morgun, with his self-loathing theories. She thought of the bath, transformed into a blackened husk. She shivered. *'It's not just you and me,'* Feodor said.

It.

She slipped the cufflink into her pocket. The tunnels waited. *'Take the first left, every time,'* Chase had said. But that was coming from another direction. In the darkness, there could be countless paths for her to wander down and never return from, but somehow, she couldn't make herself care. Immense tiredness had settled into her bones. She flicked the lighter and held it up, then stepped out into the main corridor.

The journey was curtailed by having to let the lighter die every few minutes. She lacked Chase's calloused fingertips. Each sudden descent into blackness caused spots to dance savagely in front of her eyes, and more than once she stiffened as bright humanoid shapes trailed up the tunnel towards her, gone once her trembling fingers flicked the lighter into life.

As she walked, more of those eerie painted signs appeared under the scudding light. *Loose scree ahead!* and *Whistle thrice for aid!* Her mind began to offer unhelpful suggestions, creeping subterranean predators, contaminants in the clay dust.

No different to crossing the hall in the night when Mum's out. No worse than her subterranean predator boyfriend.

Her head jangled. A wall swung out to slump against. The thought of solemn little Connie cross-legged on the lawn came to her like a memory of a real afternoon, and it scared her. The brickwork had reopened the grazes on her knuckles. She sucked them, tasted blood.

'Just a little tiny seizure,' she told herself. 'Gone now.'

As she whispered it, a drop of moisture plopped from the ceiling on to her forehead, and she jumped as though she had been grabbed.

'For God's sake, pull yourself together!' Her voice went bounding off down the tunnel without her.

Splash, went the water behind her. Aisling's breath froze in her throat.

'Go home, Feodor,' she said, certain he could hear her. 'I've made up my mind.'

The tunnels were silent. She told herself it was an animal. The play of the wind against the water. But as she stood there, still and listening, each and every hair follicle rose in her scalp as if conscious of being counted.

She let the lighter ignite again, holding it out like a weapon. 'Feodor, I mean it.'

The *slosh-slosh* of boots in water. He was closer now, closer than Sorry Street, and Aisling waved the flame about, desperately trying to focus her senses while the blood thrummed in her ears. A sound rang out, the unmistakable noise of a man grunting in pain. Not a billow of wind. Not an animal. An old wound stubbed in the dark.

The strange acoustics of the tunnels had tricked her. Unless Feodor had somehow limped past her, this was someone else. And they were in front of her.

Her fingers were burning. She had no choice but to let the light die.

And then she was running. Arms outstretched to touch the walls as she went blindly, stumbling into the first left turn she could find. No water in this stretch, but loose gravel crunching and sliding for what felt like forever, and the man sloshing through the water would have heard her miles away when she skidded on damp tiles and thudded chest-first into the wall at the end. On her knees, she managed to flick the lighter into life.

White.

A small shriek escaped before she could clamp a hand over her mouth. From the flagstones grazing her kneecaps to the rough-hewn arc of ceiling, she was inside an oppressive cocoon of thickly daubed whitewash. For a moment, Aisling was too dazzled to register that there was a door looming heavily before her, flanked by empty sentry posts slathered in the same pockmarked industrial emulsion. There was a wheel in the centre, like a submarine lock.

Printed into the steel: GIVE US THE LAW OF OUR FRIEND.

Somehow, she was on her feet. Behind her, nothing but whitewash stretching away into darkness. No Feodor, no faceless figure. Just her strung-out brain left to its own devices.

Silence seemed to emanate from behind the door. There was a slit of window above the wheel. With a vertiginous sensation, Aisling pictured a room without windows, a series of pressurised chambers. She pressed her nose to the cold glass and felt a strange temptation. She imagined herself curled behind the door, in a sterile segment of a quiet hive. No noise to keep her awake, no Beverley. Only weightless whiteness, cleanliness, and silence.

The lighter was burning her.

She had to keep her head. Sure enough, when she flicked

the lighter back into life, the obscene attraction had died and the silent white space represented a homogenous horror she turned and ran from without another thought. At the far end of the white tunnel, easy to miss, was a narrow alley of crumbly black brick stretching off to the left, and she ducked her head and took it, no longer concerned by the rotten wooden slats keeping it from falling on her head.

She wasn't sure when she first heard the hunting horns. There was a light up ahead, sickly and wavering, and she ran to it like a friend.

Caloo-calay! The horns cried. *Caloo-calay!*

Her hands touched iron rungs, and she clambered out on to grass and gravel, gasping, hackles up. Cool twilight, fresh air, a blackberry bush. Soon her mouth was smeared with juice as she took handfuls of fruit, letting the thorns dig into her split knuckles like a promise never to leave the surface again.

She was in the yard of a shabby block of tenements. Someone smoked a cigarette in the attic flats and the fragrance mingled with that of the buddleia bushes sprouting out of the rubble and trash. A radio buzzed and whined over a short burst of piano, something light and jaunty like Chopin.

Horns again, a few streets away. Somewhere, a bell tolled, calling out over the crammed houses. As Aisling managed to stand, mud-stained to the knees and shaking, a dog's head appeared over the net curtains in one of the ground floor windows. A suspicious woof brought human faces to the grubby panes and Aisling stumbled over garbage for the gate.

She burst out into the red-bricked street with its crooked

gutters and laundry-laden balconies. On the nearby canals, small boats headed for home. All the product of her own mind, of course. Though she had to remind herself more forcefully.

As she hesitated, wondering which direction to strike out in, two men in white uniforms came sauntering around the corner. They paused at the junction, raising bronze horns, and piped in unison the hunting call she had heard underground. In answer, the sounds of doors closing, of mothers calling their children. The men slid their instruments into the velvet sheaths on their backs. As they proceeded in her direction, the younger one whistled.

'Give us a smile, love.'

Hands in pockets, Aisling instinctively started to walk in the opposite direction, but he veered across the road towards her.

'Need escorting?'

'No. Thank you.'

'Where d'you live?'

'By the market.'

'Which?'

There was more than one? 'The square.'

'Well, we've just come from there. In fact, if you fancy some company, we'll gladly modify our route to get you safely from A to B.'

'I'm meeting my boyfriend. He's coming the other way. We're going to meet in the middle.'

She hated that lie. It must have sounded as hollow as she thought it did, because the man continued beside her, matching her speed.

'Well,' he said. 'Your boyfriend better not have plans to go wandering after curfew.'

His companion shouted something, and the man reluctantly slowed, allowing her to hurry away.

'Be a lousy boyfriend if he let anything happen to you in the dark,' he called after her. 'There's some proper nutters out there.'

In her pockets, Aisling uncurled her fists. Now she knew where the market was. She quickened her pace down the potholed street, ignoring the families and businesses closing doors either side of her. She had to look purposeful. The council with its promise of DAILY BREAD loomed ahead, and she forced herself not to run to it. She could sense curious eyes on her from all angles and, sure enough, when she gave in and glanced over her shoulder, the man in the uniform loitered at the far end of the long street, watching her while his friend piped the call: *caloo-calay!*

Another building was on the verge of collapse, an empty townhouse suspended, it seemed, by invisible strings. Her eyes lingered on the scorched brickwork and she thought of Feodor. *'It was an accident,'* Georgie had insisted. She twisted the ring on her thumb.

At last the market revealed itself. A man arranged painted cockleshells in a padded box, and she jogged to him.

'I'm packing up,' he said.

'No, sorry, I don't want to buy – I'm looking for someone. He's blond, sort of scruffy. And tall, only just taller than me, with a brown leather coat.'

'Brown leather?' he said, pressing brown paper over a layer of shells. 'Yellow hair? Shaggy, like?'

'That's him.'

'I'll have to think about that. While I'm thinking, though,

how's about you cast an eye over my exquisite collection of seashells?'

'No, I really—'

'These aren't just shells, madam. These are artefacts. Thousands of years old, some of these are. Properly cleaned with nice, thick bleach. See?' He held up his crusty hands. 'Lovely, lovely treasures from the deep.'

'I don't have any money.'

The man looked up. 'Then I ain't seen your mate.'

'Bernard, if your wife heard you snapping like that, she'd clip your ear.'

It was Borghese, resplendent in a black fur cloak stretching down to a pair of beautiful Cuban-heeled boots, emphasising his size and regal posture. 'Oh look, shiny pennies. None of this ever happened.'

While the man stumbled to pocket the tossed coin, pick up his shells and retreat, Borghese laced his hands before him and gave Aisling a look so long she had time to admire each of his finely-buffed fingernails in turn. Bands of jet adorned each thumb. His dark face was freshly-shaven, the skin full and soft. Even his furry eyebrows were tamed with some kind of fragrant pomade.

'Good evening, new girl,' he said at last.

She wiped at her blackberry-stained mouth. 'I'm looking for Chase.'

'You really don't have the slightest idea of how things work here, do you? Come on. I'm taking you somewhere fun.'

'Will Chase be there?'

He offered his arm, only to retract it when he saw the state of her coat. 'No, and be thankful. You need a good bath. Mucky.'

He propelled her through the market to a shop with windows draped in oily black satin. He unlocked the door and held it open for her. Inside, barely visible against the deep lacquer of the walls, were rows of funeral gowns. Hats and veils were displayed on long-necked busts staring miserably like abandoned brides. There were folded handkerchiefs on a varnished table, splayed in a washed-out rainbow from lavender to ink. In a corner, a clarinet waited beside a velvet stool where perhaps a musician would play for the customers as they picked out their sad costumes.

'Is this yours?' Aisling asked, blinking in amazement as tiny lights – *electric* lights – bloomed in glass lilies skirting the mirrored ceiling.

'Just this and most of the others.' Borghese moved to the window and pulled the curtains, plunging them into romantic darkness. 'Two of my girls are sick after going out in the fog today. Luckily for you, one of them is tall.' From the nearest rack, he swept up a mass of black fabric and pressed it to her. 'Slip it over your things. Hurry up. I shan't watch.'

Aisling stared. Layers of crêpe and tulle swelled into a haystack shape brushing the floor tiles, even against Aisling's long frame. As she lifted the dress over her head and allowed it to sink down over her she found that the ends of the voluminous sleeves were sealed with individual holes for each finger, so that her hands weirdly resembled the udders of a cow. As she struggled to smooth the billows of fabric down over her hips, Borghese returned with a vial of perfume and dabbed it behind her ears. Earth, leather, moss.

'Shut your eyes,' he said. She felt the pad of a large thumb press each eyelid, leaving a powdery substance she realised must be ash. 'There, now, did I not say you had a face for mourning?'

The figure in the mirror was a horror. The dirty red hair plastered to her scalp, the blood on her cheek, the berry juice down her chin. Black eyes, hungry, confused.

Borghese appraised her under the glow of the lily lights.

'You must be generous with your emotions,' he said. 'Sluttish.'

He slapped her full in the face. She was thrown back on to the counter, knocking over a display of hatpins. With two quick strides, Borghese had her by the shoulders. He shook her, hard.

'Where did you come from?' he demanded.

Spots flew across her vision. Borghese's bulk was formidable and the fabric of her dress easy to pinion. He gripped her chin between his fingers and turned her face to his.

'I've known the likes of you before. Nothing good comes of you.'

The shock of the slap had forced tears to the fore, and with shame she felt them spill. In the mirror, soot ran dramatically down her face.

'Pleased with yourself, weren't you, for finding your way through the tunnels? My people saw you coming. Nothing goes by without my knowledge, least of all, *least* of all, new girls.' Borghese's cavernous voice softened, but his grip remained firm. 'At this moment, a curfew is in effect. It is breakable only by special dispensation, which I naturally have. Now, you can choose to be nice to me, and I will share my privileges with you, and take you to your boy Chase. If you decide to be difficult, or to make the extremely foolish decision to run away into the streets, I can promise you now what will happen. First, you will be found. Second, your body will wash up at the old harbour by morning. No special crime, happens every night. That is what will happen when normal men find you. But if *he* finds you—'

She pushed against him. 'He?'

Borghese sighed. Her tears had dripped on to his lustrous cloak. One manicured paw disappeared into his pocket. It returned pinching a cherry bonbon. 'I can help you,' he said. 'To an extent.'

He pressed the sweet to her unresisting lips. Sour sugar.

'Now, you're going to accompany me to a lovely funeral. Here is your veil. Arrange it across your grief-stricken face, like so.' In the mirror, her face was a ghostly portrait. 'You are barely able to shuffle under the weight of your grief. You've gone without food, without sleep. You've lost the ability to speak. You understand?'

She nodded.

'No one will pay you attention. That is what you want.'

'And Chase will be there?'

He chuckled, deep and dark as unsweetened cocoa.

Borghese's body was as thick and tough as an old tree, but he strode across the deserted marketplace with elegant purpose, heels clicking on the cobblestones. Aisling allowed herself to become a reed, swaying against him, hoping the veil masked the rapid travel of her eyes. *Memorise the route*, she told herself. *Learn all the streets and alleyways.*

They crossed the main thoroughfare past a building with windows like awestruck eyes. Outlined in the smoke-charred brick was evidence of a long gone mural: GIN TILL DAWN. It was a hostel now, packed with bunk beds and bickering families. A woman hurried to the revolving doors with a loaf of black bread under her arm. As she passed Borghese, Aisling looked to the ground, leaning heavily on her escort's arm.

'Dreadful business, Mister Borghese,' the woman remarked.

'Ghastly,' he replied.

Without a glance at Aisling, the woman pushed her way into the hostel and vanished into the crowds.

'I should put you on the stage,' Borghese murmured as he led her down the steps between the townhouses, crammed stucco on stucco. Open gutters coaxed a soup of litter and rainwater downhill. The walls were choked with posters: playbills; bicycles for sale; *Have you seen this man?* under half a sad face that could have been Feodor's. It was getting colder. Aisling's skirts rustled like frosted leaves.

At the bottom of the slope a wooden arch, one winter away from rotting completely, was emblazoned with that familiar slogan, WITHIN REASON. Aisling slowed to stare up at it, imagining the hand that had travelled around town painting those words again and again.

'Words to live by. Wouldn't you agree, new girl?' Through the black gauze of her veil, Borghese's face was impossible to read. 'Or perhaps you're just a little, whisper it, mad?' He turned on one heel and lifted her veil enough to catch the flash of shock across her face. With one of his knowing smiles, he let the veil drop. 'I'd keep that to myself, if I were you.'

They took a bridge across the canal to a graveyard. On the lumpen expanse of grass and gooseweed, people congregated between clusters of headstones, the muted lowing of their anguish drifting out across the water. Borghese stopped at the iron gates.

'I apologise, but this may disturb you.'

Through the veil, she looked him in the eye. 'I'm already disturbed, thank you.'

He grinned up at the approaching night. 'That's the spirit.'

Borghese sliced through the crowd. Strange feet caught Aisling's skirts as she trailed after him.

She found herself hemmed in beside a man disguising his tears with much huffing and mopping of brow. A short woman stretched up on tiptoes. Little boys giggled behind Aisling's skirts. 'Sweeties!' one of them squeaked, and Borghese turned to look at them, his face a well-groomed mask of indifference. The offending urchin stared dumbly for a moment before shrinking back into the crowd.

Aisling had never been to a funeral. A flashback to the breakfast table, one eye on her Shredded Wheat, and the other on a magazine: *'Did you know,'* she said as Beverley pushed the plunger on the cafetière, *'Buddhist monks in Tibet learned to mummify themselves alive by drinking poisonous sap and bricking themselves—'*

Beverley raised her mug and blew steam at her. *'Why can't you subscribe to, I don't know,* Teen Vogue?'

Now, Aisling was thankful for the veil softening the scene with unreal, lacy darkness. Nevertheless, as she rose up on her toes to catch a glimpse of the crowd's centre, she found herself feeling queasy.

The body had been carried to the cemetery on a dining-room table. A torn bedsheet was tied to two of the legs. *HUGH*, read the wet paint, followed by three crayony red kisses.

Over bobbing heads and craning necks, Aisling saw the grave. No coffin, not even an especially deep hole; just a white shroud down in the dark topsoil, sliced by the gravedigger's spade. An adult body, and male judging by the width of the shoulders. Numbly, she registered fluid darkening the shroud.

Worse than the sight of the body was the mound of women kneeling at the lip of the grave. They wore gowns identical to her own, and crawled over each other, shoeless, moaning. The combined wailing and snivelling rose and fell like a cacophony of cats. It didn't seem real.

It isn't.

Borghese gave her a prod. She bent at the waist, trembling against him.

'Better,' he muttered.

Then there were the true mourners. A middle-aged man had been awake for many hours, and his eyes were fixed on the grave as if committing every fold of the shroud to memory. Beside the man a younger woman in a black summer dress too flimsy for the evening chill hugged herself. A sister, perhaps, or a girlfriend. She nodded coolly to Borghese, and he nodded back.

The nod was taken as a sign to begin, and an officiary made himself known. Far from the elegant mourning attire in Borghese's boutique, this man in his rumpled suit looked as though he had just rolled out of bed.

'I suppose now is time to start? If everyone is ready?'

The girl in the dress turned her head sharply and said something. Down the steps came a pair of youths. One of them was doing his best to keep the other from falling. As they came barrelling through the mourners, Aisling saw the marks of a fist fight colouring the older boy's cheeks. A hum of excitement gathered weight.

'He saved my life,' the older boy said in a voice too loud. 'It was coming at me, and Hugh threw himself between us. That's the truth. That's what you can tell people.'

The officiary held up his palm, but the boys would not be silent. Pushing their way through the crowd, they neared the edge of the grave. At the sight of the shroud the bruised one's forehead crinkled a deep, veiny red. His friend stood back, unable to look at anything but the body. Like Aisling, he had never seen one before.

'But you got it?' demanded a bystander with that ugly *oh-how-dreadful* tone of excitement in her voice. 'You killed it?'

'It's dead,' said the younger boy, eyes on the grave. 'He did it,' he added weakly.

The other recovered his bravado as a wave of admiration went out. Whatever 'it' was, it amounted to something big.

'We were protecting you,' he told the crowd. 'A Foreigner broke into the town, and Hugh—' his voice cracked, and he waved angrily at the grave, 'Hugh here did what he had to do.'

This was terrible and wonderful at once. Aisling was jostled as the people around her chattered excitedly:

'—climb in through the skylights—'

'—perverts, spread—'

'—boundary side, it's not safe for—'

'He was a good kid,' said the girl in the thin dress. Her quiet resignation broke the spell and the rabble shut their mouths.

'He was,' said the youth, punch-swollen nose thickening his voice until it was barely understandable. 'Foreigners don't even have family. They don't think the way we do. They come over here and help themselves to our food. Half of them are mental.'

A roar went up and Aisling was pressed against Borghese by bodies fired up with adrenaline. His big hand touched her arm. *Wait*, it said.

'Hugh was a bloody hero!' someone yelled, for the sake of shouting something.

Aisling no longer had to feign trembling. A terrible suspicion had been building in the back of her mind, and it was too large to ignore. The prayer seller had called Chase a Foreigner. She looked down at the body.

Borghese raised a finger. To Aisling's amazement the minute gesture was registered by everyone in the crowd, and even the youth fell silent as the rich baritone travelled easily across the packed cemetery. 'Friends,' he said. 'Nothing can be done for Hugh now. Allow the gravediggers to do their unhappy job. Would Hugh have wanted you to break yourself into pieces here at his graveside?'

'He would have wanted blood!' someone shrieked.

Borghese blinked slowly as if this was the most asinine thing he had ever heard. 'And he received it. The Foreigner is dead.'

'I won't stop until they're all dead,' the youth said. 'I'll walk out of here with a rifle. I'll poison the streams. I'll take them out one by one with a straight razor if I have to, for Hugh! And all the others!'

The crowd howled. Borghese smoothed the fur of his cloak and muttered to Aisling, 'Well, I'm sufficiently bored. Shall we?'

The Foreigner is dead. The thought of Chase with a gash in his golden skin made her head reel and her tongue thicken. *It isn't Chase, tell me it isn't.*

She managed to hold fast to Borghese as the mass of bodies shifted to allow them passage. But then, turning on his polished heel, Borghese froze. At the graveside, the youth had in his fist a bunch of long, dead grass. No one spoke.

Aisling caught sight of the girl in the thin dress. She had visibly stiffened. 'No,' she said tersely. 'Don't.'

Something in Borghese's body language shifted. The boy held up his fist, spilling over with long, dark tendrils. 'My granddad told me, in the old days before The Remedy, if they caught a Foreigner creeping on their land they'd scalp him. They'd take the hair and burn it in their hearths so the creatures would smell it and stay away.'

Not grass. Hair. Black, lank hair in need of a wash.

'Some of the things we left behind were good,' he continued. 'Some of them meant something. We don't have to be cold and reasonable all the time, it only makes us easy pickings for freaks like that thing that killed Hugh. Remember how Our Friend said he'd do away with all the madness? That he'd put all the defectives in The Quiet and keep the streets clean? Well, he's not here. And Hugh's dead,' he bellowed. 'Aren't you angry? Don't you care?'

The girl looked to the officiary. 'Start the ceremony,' she

said, but the little man had no hope of wrestling attention back now that the boy was holding the hank of hair high above his head.

'I took my granddad's advice. I took this off the Foreigner and tonight I'm gonna burn it and then I'm gonna go out there into the wasteland and find the rest of them. They've got houses out there. You've all heard the stories.'

A great rush of air from Borghese's lungs: 'You bloody fool.'

People were scrambling forwards to clutch at the hair. First, two or three young men came forward, then their girlfriends, then their parents, and soon the boy was handing it out, lock by black lock. Black, and not blond. Relief took Aisling so hard that bile rose in her throat and she gagged ecstatically. She buried her face in Borghese's fur, hacking, too absorbed in the joy of knowing Chase was alive to notice immediately that other people were coughing, too, and the shunting and elbowing was suddenly more frantic. People were reaching for handkerchiefs. Some had bunches of dried flowers prepared to hold to their noses. Smoke and acetate and the scent of rot.

Over the noise of the collective coughing, Borghese whistled twice, and the professional mourners fled the cemetery like a flurry of crows. 'Move,' he told Aisling as the girl in the thin dress came running.

'Mister Borghese, don't take him seriously. He needs a good sleep and a good cry, and he's too stupidly manly to do either just yet. Please.'

'Words born of grief. I understand.'

The girl's brown eyes were huge. 'You do understand? Nothing will happen to him?'

'Now why would that be up to me?'

Without another word, Borghese took Aisling by the shoulders and together they slipped away into the ruins of the cemetery. Graves old and new nuzzled into one another, arched Gothic tablets, inscriptions softening in the damp of the canals. The smell faded.

'Chase is all right,' she said. 'Isn't he? You'd tell me if he wasn't.'

He tugged her over lumps of grassy earth, fallen railings, mounds of blue dust where mosaics had been hacked away for salvage. A corridor of tall, house-like tombs was ensnared in vines and the nests of city birds.

'Lesson one, and the most important: Each and every one of those people will be gone by tomorrow.'

'Gone?'

'My girls will be all right. But the rest? No.'

'Why? And where are we going now?'

'Home.'

'You said we were going to Chase.'

'Put your veil down. And yes. I noticed you when the boy blasted off about Foreigners. So you do know something, even if you don't know what it means.' He banged on the door of the adjacent tomb, and the next, as they followed the path. 'Evening ladies, evening gents! This is Aisling. She's new.'

'What does that mean, "new"?'

'I preferred you silent. You looked magnificent at the graveside, I thought. Petrified.'

'That girl was frightened.'

'She had every right to be. She at least tried to stop him, and if asked I'll vouch for her, of course. But that scene with the hair was disgraceful. "Words born of grief." Tommyrot. The First Law concerns what? Every schoolgirl in the land learns it at her mother's knee, come along.' He sighed. 'The First Law concerns the elimination of the weakening vice: superstition. Only that which is within reason is permitted. The Laws are broadcasted continually on the wireless. The Old Remedials. You do listen to your radio, don't you, Aisling?'

She set her jaw. 'I prefer the piano music.'

'Indeed. What did I say about keeping certain things to oneself?'

The sight of the family vaults in this stretch was lifting Borghese's spirits, and his cloak flew out behind him as he strode, forcing Aisling to hitch up her skirts and hurry.

'Out with it,' he said. 'You're bursting again.'

'Are you in charge?'

His boots pivoted towards her. A rich, dark laugh. 'You are charmingly stupid. No wonder Chase is smitten to the gills.'

'But you look different to all the others. You own all those businesses. The people at the funeral, when you arrived, they—'

'Nobody's in charge. Nobody's been in charge for, well, it's a clumsy turn of phrase. You want to know who that girl was so afraid of.'

Our Friend. No, she wouldn't say it. Not out loud.

'Wouldn't you rather have a sweetie?' Through the veil, he saw her scowl. 'That's precisely your problem. Now pay attention. This is my favourite part of the stroll home.'

In the gathering darkness, they followed the avenue to a row of tombs like scaled-down mansions. This section of the cemetery had been vandalised. Some of the verdigris doors were smashed open, revealing empty shelves and fragments of broken coffins. Aisling held back, unwilling to stare at the disturbed bones of strangers.

'Early casualties of The Remedy,' Borghese reassured her. 'Long taken by the foxes; you'll see nothing grisly here. Don't pity them. They at least had the privilege of interment.'

He took her through the avenue as if on a jolly promenade. The names above the doors, once so lovingly, expensively carved, were appended with graffiti that made Darren McKinnon's efforts on Aisling's school desk seem timid by comparison.

Marchioness Marla Swinburne and her sons Dale and Christopher – *WALLOW IN HELL'S SHIT.*

The Larch family, upstanding pillars - *BUY YOUR WAY OUT OF THIS.*

Towards the end of the column, where the cemetery dwindled into scrubland, was a tall tomb of white marble veined with the ultramarine pigment she had seen in the tunnels. It featured stone lanterns, as if to guide the inhabitants' spirits home on dark nights. Aisling paused there like an uncertain guest.

'You like it?'

Olaf and Olga Craig, and their daughters, Victoria, 18, and Doreen, 12. In red paint across the door: *I BUGGERED DEAD DAUGHTERS BOTH.*

'Long, opulent lives. Parties after party, punctuated by a series of soirées to break up the boredom.' Borghese blinked placidly. 'A soirée must have no less than seven guests and no more than fourteen, lest it become an intimate gathering or a full-blown celebration, did you know that?'

Victoria Craig. Tor. In the darkness, Aisling touched her bloody cheek.

'We're going to their house?' she managed.

'My house now. Mine.'

And as they left the cemetery for the deeper darkness of the city, Aisling looked back at the dispersing crowd and prayed she had made the right decision.

23

'Welcome to the gingerbread house.'

If there was a window for escape, it had passed without Aisling ever noticing it. Borghese's home was a three-storey townhouse in a refined district separated from the rest of the town by a swiftly flowing canal. Armed men admitted them through a gate cast in the swirling style of Parisian Métro stations. Borghese offered the men coins and cigarettes wrapped in brown paper.

A whole new world of flowering magnolias and polished stone. The cobbled road was clean, and there was even a street light casting a caramel glow beside by a bubbling fountain. The dust of the cemetery left no blemish on Borghese's beautiful boots, and as he led her up the long path to his home – *Tor's home*, she reminded herself – Aisling longed for the grubby chaos of the house hidden in the woods.

Tor's elegant former life. A stained glass window depicted golden-haired women pouring silvery milk from blue pails. The delicate curves of the windows gave the house an organic, beehive-like appearance. Aisling could almost have imagined honey oozing out to greet her from the front door if it weren't for the security portcullis that clunked and wheezed as an unseen individual granted them access. The instinctive fear of the closing of doors returned in a rush, and Aisling stiffened as they entered the hallway. But no chains or guards were waiting. The buttery scent of hot toffee wafted up from the kitchens below stairs. Aisling pulled away the veil.

'Chase?' She called out. 'Chase, I'm here.'

Borghese's dark face crinkled with affront. 'You don't come into my home and bark,' he said. 'Wait here. And take those off. They're expensive.'

He went off down the hall while she struggled out of the heavy mourning weeds and dumped them on a chair overlooking a nest of gilded frames on the wall. Each held a newspaper illustration of a younger, leaner Borghese in a series of increasingly elaborate costumes: lifting a dumbbell, receiving a kiss from a girl in a feathered leotard. *Stupendous Scipione!* declared a flier. *Borghese the Bull! Watch as he shoulders the weight of the world!* And then: *From strength, sweetness – celebrated strongman leaves sideshow for the confectionary business.* Borghese, broader, older: a calmly confrontational portrait of a knowing man with slicked-back hair. How did anyone summon that kind of confidence?

'May I take those, miss?'

Borghese's elderly assistant Wilson was there, holding out his hands for the clothes. Two of his fingers were missing. There was a glint of insolent fascination in his eyes as he took in the blood on her cheek and the smeared kohl.

'Anything you need at all, miss,' he said evenly. 'Just you ask me.'

She looked to the stairs. An overstuffed baroque chair was mounted to a rail, a sort of homemade stairlift, and her eyes followed the rail up the wall where it travelled its fixed course. Light filtered down from somewhere higher, an attic room, perhaps. 'Chase, is he here?'

Wilson's face scrunched as if she'd just asked for full access to Borghese's underwear drawer. 'The Foreigner? Not down here. Not with all the silverware.'

'What is a Foreigner?' she asked.

Wilson smirked and tucked his chin over the billowing mound of fabric. 'I reckon you's one,' he said as he walked away. 'You's got that look.'

He bid her follow, and they found her host in a cosy living room facing out on to a long garden where wisteria rambled in the darkness. An ancient woman snoozed on a sofa of yellow velvet. She wore the neat, long-skirted uniform of a maid, but her horny brown hands and straining neck made her seem like a creature uprooted from the forest.

Borghese was kneeling next to the sofa. 'Francesca?' he called softly. 'Francesca, have you swept the fireplaces today? How are your knees, dear?'

As her chalky eyes fluttered and settled on Borghese, they widened with delight.

'Good evening, sir! Fireplaces spick and span, sir. The knees are as they always are, but I shan't complain, sir.'

Borghese hummed adoringly. 'There's my good girl.'

Dominating the room was a portrait over the marble fireplace: a broad man in blustering military uniform, his corseted wife and two daughters. Aisling recognised the young Tor at once, although in her yellow frock and pearls the round face seemed too haughty for a true likeness. Her shoes, Aisling noticed, bore signs of fire damage, the barest lick of hot smoke. Aisling drained her own face of expression and said nothing.

The old woman, however, had noticed her. 'Ah! The young mistresses are back? Good evening, Miss Victoria. Shall I have Lisa bring you a slice of pie from the pantry?'

Aisling caught Borghese's warning expression and tried, despite her filthy face, to respond like a lady. 'Oh,' she said. 'I'm all right, thank you, Francesca. Maybe later.'

'I did the fireplaces today, miss, spick and span.'

'Good girl,' Borghese said. 'Don't tell the other staff, but I think you're the best parlour maid a gentleman could ever wish for. And do you know, I would like to give you the night off. Fully paid.'

The old woman curled in on herself with pleasure. 'Oh, sir!'

Borghese patted her bony knee. 'That will be all, Francesca. Come along, Victoria. Bedtime.'

'Beauty sleep for the belle of the ball,' Francesca smiled.

'It keeps her placid,' he muttered he as tugged Aisling upstairs. 'As a girl, she was a maid here under the Craigs until a misfortune of fertility befell her. She's entirely unaware that I am her son, so I expect you not to say anything to agitate her.'

'I'm very sorry.'

'Don't be. She is the most fortunate demented old woman in the world.'

Borghese caught her glancing back over the bannister to

the portcullis barring the front door and gave her a soft clip around the ear. 'Don't be a silly bint.'

On the second floor, he took a key from his waistcoat and unlocked a door.

The room was a crash site. Books strewn, clothes pouring from the wardrobe, a stack of paintings overturned. In the midst of it all was the dishevelled Chase, slumped with his knees to his chest on a shabby satin day-bed. He smoked something herbal, eyes red-rimmed and wet. When he saw Aisling, he almost slipped to the floor, disturbing a set of handcuffs dangling from the arm of the bed.

Borghese smiled grimly. 'Earlier on, we had to resort to crude measures. His virtue's intact, don't worry.'

'You're hurt,' Chase said. She watched his unsteady journey from bed to doorway with anguish, and when he fell against her she thought he was drunk or dying.

She returned his embrace with a fierceness that shocked her. 'I had to find you. What's happened?'

He was shaking his head, a reedy loll of exhaustion. 'You shouldn't have come.'

Borghese pushed past to retrieve the smoking cigarette from the rug where it had fallen. 'Jobi happened,' he said, taking Chase's drooping chin and inserting the damp end back into his mouth. 'He's downstairs, new girl, if you fancy meeting him.'

'Chase, what happened?'

'The crucial details?' Borghese said. 'Jobi, indiscreet little urchin, got himself caught. They hanged his body from a lamp post last night. We, meaning Chase, spent this morning trying very hard to get ourselves caught in turn, cutting the body down in a loud and obvious fashion until a thoughtful someone, meaning I, intervened.' He saw Aisling's expression and raised his thick brows. 'Dead. And now he's on my kitchen table, because I'm an all-round accommodating chap.'

'The funeral.'

'Jobi's brave and glorious slayer. As for, "He threw himself on the creature's knife," Jobi gave him a pair of forceps to the eye, most likely from a prone position, deep enough to kill instantly. The gang had already broken in and done for the surgeon before moving on to him. An illegal surgery in the front room of a two-up two-down. They wanted a cage-fight, and they got one.'

'Surgery? I don't understand.'

'You don't understand anything.'

Chase was taking in air by the gulp. She went to him, surprising herself by stroking his matted hair.

'I don't know what to do,' he whimpered.

'I know some people,' Borghese said. 'One can dispose of anything these days.'

Chase flew off the couch. 'No! No doctors, no students. He gets buried like anyone else.'

'Yes, because this is the time to be picky.' Borghese swept off his fur cloak. He was huge, even without it. 'This could cost me my neck. It's already cost Jobi his. Now sit down or I'll have you restrained.'

Chase fell back on to the bed. When his eyes met Aisling's they were glassy and dazed. 'His tongue was all puffed up. And his eyes, they... My oldest friend...'

She helped him settle down on to sofa. His hand, as he offered her his cigarette, was heavy and pliant and cold. 'You should take a puff. Do you good,' he croaked. She leaned in close for him to slip it between her lips. 'Don't inhale too hard, you'll burn your throat. Good.' Then, against her neck, a lucid whisper: 'Careful what you say here.'

She sucked on the cigarette, and the smoke hit the back of her throat like the gnash of teeth. *'They give you wrinkles, but they keep you thin,'* echoed the voice of her mother. This didn't smell like Beverley's Misty Menthol Lights. This was one of those roll-ups she absolutely did not want her daughter to be seen smoking.

Chase jerked his chin at Borghese. 'You gonna feed us, or what?'

He sneered. 'Oh, certainly, sir. Red or white with your filet mignon?'

'Look at her. She's filthy. What've you done to her?'

'The bathroom is on the next floor. I'll have Wilson prepare hot water.'

'We're staying together,' Chase said.

'The finest bathing facilities you'll ever lay eyes on, and you want to squat over a bowl?' Borghese sighed. 'I'll feed you. You can sleep in this room. And tomorrow, while arrangements are made, we will pretend to be civilised adults and formulate a way to get you out of town unnoticed.'

Aisling caught up with him as he went to leave. 'Don't lock the door.'

The key paused between his fingers. He regarded her with his great brown eyes, lashes thick and wiry like a desert plant. He slipped the key back into his waistcoat.

'Wilson is quicker than he first appears,' he warned her. 'And unlike me, he is no gentleman.'

>•<

Wilson brought them bowls of pasta and they stuffed their mouths without considering it could be drugged.

'I don't care if we stay up until dawn,' Aisling said, attacking the most glorious hot food she could remember tasting. 'Tell me everything.'

Chase licked tomato sauce from his chin. 'Who've you been talking to? Not him downstairs. He's the tightest-lipped bastard in the whole world.'

'I might have met someone who knows you.'

Chase paused, fork in mouth. 'You followed the path I showed you?'

'I tried to. And I found my way in the end, but I took a longer way through the woods.' It was hard to swallow. 'I don't want you to be angry.'

His green eyes were wary.

Why was she afraid to say it? 'Feodor.'

They finished all the food they could eat, and shortly, Wilson brought hot water and cloths. Chase stripped off his shirt and began to wash. His grief for Jobi was nakedly apparent, slumping his shoulders and dulling his eyes. Aisling turned her back and went to the window. In the reflection she saw him, golden and wiry, bruises like spillages, and she refocused politely on the smoking paraphernalia discarded by the bed. Papers and scraps of herbs, perhaps the same ones the prayer seller had used to send her message to Robert off into the atmosphere. The world beyond the canal was dark and silent. A splash and a cold intake of breath, and Chase's back shimmered palely against the glass.

If I were normal, I'd be able to comfort you, she thought. *But I've made it worse. For you, for Tor, for Robert and Edythe and Beverley.*

'I'm ready to tell you something,' he said.

Downstairs, a door slammed. She turned, eyes averted.

'Look at me.'

The boom of Borghese could be heard through the floorboards, something peevish about 'stains' and 'unacceptable'. Her eyes drifted anxiously. Chase caught them.

'The surgeon Jobi was seeing, he was going to do something I've wanted since I can remember. Now I know when I show you this, you'll likely leg it out that door. But I need you to remember that I never asked for it, it's done to us at birth. And that I like you a lot, and I think you deserve to know. That's not to say I'm forcing you to accept it. It's just necessary. The honesty. Y'see?'

He was shivering. Before she could answer, or perhaps before he lost courage, Chase ducked his head under the water and emerged with the blond straggles plastered to his scalp. An arc of water shot across the floor, wetting her toes. Instead of reaching up to smooth the hair down over his ears in that gesture so familiar, he knelt with his hands in his lap, breathing unsteadily as she stared, uncomprehending.

Along the hall, Borghese demanded a hot rum and blackcurrant from no one in particular.

Chase stared at her, the ridges of his ribs hitching unevenly.

'Say something.'

'They're not real.'

'I wish.'

'Can I touch them?'

'No. Yes. Gently.'

She reached up to the mass of dripping hair and carefully turned his face away. He flinched.

'You're disgusted,' he said.

'No. They're beautiful.' And she was smiling, because she'd seen them, of course she had, up the tower as the wind blew their hair around that first morning in the town. She hadn't allowed herself to believe something so wondrous and absurd. 'So this is what a Foreigner is.'

'You're never going to accept this. Are you?'

'You'd be surprised what you can just accept.'

The bedroom door cracked open. They sprang apart guiltily. Borghese had a large glass of something steaming in one hand and a book in the other.

'I'm retiring with a hot toddy,' Borghese announced. 'I'm expecting complete silence from both you guttersnipes, all night.' He paused at the sight of Chase's dripping flesh and grimaced. 'Despite what you might have planned.'

He closed the door without locking it and thumped off down the hall.

Again, the sight of Chase's long, delicately pointed ears greeted her ridiculously. She blurted: 'You're like a fairy.'

A wince of pain and he began pulling wet hanks of hair over them.

'I'm sorry. Is that a bad word?'

'S'all right. You didn't know. We're born like you. We have them split and sewn back up in points when we're small. The scars don't show by the time you're my age.' He wiped at his wet cheeks. For a moment, he looked as if he might summon the old fun, the ragamuffin insouciance of that night with the fireflies in the garden, but the glow was gone almost as soon as she recognised it. 'A Foreigner's someone from the wasteland. A few normal people live out there too, dotted about, like Tor. But Foreigners are different. We're blood. Yeah? Tribal, like. I was born in the commune. I don't know who my parents were. We don't have family trees or personal fortunes or none of that stuff. And we don't mix with people.'

'People?'

'You're people. We're not.'

He dried himself off and dressed. The gold earring glinted and she stared, unable to look away. The room felt too small for her, a doll's house, and she looked to the lock on the door. Chase checked it for her. Unlocked.

'Blood's one thing,' he said. He tapped the side of his head. 'But what's in here, that's yours alone. You know it. Years ago me and some of the others would sneak into the town, and if anyone noticed us they didn't say anything. Not dangerous like now. Plenty of our lot ended up in The Quiet. I had a few close calls, but Jobi always got us home safe, until the elders found out and gave us a good whipping. We're not to mingle. That's how it's always been. But I loved it here. I loved the people. I loved the pubs, and the old men who'd talk and talk and read from the papers if you asked them. Like you do. And then I met Tor, and she was nice to me even though she knew what I was from the start. She treated me like, well, I guess like a mother. I could pretend.

'Having her house in the wasteland to go to got me thinking. I could get out. Or come and go. It's boring staying amongst your own. Jobi had friends in safehouses, he'd be away for weeks, and he'd get away with it 'cause the elders liked him. They didn't know how much he hated being a Foreigner. But me...'

'You're not a good liar.'

'The more I was away, they worse they made it for me,

coming back. And things in the town…' Chase's foxy eyes were pleading. 'Do you have any idea what he does to people like me? To people like you?'

She had an inkling.

'I couldn't go in to watch people any more, just to grab things Tor needed. The commune, they wouldn't have me. They said I rejected them, so why should they accept me? But then there was you. And you didn't twig. You were the only person in the whole world who didn't care what I was, even when it was bleedingly obvious. I guess that's part of you being, y'know,' he stuck a finger to his temple and pulled the face. 'You were gonna teach me things.'

'I will.'

'The surgeon Jobi was seeing, he was going to give us rounded ears. We found each other after Tor threw me out, and he told me it was all arranged. We just had to decide who went first. It was one of these underground jobs, an operating table in some guy's parlour, and it was too risky to have us both there at once. So we had a race for it. First one to the dock gets proper people-ears! He was always quicker. His face when he reached the dock. His laugh.'

The strip of golden light under the bedroom door winked out.

'I went and laid low while Jobi skipped off to find the surgeon, but as he went around the corner I saw them coming out of a pub. Three of 'em. That walk they do when they want to look big. They'd watched us running past. We must've looked happy. They get suspicious when you look happy.'

Aisling thought of the things she wanted to say versus the things that might have helped. *You don't need to change for me. You're perfect as you are.* No use, any of it. With a tremble they could both see, she reached out and laid a hand on his.

Later, the cold forced them into bed. Chase fidgeted on the mattress.

'Foreigners don't do beds,' he said.

'Do you want to talk about Feodor?'

He stared up at the ceiling. 'I hate that he's even been near you.'

'He's ill. I think he could actually be dying.'

'Yeah? The right people, for a change.'

And I had an episode. In the tunnels. I went back to my aunt's house. I'm getting sick again.

No use saying that, either. *When it comes, it comes, and that's the end of it.*

Where will I end up this time?

'This was Tor's room,' Chase said, staring up at the ceiling boards where their friend had painted constellations decades ago. 'Her whole family died during The Remedy. Decadents, see. Tor only escaped 'cause the mob took one of the maids, thinking it was her in disguise. When this is over, I want to go back to her. What do you want to do?'

'I don't know.'

'Go back to your people?'

'He said I couldn't go back.'

'Feodor? If a scrap of truth passed his lips, he'd choke on it.'

Aisling stared up at the painted stars. 'I think about my mum sometimes. How she'd cope without me. But if I woke up tomorrow in my aunt's house, under that itchy blanket in that horrible room, I don't know what I'd do. I've been trying to stay rational. But I don't know how I could bear it if none of this was...' She pushed at her eyeballs with the heels of her hand until lights blossomed. A grassy, hot smell intervened, and she looked around to find Chase had lit another joint.

'Real and unreal don't mean nothing.' He smiled weakly, and took a puff. 'There's just what you experience and what you don't. Temporary, that's a word you can work with. Everything's temporary. Bad stuff and good. Jobi used to say that.'

She sucked on the joint. Falling asleep in a stranger's house after smoking some nameless herb, what were the neighbours going to make of that?

Sod the neighbours.

She wished she'd thought it sooner.

'I s'pose I could be anywhere,' she mumbled.

'I s'pose.'

'Sleeping in a hospital somewhere. Another backless gown.' She almost giggled. Her brow crinkled. 'Feodor says there's a barrier I slipped through to get here. A door. But I saw you turning cartwheels in my aunt's garden. How did you do it? Go back and forth like that?'

'Didn't know I'd done anything.' He rubbed his neck. His body hurt. 'I reckon you're far-sighted. Full of dreams and messages like them blind scribes. Maybe I was sent, eh? To come and get you out of the mire, like your Little Boy Lost.'

She stretched beneath a bloom of smoke. Yes, it was a good thought. But there were thoughts waiting behind it, crowding closer, too large for the room. 'Something terrible happened in that house, Chase. I can almost see it.'

When Aisling settled down to sleep, Chase smoked the

last of the joint down to a stub. 'Always your aunt's house,'
he said. 'Why'd you never tell me about your own?'

24

Sometime in the night, Aisling stirred. Chase had migrated to the floor, and she was relieved to see him sleeping soundly, eyelids fluttering in the passing breeze of a dream.

Her bladder called. Stepping over Chase, she went out into the corridor, and followed the stairs to the next floor in search of the bathroom.

As Borghese had boasted, it was the finest bathing facility she had seen outside of an advert for a luxury hotel. The bath took in a panoramic view of the town through an enormous window draped in a froth of white lace. The memory of Edythe's charred bathtub loomed painfully, followed by something else, something black and treacly that forced the blood up into her ears.

She went to the window and rested her forehead on the cold panes. Outside, in the perfect stillness of the street, the single street light lured moths. As she watched them blunder into the flame, her mind turned to the wasteland. How was Feodor faring in the dark?

Her hands were beginning to heal, she noted. Like watching footprints wash away in the surf. The thought of dead Jobi on the kitchen table was enough to stop her from lying down to sleep again, and so she remained at the window, dragging her knuckles across the fogged panes. A quick punch or two would split the skin nicely, she thought.

Rubbing away the steam with her sleeve, she almost missed the shadow beneath the lamp post. Hunched shoulders. White face tilted up to where she stood, framed in the window by Borghese's electric lights.

Aisling raced back to the bedroom. Chase was awake in an instant, up at the window with her. 'What?' he grunted. 'Who?'

Cobbles glistened in the early morning damp. In the guard station, the night watch stood firm, the flicker of a cigarette illuminating half a face. The cool air creeping through the casement prickled Aisling's skin, and on the air the faintest whiff...

'There.'

He was coming their way. Big-shouldered, head bent, lurching as if each step sent shots of pain up through his feet.

Quick and silent, Chase snatched up both their coats and dropped Aisling's over her shoulders. 'You've got that knife I gave you?'

'I'm not hurting anyone.'

At the front door, a polite *knock-knock*.

'We're gonna get out of here, all right?' Chase said. 'By whatever means.'

No time for anything else. Borghese was there in a plum dressing gown as Wilson, over his shoulder, went down the stairs like a hound. Without a word, Borghese reached up and yanked hard on the chandelier over the bed. An answering crunch came from the wardrobe, and he spread his great arms to herd the pair of them, struggling through the layers of perfumed taffeta to a small, open hatch at the back.

Before he could shimmy through after Aisling, Borghese caught a handful of Chase's hair.

'Make a sound,' he hissed, 'and I will hurt her. Not you. Her.'

Crawling blindly, Aisling's hands touched a ladder. She saw Chase's face all around her. Mirrors. The real Chase followed her, step by wobbly step, to the crawl space above Tor's bedroom and the adjoining room. For a moment they could only breathe, unwilling to take in the claustrophobic dimensions vibrating with the thump of Borghese's feet hurrying down the staircase.

Chase pushed his face to the floorboards, searching for a crack to look through. The mirrors provided light and magnified views into other areas of the house. With them, Aisling could see far down into the kitchen, and, sure enough, on the rustic table was the body of a boy, long and wiry like Chase. His black hair had been roughly shorn to a prisoner's crop, leaving a few long strands plastered to his swollen face. Wilson hurried into view with a long hessian sack. When he grasped the body by both ankles, Aisling moved so Chase would not catch an accidental glimpse.

'Look,' she said. In another mirror was a clear view of the entrance hall. They were treated to the sight of Borghese anxiously smoothing his clothes. When he raised the portcullis and opened the front door, his broad silhouette was the picture of poise.

'I wasn't expecting you, my friend.'

Chase jolted. In the four-handed scramble to reset the mirror, there was a deep whirr as somewhere a generator groaned into life. *Tickety-thump-tickety-thump.* The stairlift. As it coiled up higher into the house, she and Chase strained to make out a second voice, a soft, laboured tone, whistling on sibilants.

'So sorry to make a nuisance of myself.'

Aisling felt it through her haunches. They were directly beneath them.

A tumble of boots and doors and creaking bed. Face to the floor, Chase's spine arched. For a moment she was sure he was about to yell, but his body had seized up like a cat's. There was nothing to do but join him there, trying to see.

Below them, a bedroom, floral, clean. Temple to temple, up against Chase, she could see nothing but Borghese's hands guiding someone, and when she shifted for a better view, the floorboards groaned loudly.

'Bloody—!' Chase hissed. 'He'll hear. Are you crazy?'

'No, I'm like that.' Stung, she stuck a finger to her temple and crossed her eyes.

He appeared to shrink as he reached around to hold her. 'Don't let him hear you say that. Don't even joke.'

In the bedroom below, the smell of acetate was so strong Aisling almost expected the flowers on the coverlet to wilt. David was making polite conversation between gasps for air. 'How does your mother fare?'

'Her arthritis makes walking impossible. Her lungs vary with the weather.'

'Her mental condition.'

Aisling could see Borghese's velvet shoulders stiffen. 'Our arrangement—'

'Our arrangement stands.'

'Having her here harms no one. She can't so much as shuffle to the toilet.'

'Some would argue she was better off elsewhere.'

'Our arrangement,' here Borghese's voice wavered, a tug between propriety and emotion, 'stands.'

Squinting down, Aisling's tongue seemed to thicken like poor Jobi's, bundled into a sack under the kitchen sink. Splayed out on the coverlet: David. Prim and hairless as he had been in Edythe's house, chatting casually about the wallpaper. David, stinking and ill as he had been down in the cellar, saying frightening things she couldn't understand. Against the floral coverlet, he was nothing but bones and tight skin and eyes like great revolving marbles. So sick she was afraid to be in the same airspace as him. Chase felt it too, and was aghast. He had no idea.

Borghese removed David's black overcoat with a release of stale air and David sank back uncomfortably into the bed. With the utmost respect, Borghese unbuttoned the thin black dress shirt with its cuffs tight around the bulging tendons of his wrists.

'You've lost a cufflink, my friend.' Borghese held the remaining silver cufflink close to David's face where he could better see the tarnished green jewel. Up in the rafters, Chase felt Aisling's heart lurch. He squeezed her arm reassuringly, but received nothing in return.

David weakly batted the cufflink away. 'Perhaps your mad mother can play with it.'

Borghese did not react. 'I'll have Wilson fetch you new

shoes. I'm sure one of my shirts will do until I can have my tailor make something more appropriate.'

'Wilson, yes, I noticed your man Wilson up to something. Down in the hall.' David gave a big sigh, as close as he could get to laughter. 'Don't look so alarmed, Scipione. I don't mind what you do behind my back. Within reason.'

'Are you hungry, my friend?'

'Do I look thinner?' Lost teeth in his mouth, like broken windows.

Aisling did not see the suspicion rising slowly on Chase's face as he looked at her. Her eyes were transfixed to David.

'I want a smoke. Would you? Yes. Prop me up. They're in my coat.' A crushed carton with a picture of a camel in a yellow desert. Borghese took a thick brown cigarillo from the packet and lit the end. The friendly scent of Robert blossomed out over the mildew. Up in the rafters, Aisling's head spun.

'This has been the most appalling day in years,' David said, exhaling smoke.

'The mourners would like you to know that what was said was said in grief. The boy wanted to let off steam.'

'Ah, but he was right. They're coming in from the wasteland every day now. Foreigners creeping in through the gaps in the walls. Like bacteria. The one they killed ended up swinging from a lamp post outside the old town hall. The body's gone now. Anatomists. I wonder what they'll find inside him.'

'Can I tempt you with something to eat?'

'I can't chew. Even soft bread, it hurts. Everything always hurts.' His hand gestured vaguely at a sore spot under his knee and Borghese rolled the loose trouser leg up to where a bruise blazed yellow-black against the pallid flesh. 'She kicked me. Weeks ago. Look at it.'

'Who kicked you, friend?'

'I don't know who she is. Not really.'

Borghese was horrified. 'Someone assaulted you?'

David shrugged. The pain on his face indicated he instantly regretted the motion.

'With your permission, I will find this person and bring her to justice.'

'She didn't know me, Scipione.'

'How could she not know you?' Borghese was incredulous. 'A precedent must be set. You said it yourself, we only improve ourselves by plucking out the rotten element, and if someone has the temerity to attack you—'

'Don't flatter. The younger generation barely know me from nursery stories, let alone... No, it was different, this particular situation.'

'But even so.'

'It was my fault.' He sighed. 'I frightened her. I have always been frightening, have I not?'

From the mirrored dresser in the corner, Borghese fetched one of many bars of chocolate wrapped in foil. 'Sweetness for bitter times,' he said, and warmed the chocolate in his big hands until it melted. David opened his parched lips and licked the proffered wrapper. His eyes rolled back and met Aisling's through the cracks in the ceiling boards. Her heart in her throat, Aisling prayed he hadn't registered the sight of anything but warped mahogany.

'All my work with this place. The Remedy, the methodical cleansing, everything I did, and still this.' His eyes protruded, taking in the remains of his body. He coughed out a laugh. 'Physician, heal thyself, hm? I've searched for that girl. I allowed myself to believe she was a good omen for me. Oh, don't look so alarmed. No, I toyed with that heretical idea. She was like me, Scipione. Yet the more I think of her wildness when we met that night in that house, the more I think she...' His Adam's apple bobbed in his throat like a snake attempting to swallow an egg. 'She was so young, Scipione. So out of place. Do you know, Scipione, that I was young once? And unwanted?'

Borghese silently took in every word. The sugar was a shock to David's emaciated system. He chased the high with a suck on the cigarillo and bared his gappy gums with a smile.

'These kill you,' he said. 'Did you know that?'

'If you dropped it in a hay barn, I'm sure.'

The sugar-glaze temporarily faded from David's eyes. 'Ah, see,' he said. 'That's where you're wrong.'

Borghese left the room to fetch a silver vanity case. He lit a candle beside the bed and began laying out equipment: a spoon, a packet of chocolatey dust and a hypodermic needle.

'I want to divulge something,' David said. 'Will you let me?'

'I'm in no position to deny you anything,' Borghese said, with perhaps more bitterness than he intended to betray.

'Have you seen these cigarettes before?'

'It's not a brand I know.'

'I buy them from a corner shop on a noisy street in a place you'll never, ever see. Lots of immigrants there, now. Poles, Romanians, all kinds of Indian and Oriental.' He chuckled weakly. 'I was a novelty, once. The sole interloper in that English village. My mother thought starvation was the worst fate a child could face. She never stopped to think what it does to someone, to be the one white bird in a flock of black.'

Borghese coaxed the flame higher, then warmed the spoon above it. David watched, his big wet eyes appearing to melt in the flickering light.

'You remember, of course, the beginning, how they welcomed me as a traveller,' he murmured. 'Lately, I have found I can go anywhere I like. I walk and I walk and I find myself displaced. Isn't that lovely?'

Borghese judiciously ignored the blisters on those big, bare feet. He took a pinch of the brown powder and let it fall into the bowl of the spoon. Shortly, it bubbled and puckered like caramel.

'It is as if the universe is experimenting with me,' mused David. 'Picking me up, putting me down. To see if I suit the place.' His tongue slithered over the crust of his lips as he watched the bubbles being tapped from the needle. 'What if I don't suit any place, Scipione?'

In the cushion of Borghese's lap, David's arm stretched out, grey and veiny. Borghese pressed at the crook of the elbow and for a second Aisling was sure he was about to caress it. He angled the needle and drove it into the flesh.

'You need a long sleep, my friend. And when you wake, new clothes, good food and medicine to restore you. Anything you need, this house is where you'll find it.'

>•<

An hour after David slid into drugged unconsciousness, Chase was restless. Dawn was on the way, and the stirring birds agitated him. He squirmed on his back, stretching his long legs, kicking at the air. Aisling ignored him. The grain of the floorboards was digging into her face, but she kept her eyes on the man on the bed.

Borghese had disappeared. Gone to dress, gone to dispose of Jobi while Chase was safely stowed away. Wherever he was, he had left David unguarded, and the adrenaline shooting up and down Aisling's spine was becoming too much to bear.

David, what did they do to you?

Chase kicked, his grimace returned by dozens of mirrors.

'I can't go to gaol,' he said. 'I can't. There's things I've not done.'

Seeing David's missing teeth had set the cogs turning in his head. *Go on, go down to your friend*, he seemed to say. Beverley had been right about men, at least on one count. Easily spooked.

In his sleep, the grey areola of David's eyeball emerged from under the twitching lid. Somehow, he even looked like the house in Suffolk: mismatched, awaiting repair.

He told Borghese he could go back.

'He's gonna turn us in,' Chase said. 'We're dead.'

Aisling struggled past Chase's unresisting body to the hatch leading back out into the wardrobe.

'You'll never get out,' Chase muttered, but she soon found the latch by rejigging the mirrors for light. Through the crack in the wardrobe she checked Tor's bedroom was empty, and then carefully, so as not to jostle all those noisy fabrics and coat hangers, slid her way out.

Neither Borghese nor the swift and dangerous Wilson were about. Down in the garden, starlings raided the apple trees. The floorboards creaked benignly. No one was going to grab her from behind, she realised. She was free to do this.

The door opened up into a clean, high-ceilinged bedroom. That same old weighty fuel-stink. It clung to her tongue as she licked her dry lips.

David sprawled, twitchy. He lay there in his tatty trousers, a dried-up husk of the man in Edythe's photograph. Lips pulled back from bloodless gums in a corpsey snarl. What was that he said about a mother? She tried to imagine him as a boy of her age. Too strange a task.

She moved to the end of the bed for a closer view of his cracked leather feet. That compulsion to go somewhere, and now, she knew it intensely. Perhaps that was all she needed to know about him.

A familiar glint under the bed. Lodged between the corners of two old suitcases was one of the Reverend John Enright's emerald cufflinks. Slipping it into her pocket along with its twin and that wretched tooth, she sat on the edge of the bed.

'David. Your omen's here.'

It was loud enough to stir him.

His eyes rolled over her. She thought of stories of the guillotine, how severed heads reacted to slaps and jibes long minutes after the moment of the blade.

'Hullo?' he whispered.

'You're writing a book,' she said. 'About Russian immigrants.'

David stretched, letting his neck loll back on the pillow to get a better view of her. 'Ah,' he sighed deeply. 'That's something I say. When I go. Visiting.'

'You visit lots of people?'

'Oh, many. I like to talk.' His mind drifted; he was evidently still under the lingering hold of the drug. 'Is that surprising?'

'Tell me what happened at the vicarage.'

He seemed not to hear. 'Your uncle was a good boy,' he sighed. 'Tin Hussars all over the parlour floor, me with my big feet.'

His hand slid over the coverlet towards her. She moved back.

'I saw you,' he said. 'In the tunnels. You needn't be afraid of me. We're very much the same, you and I.'

A long sssss in 'same', with a sleepy bubble of saliva. He was a pitiful sight. But then her mind jumped back to picture the tooth spat out on Edythe's cellar floor, now nestled against her hip. Him laying his hands on her, uninvited. She held up the cufflink.

David wheezed at the sight of it. 'I'm sorry Edythe flew off the handle. To be quite honest, I don't know what I was trying to accomplish, moving things around, like some petty ghost. I think that's why ghosts do it, you know. To be remembered.' The hand made its way across the coverlet to touch her, and again, to his drowsy dismay, she moved away. 'Did they ever mention me to you? Surely some memory was jogged when they led you up to that bedroom, or allowed you into the bathroom, where...' Suddenly, puzzled: 'How did you get here? Here. Do you remember?'

She pictured him gripping the beam across the priest hole, working it with his ropey arms to reveal the dark slit, a fitting home for his writings, his theories, the poison he fed himself. She could see it, now. At the vicarage, he was a hairless, gap-toothed melancholic. Here, he was in charge.

David gazed out over her head. 'Leviticus: *Then the priest shall command that they wash the thing wherein the plague is, and he shall shut it up.*'

'We are not the same,' she said.

The dreamy haze hitched. He wasn't looking at her. Over her shoulder the door was opening. The tall shape of Chase emerged, and perhaps it was the murderous look on his face, but David was painfully awake and shrinking away.

'I didn't realise you two were mates,' Chase said.

David's fingers had coiled themselves around a strand of her hair. She snatched it away in disgust.

'You'll stay with me?' he whispered up at her. 'My sky woman. My messenger. You won't abandon me when I'm—'

David wrenched his head off the pillows to breathe something at her, but Chase was bodily removing her from the bed. She shook him off. 'What are you doing?'

He leaned over David. 'My friend died yesterday. The Foreigner. Yeah?'

David did not comprehend. He wriggled backwards into the pillows, goggling at Aisling and Chase as if they were twin nightmares.

Chase shot a green look at Aisling. 'Wait for me outside.'

'What? No.'

It wasn't a request. The bed creaked as he got up on to it. There was a bright, shivering look in his eyes and, when David made a weak attempt to shuffle away, the younger man straddled his chest.

'Chase,' Aisling said. 'You're hurting him.'

When the knife appeared, David made a sound halfway between laughter and fright.

'Chase, what are you doing?'

He placed the tip of the knife in the hollow between David's heaving throat and sternum, and positioned his fist on the end of the handle, like a chisel.

'Say his name for me.'

David croaked.

'Jobi. Say it.'

The weight of Chase on his chest cut off David's air. Blood beaded sluggishly at the base of his neck. A thought leaked into Aisling's head that if Chase opened the jugular, petrol would ooze from him, stinking and syrupy. Embellishment, she told herself. But the thought was a stain that wouldn't shift.

David gestured with his eyes. 'You would… in front of?'

'Aisling, go out and shut the door.'

David grunted as Chase's weight intensified against his ribs, and Aisling realised she was tensed for a crack as much as a stabbing.

'Chase,' she pleaded. 'This isn't you.'

'You taught them what to do,' he told David. 'Those boys. You made the rules. *"The Twelfth Law concerns Foreigners, wastelanders, the transient. Any individual rejecting the Reason and protection of Our Friend undermines the safety and happiness of others through the spread of decadent, superstitious ideologies."* We memorised that. *"Incarceration, re-education, removal."* Yeah? And the rewards for turning us in, the medals, the nice houses. We all know Borghese didn't get this place by selling sherbet.'

'Chase, he's drugged, he's really drugged.'

'Say his name.'

David struggled. The cartilage of his throat bulged as

he strained his neck away from the thirsty blade. He was trying to speak. A rattle in the lungs. 'She,' David hissed, 'will leave you behind.'

Chase punched him so hard that the whole bed rocked.

A volley to the face and chest. 'He stuck by me, he made me laugh, he knew what I wanted and he wanted it too and you killed him with your stupid rules and his name was—'

The shout did it. At the bottom of the house, a rumble of movement. Aisling caught Chase by the coat and tugged as hard as she could, but he was all muscle and heavy with grief, and her hand came away slick with a splash from David's broken nose. Panting, Chase regained his grip on the knife and placed it against the pulsing jugular.

All too soon, the door hit the wall. Borghese's face flushed deeply at the tableau before him. But rather than throw himself at Chase as Aisling expected him to, or even tell him in a coaxing voice to drop the knife, the confectioner did nothing. The look on his face was unmistakable. He thought David was dead.

They all saw it: relief.

Then, just as Borghese was about to recover himself, the battered body beneath Chase's wavering knife shifted like weed in a lethargic tide. Slowly it opened its eyes to regard Borghese, and it clearly took all his self-restraint not to recoil back into the door frame. Borghese fixed Chase with a wild, imploring look. The knife hung above David's thorax, and Chase could have killed him several times over, but the energy was waning, and the strange, unspoken exchange was coming to some kind of end.

Chase couldn't do it.

At first, Borghese could only manage a sob into his

dressing gown sleeve. The atmosphere loosened. They all became aware of their own muscles aching, of the heat in the room and the slow *pat-pat* of David's bleeding nose. There was a commotion outside the house, far below in the upmarket, pretty street.

Borghese addressed David: 'There's been an incident.'

>•<

Despite being unable to hobble to the toilet, Scipione Borghese's elderly mother was twirling her way across the broken glass in the street like a ghostly ballerina.

In her nightgown, hair streaming, she was beautiful, Aisling thought as she trailed after Borghese and Chase, down the stairs and outside, into the heat emanating from the burning guard post. The younger guard hunched cross-legged on the kerb, wrapped in somebody's least-favourite blanket. In his singed uniform, he whined at anyone who came too close: 'Not again. Not again.'

Someone had hurled a makeshift bomb. Rainbow pools of sticky liquid still burned with acrid smoke and somewhere a baby was screaming. All the lights in all the houses were blazing, faces at every window. The street was a beacon in the electricity-free landscape. People from the town were already venturing out on to the bridges to look. The remaining guards stalked the perimeter.

'Oi!' someone called from the darkness beyond. 'D'you need someone to fetch a doctor?'

'You are in breach of curfew. Clear off!'

Wilson had taken up the role of leader to the servants of the street, working to stamp out the pockets of fire while their masters cleaved to their doorsteps in their pyjamas. He shouted to Borghese, 'You ought to go inside, sir. He's still in the area, sir, he can't've gone far.'

'Francesca, please, come in now. Be a good girl.'

The old woman danced on, regardless. In the red glimmer of the flames her face shone like china, and she laughed joyously as she collided with Aisling, bone on bone.

'For you, Miss Victoria. The gentleman caller insisted.'

It was a thick wedge of folded paper.

'Gentleman?' Aisling's throat was sore.

'He was anxious to see you, miss, but I knew you'd have none of it, so I told him you was busy with the other gentleman, the slaphead, and he took fright, miss, it was terribly funny. You do keep them on tenterhooks, don't you?'

It was one of Georgie's plans for the smokehouse. As Francesca went twirling off, evading the open arms of her son, Aisling took the paper to a dark spot away from the chaos and sat on the kerb to read.

I thought I'd try writing to you the direct way for a change.

Feodor's blocky, difficult handwriting was immediately recognisable. Before she had a chance to decipher the next line, Chase was beside her, looking ten years older, stubbly and gaunt. She hid the paper in her sleeve.

'I couldn't do it,' he said.

'You don't need to apologise.'

'You can share stuff with me. That's what friends do.'

'Is it?'

'Yeah, I think so. Jobi did.'

The new day was coming in fast. People in the poorer part of town were waking up to the commotion. Wilson, boots thick with oil, raised his hand to Aisling. With his finger-stumps he indicated the break in the fence beside the unmanned guard post. His master's back was turned.

Aisling helped Chase to his feet.

'We should go.'

25

They holed up under an iron bridge in the meatpacking quarter while the morning rush thumped overhead.

Beside her, curled in on himself with the dust of sleep crusting the corners of his eyes, Chase looked like a drowned urchin. Above them someone shouted a greeting to a friend, and he jerked awake, hand going straight to the knife in his belt. She placed two fingers on his back and he settled down.

Lying there in the silt, she tried to count the months she had been there – there there, with Chase and the rest of them. Was she eighteen yet? Something in her bones was changing.

Aisling fingered the folded paper in her pocket.

Did you like the warning shot? Feodor wrote. *I put it together a bit quickly, but the alcohol went nicely with the sugar. The things you don't forget, eh?*

Thanks for putting me into bed. Georgie says it's my

kidneys. He says he'll feed me boiled barley and vinegar for a week and I'll be fine. Funny how being sick makes you see things sideways.

I've got him here, and he's being a good boy. Where? Not telling. Not in the chapel. I dragged my corpse out to look for you soon as I could, and it turns out Georgie had the same idea. Quite a shock I gave him, pouncing on him like that.

You know the first thing he said to me? 'We planted a tree.'

Apparently, after Tor told everyone I'd died, she thought it would be nice to set up a little memorial to me in the garden. Like you do when the family dog dies, you know. And then, do you know what he said next? 'Will you let me shave your face?'

I've spent years picturing what it'd be like if I ever saw any of them ever again. I've rehearsed it every which way, and I still wasn't right.

Not as good as Tor's reaction, though. I went back to the house the night you'd gone off for a jolly with Chase. She came outside in her nightie before I'd even knocked on the door, like she could smell me. She said, 'Please go away.'

We're the same, you and me. Tor mothers people. She wraps them up tight and tells them nothing will ever go wrong again, so long as you do what she says. And you love it at first, because it's a kind of freedom, isn't it, deciding to give up? But that doesn't last. You get that feeling. You know the one. Hurts, doesn't it?

She never understood what I had to do, or why. 'Rada's not your sin,' she'd say. 'Not yours to atone for.'

You see why I couldn't stay.

He's taken to long walks, Our Friend. I've taken to following him. You're the sign he's been waiting for, Aisling, whatever that means. I don't think even he really knows. I remember his broadcasts on the radio: 'The Sixth Law concerns vitality of the body as manifestation of mental fitness, the Seventh Law concerns the role of dress within a functional society, the Eighth Law concerns the sexes and the occupations thereof.' Within reason, right? He had families informing on each other, anyone the slightest bit weird dragged off and never seen again. Openly talking about omens, that'd be suicide. But he's scared of you. You know something about him.

I used to believe I could make stuff better by burning it to nothing. And then I thought I could do some good, instead. Punchline is, I still ended up burning the place down. But now you're here. And like Our Friend, I'm beginning to wonder what that means.

When she finished reading aloud, Chase sat scratching scales of dried blood from his hands.

'Feodor damn near burned the whole world.' He paused as some people tramped over the bridge. Thumping boots on iron. 'People took to boats to get away. Just floating out in the harbour, watching their homes go up. Georgie? Well, you've seen his arms.'

'He told me it was an accident.'

'Remember how Our Friend just turned up in the mire one day, and no one knew where he'd come from or how? So did Feodor. Supposedly. I thought he was soft in the head, looking for attention. But people notice new faces here. Rumours spread, and Feodor fell for them. Decided they suited him, anyway. He said he'd been put here, by destiny, or some such nonsense, to get rid of Our Friend, to sort the place out. Arthur saw the danger and got me to take him out to live with Tor, and it was good for a long while. We all liked him, moody so-and-so. But he couldn't resist the fame. A lot of people believed in him. A lot died. Not that he hung about to see it.' He rested his head back against the rusty legs of the bridge. 'And now he's got Georgie.'

'Did he ever talk to you about the girl?' she asked. 'Rada?'

'Only every waking bloody moment. He was cracked, Aisling. The things he used to say.' He took the letter from her, held it to his nose and sniffed. 'Come on.'

'What?'

'Little shit's told us where he is.'

The tide was low. Chase led her to the entrance of an unfinished sewer at the back of the terraces where ragged chickens scratched about in the weeds. They had to clamber down a rickety maintenance ladder to swing themselves inside the opening, and they steadied each other as they wobbled, not meeting eyes. They sloshed through the sandy puddles, half certain arms would come out to meet them around the next corner, and that Borghese would be there in his fur coat like a bear come to maul.

'This'll be over soon,' Chase chattered. 'Georgie will build his smokehouse. We'll spend the autumn stocking the cellar, and I can show you how to take care of the chickens, if you like. Maybe you can teach me some reading. That'd pass the cold months well, wouldn't it? I'm not too slow a learner. 'Cause you'll stay, won't you?'

You won't go leaving me? his face seemed to say. *Us?*

'No, I— I want to go back with you.'

'Well, good. That's a promise, then. Good.' He wafted his lighter across a sign reading ALL THE FUN OF THE FAIR and tugged her gently down a side alley. A rusty drainage pipe leaked steadily on to their heads. 'I'd like to know, one day, why Feodor said you two are the same. Why you have Our Friend's tooth. I mean, not just now, if you're not ready yet, but friends share things, so tell me one day. Soon-ish.' *Immediately*, said his face, turned down to look at the water stagnating in the black earth underfoot. Suddenly he stopped walking and turned to her, arms hanging by his sides. He was dirty and bloody, eyes glassy-wide with loss.

'I really love you, you know. I just do.'

She was too stunned to speak. Whatever happened now, she was still glad they had met, glad he hadn't done something he would regret, that would change him. But what had Tor said? *'Because you're happy, it can't be real?'* Because he likes you, because he doesn't just tolerate you, he can't be…

Her mouth moved of its own volition. 'I'm tired, Chase.'

But Chase was close to angry tears. 'Me too. But I bloody well mean it.'

They stood there in the tunnel, panting.

'We good?' he said.

'We're good,' she said.

They moved off. The brickwork ended and the tunnel became little more than an underground trench propped up with wooden slats and a prayer. The ground took a sudden slope. The two of them slipped on the sandy scree. Overhead, the drainage pipe was even leakier here, with dripping tentacles of algae and a straining, ticking sound that made Aisling nervous. Chase gestured. No more talking. They edged their way down the squelching duckboards towards a mound of sandbags under an industrial door weirdly suspended at head height. On the steel, someone had chalked a skeleton grinning over a martini glass.

With a nod to Aisling, he let the light go out. Violet sparks before her eyes. She could hear Chase straining with the door's wheel mechanism. In the dark, the dripping of the pipe overhead set the nerves at the base of her spine shivering. She felt suddenly drunk, as if she'd had a teacup of Robert's whiskey. Something like a memory, half a memory, of white enamel and a scummy residue that meant something dreadful she couldn't define.

The door was open. Chase came back up the slope for her, offering his arm, but the weight of the two of them on the duckboards dislodged a stake propped against the ceiling. Something groaned. Chase flicked the lighter, looked up.

'Balls.'

There was no use running. Without support the drainage pipe sagged ominously, and with a heaving moan the rusty segments cracked apart and belted them with sheets of freezing water.

Aisling was forced to her knees by the weight of her coat. The duckboards shifted as the sandy ground became a quagmire. Chase dropped the lighter. She heard him curse every whoreson plumber in the land as the water kept coming, rolling down the slope, dragging them both with it.

In the slide, Aisling's pockets tipped out. She swept her hands around in the dark for the tooth and the cufflink. Mud in her shoes, her sleeves, her hair. Black-tasting, sucking and thick. Wrist-deep, she scrabbled for David's tooth. Handfuls of nothing. Her breath caught in her throat like a bone.

Why not let it go?

The mud was deepening fast. Chase was calling to her, swearing and coughing as they slithered to the bottom of the tunnel, pinned to the sandbags by the force of the downpour. Breathless and blind, Aisling's fingers tightened into claws. With horror, she realised what was coming. *Alert a friend or carer, if you can*, the pamphlets always said. *Avoid fractures and burns with these simple adjustments around the home.* She tried to shout to Chase, who was just a few feet away in the dark, fighting not to sink, but her tongue was clotted with mud. Over the noise of her body, thoughts of drowning scrolled like a news bulletin from a distant country.

You can't drown in make-believe mud, Sweets.

Beverley, as if she were here, lighting up a cigarette. Grit worked up into her nostrils and down her throat. Make-believe mud for make-believe seizures? Chase, shouting her name. The walls wouldn't hold.

She was just so tired.

So why not?

The mud held her tight. Face down and jerking, deaf to Chase as water rose over her ears, the next thing Aisling knew with any certainty was pain. Something in the dark, something needle-sharp. In the haze of the seizure, it drove into the tender skin of her temple, and she thought of sharks swimming in the slurry. Pinprick. Intravenous. Doctor Ross and his wide white mouth.

A shove from below forced her body to the surface, spitting and retching. Pain drilled through her head. The water had stopped.

In the deluge, one of the duckboards had slid down the slope and under her. She floated there, half insensible, asking herself her own name, the day of the week, how many months until Christmas. With a shaking hand, she pawed at her forehead, and plucked out David's tooth. The following glut of blood made her shudder. Some of the struts steadying the walls had half sunk in the mud, and she dimly noticed the ceiling's worrying new shape, sluggishly dropping clods and stones. No candles were lit, she realised. Yet she could see.

'Please.'

Not Chase's voice. Aisling dragged herself up the duckboard and on to semi-solid ground. Alleys she hadn't noticed before branched off from the main tunnel. No sign of Chase in any of them.

The voice again: 'John.'

Blood in her mouth. The light grew brighter, as if a hand had swept aside a curtain.

'Whatever it is,' she croaked, 'I don't want to see it.'

'John, please.'

David. Standing in the tunnel's highest point. He was shaking his head, staring out in her direction, unseeing.

'I said no!' Aisling hurled a stone. It bounced off the wall. David didn't flinch.

'John, she's lying. I wore them once, yes, but John, you aren't listening. Why would I steal? When I live under your roof, why?'

Aisling pressed her face to her knees. It could have been over by now. What did it take to drown, a minute? Two? Already she lacked the courage to try again. She shut her eyes, the tooth tight in her fist where her blood already dried and cracked.

'She planted them in my room,' David insisted. Still standing there. She forced herself to look. His body, long and cringing, was different. A young man's frame, with all the vigour sucked out. 'She is lying.'

Aisling tried to think of something beautiful. Egypt at night. The Northern Lights. The last beautiful thing she could recall was the way the grass felt under her palms in the vicarage garden, with little Connie smiling in the smoke.

Her eyes cracked open.

David's hands trembled, outstretched as he pleaded with someone just over her head. His cuffs, ink-blotchy, gaping like mouths. As she neared him, she saw the last remaining wisps of hair plastered to his damp brow. Repellent. But she didn't think, just touched him. Put out her hand to his face as she had to Feodor before him.

He didn't smell of petrol, she realised as her fingers brushed skin. Not yet.

26
DAVID

'Alopecia,' declared the Reverend John Enright, taking a sip of the over-stewed Earl Grey that Effie had brought out into the conservatory. 'Sounds rather like a furry animal one would find in the Andes.'

The Bloom sisters had come up from the village on their pushbikes, dolled up like they'd arrived in a Bentley. Fanny wore red nail polish for the occasion and smiled benignly while the younger sister, May, stared at the young clerical assistant sitting uncomfortably with them in the vicarage conservatory. That hairless head. It put her off her scone. Only last Christmas, David had slicked down what little thatch he had with pomade, and he'd overheard her calling him a spiv. Now, his gleaming head looked strangely too large, like the bones of his knees bulging in his black trousers. All hair, every strand of it, gone.

It was a tragedy. A fascinating one.

David flexed his neck. Since losing his hair, the worst

thing, the worst in a long list, was—

'The eyelashes went not long after his eyebrows,' said the Reverend Enright. 'Every bit of grit floating by lands directly in his eyes now, poor chap.'

David squirmed.

'You shouldn't rub it,' said Fanny.

The Reverend nodded as if she'd made a vital medical observation. 'No, you'll risk infection. Fanny's quite right.'

David shook his head. Disagreeing or shaking away the dust, it was unclear.

'No one knows what causes it. It has been known for people with this condition to find the hair growing back, as if returning from a short holiday. It isn't infectious. Perhaps I'm simply working him too hard.' The emerald cufflinks John saved for special engagements glinted prettily as he lifted his teacup. And he made vanity jokes at David. *'God's way of saving you money on Brylcreem, dear boy.'*

May continued her unabashed staring while her sister droned on in her farmer's accent. 'I heard about a girl from Ipswich who had a terrible rash all over her face. They tried all kinds of grease and light and disinfectant. In the end, they sent her to a nice little village in Switzerland. Good air healed her up beautiful.'

'David is up to date with all the latest scientific literature,' the Reverend said, as if it were funny. He had seen David's American Eugenics Society quarterlies, along with the manifesto of Le Corbusier and the decrees of the Spanish Anarchists David criticised mildly in half-written essays John assured him no one would ever read, piled up in the little room at the top of the house where he slept.

'You could try a hat,' May said, and Fanny stifled a laugh.

'No, I mean it. With a big peak, some netting, or summat.'

'You can take up beekeeping,' added John, and how the ladies loved that idea, buttering their scones and stirring their tea. It was a skill of theirs, David thought, somehow ignoring the object of their discussion, as if he were an amputated limb sealed in a jar. The image made him curiously wistful. To take up a knife and slice away contaminated flesh, David thought. How marvellous that would be.

'I'd've thought your stock were hardy, Mister Morgun, what with all that snow,' Fanny said. 'Siberia, weren't it, where Mister Carey found you?'

David cleared his throat to speak. An unbecoming noise, not suited to the living evidence of the late Mister Carey's Christian charity. Siberia? Fanny was only a couple of thousand miles off. And not so much 'found' as snatched from death's teeth, if one believed the Reverend Enright's version of events. David was Mister Carey's mercy mission. The sermons the Reverend squeezed out of his mere existence – he was wrung dry.

'Excuse me.' David screwed up his fist and rubbed his eye. Itchy, itchy.

'Oh dear,' said the Reverend Enright, smiling. 'And of course, nowhere on earth is as dusty as a vicarage in summer.'

'I'll come and clean, if you like,' May offered, mainly because the work would afford her further glimpses of that weird, bald head.

David folded his hands in his lap and studied his smooth wrists. It had started with hairs on his shoulders, fallen from his head during services. In the bath, the translucent fluff on his chest and thighs slipped away with the soap suds. Months of toothache. A mystery, the dentist said, a painful mystery that stopped him sleeping. *'God's way of telling you to stop scoffing toffee, David.'*

David didn't believe in mystery ailments. The swoons of weak women, neurasthenia, *J'ai mal au coeur*, all bunkum. David believed in a cause for every event. He knew, for example, that the revolution caused the civil war, and the civil war caused the famine. He knew the famine caused his father to die, and his mother to give him to the Englishman. Mister Carey said she had the Red Cross's details. Mister Carey said she would send for him. Kindness caused Mister Carey to lie.

David looked to the garden, fenced off from the stretching fields beyond. If it were up to him, he'd build academies here. Grand libraries. The young people would have no need to leave the way they did, haemorrhaging into the cities where life could be found. Mister Carey called him a bright lad. He could go away to study, he told him, become a chemist, or an archaeologist, or a plastic surgeon. *Stay here*, a weak part of David said. *Just in case.*

In case of what? Here he was, taking tea with the Bloom sisters in a conservatory belonging to a man he despised. He was bald and sore and hadn't felt an emotion in nearly a year.

What use had he for a mother, he reasoned? Him, a grown man. When Mister Carey died he went through every scrap of paperwork in the house. What use was sentiment, he asked himself, when the search yielded nothing? Sentiment leaves a man vulnerable. It dampens the brain.

May's infernal Suffolk accent cut through his reverie. 'I can't imagine having no eyelashes.'

'But you pluck your eyebrows,' Fanny said. 'And draw them on.'

'I don't,' said May, and licked jam from her thumb. Overweight and under-educated, the Blooms, and propagating like horseflies since the Norman conquest.

Effie the maid sauntered in to ask if everyone had enough butter. She glanced at him. He evidently had crumbs around his mouth, because her nose twitched the way it did when the children were small and wet their beds.

David wiped his face. 'May I— May I be—' it hurt, the grit, right under his eyelid, and the toothache, and the staring and— 'May I possibly be excused?'

'I should say so,' the Reverend said. 'You're putting our guests off their elevenses.'

'Oh, it isn't his fault,' Fanny said. 'You mustn't mind us, Mister Morgun. You have a good scratch.'

May giggled. She actually giggled. A ball of anger walloped David in the stomach and he stood clumsily, making the wicker chair crunch as if he were too heavy for it while she sat there, prim as a kitten with her fat ankles and her cheap dress.

He fled to the hall, trying to ignore John switching on his sermon voice for the benefit of the ladies. ('Of course, the story of Job teaches us that the very kernel of suffering, humiliation…'). *Shut up shut up.*

Here was the staircase, and the window where the rain battered darkly and too often. The photographs above the door. Mister Carey, chuffed to bits with his Red Cross armband, and David a blur at John Enright's left hand. The volunteers came to Russia from every nation imaginable. Scraps of memories wrapped in hunger. In Saratov, the bony dead were piled like lumber. He was sick on the boat, swaddled in someone else's coat. Before those black waves, mother meant hard hands and the taste of boiled cabbage. Of a sister, he recalled mere morsels. His father, slivers of nothing.

Mister Carey's mercy mission.

What are you, David? A gangly man with no hair struggling to find the lavatory. He passed the children's playroom where Edythe liked to arrange her dolls in rows while Connie scrawled on reams of paper. Robert, at sea now, had left his books all over the floor. He tried to read David's, once, necessitating a better hiding place in the cellar. The children knew what the bedroom at the end of the house meant: a place for the oafs and the quislings, the guests they didn't want.

He was becoming hysterical again. The boy wasn't a bad piece of work. And Connie laughed a lot, but rarely at him. Where was she, sitting in the garden? Had she seen his latest humiliation?

Edythe, though. It wasn't the girl's strangely aggressive neatness, or the wifely way she doted on her father, polishing his shoes because Effie was a slapdash country slut who tripped up the stairs twice daily. There was something, half-imagined maybe, projected at him through her blue stare. *Make one false move*, it said.

Oh, and he had.

There was the lavatory. There was the mirror. He closed the door and forced himself to meet his own eyes.

He had always been ugly. The baldness shouldn't have hurt him like it did.

This is God's way of telling you to stop— Stop— Stop—

Would he ever forget the afternoon Edythe had caught him trying on John's cufflinks? A moment of indiscretion in the privacy of his bedroom. Standing in front of the mirror, puffing out his chest to give the impression of musculature. The very second he fastened them to his cuffs, she revealed herself. And against all his principles he had grovelled. *'Please don't tell, I shan't do it again.'*

What a telling off it had been. In the kitchen, in front of all three children. In front of Effie, even. There was no section of the household who did not know he was a thief and a snake and embarrassingly vain.

That was before she showed them his notebook.

The face in the mirror was contorted now. Crying without eyelashes, nothing to hold back the water. A wet, white face with bones too big for the skin. *'Karloff, good heavens, it's uncanny!'* the Reverend exclaimed, returning from the Alhambra in Bury St Edmunds with the children one evening. *'RISE, Imhotep! Rise again!'* And the four of them collapsed laughing as David stood on the landing in his dressing gown with his cup of evening tea. He managed to speak – what was a servant of Christ doing at the pictures, watching a walking corpse? – and they had howled all the louder.

Nothing happens without cause. And so David had fought with all he had: clean living (not so much as a sip of Communion wine!); academic periodicals, food for the mind; morning calisthenics on the lawn until Edythe started waking up early to applaud him from the window. Hair in his tea. Sores in his mouth. A good man would have rallied. A good man would be well. There must be something within him. Something innate.

He sat on the lavatory and shakily took his cigarette case from his pocket. It looked suave no matter what contrary story his body told. Even the Elephant Man kept a vanity case.

Downstairs, the conservatory hummed with pleasant conversation. A sob thrust its way past his sore teeth. That ridiculous head, shaking at him in the mirror. A ball for kicking, a ghoul from the pictures. He reached over and locked the door, careful not to get his shoes on the fluffy white bath mat. It must have been Edythe's choice, it showed dirt so easily. She had taken over Effie's duties up here, he noted. An impressive array of bleaches and carbolic fluid lined up beside the paraffin heater. David squinted. Alphabetical order. He could have laughed.

Wash me thoroughly from my iniquity and cleanse me from my sin. He turned the stubborn faucet. They'd not come looking if they heard him drawing a bath.

His mother. Rada. Yes. He heard his father calling that name. '*Rada, kotyonok. My kitten.*' He saw her tracing the cracks in the walls the night of his sister's quiet death. '*You'll have more, lapochka,*' someone said. And did she, his mother? Did she feed herself, and live and meet another man? Have a girl to replace the lost one, and a boy to replace him?

He flicked his lighter with slippery fingers and lit the cigarette.

She was young. Tough, too, if she could put her little boy on a boat and watch him go. The first puff of smoke bloomed into the small room. No. If she'd lived, she would have looked for him. It stood to reason.

Or perhaps, even then, she saw his defects.

He sucked on the cigarette too heavily and burned the back of his throat. The pain caused the cigarette to drop from his slickened fingers.

If it were up to me.

A thin stream of smoke wafted against his face. Edythe's bath mat would be spoiled. With one hand rubbing his swollen eyelids, he fumbled for the cigarette.

If it were up to me.

The smoke became more forceful as Edythe's bath mat caught the flame and held it. Slowly, David stood and faced his reflection.

It never will be, it said.

He took the bottle of Aladdin Pink Paraffin from Edythe's neat rank and emptied the acrid fluid on to the floorboards.

27

Chase's arms locked around her, straining in an awkward embrace as they struggled together on the wet scree.

'Hey. Hey, I'm here,' he was saying in the dark. 'Where the hell did you go?'

Aisling's knees had given way. She was wiping at her sodden coat frantically, swearing in short bursts of laboured breathing. For a moment she couldn't be sure of where she was, and that was the worst of it.

'Turn the light on. Turn it on.' The words were slurred.

'It's wet, it's buggered. I can't.' He let her touch his face. His stubbled jaw, his cheekbones, the distress on his brow, all there. 'One minute, you were behind me, then you just— The water, you— Is that blood? Are you bleeding?'

Smoke in her eyes, paraffin. 'Oh God,' she gagged. 'Oh God, that poor man.'

Chase found dry matches in one of the candle sconces. He cupped the weak flame, checking her wound. Behind him, the main tunnel had almost completely collapsed. He saw her staring at the spot they'd stood in, overcome by rocks and timber.

'I couldn't hear you.' Chase tried to hide the tremor in his voice. 'We can't go above ground. Borghese's sent out dogs. There's wiggle room. We can make it if we crawl. Can you move?'

Her ankles thawed and she sunk back to the ground. Chase prised open her fist, baring the tooth as wetly bloody as if freshly pulled from David's mouth.

'It's this,' he said angrily. 'It's doing you harm.'

He tried to take it from her. Blood and bone, she snatched it away before it could burrow into him, too. She glanced back the way they came. No David now, no voices. Only distant hunting horns.

On the shore of Lake Nero, Red Cross letterheads sank in the black water.

>•<

Waiting for them beyond the rubble was a high, cone-shaped chamber. In the centre was a vast well. Aisling could feel the chill radiate against her skin. A coin of light from above touched the centre of the water, rippling like a pulse.

'It's a spring,' said Chase. 'The gin factory up top used it for their distilling. That's where they lowered the buckets, look.'

His voice only wavered a touch. The crawl had felt like days, what with Chase halting them, breath held, at the slightest sign of soil trickling from above. Aisling no longer lived in her body. Let the ceiling fall in. She could comfortably have lain in the dark forever, knees to her chest like a priest in a cellar.

There was a stone staircase spiralling up the tapering walls, and they took it slowly, mindful of the mildew slickening the steps and the easy drop to the flagstones below.

Chase put Aisling in front of him, promising to be a cushion if she slipped. What had just happened to make her so pale? She had that closed-off look he didn't like. Eyes hooded, breath shallow. She had no idea she was doing it, but it made him feel see-through, somehow, and it hurt.

He would get her home, and he would get Georgie home. Everything would be fine.

As he followed Aisling up to the factory floor, the turquoise walls held a melancholy familiarity to Chase, dull with dust where the white mosaic spelled out The Superior Botanical Nectar. That black forelock of Jobi's hair tickling the rim of a bottle. *'What's "botanical" mean, anyway? 'S'it like, 's'it like medicine?'* Giggles and burps. *'Dunno, but it's nice, isn't it!'* Before the curfew was imposed, the dance halls welcomed revellers long into the night. Sloe and juniper on the evening breeze. He and Jobi took turns to snatch a bottle for the night, sniggering over it down by the harbour, becoming over-sentimental on the third tot and crawling to sleep side by side in a stranger's garden.

The lump in his throat hardened and faded away. These were his memories and no one could steal them.

The place was in a poor state. It shouldn't have surprised him, given the condition of the entire bleeding world, but there was something especially sad about the cobwebs draping the gigantic copper stills.

'Wasn't so long ago, even,' he said to himself. Aisling didn't hear. She picked her way across the chequered floor with an odd, tottering walk that made him hurry to her, stopping a few feet behind so as not to seem as oafish as he felt.

'You all right?'

At the soft questioning, Aisling dragged her gaze away from the deep water below. There was soot coating every surface. She felt herself gag.

'I've got to get you home,' he said.

She gave a quiet little laugh. She looked as gaunt and exhausted as when he had first set eyes on her, and it put a flutter in his pulse.

'What happened down there?' he said. 'Come away from the edge.'

There was an edge, of course there was, how had she missed it? The railings had long ago been scavenged, leaving a straight drop down into the black spring a hundred feet below.

'Would you do me a favour and stay close to me? And if something happens, just get somewhere and lay low.'

'I did. Down in the cellar. I didn't know what else to do.' Aisling laughed again. She heard it come out of her. 'What if all this is…? What if all this *is*?'

'You're beginning to scare me. You don't want to scare me, do you?'

She touched the heel of her hand to her bleeding head and squinted. 'What's that noise?'

There was an owl in the rafters. A squeal of radio static startled it from its sleep. Aisling stared up at the ruffle of white wings as Chase bounced on his heels, straining to locate the source of the voice filling the factory.

'We insult the marvellous machine of the body with our

addictions, our slothfulness, our wanton or miserly way with nourishment,' came David's schoolmasterly tones. 'The corruption of the senses blocks the avenues of the fort of reason. This civil war inside a man leaves him vulnerable to physical and intellectual weakness. Give us health, give us reason, give us the rule of Our Friend.'

A crunch of interference. Then the sweet twinkle of waltzing piano.

'Shit,' said Chase, as his hand went to his knife.

They found Feodor deposited against one of the huge copper stills, tonguing an empty bottle of something labelled Saucy Nick's Bone Dry. In his lap was a radio, and he played with the tuning knob with one grubby hand.

'It still works,' he said, seeing the two of them. 'One of the first things I did was hijack Our Friend's frequency. Me and some guys set up a transmitting station in an attic and just blasted all over him at regular intervals. Doesn't take a genius. I used to do it to the drive-thru Maccy D's at home.'

The black cloud of curls was filthy still, but the contours of his face were clean and freshly shaved. He looked stronger than Aisling had left him. That terrier demeanour of coiled energy and darting eyes. A surprising relief.

'I do "Chopsticks" in a bit, too. We creased up! Cutting him off mid-flow with "Chopsticks".'

Chased scrunched up his face in disgust. 'Are you drunk?'

The bottle of Saucy Nick's went spinning over his head. It shattered against the slogan on the wall, and the owl took flight up and out of sight.

Feodor dropped the radio, killing the sound. For a moment, it looked as if he was considering standing up and hitting Chase, but he saw the blood and mud on their clothes and was still. 'Made friends?'

'Bit of a scuffle,' Chase said.

Feodor nodded warily. 'Our Friend. But you didn't kill him?'

Chase examined his boots. 'No.'

'Meow.'

'What?' He looked up angrily.

'Pussy.'

A glut of cloud skimmed over the sun.

'Probably a good thing, though,' Feodor said. 'When it happens, it needs to happen publicly. People need a big show to make them change.'

'And you'll be the one to make this big gesture. 'Cause you're so bleeding good at them.'

Feodor shrugged. 'Yeah. Well, sorry about your mate.'

The unexpected sincerity of the remark seemed to hurt Chase the most, and a blush spread down his collar. Just then, Feodor heard something. His head twitched, listening keenly, but his shoulders soon relaxed and a smile tugged at one side of his mouth.

'Here he is! Here's my little mate. Find anything good?'

Georgie pottered out from an adjacent storeroom, looking unbearably young with Tor's pistol tucked into the waistband of his trousers. He had an armful of grubby mixing flasks gathered to his chest. He was delighted to see Aisling and Chase.

'Look! We can do all sorts of things with these. I'm a scavenger now, too, Chase. You've got competition.'

'Hey, buddy,' Chase said, with his best impression of a casual grin. 'Why don't you take Aisling down to the tunnels, and I'll be with you in a bit?'

'Oh, are we not all going?' Feodor asked, eyes like flint.

Georgie put down his flasks. He arranged them into a neat line, like trophies. 'Chase, I've been talking to Feo and everything's fine. I think we could all do very well together at the house again. He can't go on living the way he does. The winters are getting worse, and I think—'

'No.'

Georgie's soft face was stunned. 'His kidneys need treating.'

'Go on. Out you get.'

Feodor rubbed against the still, dealing with an itch. 'Got enough crazy people in that house, I s'pose.'

Chase gave him a dangerous look. 'Do you want a thump?'

Feodor smirked. He saw the atmosphere between Chase and Aisling. 'You gonna rein this one in?' he asked her. 'I take it you were the one who stopped him chucking Our Friend out the nearest window. The old woman told me you were up there chatting away to him quite happily. Just what I told you not to do. It's like you're thick or something.'

Chase reared up. 'There's nothing wrong with her.'

'Our Friend likes her.'

Georgie broke in: 'Tor was so terribly worried when you left, Aisling. It doesn't feel like home without you there.'

Feodor whistled flatly. 'Home. Where's that then, Aisling?'

'Don't pretend Tor just chucked you out,' Chase said. 'You ran.'

'So did she.'

'That's different.'

'Same,' he said, still looking at her with an over-familiar coolness that both infuriated and unsettled Chase. 'We're from somewhere else altogether, her and me. Ing-er-lund,

Chase, an island where it rains a lot and everything's made of concrete. In England, if you go about like her, talking about boys no one else can see appearing into your bedroom at night, you get escorted to a nice hospital where they let you spend a few months playing board games and talking about your feelings before letting you out into the community where everyone politely keeps their distance and says, "Well, she's a nice girl, but you wouldn't want her babysitting little Timothy." Not like here. Where they dangle you from a lamp post.' He turned a sweet look on Chase. 'Condolences.'

'I don't understand,' Georgie said.

Neither did Chase. He looked like an overgrown lost boy.

'What else hasn't she told you?' Feodor fired at him. 'You don't know. Doesn't that worry you a bit?'

'I don't care where she's from or what you think's wrong with her. Georgie, come here.'

Feodor caught a handful of the boy's tunic. 'No, Georgie, why don't you stay over here with me? We're mates again, aren't we? Mates don't just ditch each other.'

Aisling managed to speak. 'I have to talk to you.'

'To me? Try talking to him, he looks like he's going to cry.'

'You killed people,' Chase yelled suddenly. 'Look out that window. Look at all those husks. Those were houses. At least two schools. You burned them down because you thought you were special.'

For the first time, a glimpse of real discomfort passed over Feodor's face. 'I never set out—'

'You just chucked a bomb at a guard post!'

'What, that little whizz-bang? Hardly Hiroshima. Sorry, only she'll understand that.' The snapping terrier was back and grinning at her. 'Maybe you can explain that to him when you tell him why you've got Our Friend's tooth in your pocket like some creepy love token.'

'Do you want me to feel sorry for you?' Chase growled. 'Better luck next time, Prince Paleface, or whatever the hell they called you.'

'Oh, don't bicker,' Georgie said. 'You always bickered. You think I don't remember what it was like, before the fire. You and him snapping and making up eleven times a day, and Tor making you sit at either end of the table so you wouldn't kick each other all through dinner. I may have been small but I was there too, so you can stop pretending this is all about you, thank you kindly.'

In any other circumstances, a telling-off from Georgie would have been adorable. When no one laughed or attempted to contradict him, the boy turned his gentle eyes on Feodor.

'You said you needed to go away and see some friends that night. I said, I'm your friend. You can take me. You made me stay anyway, but you've not always been good at hiding your tracks. So I waited for Tor to nod off after dinner and I took the tunnels down to Arthur's shop. But you weren't there. No one was. Just a dripping white cross on the door. They'd been taken to The Quiet. Even Eva, with her baby. There were posters on all the windows, a warrant out for Germaine's arrest. I knew at once you were in trouble, Feo, but there were people running all over the place, breaking curfew, carrying bags of belongings. Oil, they were saying, it's made with oil. And I didn't know what that meant, except Tor filled our lamps with oil, at home, and I knew you liked to do the lamplighting, once dusk came.

'I took the back alleys out to the factory quarter, where the worst of the fuss was. Warehouses were burning. There was glass everywhere. But then I spotted Germaine, shaking in a doorway. He was going to get out, he told me. He'd robbed a grocer's shop to pay a guide to sneak him into the wasteland, but the watchmen saw the lamplight and he had to grab the cash box and run. He thought he'd lose them in the factory quarter, but the closer he got the more people he saw, breaking curfew. One of the factories was surrounded. He said it was you, Feo. You'd rallied them against Our Friend. The factory made the whitewash for The Quiet, and you and your dissenters had thrown it all down the steps and into the streets. And Germaine saw you standing there, applauded and loved, and he thought of Arthur and Eva gone forever, and it didn't matter that the night watch were still chasing him. He ran up those steps to the factory gates and he hit you with the cash box so hard, he could have killed you. He hoped he'd killed you. But your followers threw themselves at him, and they would have finished him had the night watch not come tearing around the corner, arresting anyone they could catch. Before they could get up the steps, you snatched up Germaine's lantern and threw it at the watchmen. The lantern exploded and the people scattered, but the whitewash, it was made from oil. All those barrels of paint pouring into the gutters. It went up so fast, Germaine lost some of his hair as he fought his way out of the crowd.

'"You shouldn't be here," he told me. He said you'd ruined everything. That by tomorrow there wouldn't be a world left to save. And as he said it, one of the slum boys racing by saw the cash box under his arm, and he ran up and sank a screwdriver into Germaine's neck.

'Germaine was on the ground. I was all wet. And I couldn't work out why. The fire had spread across the canal. It was loud. I could feel the heat on my face. Windows were popping like party balloons. But then I saw you, Feo. I saw you go up a drainpipe. I saw you running to the wall. And I chased you, because you looked so frightened and everyone was cursing you because the world had at least been stable before you arrived, and I know you only wanted to make it better, but...' He placed two fingers gently on Feodor's sleeve. 'The fireworks emporium exploded just as I was catching up with you. I thought I was flying, and then I was flat on my back. I remember fireflies. I remember you climbing over the rubble away from me. The firefly smoke. You disappeared in it.'

Georgie rolled up his sleeve to show them the puckered pink satin of his arm. Feodor squeezed Georgie's waist in a half-hug. His face was blank with shock.

'It was meant to be a stunt,' he murmured. 'I didn't know it was... I didn't know you were even...'

Georgie covered his scars. 'It took months for Tor to heal my skin, but the hurt inside of me, only I could heal it. And I chose to do it. You never set out to hurt me. If I let myself be dragged under by blame and bitterness, who would I be now?'

All at once, they looked like strangers to Aisling. Far away folk with a history of their own. She put her palm to the gash in her head. The little veins in the soft place between forehead and cheekbone throbbed.

Chase cut the moment. 'I don't care about your noble intentions,' he told Feodor. 'You're not welcome in that house. You're not welcome around my friends. And if you've been living in a pit for the past few years I'm a happy man, because it's all you deserve.'

A dark lock of hair slid across Feodor's eyes, and he let it hang there. 'Well,' he said. 'That's what I get for trying. I'm the blighted youth, aren't I, Chase? Everything I touch turns to rot.'

'Georgie, get over here,' Chase said.

But Feodor backed off. Even thin and crackling with nerves, he was stronger than Georgie, and he fastened the boy to him with one arm across his chest. He reached around, pulled Tor's gun from Georgie's waistband and held it to his throat. Surprise flickered across the boy's dusky face; disappointment took its place.

'What are you doing?' Chase said.

'What you expect of me.'

He's going to shoot him, Aisling thought. *He's going to shoot him and it's going to be real.*

'Tell me about Rada, Feodor.'

Chase tried to step in front of her, but she dodged him, sidestepping across the black tiles.

'You wanted to do some good. To pay for her death.'

'Don't turn your child psychologist crap on me. I will put a hole in him.'

'No, you won't. It was natural. To want to help.'

'No, see, I've been thinking,' he said. 'That's why you're here. You're going to help me find Our Friend and I'm going to finish what I started. That's what's supposed to happen. That's the point of it all. That's the point of me.'

'Listen.'

'I'm going to lure him to you.'

'Feodor, there's no point.'

'And when I've got him, I'm going to stop him hurting anyone else.'

'He's dying.'

Everyone was silent. In Feodor's grip, Georgie was frozen, like a snared animal.

'Rubbish,' Feodor said at last.

She held out the tooth to him. A hole had appeared since she had last looked at it, festering through the middle, and the stench of fuel was rank.

'His name is David. He lived in my Aunt Edy's house, before all this. A long time ago, before I was born. But we talked. I touched him, just like I touched your nose.' She shook her head. 'I can't explain that. But when I was alone with him last night at Borghese's, he said "we are the same". So did you, do you remember? And I see what it means, now. We all slipped through some kind of door, but that isn't important. It's ripples. Connections. We're all touched.'

Feodor gave a little snigger into the soft crook of Georgie's neck. She remembered recording his words: *I laugh when I'm frightened.*

'I'm touched,' he said. 'I'm filthy. You read the walls, you know what my dad got up to. If Yuri hadn't killed Rada, he would never've run to England. He wouldn't've met my mother. I'm alive because Rada's dead. It's all over me. And Our Friend's right, filth spreads.'

'I know something you don't.'

A gust of wind forced itself through the broken windowpanes and swept up the matted locks of Feodor's hair.

It was as though they were her own memories. She

described the room with the pockmarked walls and the beds that never got warm, the foreigners who came prepared for hunger, but not for burying the dead. She spoke as gently as she could, trying not to look at Chase's stricken face. *Why couldn't you have told me that?* he seemed to say, and she didn't know. When at last she told them about the great ship that took the child away, her stomach roiled with the knowledge of what waited for the boy in Suffolk. Georgie, when she described Mister Carey who'd taken David in, gave a tiny smile.

'Like Tor,' he said, but Feodor silenced him.

Aisling wiped the crusts of blood from her temple and looked Feodor in the face. 'Rada was David's mother's name. She survived the famine and had more children.' She swallowed, breathed deep. 'Your Rada was her granddaughter. David's niece.'

His face. Total dismay.

'David,' he said, almost whispering, as if the name were wicked for being so ordinary.

'All that time, waiting in Suffolk for his mother to come and find him, he thought he was unworthy of her. But your Rada was looking for David. And she found him.' *And then your father.* It wasn't necessary to say it. It would have been cruel.

'This is— This is worse!' Feodor shrilled, laughing. 'Yuri drowned her before she could do anything about it. It's his fault. All of it.'

'No. It was too late. By nineteen forty-eight, David was gone. There wasn't a body. The firemen said it wasn't impossible. The villagers swore they'd seen him hanging around the house for years afterwards, watching the children in the garden. But it was just gossip. David vanished. Like we did.'

'And here's you,' he said, 'trying to stop me from stopping him.'

'No. It's like Georgie said, David chose bitterness. David had a choice, and so do you.'

Even as she said it, it chimed like a lie. David had his whitewash, his clean quiet chambers, but the black pitch in her head was just the same, drowning out all the beautiful places she'd ever longed to see, the adventures she hoped she'd have. Even her past was viscid and dark, as if she had sprouted out of the mire, a shameful thing like the blighted youth in David's notebooks. *'When you get better,'* said Beverley, *'everything will fall into place.'*

Get better. Go away. Whichever.

Feodor was turning it over in his head. His fingers played over the soft folds of Georgie's tunic as if fluttering out a tune. 'A vicarage in Suffolk,' he said slowly. 'And an Auntie Edythe.'

His hand clamped to Georgie's jaw, wrenching back his head to allow the pistol access to the soft groove of his throat. To Aisling's dismay he was laughing, shaking with it, and the finger on the trigger jerked with every intake of breath.

'You're not compos mentis, Aisling. He knows, Chase the Wonderdog. Look at how he's looking at you. But you know what's really funny?' His red-rimmed eyes glinted fire. 'I know something you don't know. I've had plenty of time to think this over. Loads of time to wonder who you remind me of. Lanky legs and ginger hair and a bitch of an aunt out in the sticks. Does the name L mean anything to you? L as in Eliot? Talk about ripples. Talk about connections. He didn't make it to Patagonia, you know, but he did make it to my neck of the woods. Two hours away from you, by train. Nice girlfriend. Nice kids. He told me all about them when he wasn't busy necking me. He had a nice, not especially interesting life without you. David's mother might've been looking for him, but your dad sure as hell wasn't looking for you.'

Aisling's open hands drooped. She looked to Chase, and he looked back long enough to bare the embarrassment and the shame before his eyes slid across the tiles and away.

Chase was pleading with Feodor now, pleading with him to spare Georgie. He had hurt nobody. Georgie was a good boy. He'd had enough violence in his life, and so had Chase and so had Feodor, they'd surely all had enough.

Something deep in the centre of Aisling clenched. A longing for warmth, for quiet, for locked doors she had the key to. Not the stifling inertia of Edythe's vicarage. Not her old back bedroom with the map of the world and the tear running up through New Zealand. Not even the house in the wasteland where safety was guaranteed at a price. Something for herself. Where was that kind of freedom?

Chase had planted himself in front of her now, squaring up to Feodor who backed towards the drop in the centre of the factory floor, stroking Georgie's flushed neck with the barrel of the pistol.

'You don't want to believe me, do you?' Over Chase's shoulder, Feodor flashed Aisling a slice of crooked teeth, the grin of a wounded thing. 'That's us even, then.'

Down in the black spring, the coin of light shivered.

'You told me to test myself,' Aisling said. The words slid

under Chase's curtain of pleading, but Feodor heard them and his eyes flicked up to meet hers with belated clarity as a veil of cloud cast the distillery into shadow.

It took two long steps and a cool gulp of air, and she was flying.

Aisling watched her feet leave the black tiles. Her coat was a flag fluttering in the wind. It masked the gunshot overhead. Dropping through the dark chamber with her legs above and her hair streaming, she thought with a flash of pleasure that she must have looked like one of Blake's strange angels twirling out of Heaven and into the black sea of Hell. What had Connie said, holding her letter to God, pink and copper and violent blue, with the tiny body falling from the clouds?

Were it not better to believe Vision with all our might and strength, tho' we are fallen and lost?

Aisling had time to smile.

My decision. Mine.

Verity Holloway

28

Horizontal? Vertical? Water flooded into her sinuses. Unspeakable, lung-hardening cold. After the initial roar of the water enveloping her there was a high-pitched ringing, then a deluge of silence. Her heavy coat and boots dragged her down as the water tugged at her eyelids and forced them to open. The light of the factory above, white and icy, was morphing into a warmer glow, a dreamy fireside colour swelling out towards her, and she wondered calmly if this was death. Because, if so, it wasn't half as bad as having a seizure, and that would be a great line to toss around in order to sound brave and interesting when she got better.

When?

She surfaced with a gasp the size of a scream. Dry air against face, head, shoulders, flailing arms against the enamel sides of a bathtub. The light fitting swung. At first she doubted herself, but as the oxygen flowed slowly back into her brain she realised, yes, it was the bathroom at the end of the hall in Edythe's house, white and undamaged.

She was lying fully-clothed in a draining bath scummy with used soap suds. On the floor beside a paraffin heater was a magazine mottled with moisture. On the cover a red-lipped woman purred at herself in a mirror. *You'll be a little lovelier each day, with fabulous pink Camay!*

The water drained around her. Aisling hauled herself out of the bath. Stuck to her sodden clothes, pats of colourless sudsy hair. Some of it plopped on to the tiles.

Dripping and dazed, she turned right out of the bathroom door. It was early evening, and a light pattering of rain was the only sound there to greet her. She took the stairs to her old bedroom. They seemed darker somehow, and she noted the unfamiliar wallpaper and an oily scent far removed from Edythe's clinical cleanliness. Masculine, like a charity shop armchair.

There was no point in being frightened, she understood that much.

At the door, she paused to listen. A gulf of floorboards between her and whoever was inside. But there was someone. She could almost see them on the narrow bed where she had lain awake so many nights, waiting for life to change. A wet pat of hair lay at her feet. She rubbed it between her fingers, ghostly fine. And then she heard it, the smothered sound of someone who didn't want to be heard crying.

The moment she touched the doorknob, the sounds ceased. She pressed her face to the hinges.

'She was looking for you, David,' she said. 'Your mother wanted you back.'

Her ears were blocked with water. Her tongue billowing in the rush. It washed across her eyes and she was blinded by it, whisked out and away from the house, and with a violent tug of tidal power the water drew her down, deep down, to where all was black and viscous and too hot, and then—

Surfacing.

The ceramic pink pig on the end of the bathroom light cord swung where Beverley had thrown open the door. Its smiling face bumped against the wall, threatening to crack. Aisling was in the bath. Not the curved, clean bathtub at Edythe's house but her own, the plughole clogged with auburn hair and dead tea lights lining the sides. A froth of white bubbles crackled around the bones of her bare shoulders. A cotton ball soaked in TCP. A quarter past ten, a Tuesday.

Oh. She remembered.

Beverley was there in her pyjamas. Under the reek of astringent, Aisling detected the jasmine moisturiser Beverley always applied before bed. Her skin was oily with it, her eyes pink where the remains of her workday mascara clotted angrily.

'You must never, ever lock this door.'

Very quietly, someone said, 'It's the truth.' A girl of fifteen. Aisling, or someone who looked like her, with a hot pink gash over one eye. She only made it angry, dabbing it like that.

In her mother's hand, the old journal with the galloping horses on the cover. Those guilty pages left open on her bed.

I must have made him—

I must have given some signal—

I need to tell—

I can't—

I can't—

That confession in biro: *I, I, I.*

Beverley breathed noisily through her nose. The nails of thumb and forefinger *snap-snap-snapped*. 'Why did you lock this door?'

'I'm not making it up,' said the girl.

'You didn't even tell me,' Beverley said. 'That's the worst of it. You couldn't come and stand in front of me and say it. You had to write it all down so that anyone could find it, and then slink off to the bathroom, locking me out like a stranger.'

'I—' The puff of breath barely stirred the bubbles clinging to her chest.

'Stop it!' One shout, the only one. 'No. You don't get to talk now. You don't get to make allegations that could ruin Malcolm's life. And what about my life? You're not even upset. If any of this were true, don't you think you'd be crying?'

It was true, the girl thought. If she were normal at all wouldn't she wail now, pull at her hair, scrub at her skin with the TCP until the oily cling of it came clean away? She stared at the light brown hairs flattened to her knees as the core part of her tremored lightly with the ripples in the bathwater.

I can't sleep, can you? Look, you're wide awake. Look at your feet. Hanging out the covers like that. Look at these feet.

'I can see what you're thinking every time it all fails for me,' Beverley said. 'You put your arms around me and you act like you're sorry, but I see exactly what's going on in your head. You want me to yourself. You don't know what it was like in that house before you were born. Your stupid arsehole father. When he yelled and he shoved. Those steep servants' stairs. And just when I thought it was all getting better, he left me with you. And now you tell me that someone who really loves me—'

Words gave way to a thin wail. Aisling had never thought for a second she wouldn't be believed. *Never write as 'I' again, never be so stupid.*

Beverley gathered herself with tearful dignity, clutching the journal that would shortly find its way into the recycling bin. 'You are going to go to bed,' she said. 'And I am going to go to bed. And tomorrow... tomorrow, everything will be fine.'

And with that, Aisling's bones turned to treacle. The door swung shut as if kicked, and a hot black wall of water came barrelling out of the walls, the toilet, the window, to take her, drag her, up, up, she couldn't tell how far up, until the air hit her face and she met Feodor's eyes, wild with fright and reddened from having dived down to meet her in the freezing distillery well.

Despite his diminutive frame, Feodor had hauled Aisling's body half out on to the concrete, and she crawled after him, moaning with shock and cold. The weight of her sodden coat was tremendous, and it fell off as soon as she struggled out of one sleeve. Feodor sat crumpled, limbs akimbo, mouth agape. His clothes clung to his bones, like a child in the aftermath of a disaster.

She thought she could stand, but when she rose up to her full height she tottered as though the floor had lurched. She fell hard on to her knees, and revelled in the shock it sent up through her bones.

She hadn't died. And away from the brink she found she wanted to live. But Feodor sat still, looking dumbly up at her.

'I didn't even think about it,' he said, very quietly. There was a note of wonder in his voice, and it pricked at her. She was raring to go, anywhere, now, and there he was, just sitting.

'He let Rada drown. I didn't.'

The chamber echoed with the rasp of their breathing. Again, Aisling tried to stand, zigzagging across the floor like a gull riding a thermal.

'But I'm dirty,' he said dully. 'All over.'

'You will be,' she panted, 'if that's the first bath you've had in years.'

She offered him her hand, and he took it. Feodor staggered to the foot of the steps and shouted up to the factory floor. 'Georgie?'

'He's hardly going to talk to you, is he?'

'I dropped the gun. It went off.'

A distant pang of fear.

Shortly, a dark head peered over the edge. They couldn't read Georgie's expression. He called down to them in a high, boyish voice: 'Are you all right?'

Oh, thank— 'We're wonderful,' Aisling said. 'You?'

'I think— I think we are. I think, oh, but—'

Feodor was very still.

As he said it, a glass flask went shooting down into the chamber and smashed at Feodor's feet. The shards flew up and stuck in his hands as he shielded his face.

'Is she all right? You stupid little idiot, is she all right?' Chase came thumping down the steps, one hand clamped to the side of his neck, streaming with blood.

'She's fine,' Aisling said. 'You're hurt.'

'Two inches to the left and he'd've shot my throat out, the

scrawny little pox-ridden shit. Happy?' He flicked a palmful of blood at Feodor, who accepted it full in the face. A red rivulet trickled down his nose as he regarded the glass in his palms with detachment.

Aisling went to Chase and carefully prised his hand away from his neck. The bullet had skimmed the collar of his coat and taken a chunk out of the leather. An inch of skin was sliced away and the bare flesh beneath was dark and wet and strangely exciting. *Look at yourself,* she wanted to say, *look at this muscle and this pulse.* 'You'll have a nice scar.'

'So will you,' he said. She had quite forgotten about her head. 'Proper villain scar.'

He unfastened the chain around his neck and pooled it in her open palm. Mucky silver clotted with blood. She put it in her pocket along with the tooth. Just as well she didn't have the Blake book with her. It would be ruined. But she had the poems in her head now. She would manage.

Chase struggled to catch his breath. 'You fell a hundred feet. You should've broken your neck.'

'I survived,' she said, and meant it. 'But Feodor fell, too, and—'

'Yeah.' He regarded the bedraggled creature picking at the glass in his shivering hands. He was deeply grateful for Feodor dragging her out, Aisling realised, and unable to express it.

Georgie trotted down the steps to Chase and assessed the bleeding. 'We need to get that clean. You'll already have all kinds of horrors in it.'

Feodor had slunk away to tremble against the wall. He excised a slice of glass from his thumb and let it fall.

Georgie was unafraid. His look was pitying. 'Chase?'

Chase set his jaw. With a hand clamped to his wound, he approached the other man. 'You 'eard.'

For a moment, Feodor simply stared at him, as if expecting a blow.

'I said you're coming with us. The lotion he uses stings like buggery. I want to see you squirm.'

Feodor wouldn't move until Aisling shuffled to him in her wet clothes. He squinted up at her as if she were made of light.

'He'll still lock you up if he catches you,' he said. 'Our Friend. You know that, right?'

A realisation had been brewing ever since her body hit the water, and now it swelled within her.

Neither David Morgun not Edythe Enright nor Doctor Ross would ever be able to send Aisling Selkirk away. That person had fled. It would be like trying to lock up a spirit. And Aisling felt happiness for that other girl, that very young person who had felt defeated and afraid. Even now, if she were to jolt awake and find herself on the bed in that nasty little room at the top of Edythe's house, she would weather it and she would live.

A hazy Mexican vista exploded into her mind's eye, crimson chrysanthemums drenching the drab slate chamber around her. She looked down into Feodor's pale face; his huge, red-rimmed eyes. There are so many things to do with life now, now, why give others the privilege of snaring you?

'I know it's hard to believe,' she said, 'but I think we might be okay.'

>•<

Feodor fainted twice on the way to Tor's house. On the second occasion, Chase declared that if the little sod were a horse, someone would donate him to the glue factory.

Georgie worried his lip. 'I wonder what Tor will say.'

'I won't go back,' came Feodor's voice, muffled in the wet crook of his arm. 'They can't make me.'

Chase sighed. 'Well, make up your mind, 'cause I'm sick of carrying you.'

'He means London,' Aisling explained.

'I'll make a note of it. No gallivanting off to imaginary cities this evening. However,' he bent as far as his wound would allow to address the young man shivering on the ground, 'some of us have been shot today, so if you'd like to get a move on, that'd be grand.'

'Listen to me,' Feodor panted. Aisling knelt. His forehead was hot under her palm and he swallowed the staccato that had crept into his voice. 'You said he knows how to go back. I don't want to. I don't. But. Our Friend. Do you think if he really does know he'd tell us?'

Chase growled. 'If we both took a leg and dragged, this would be over a lot quicker.'

Aisling slipped her arms around Feodor and hauled him to his feet. She didn't want to accept the smell of paraffin thick on the breeze.

>•<

Glass of wine in hand, Tor sat at the garden table. She wore a sleeveless dress of lavender cotton with a fringe of tassels around the hem, one of the few she managed to rescue all those years ago, patched and let out until it resembled a faulty parachute. The mauve ballet pumps looked rather less elegant than they once did, what with the swelling of her ankles, but nevertheless, a quick dab of her dwindling supply of make-up had hidden the rings beneath her eyes. She felt cool and refined.

When her four young wards came clattering over the roots of the boundary tree, Tor took a sip of wine, noting its golden flavour. Perhaps Georgie could construct an ice house for the chilling of future bottles. When she suggested this out loud the four of them looked at her with such astonishment that she fully expected them to drop Feodor and let him roll down the hill.

Tor gestured with her glass at the pile of cushions in the patch of late sunshine where a pot of sandalwood incense fumed headily. 'Help yourself to supper, everyone. Wash your hands first.'

Feodor stared at the dishes of dried fruit and pickled eggs as if he had been presented with a mound of jewels. There was a little cheese sliced into slivers on a saucer, and he reached for it uselessly as Chase dragged him past the table and dropped him on to the cushions.

'Get it yourself, dickhead.'

When Aisling presented herself, wet and smutty with charcoal, at Tor's table, the two women regarded the changes in each other.

'Your old maid called you the belle of the ball,' Aisling said.

'I thought it important he saw me at my best.'

Tor fingered the string of pearls around her neck as Chase stole a boiled egg from her plate and bit it in half.

'The Lash,' she told him. 'I've been watching the chickens,

and I'm now almost certain The Lash lays the best eggs. I'd rather hoped it would be Sodomy. I thought that might appeal to a certain puerile someone I was rather missing at the time.' She tucked the curve of her black bob behind one ear and called out to Feodor. 'And you over there, young man, dampening my best cushions. I thought I told you to go away and sort yourself out.'

Feodor, with that black-eyed, brooding look that turned him into an Orthodox Jesus, slid a glance at Aisling. 'She sorted me out,' he mumbled.

'I thought she might. Chase, take him a bowl of raspberries, before he expires.' As he grudgingly did so, Tor gestured for Aisling to come closer. 'I've made him comfortable. I don't know how long it might take.'

The fumy evening breeze was wretchedly cold against her wet body, and she could not concentrate. 'He's just in shock,' she said, with a glance at Feodor. She misunderstood.

Tor went on. 'I must say, I didn't know what to do. If I'd known the confectioner knew we lived out here, I'd have, well, I'm sure you grasp my meaning. He was asking for you.' As Chase returned with the stained and empty bowl, she smiled up at him tiredly. 'Came back to eat all my preserves?'

He shrugged. 'Fancied a bit of fish.'

'I'm sorry to hear about Jobi, dear. I know you loved the silly ass.'

In his grief, he didn't wonder how she knew. 'I'm gonna help build the smokehouse. I reckon I can salvage us a rowing boat. I could stay on. More permanent, like. If you'll have me.'

'Sounds ideal. Aisling, why don't you go inside and change

into something dry? Fetch a jumper for our guest.' Over her glass, she gave her a long, steady look.

The house seemed smaller than Aisling had left it, cluttered with chintz and garbage. Sheets of Georgie's plans stuck to the soles of her boots. The holes in the wall, covered with corrugated iron and planks of wood, were sure to let the snow in, come winter.

Tor had put David in Aisling's bed. She could smell him, though the repugnant tang of paraffin was earthier now, muted by the incense burning in the garden. She edged towards the steps leading down to her bedroom. It was dark in there, she could see nothing but the faint glint of evening light on the pickle jars. She wondered what it was she wanted to say to him.

She hesitated at the steps. Off came the heavy coat. She turned away and climbed the ladder to the platform where Tor slept. Amongst the musty jumble of once-luxurious fabrics, she found two thick jumpers for herself and Feodor beside an open tin of charcoal pencils. No sound came from the lower bedroom. Not the slightest sigh. Tor's family were taken from their home and killed for this man. Jobi had been stabbed for him. The prayer seller's brothers were never seen again. *Do you know what happens to people like you?*

Who created that category? If there was one thing she could say to David – who would put it in his notebook as a prime example of the broken reasoning of the sick, she was sure – it would be that whatever group of people he decided to lump her in with, she would never have to accept it. If she saw herself as an explorer criss-crossing her way across the world, however blindly, then that was what she was. Regardless of the doors locked around her.

One glance back at the garden. Outside, Rum, Sodomy and The Lash chuckled over their feed. Georgie was showing Tor the wound to Chase's neck, fussing over his every flinch. She saw Feodor off to one side, knees clutched to his chest. He glanced in her direction, a stealthy look, and a hank of damp hair slid across his face.

Down into the dark.

29

Tor drained her second glass of wine. It soaked her with the sense of serenity that had once been with her every day. Untrustworthy. She put down the glass and glanced back at the house. A trail of smoke from the chimney where she had warmed her lunch. No sign of anything dreadful. Aisling could take care of herself. That, of course, didn't mean she would be forced to. But Tor had seen this time and time again.

Feodor, fortified by the fruit he had eaten, lingered against the rough door frame. Sensing he was being watched, he glanced up. Perhaps it was the wine, but Tor smiled at him. He managed to hold her gaze before slipping inside.

Down in the lower bedroom, Aisling sat on the steps with her chin on her knees.

David had died very recently. His grey eyes were open, looking out into the smoky garden.

Tor's drawing equipment lay beside him. A charcoal stick worn to a stub, a scrap of paper taken from Georgie's plans. The bulbous-boned likeness of David swaddled like a starving baby. Tor had offered him painkilling tea, washed his feet, given them socks. On top of the blanket one of his hands was arranged as though it had recently been held. In his lashless eyes, Tor had captured the faintest glimmer of surprise.

We embellish what we don't know.

But he was dead, and it was done.

She stood and wiped her face roughly with her palm. When she turned, she found that Feodor was in the doorway. He was wearing one of the knitted jumpers she had picked out, and it dwarfed him.

He said, 'I kind of pity him now, knowing.'

'I don't think he wanted pity.'

'No.' Feodor went past her, down into the room. He looked at the body. 'It's stuck in me. Everything. Dirty roots. Like that bloody tooth.'

'What do teeth do?'

He shook his head miserably.

'They get old. And they drop out.'

Feodor sat on the floor beside David's body and began to cry.

Later, when the fireflies played around the tree roots, Chase took Aisling down to the shore of the lake. He brought a lamp with them, revealing the secret perambulations of foxes and badgers and tiny scavenging birds.

'If you keep going,' he said, 'there's a cove where the turtles come out to lay their eggs at night. It's the right time of year. We might see some.'

They walked the length of the shore together. Chase had packed a bag with a picnic blanket and some leftover seed cake. Aisling offered to carry it and save his wounded shoulder, and he let her, but only just. They clambered over a groyne of rocks and came to a scrubby stretch where sea kale sprouted out of the sand.

'Gimme some of your Mister Blake, then,' Chase said. 'Teach me something.'

From memory, she obliged him:

'O, what land is the Land of Dreams?
What are its mountains, and what are its streams?
O Father, I saw my Mother there,
Among the lilies by waters fair.
Father, O Father, what do we here,
In this land of unbelief and fear?
The Land of Dreams is better far
Above the light of the Morning Star.'

In the lamplight she could see his smile, faint, weary, but real. She took the tooth from her pocket, stuck to Chase's bloody chain. She knelt where the water lapped the sand.

Tomorrow, they would bury David. Georgie wanted a crowd of apple trees where the boundary tree stood. There would be no more mire for David; they would lay him down in an orchard.

She lowered her open hand into the gentle waves. The tooth rocked there in the hollow of her palm, shedding swirls of blood as she watched the white flash of a magpie leaving the woods to disappear out over the lake.

'Can I ask you something?'

'As long as it's not too taxing,' Chase said.

'What's beyond all this?' She stood to gesture at the dark

horizon where water and sky became indistinguishable. 'I know you said you don't know. But I can't understand how you wouldn't be curious.'

In the shallows, a large flat rock held a pool of water. In it, a tall figure with frizzy hair, a straight spine and a stripe over one shoulder where a heavy bag hung. She didn't immediately recognise herself. Not ready to roam, but roaming. One day you're tramping through a tunnel marked with strange signs, she thought. The next, you're older. You're sturdier, and the things that scared you no longer do. You wonder how you got here.

She fed the chain through the tooth's rotten hole and held it there, in front of her face, before fastening it around her neck.

Dear child, I also by pleasant streams
Have wandered all night in the Land of Dreams;
But though calm and warm the waters wide,
I could not get to the other side.

A gust of wind rolled in from the lake. The lamp flickered out, taking the reflection with it.

'Chase?'

ACKNOWLEDGEMENTS

It's hard to remember a time when I wasn't writing *Pseudotooth*. Chase has been with me since I was in school uniform. I can scarcely imagine how many people I need to thank, so this is by no means a complete list of the people who've been good to me over the years.

In no particular order…

My partner Gabriel for being my constant support crew, emotionally and technically. You've been here through the happy times and the lows, and now it's all finally happening. Thankful Kakapo.

Mum and Dad who brought me up on books and stationery and encouraged me constantly. Even though Mum isn't close by to see it, I know you're both proud.

Sally Cline, my undergrad writing tutor and later my Royal Literary Fund mentor. You were exactly the teacher I needed, especially when I was being a will-o'-the-wisp.

My two first readers, Thora and Rachel, who trawled through one of the enormous early drafts when I could no longer see it clearly. You managed to be incredibly constructive about it and continue speaking to me afterwards.

Thank you to George and Gary at Unsung for helping me untangle that original submission until it became the book I'd wanted to write all along.

THE ARRIVAL OF MISSIVES

BY ALIYA WHITELEY